About the Author

David Munro was born in Edinburgh and lived there until the age of 27. He was employed by a major brewery within the capital and relocated to Aberdeen then Glasgow. He attended university and college to attain Chartered Marketer status. As David is an arts professional and with experience of different cultures, this lends itself to creative literature. *The Time Jigsaw Deliverance* is his anticipated sequel to *The Time Jigsaw*.

Dedication

To Miss Todd, Mrs Murray and Mr Miller who were my school teachers at Granton Primary, Edinburgh, from 1960 to 1966. My gratitude for their tuition and guidance.

David Munro

THE TIME JIGSAW DELIVERANCE

AUSTIN MACAULEY
PUBLISHERS LTD.

A CIP catalogue record for this title is available from the British Library.

ISBN 978 1 78455 793 5 (Paperback)
ISBN 978 1 78455 863 5 (Hardback)

www.austinmacauley.com

First Published (2015)
Austin Macauley Publishers Ltd.
25 Canada Square
Canary Wharf
London
E14 5LB

Printed and bound in Great Britain

Acknowledgments

Elaine Scott

Chapter 1

The Big Apple

Elizabeth Carsell-Brown alighted from the train at 42nd Street subway station, walked up the steep concrete staircase and reached the main exit. As she emerged from the station, a wall of noise engulfed her. On the crowded sidewalk, Elizabeth bumped against a male passer-by.

"Watch how you go lady!" he cried.

"Sorry," said Elizabeth.

The man shook his head and walked on.

Elizabeth sighed. New York does not compare to anywhere I have been. Since I came here, seventeen years have gone by and still I feel uneasy. Those gigantic grey skyscrapers intimidate me. Ah! A man· sells newspapers on the street corner.

"Read about President Hoover's inauguration, read all about it!" shouted the newspaper-seller.

Elizabeth walked towards him. He has a determined expression. "A New York Times please." Elizabeth smiled.

"Okay lady." The newspaper-seller thrust an edition at Elizabeth.

She took the newspaper and put it under her arm. "Thank you."

"Three cents."

Can't you say please? Elizabeth opened her bag, then a purse inside it. "Do you have change of a dollar?" Elizabeth took out the dollar note and held it in her hand.

The newspaper-seller frowned then checked his tally of coins in a small wooden box. "Just."

"Oh good, here you are." Elizabeth handed over the note.

He gave her a bundle of dimes, nickels and cents. "You'll have change next time!"

Elizabeth put them into the purse, closed her bag then started to walk.

The newspaper-seller pointed. "Mind that crack on the sidewalk lady!"

Elizabeth looked downwards. "Thank you."

"You're welcome."

Elizabeth stepped over the crack and walked on.

"Dames." The newspaper-seller shook his head, turned around to face the busy street and shouted. "Read about President Hoover, read all about it!"

A man approached the newspaper-seller. "A Times, Mac."

"Okay, buddy." He gave him a newspaper.

The man handed over three coins.

Elizabeth continued along the crowded sidewalk and observed a place of refuge. An advertising board outside a building stated excellent food and hot drinks.

Ah! Here is Delmonicos. I'll pop in and have a coffee – I need to escape from the hustle and bustle. Elizabeth pushed the entrance door, walked inside then looked around the establishment. It's also busy!

A sturdy dark-haired woman with a fawn knee-length overall spotted Elizabeth and came towards her.

"Can I help you, honey?"

"Do you have a table for one, please?"

"Dis way."

The waitress led Elizabeth to a small table with a red and white square tablecloth plus two dark wooden chairs.

"How about dis, will it do?"

"Yes."

Elizabeth sat down then laid her newspaper and bag on the spare chair. She unbuttoned her cream coat then removed her light blue cloche hat and placed it on the table.

"Ready to order?" said the waitress.

Elizabeth nodded.

The waitress took out a small white order pad from her breast pocket and removed a small pencil from behind an ear. "What'll it be?"

"A coffee, please."

"Just cawfee?"

Elizabeth nodded.

"Black or white?"

"White, please."

"Sure you don't want nothin' to eat?"

"I am sure."

"Be back soon." The waitress walked to the counter.

New Yorkers endear me with their variety of accents. Elizabeth cast her gaze around the establishment. It is busy for lunchtime – even in Midtown Manhattan.

The waitress returned and laid a cup of coffee on the table. "Sure I can't get you anythin' to eat?"

Elizabeth smiled. "I am sure. The establishment is busy."

"A local publishin' company went bust last month. Employees come here to pass away de time. It's same story all over dis part of Noo York." The waitress departed.

Elizabeth dragged the white cup and saucer over to her, lifted the cup, took a sip of coffee then looked around the vicinity. She put down her cup onto the saucer then picked up her broadsheet newspaper from the chair. She noticed a man look towards her table.

Let us see what if any positive news may be in today's New York Times.

"Can I take this spare chair, lady?" said a clean-shaven stocky man.

Elizabeth lowered the newspaper then looked up. "Yes, of course."

"Thanks."

He took the chair over to another table and placed it on the grey-tiled floor. He sat on it then started to chat with his group of acquaintances. Elizabeth continued to browse through the New York Times. It included President Hoover's inauguration, criminal activity, economic gloom, baseball and a page on culture.

At least there is the crossword puzzle. Elizabeth picked up her cup, took a sip then laid it on the saucer.

Twenty minutes later, the same waitress returned to Elizabeth's table and lifted an empty cup and saucer.

Elizabeth looked up then laid her newspaper on the table.

"More cawfee?"

"No, thanks, I am about to leave. Can I pay you here?"

The waitress looked at the counter then her customer. "Pay at the till."

"Fine."

Elizabeth rose from the table and buttoned her coat. She put on her hat, lifted the bag then walked to the counter. When she reached it, Elizabeth heard a cry.

"Hey!"

Elizabeth turned round.

"Your noospaper." The waitress walked to the counter with it in her hand.

"Thank you." Elizabeth took the newspaper from the waitress.

The well-built unshaven man behind the counter rubbed both large hands down his long white apron then picked up a receipt on the counter.

"Fifteen cents lady."

Elizabeth opened her bag then the purse inside it and took out a bundle of coins. She gave them to the man and smiled. He took the coins and looked at Elizabeth.

"There is twenty," said Elizabeth, "keep the change."

He nodded. "Danks, lady."

When Elizabeth left the establishment, a tall man in a dark suit and hat brushed against her then walked on through the crowd. Elizabeth discovered her bag had been stolen. A white-shirted man ran past her and caught up with the dark-suited individual. The two men had a conversation then an object was handed to the white-shirted man. As he walked back to Elizabeth, she recognised the person who retrieved her bag.

"Here you are, lady." He handed over a black leather bag.

Elizabeth put a hand on her chest. "My goodness! It all happened so fast."

"Can't be too careful, petty thieves are everywhere."

"Thank you."

"When you took out your purse in Delmonicos, I saw him stare through the window. He waited till you left then made his move."

"I am grateful. Can I give you a reward?"

"No need."

Elizabeth stared at the man's shirt. "Do you not feel cold?"

"This is March, lady – it's springtime in Manhattan." The man smiled then walked back to the establishment.

Elizabeth now wanted to venture home and quick. She proceeded to the nearest taxi rank and spotted a stationary vehicle. When she approached it, a man entered and the taxi drove off. Elizabeth reached the rank and another taxi appeared then started to slow down. When it stopped, the white-capped driver opened the passenger door from where he sat.

"Where to, lady?" said the driver.

"Upper East Side, please."

"No problem."

Elizabeth stepped into the cab, sat in the rear passenger seat and closed the door.

"Which part, lady, park or river?"

"27th East 62nd Street." Elizabeth sniffed the air. The previous passenger must have been a cigar smoker.

The taxi moved off and navigated a route through the busy Manhattan traffic. After a few blocks it came to a sudden halt. Due to a traffic light delay, irate automobile drivers pumped their horns. The taxi started to move at a slow pace then once more came to a halt.

Elizabeth said, "What is the problem?"

"A taxi has collided with a bus," said the driver.

Elizabeth peered out the small rear window. "A queue of vehicles has formed behind us." She looked ahead.

"The taxi driver can't blame the snow – it's gone."

Elizabeth smiled. "I hope that is the last of it."

"Did you take in a Broadway show, lady?" The taxi driver glanced behind.

"No, not today." Elizabeth sat upright.

"I hear audiences are poor."

"People don't have the money to spend on entertainment just now."

"Hotel accommodation appears okay."

"Is it?"

"Oh yeah, lady. My last passenger told me his company is goin' to build the tallest buildin' in the world and it's a hotel!"

"In New York?"

The taxi driver nodded. "Right here in Midtown, work starts next year."

"It will no doubt create jobs for the unemployed."

"I trust our noo President has other solutions to help the economy."

"It is not in the best of health. Perhaps Governor Roosevelt will improve the city's situation?"

"He's a good guy – he'll do his best."

Let us hope so.

"Did you say somethin', lady?"

"Just thinking out loud."

"My wife's just lost her job in a factory which makes shoes."

"Where is it located?"

"Brooklyn. Two hundred and eighty people out of a job – just like that! My kid brother is on short time down at the docks."

"The future appears bleak."

"My kid brother makes sure he has enough cash to watch the Yankees."

Elizabeth smiled.

"I'm a Giants fan but I make allowances for my kid brother."

Elizabeth laughed.

The driver sighed. "At last."

The taxi moved off and sped through the heavy traffic however, it again halted at a set of lights.

The driver glanced behind. "Where you originally from, lady – England?"

"Across the border."

"The Bronx?"

Elizabeth laughed. "Scotland, it borders with England."

The taxi driver laughed. "Just kiddin', lady. My wife's family came from Scawtland."

"Oh, where about?"

"A place called Fawrt William." He turned his head to face Elizabeth. "Is it a garrison?"

"You are funny. No, it is a small town in the Scottish highlands. It lies near a loch."

"A what?"

"Similar to the sea."

"I learn somethin' noo every day." The driver observed the lights straight ahead.

Elizabeth smiled.

"You know, lady, my bank manager, he also says I'm funny."

"Why?"

"I asked him for a loan of five hundred dollars. After he stopped laughin', asked why and what collateral I had."

"What did you say to him?"

"The cash would be used to invest in the stock market and as collateral, my taxicab."

"Did he approve the loan?"

"Oh yeah, he told me the stock market's a safe bet."

As the traffic lights changed from red to green, the taxi sped off and headed for Upper East Side. Thirty minutes later, the taxi arrived at its destination.

"Here we are, lady."

"That was quick! Just round the next block, please."

"Sure." The driver brought the vehicle to a stop and applied the handbrake. "One dollar eighty-five, lady."

Elizabeth went into her bag, opened her purse and brought out two single dollar notes. "Keep the change."

"Thanks, lady."

The driver vacated the cab and opened the passenger door. Elizabeth got out and the driver shut the door then tipped his white cap at her. He returned to his driver's seat, closed the door and released the handbrake. The taxi, with its yellow body, black roof and mudguards, moved off into the Upper Manhattan traffic. Elizabeth searched through her bag for the entry key.

"Afternoon, ma'am," said a passing gentleman. He removed his hat.

Elizabeth acknowledged the gentleman, put her key into the main door lock then turned it. She pushed the door forward and entered the building.

A woman walked down the stairs. "Don't close the door, Beth."

Elizabeth looked up.

"Did you have a good time today?"

"Yes, thanks, Molly."

"Did you go to Delmonicos?"

"Yes, a popular place."

"A good sign Beth." Molly smiled. "See ya." She departed and closed the door behind her.

Elizabeth walked up two flights of stairs to her apartment. Once inside, she laid her bag and newspaper on a table, took off her hat and coat then hung them on the hall coat stand. A glance at the wall clock made her frown.

"It's stopped again."

After she fixed the clock, Elizabeth prepared dinner in the kitchen. James would soon be home from work. She heard the apartment door open and wiped her hands on a white towel.

"Is that you, James?" Elizabeth walked into the hall.

James removed his hat, coat and jacket. "Who did you expect?"

"Oh, a dashing gallant movie star!" She kissed her husband on the cheek.

James smiled. "I do have something in common with Douglas Fairbanks."

"And what could that be?"

"We're both British and sport a moustache."

"There is also another similarity."

James hung his coat, jacket and hat on the hall coat stand. "And that is?"

"Tell you later." Elizabeth walked into the kitchen.

James followed, sat down at the table, picked up his spectacles and put them on. Whilst Elizabeth stirred a pot of stew, James picked up her newspaper and started to read.

"Not much good news today."

"The economy goes from bad to worse to disastrous! The financial section in this edition reiterates that. Perhaps our new President will make a difference."

Elizabeth sprinkled salt into the pot. "Has Mr Alder paid his account yet?" Elizabeth turned to face James.

He looked up. "Not yet, Elizabeth. I've sent him two reminders and threatened legal action."

"It's a lot of money that he owes."

James smiled. "Cash, Elizabeth, we are in New York."

"You mean 'Noo' York."

James laughed.

Elizabeth wiped her hands on the white towel. "Whatever, he should pay his debts."

James put down the newspaper. "Nobody pays their debts on time – if at all!"

Elizabeth sat down at the table opposite James. "What do you mean?"

He sighed. "It's not just Mr Alder – there are others."

"How many?"

James loosened his dark blue tie. "Another seven clients, maybe eight."

"How can the practice survive if there is limited income?"

"I will chase them up Elizabeth."

"You must be assertive."

"This isn't Scotland. The Americans act in a different way to threats."

"How?"

"They don't give a hoot! Any warning letters no doubt end up in a bin."

Elizabeth sighed.

"I'm hungry, Elizabeth, let's eat. It has been another long, tiresome day." James removed his spectacles then rubbed his eyes.

"Your business finances may not be healthy, however, your appetite is."

After dinner, James and Elizabeth relaxed in the living room. Elizabeth read a novel and James settled for the New York Times. An unfamiliar noise broke the silence.

"What was that?" said James.

"I'm doing my best to concentrate on this story."

James put down his newspaper and stood up. "I will check."

"The noise appeared to come from downstairs."

James went to the apartment door, opened it and looked along the white-walled landing. He closed the door, returned to the living room and sat down.

"Maybe a door was slammed shut by a draught."

James picked up his newspaper and turned the page.

"Any interesting articles?"

"Not really, just the norm." James looked at Elizabeth. "What book is it?"

"Beau Geste. It's about the French Foreign Legion in North Africa. It was made into a film three years ago."

"It must have a good storyline."

Elizabeth looked at James. "Yes, it has."

"Ronald Coleman played the starring role."

"Georgina and Dale went to see it."

"How is his business faring?"

"Georgina has not spoken about it for some time. I believe the company may be in trouble."

"Not many people can afford to spend whatever money they have on furniture, Elizabeth."

Elizabeth looked towards the living room window. "I suppose there are other urgent necessities. I perceived from Georgina that Dale must obtain capital from somewhere, somehow and soon."

"Any business in New York requires capital to help their cash-flow situation." James glanced at Elizabeth. "Due to the lack of investment, little or no funds are available."

Elizabeth stared at the door. "Who can that be?"

"I'll answer it." James stood up then walked to the door and opened it.

"Sorry to bother you sir," said a black uniformed police officer, "did you by any chance hear strange noises this evenin'?"

"Why yes officer, about fifteen minutes ago – a loud thud. I checked our landing however, everything appeared normal."

Elizabeth put down her book, stood up and walked to the door.

"Why do you ask?" said James.

"One of the apartments has been broken into and valuables taken."

"Which one, officer?" said Elizabeth.

"Lockwood."

James turned to Elizabeth. "You were correct."

"Sorry, sir?" said the police officer.

"My wife thought the noise came from downstairs."

"Yeah, sir. I have spoken with another neighbour and he confirmed that."

"Did nobody downstairs enquire about the noise, officer?" said Elizabeth.

"No, they didn't ma'am. Both neighbours on that landing had a radio on."

Elizabeth looked at James. "The volume must have been high!"

The police officer tipped his hat. "Be vigilant and if you hear or see anythin' suspicious, let us know." He walked along the black and white square tiled landing then down the staircase.

James closed the door. "How did the thieves enter the building? The main door remains locked at all times and can only be opened with a resident's key."

"Where there is a will, James."

"Yes, Elizabeth, there may indeed be a way."

"James, I have just remembered."

"Yes?"

"The Lockwoods went on a vacation."

"I'll contact the local police station and let them know."

James picked up a directory from the hall table then looked through it. He found the number and laid the directory on the table. With his left hand, James lifted the black handset from its cradle base. On the base, he dialled the number with his right forefinger then put the receiver to his left ear.

"I like this new telephone, Elizabeth."

"At least the receiver and transmitter are on the same handset – it's less cumbersome."

"Yeah?" said a voice.

"Police?" said James as he spoke into the transmitter.

"Yeah, this is Sergeant Mullen, what's the problem?"

"My name is James Carsell-Brown. This evening, an apartment was broken into within our block."

"I'll send someone round, sir."

"Someone has been here, I have information on the family who live in that particular apartment."

"What information would that be, sir?"

"They are on vacation and may not be back for another week."

"Give me the address of your apartment block sir."

"25 East 62nd Street."

"Name again, sir?"

"Carsell-Brown, we are on the second floor."

"Is Carsell your first name, sir?"

"My surname is Carsell-Brown."

"Got you. First we've heard about an incident tonight in that vicinity. Was it a police officer you spoke to?"

"Yes."

"Can you describe him?"

"He wore a police uniform, average build and height."

"Ninety-five per cent of our precinct officers fit that description, sir. I'll send a couple of my officers to take a statement from you."

"Thanks."

"And sir, check their NYPD IDs."

"I will Sergeant, and thanks."

"No problem."

James replaced the handset into the base cradle then turned towards Elizabeth. "I believe our police officer may have been an impostor."

Elizabeth put a hand on her mouth. "Gosh!"

"If we had been out then our apartment may also have been robbed."

"How daring."

"Desperate times produce desperate acts, Elizabeth."

James dashed into the subway station and glanced at his wristwatch. He stood anxiously in a queue at the ticket desk tapping his right foot. He purchased a return ticket then rushed down the staircase and onto his destination platform. James boarded the eight-carriage morning commuter train bound for Lower Manhattan then all carriage doors closed as one and the train departed.

Phew! Just caught my connection in time, glad the conductor held off for a few seconds.

James looked around the carriage and spotted an empty seat. He sat down, put his black briefcase on the floor and opened his Morning Dispatch edition at the financial section.

"Excuse me, Mac."

James put down his newspaper and looked at a young man who sat opposite. "Yes?"

He leaned forward. "How did the Yankees fare last night?"

James turned to the sports page then looked up and down the columns. "A win."

"How many home runs did Babe Ruth get?" said a white-haired man next to James.

James looked at the page's match report. "Two."

The man nodded his head.

"Is that good?" said James.

"Don't they play baseball in England?" he said.

"I'm not from England," said James.

"You ain't from America either," said the man, "your accent's a bit of both."

"I'm Scottish."

"The Philadelphia Athletics is a good team, it goes well for the new season," said the young man.

"Has it not started yet?" said James.

"Not until the 16th of this month," he said, "they played a 'friendly' last night."

"To test the water?" said James.

"Test the what?"

"Before the season begins, find out how the competition performs."

"Yeah, I see what you mean." He leaned forward. "Why do Brits not play baseball?"

"We play football in the main."

"Where's that located?"

James smiled. "All over the country."

"Gee!" The young man tipped his grey fedora hat.

"However, no baseball."

"That's a shame." He glanced out the window. "My stop, see you, Mac." He stood up and went to the carriage exit door.

The white-haired man stood up and sat opposite James.

James put his briefcase on the vacant seat, picked up the newspaper then gazed out the window. Until Elizabeth's birthday, just eight more days. What shall I buy her?

"Excuse me, is this seat taken?"

A lady wearing a white blouse under a pale blue coat and white cloche hat stood over James. He removed his briefcase from the seat.

"Thank you." She sat down.

James opened his newspaper and started to read. She has a lovely tan.

"Nice morning, lady?" said the white-haired man.

"I hope it stays that way."

James turned to another page. She's Italian.

"Tickets, please." said the dark blue uniformed conductor.

James put a hand into his coat pocket.

The conductor approached James. "Ticket, sir."

Where is it? James fumbled inside one pocket then the other. "Can't find it!"

"There it is." The lady pointed. "Next to your left shoe."

James picked the ticket up from the carriage floor and handed it to the conductor.

He took the ticket and clipped it with a metal implement. "Thanks."

James glanced at the lady.

She smiled.

The train rolled through Midtown then Lower Manhattan at full speed. Commuters boarded and left the train at every stop.

James looked out the window. My stop, Wall Street. He held his newspaper, picked up the briefcase and stood. James looked at the lady.

She smiled.

Nice white teeth.

James alighted from the train and walked up a stairway to the exit. He could smell tobacco on his coat – the white-haired smoker who sat nearby. James departed Wall Street Station, walked along the main street then took a short cut down a deserted narrow alley.

"Gotta light, Mac?" said a man wearing a grey cap and jacket. He held up a cigarette in his left hand.

"Sorry, I don't smoke,"

The man took out a gun from his right-hand jacket pocket. He glanced towards a doorway and pointed the gun in its direction. "In there – now!"

James walked into the doorway. He gripped his briefcase. "I have no money."

"Then I'll have the briefcase."

"It just contains paper documents."

"Give it to me now or else."

"Drop the gun!" cried a male voice.

James looked sideways.

Two police officers with stern expressions and guns in their hands stood at the entrance of the alley. The man ran off with the gun still in his hand.

One officer put away his gun into a black holster then stepped forward. "You okay, sir?"

"Yes." James took a deep breath then stared down the alley.

"He'll be picked up."

"You came just in time." James took another deep breath.

"We received a tip-off."

"A tip-off?"

"A woman called our station two hours ago."

"How could she have known? The incident has just happened!"

"Maybe the person knew of the robber's intentions sir. At least you're safe."

James nodded. "Yes, and thanks."

"Take care, sir."

Both police officers headed down the alley. James composed himself and continued on his way to the office.

That incident has given me a shake. It is unthinkable that this can happen in broad daylight in the midst of Wall Street.

After a brisk walk to his office building, James entered and looked at a dark-uniformed doorman who stood in the foyer.

The doorman smiled. "Good mornin', Mr Carsell-Brown."

Not really. "Morning Lloyd."

"The elevator has been repaired."

About time.

Since it was in operation, James took the elevator to his office floor instead of having to walk up several flights of stairs. Other office personnel from various floors shared the elevator with him. By their demeanour, they appeared more nervous than he did! Men puffed on a cigarette and women had strained expressions – perhaps due to their company's business downturn. After a lengthy wait James reached his floor, got out and left an intense atmosphere within the elevator. He took a deep breath then walked along the corridor to his office. Before he entered, a colleague greeted him.

"Jim, Bob wants to see us in his office," said Tom.

"What, now?"

"Eight-thirty."

James looked at his wristwatch. In thirty-five minutes.

"Could be interesting, Jim."

"I'll bet."

"You don't look too good."

"On my way here I had a bad experience, tell you about it over lunch."

"Okay."

At mid-day, Tom and James walked to a local restaurant two blocks from their Wall Street office. The establishment became a refuge for businessmen to meet and discuss various topics that included the economy, automobiles and baseball. When they entered, Tom looked around the restaurant.

"Not much wrong with this business."

James pointed. "There's an empty window table."

Both men removed their coats and hats, put them on a nearby coat stand then sat down. After a few minutes, a black outfitted waitress appeared. James and Tom ordered lunch and a glass of soda water.

Tom once more looked around the restaurant. "Too much smoke." He stood up, went to the window and opened it then sat down.

"I would imagine the pressure of business survival does not help."

"Yeah, Jim, no doubt."

The waitress returned and from a circular shiny silver tray, placed two drinks on the white tablecloth.

"Thanks," said Tom.

The waitress smiled. "You're welcome." She walked back to the counter.

James looked at Tom. "Polite."

"He smiled. "She has other attributes!"

"I believe so however I am married." James lifted his glass then took a sip of soda water.

Tom lifted his glass. "Here's to when I get hitched again." He drank the contents then laid his empty glass on the table.

James took another sip.

Tom held up his hand.

The waitress looked across to the table.

"Same again, miss!" cried Tom.

She nodded.

James drank his soda water then laid his empty glass on the table. "What about the meeting this morning?"

"Bob looked strained – and who can blame him. Because of clients' unpaid fees, we have a cash flow problem."

"Will there be staff cuts?"

"No question about it, Jim."

The waitress arrived and laid two drinks on the table. She lifted the two empty glasses, put them onto her tray then departed.

Tom lifted his glass and sipped his second soda water. "What happened to you this morning?" He replaced his glass on the table.

"I was held up."

Tom sat back on his chair and looked at James over his gold horn-rimmed spectacles. "Held up?"

"After I left the train."

"Gee!" He rubbed the back of his bald head.

"Two police officers appeared and the thug ran off."

"You're a lucky guy."

"One of the officers said they had received a tip-off."

"Whoever it came from, you owe them – big time."

James nodded.

Tom looked towards the counter. "Good, here comes our food."

When five o'clock came, James left his office premises and walked through crowded sidewalks full of commuters heading to the local subway station. From now on there would be no more short cuts down an alleyway. James boarded the packed northbound train however, no seat on this occasion. Passengers filled the corridors of this rush-hour express.

Dash! I forgot to buy Elizabeth's birthday present. I'll buy the necklace tomorrow.

James looked around the carriage and did not spot any happy expressions, even though the working day had ended.

Maybe their firms find themselves in a similar predicament as mine. Would the situation be any better in Scotland? Should Elizabeth and I have stayed there? As time passes, I miss the picturesque green valleys, hills and lochs. Also no congestion in Ardrishaig, just an abundance of space. I hope for a better peace of mind ahead.

James took a newspaper out of his briefcase and started to read. He balanced himself against the carriage exit door. After five minutes, he shoved the newspaper back into his briefcase.

"You okay, buddy?" said a fellow male passenger.

"Yes, it has been a difficult day."

"Hard times?"

James jerked forward towards the stranger. Those damn bends.

The passenger laughed. "Even the train driver has an off-day."

James smiled.

The fellow passenger looked out of the carriage window. "My stop." He turned to James. "Take care – don't do anythin' stoopid."

"I promise."

The jovial stout stranger left the train, adjusted his grey fedora hat and walked up the stairway towards the station exit.

I must have a severe depressed look on my face.

"Ticket, sir," said the conductor.

James handed his ticket to him.

"Thank you, sir." The conductor examined the ticket and gave it back to James.

As James put the ticket into his coat pocket, the busy commuter train slowed down and went through a tunnel then stopped. James looked out the carriage window and observed Lexington Avenue station.

My feet ache and I still have to climb that steep exit stairway.

Whilst he walked from the subway station to the apartment block, James swithered whether to tell Elizabeth about what happened earlier in the day. He entered the building, went upstairs to the second floor then opened the apartment door.

James closed it and laid his briefcase on the brown hall carpet. He put his coat and hat on the coat stand then went into the kitchen.

"Did today go well?" said Elizabeth.

"Okay. Just a light meal for me tonight."

During dinner, James did not appear in the mood for a conversation. Elizabeth would enquire about the firm and receive short answers.

"Are you not hungry, James?"

"No." James pushed away his half-full plate.

"What's wrong?"

James sat back on his chair.

"Well?"

"After what happened today, Elizabeth, I don't have an appetite."

"The usual client problems?"

"Yes." As she will worry, I won't tell Elizabeth about this morning's incident. James looked towards the living room. "Is the concert from the Capitol Theatre being broadcast tonight?"

"Not sure." Elizabeth lifted dishes from the dining room table and took them into the kitchen.

James walked into the living room then switched on the radio. He turned the reception knob back and forward. "That's it."

Elizabeth entered the living room. "You have a signal?"

"Yes, no problem this time. It's a clear night which helps." James sat down on the couch."

Elizabeth sat next to him. "What happened today?"

He looked at his wife and shook his head. "Don't concern yourself, Elizabeth."

"You have that puzzled expression." Elizabeth stood up, turned the radio volume knob anti-clockwise then returned to the couch. "Well?"

"Cuts will be made in the firm. A meeting took place this morning."

"Do the cuts include you?"

"I don't believe they do, however, anyone over fifty will be considered."

"Until then, you only have two years."

"Right, now I feel nearer sixty!"

Elizabeth smiled. "Do you want a whisky?"

"Yes, thanks."

Elizabeth went into the kitchen and returned with a half-filled glass. "Iced tea." She smiled and gave the glass to James.

"We're not in a public place, Elizabeth, you can mention alcohol."

At last, a smile.

"You don't look thirty-five, let alone forty-five. Since we married, your slim waistline has not changed."

"Because I take care of myself. You must eat more – look how thin you are! Also, my brisk walks through the park are beneficial."

"Are you not having a gin?"

"Not now, maybe later."

James sipped his whisky. "How would you like to celebrate your birthday?"

"I'm not sure."

"How about dinner then the theatre. Georgina and Dale can join us."

"Splendid."

James sipped his whisky and sat back on the couch. "Do you think of home, Elizabeth?"

"This is our home."

"You know what I mean."

"Sometimes, however we are not ready to retire and return to Scotland yet."

James stood up, went to the radio and turned up the volume. "That's better."

Elizabeth returned to the kitchen and James listened to the concert. He reflected on the incident, which occurred prior to his arrival at work. Should he tell Elizabeth about being confronted by a robber and what purpose would it serve? After all, Elizabeth's concerns would be compounded given the firm's financial predicament. Perhaps tomorrow will turn out better for both of them.

Elizabeth caught the mid-morning train for Lower Manhattan to Chambers Street station. She alighted from the train, walked up the concrete stairway then out of the subway exit. A blast of air ensued and she held on to her hat.

Those balmy breezes! Elizabeth looked at her wristwatch.

Mr Arbington had asked her to visit him around eleven-thirty. The gallery was two blocks from the station and situated on 45th street. Elizabeth arrived at the Julien Hartley Art Gallery in good time for her important appointment. As she entered the gallery, an elegant lady in a short navy dress with white pearls round her neck came forward.

"Can I help you, madam?"

"I have come to see Mr Arbington."

"Is he expecting you?"

Her short jet-black hair enhances a powdered face and deep red lips. "Yes."

"Wait here, please, I will let him know you have arrived." The lady walked along a narrow bright corridor.

Elizabeth walked towards a display of paintings and adjusted her hat. She could hear footsteps behind her become louder and turned around.

"Hello, Elizabeth, good to see you. Well I hope?"

"Fine, thank you, Mr Arbington."

He brushed a grey hair of his black double-breasted chalk-stripe suit. "What can I do for you?"

"Has there been interest in any of my paintings which I submitted?" Elizabeth gripped her bag.

"Yes, as a matter of fact."

"Oh?"

"Someone has declared an interest in one of them." He coughed.

"The landscape scene of a loch and hills?"

"No, my dear, the coachman."

The coachman?

Mr Arbington smiled. "You look surprised."

"When will you be able to complete the purchase?"

"I believe in a week, perhaps two."

"Terrific!"

Mr Arbington raised his grey eyebrows. "I could tell the person liked it." He rubbed his hands.

"How?"

"The lady studied the painting for some time. Whilst I spoke to her, she appeared enthusiastic. When the deal has been completed, I will telephone you."

"Thank you."

Mr Arbington led his guest to the door. "Nice to see you again, my dear."

Elizabeth walked down the six steps then looked towards Mr Arbington. He smiled and waved then went back into the gallery. As Elizabeth made her way along 45th street, she gazed at the array of shop facades.

I wish the lure of the fashionable clothes shops would not be an enticement. But if I sold several paintings then James and I would have more capital and less stress. Here is a furniture shop – I cannot resist them either! It won't do any harm to enter and look around.

"Yes, ma'am, can I help?" said the male sales assistant.

"I'm just taking a look around."

The sales assistant returned to another customer.

That's a nice oak mirror. Elizabeth moved closer to it. Maybe an antique. She lifted the price tag – 89 dollars!

"An antique, ma'am," said the sales assistant, "excellent craftsmanship."

He was quick to return. "It would look perfect in my hall."

"It is a good price for a quality product, ma'am. Look at the oak surround." He moved his hand round the top of the mirror.

"I agree." James would not be pleased if I spent almost ninety dollars on a mirror.

"You don't have to pay for it all at once."

Elizabeth turned to the sales assistant.

"You can pay for it in a series of instalments."

"You supply a credit facility!"

"Oh, yes, ma'am." The sales assistant smiled.

"I will speak to my husband and get back to you."

"No problem, ma'am, see you soon." The sales assistant walked Elizabeth to the shop exit and opened the door. "Bye."

Elizabeth walked slowly back to the subway station. When she turned a corner, noticed people had gathered near the station entrance. A group of dark-uniformed police officers ushered them back. Elizabeth approached a woman onlooker and asked the reason for the commotion.

"Maybe someone has been robbed?" She popped her head up over another onlooker.

Elizabeth moved her head from side to side.

"What's up?" said a short man behind Elizabeth.

Elizabeth tilted her head down toward him. "A police incident of some sort."

"Terrific! That's all I need." He looked at his wristwatch.

From a distance, the clanging sound of bells could be heard. They became louder and a black van with its distinctive red cross on the side appeared then screeched to a halt outside the station. Two men in white jackets and black trousers immediately got out. As they rushed into the building, one carried a medical bag and his colleague a folded-up stretcher. The police officers cordoned off the entrance.

"What has happened?" said a woman in a white fur coat and large white hat.

Elizabeth looked at her. "An accident I believe."

"I will be late for a theatre appointment." She checked her trim gold wristwatch.

"Someone's comin' out!" a man shouted.

The medical personnel came out with a body on a stretcher covered by a grey blanket. As they took the stretcher into their vehicle, a pair of men's black shoes protruded from the blanket.

A police officer blew his whistle and people dispersed from the scene. The ambulance sped away through the Downtown Manhattan traffic.

Elizabeth entered the subway station, walked down the steep staircase and onto a platform for her designated train. Both platforms soon became congested with delayed passengers who awaited their respective north and south arrivals. Elizabeth heard the rumble of a train within the entrance tunnel become louder, then two headlights became larger and brighter. In anticipation of the train's arrival, passengers on the platform edged forward. A silver-grey train emerged from the dark tunnel and came to a halt. When the carriage doors sprung open, passengers left the train. They shuffled and manoeuvred past people who started to board the train. Much to her delight when Elizabeth boarded she managed to grab a seat.

"You gotta light, lady?" said a dark-bearded man who sat opposite.

"Sorry, no."

He leaned to the side. "Gotta light, Mac?"

"Yes." The clean-shaven man pulled out a box of matches from his raincoat pocket then handed it to the other man. "Keep it."

"Thanks."

"Glad to oblige, I work for a tobacco company!"

The bearded man smiled.

Whilst the train travelled through the borough of Manhattan, Elizabeth read a fashion magazine left on her seat by a previous passenger. Photographs of slim young women in short skirts were prominent. As the train pulled into a station, Elizabeth looked out the carriage window. A group of passengers rushed onto the crowded train. Due to the congestion, people had to stand huddled together in the carriage passageway.

Elizabeth looked up. Thank goodness I found an empty seat. To stand and endure a stuffy carriage for my length of journey would be uncomfortable and intolerable.

The train moved off and Elizabeth returned to her magazine. She read with intrigue and interest the predicted fashion trends for 1930. When the train emerged from a long tunnel, bright sunlight shone from the Manhattan skyline into the carriage. To deter the glare of the sun, Elizabeth pulled down a window blind. She continued to read and enjoy the magazine content.

After she stepped off the train, Elizabeth went for a stroll through Central Park then returned to her apartment. She prepared dinner then sat down at the kitchen table to scrutinise energy bills for the last twelve months. Elizabeth heard the apartment door open, stood up and put the bills into a table drawer.

"James?"

"Yes, Elizabeth, just me." James removed his hat and coat. "Did you have a good day?" He put both garments on the coat stand.

Elizabeth kissed her husband on the cheek. "How did your day go?"

"One of the staff has been dismissed."

"Who?"

"Al. He took it badly."

"James, he may not find another job. How old is he?"

"Fifty-two. Since his wife passed away six months ago, he has not kept good health. He did not need this – it's a kick in the teeth." James walked into the living room.

Elizabeth went into the kitchen and set the table. "James!" she cried.

"Yes?" He walked into the kitchen. "Why are we having our evening meal in the kitchen, Elizabeth?"

It feels warm and cosy in here. Besides, we won't have to heat the dining room therefore save money on our fuel bill."

James smiled.

"Tell me about Al."

"He went into Bob's office at nine o'clock, came out five minutes later in shock and left the office. Why do you ask?"

"It's maybe nothing."

"What Elizabeth?"

"I was in Lower Manhattan this morning to see Mr Arbington about my paintings. After I left his premises and reached Chambers Street station, it had been closed to the public."

"Why?"

"A fatality."

"What happened?"

"Not sure. A body was taken away by an emergency ambulance crew. I'm sure it may have been a man."

"You believe it could be Al? He looked upset but strikes me as a responsible fellow. Would you like me to telephone him?"

"Just to make sure he is alright. This morning would have been traumatic for him – so soon after the death of his wife."

James went into the hall, lifted the handset then dialled Al's number.

Elizabeth followed.

James turned to Elizabeth. "No answer."

"Try again later."

James replaced the handset into the cradle. "He may be at an illicit club getting drunk."

Elizabeth frowned. "Let us hope so."

James stood on the station platform along with other frustrated fellow passengers and looked at his wristwatch.

"Damn!" The train is fifteen minutes late. Not the ideal start to the working week.

Another five minutes passed and agitated commuters exchanged grievances with one another about the service. Their comments not complementary of the New York rail network. Rather than take another glance at his wristwatch, James fiddled with house keys in his coat pocket.

I will be fortunate to make Lexington Avenue to Wall Street in time for eight o'clock! The other platform had also filled up with commuters for the northbound train. James heard a train's echo within the tunnel. He moved a step forward and looked towards the tunnel's mouth. Many commuters had the same impulse. A train soon emerged then came to a halt at the busy platform. People dashed for each of the eight carriages. James boarded and edged himself near the doorway. The train conductor will have a tiresome time manoeuvring his way through these packed carriages! The train pulled away from the empty station platform and into another tunnel. After a couple of minutes, the daylight appeared and any passengers fortunate to find a seat, started to open and read their morning newspaper. James held onto an elevated metal handrail with his left hand and gripped the briefcase with his right. Two stylish young women in their early-twenties stood next to him. Even with their sophisticated appearance, they did not receive the offer of a seat. As the train moved to and fro, both women held onto their metal handrail to steady their stance. The topic of conversation revolved around a plush restaurant near the Plaza Hotel in Midtown. The decor, intimate atmosphere and excellent cuisine received lavish praise from both young women.

James glanced at them. Please mention the name again, I didn't catch it. This would be an ideal place to celebrate Elizabeth's birthday.

"Wouldn't it be terrific if they served alcohol?" said one young woman.

"It does have everything else," said her companion.

"There's still a shortage of single men."

Her companion quipped, "That's not stopped you in the past!"

"Behave, Gloria." The scarlet cloche hat she wore turned in the direction of James.

Her friend whispered, "sorry, Anne."

I tried to look uninterested.

"Mary attended a birthday celebration dinner at Vicini's last month." The young woman adjusted her light blue cloche hat.

"And?"

"She loved it!"

"Gloria, does Mary drink?"

"Oh yes, orange juice." She laughed.

"You mean a Bronx cocktail?"

"You bet! Orange topped up with plenty of gin and vermouth. I could go one right now."

Her companion laughed.

This is different from my normal journey to work – and enjoyable! However, I must remember the restaurant name – Vicini's.

"Anne, did you read that the Graf Zeppelin may return to New York?"

"No, Gloria, when?"

"Sometime in the summer, it hasn't been confirmed yet."

"I would love to fly in an airship, have dinner and admire the view."

"Once they become popular, more flights will be available."

"Then maybe the cost of a ticket will become affordable."

"What destination would you choose?"

"Maybe London or Paris?"

"Anywhere else?"

"California. I may meet a movie star." Anne smiled.

Gloria looked along the carriage. "Here comes the conductor."

Anne searched her pockets. "I can't find my ticket!"

"He has a grumpy expression."

"It's not funny."

James spotted a ticket on the carriage floor and picked it up. "Could this be your ticket miss?" James handed over the ticket.

The young woman examined it. "Yes, thank you."

As he eased his way through the carriage, the conductor clipped passenger's tickets. The two young women continued their conversation, which for James brightened an otherwise regular mundane journey to work. The train drew in to a station.

James looked out the carriage window. Wall Street, what a pity.

"Excuse me, please," said the conductor. He retraced his steps through the crowded carriage.

James squeezed past both young women in order reach the exit door. They smiled at him and had a scent of sweet lavender. He left the train, walked up the stairway and exited the subway station. Commuters late for work quickened their steps en route to various office locations. James looked at his wristwatch and it confirmed he was late by ten minutes. He entered the building, took the elevator and soon arrived at his office. Clara, senior secretary within the practice, greeted James with a grim expression.

"Jim, Bob wants to see you in his office

James gripped his briefcase. "Now?"

"Right away."

James put down his briefcase next to his desk and walked along the corridor. He stood outside Bob's office and knocked three times on his door.

"Come in."

James opened the door then walked into the austere office.

"Jim, take a seat."

James closed the door. Bob also has a grim expression.

"Bad news Jim, it's Tom." He sat back on his brown leather chair.

"What's up?"

"An accident at a local subway station."

"Which one?"

"Chambers Street."

"What happened?"

"Tom was hit by a train."

James slumped down on the chair. "Hit? How?"

"Two commuters told police officers that Tom jumped in front of a train."

"Suicide! Not Tom."

"Suicide is the opinion of our NYPD. In the meantime, can you take on some of his clients?"

"Yes, of course."

"Clara will give you the files." Bob stood up and walked towards James.

James stood up.

"It's a shock Jim, however we carry on." Bob opened the door.

James walked back to his office, entered it then sat down.

Clara knocked once then entered. "Jim, these are some of Tom's files." She put them on his desk.

"Thanks Clara."

"Can I get you a coffee?"

"Yes, thanks."

"Coming up."

When Clara left, James sat down and stared at his office window and the Lower Manhattan skyline.

Why Tom? Such a waste of life. In my conversations with him, I did not detect any woes or stress.

Clara walked into the office. "White with two sugar." She put the cup down on the desk. "If you need anything, just call."

"Thanks."

She smiled and departed.

James browsed the bundle of Tom's files. Of the six, four clients were local and the other two resided in Long Island and Staten Island. Three of the businesses related to import/export of goods, two in retail and one practiced as a designer. The files appeared up to date with regular correspondence between Tom and his respective clients. However, all still had to settle their account. Four made a part-payment, the other two had not paid any of their outstanding debt. One of them a retailer and the other an importer/exporter.

Clara knocked on the door and entered. "Jim, this relates to 'Joes' – one of the retailers." She held a cheque in her hand.

"How much?"

"Two hundred and fifty dollars."

James looked at the account. "Another part-payment, still one hundred and fifty outstanding."

Clara smiled. "At least a payment has been received."

"Did Tom mention one of the importers/exporters – WNY Trade?" James reached for their file and browsed through it. "He met with this client on the 1st of March."

"What was the outcome Jim?"

"According to Tom's notes, payment is to follow." James looked closer. "Two thousand dollars!"

Clara leaned over. "Wow!"

"That could be why he met with the client – to apply pressure for payment. It's a large amount of debt."

Clara glanced at the office wall calendar. "The meeting didn't pay any dividends, that's just short of six weeks."

James stood up. "I better let Bob see this." He lifted the file from his desk. "He may also want to pay the client a visit."

"I agree."

James walked back along the corridor to Bob's office and gave his distinctive knock on the door.

"Come in."

James entered Bob's office and laid the file on his desk. "Two thousand dollars has still not been paid."

"Which client?"

"WNY Trade. Tom contacted them six weeks ago."

"West Midtown?"

James nodded.

Bob opened the file. "I'll contact them."

"Do you want me to accompany you?"

"I'll give them a call. Maybe there's been a glitch of some sort."

James left the room, closed the door then walked to his office.

"Can I have a word, James?" Clara stood in the doorway.

"Of course, have a seat."

She sat down opposite James. "It's about Tom."

"Go on."

Clara moved her chair forward. "Lucy?"

"The office junior?"

Clara nodded. "She told me that one of her friends spotted a man being chased inside Chambers Street station."

"Chased?"

"By two men."

"What happened next?"

"He stumbled and fell onto the railway line. He managed to stand, then a train came through the tunnel and hit him."

"Yesterday morning?"

"Yes."

"Did she inform the police?"

"No. Lucy said her friend didn't want to become involved. She's just fifteen."

"It's not like Tom to run away from anything or anyone!"

"Lucy also mentioned her friend did not like the look of both pursuers."

"Two witnesses told NYPD that Tom jumped in front of the train."

"Maybe that's how it appeared."

James sat back on his chair. "Does Lucy's friend stay locally?"

"No, that particular day she visited a Downtown museum for a school project. She stays in Long Island."

"Thanks for letting me know."

Clara stood up and left the office.

James gazed out his office window. Who could the pursuers have been?

For the remainder of that day, James studied Tom's files. They became a source of information from where a lead to Tom's death may be discovered. Just after five o'clock, James departed the office and caught the train from Wall Street station. On this occasion, he managed to find an empty seat. He sat down, put the briefcase on his lap, stared out the carriage window and pondered about the day's events.

I knew Tom's marriage had fallen apart and this may be perceived why he committed suicide. However, given what Clara told me, another reason for Tom's death had surfaced. Could the pursuers that Lucy's friend spotted be connected to the firm WNY Trade? After all, they do owe a large sum of money to us. Maybe Tom became too persistent and assertive in his effort to collect payment. Had there been any method of unofficial contact? It is a pity we had not discussed the situation over our frequent lunches together. When Bob contacts them, I await with anticipation the outcome. I suspect he will have to converse in their "hell's kitchen" language. I checked my wristwatch – should be at Union Square station shortly.

A man stood up and made his way towards the carriage door. Two male passengers moved forward to take the spare seats, however, a teenage boy was there first. The train pulled into the station and came to a halt. The carriage doors opened and a hesitant elderly woman passenger proceeded to alight. A man rushed forward and sat on the vacant seat. A middle-aged woman boarded the carriage and looked for somewhere to sit.

James stood up and looked at her. "Excuse me."

"A gentleman. It's a rarity on this train! Thank you." The woman sat down.

James held a carriage handrail. Elizabeth's birthday on Friday and I forgot to buy a card. Thank goodness for the newsagent adjacent to my station destination. When I leave the train, I'll head straight there. At least a table has been booked at the restaurant.

Chapter 2

A Cruel Deed

Whilst in his office, James sipped a cup of coffee and read the morning newspaper. Financial articles continued to have an optimistic viewpoint about a recovery in the American economy. There came a knock on his half-open door and Clara stood at the entrance.

"Jim?"

"Yes, Clara."

"Bob would like a word."

"Now?"

"As soon as possible."

James looked at his wristwatch. "I'll see him now."

"Okay."

James put aside the newspaper, finished his coffee and laid the empty cup on his desk. He stood up, walked along the corridor to Bob's office and knocked on his door.

"Come in."

James opened the door. "Clara mentioned you wanted to see me, Bob?"

"Have a seat."

James sat down opposite Bob.

"I've spoken to a Mr Ryan of WNY Trade about the money his firm owe. He is the person Tom met with at their premises. A cheque for the full amount should be here tomorrow or at the latest, Monday."

"How did he sound?"

"Okay. He apologises for the delay – cash flow problems." Bob passed the file to James. "If no cheque has been received by Tuesday then let me know."

James stood up and lifted the file. "Will do." He left Bob's office and closed the door.

Clara approached James in the corridor. "Everything okay?"

James smiled. "Yes, fine. I will take an early lunch today – be back at one."

"If anyone calls, I will let them know." She picked a grey hair off his navy blue suit jacket and walked on.

After he attended to several customer accounts, James glanced at his wristwatch – ten minutes to twelve. He put on his hat, left the office then walked down the stairs and onto the main street.

"Gotta light, Mac?" said a male passer-by.

"Sorry, I don't smoke."

The man walked on, complete with an unlit cigarette in his mouth.

When strangers come up to me, I now feel apprehensive. It's hard to forget being held up at gunpoint.

James continued his walk to the restaurant and arrived there within ten minutes. He entered the establishment and discovered plenty seats to choose from. An advantage of taking an early lunch. However, no Tom to discuss office politics, gossip and speculation. James chose his favourite window seat, sat down and took of his hat then laid it on an empty chair.

A waitress approached. "Hi, what can I get you?"

James looked at the menu.

The waitress held a writing pad in her right hand and pencil in the other.

"Vegetable soup for starters then a plate of macaroni, please."

"Tomato sauce with the macaroni?"

"No, thanks."

"Coffee?"

He nodded. "White please."

"Back soon." The waitress departed.

James looked out the window and observed the public pass in both directions. A cultural and gender mix of New Yorkers filled the wide sidewalk on this sunny April lunchtime.

"One vegetable soup."

"That was quick!"

The waitress smiled and laid a bowl down on the white tablecloth then walked away.

Forgot to ask the waitress for a roll.

The waitress returned. "Just in case." She laid a small white plate with a roll on the table.

"Thanks."

She departed then served another customer.

James finished his starter and moved the empty soup bowl aside. He noticed a lady with dark hair and wearing a mint green coat walk out of the restaurant.

Where have I seen her before?

"Macaroni." The waitress laid down the plate then lifted the empty bowl.

"The lady that just left, is she a regular?"

The waitress shook her head. "More coffee?"

"No, thanks."

She walked away.

A short time later, James finished his lunch and sat back on the chair. He looked at his wristwatch – it would soon be time to head back. He stared at the empty seat opposite where Tom would have sat. He picked up his hat and put it on then walked to the counter. Whilst James paid his bill, the restaurant filled up with more lunchtime customers. As he left, the waitress switched on the radio and the sound of jazz music engulfed the restaurant.

It is the roaring twenties.

James returned to his office, entered the building and took the elevator to his respective floor. When he came out of the elevator, James spotted Clara and walked towards her.

"Have an enjoyable lunch, Jim?"

"Yes, thanks."

"Bob told the staff that Tom's funeral is on Monday at Trinity Church. He just received word from Tom's wife."

"Lana must be devastated given the circumstances of his death."

"Tom didn't stay with her?"

"They were separated and soon to divorce."

"I'll see you later, Jim, may as well enjoy the sunshine on my lunch break."

"Bye." Elizabeth's birthday on Friday and Tom's funeral on Monday. Such a contrast in emotions.

James looked out from the apartment living-room window at the street below. He then walked into the hall, stared into the mirror and straightened his tie.

"The taxi will be here soon, Elizabeth!" he cried.

"Almost ready, just another few minutes."

James glanced at his wristwatch. "You said that fifteen minutes ago." He heard a vehicle pump it's horn and once more looked out of the window.

"Is that our taxi?"

"Yes, it is."

Elizabeth came out of the bedroom and smiled. "Ready."

"You look radiant." James kissed her on the cheek.

"Mind my make-up!"

James smiled. "No damage done, let's go."

"James?"

"Yes, Elizabeth?"

"It's nothing."

"Are you sure?"

Elizabeth nodded.

The couple left their apartment, walked along the landing and down the stairs. The taxi driver again pumped his horn then James and Elizabeth emerged from the building. When they reached the taxi, the driver started its engine. James opened the nearside passenger door, Elizabeth stepped inside and sat on a black leather seat. James followed, closed the door then sat next to his wife.

"Where to, sir?" said the driver.

"Vicini's, please."

The taxi driver nodded.

He released the handbrake and the yellow and black taxi moved off. The driver glanced behind at James.

"One of Midtown's finest restaurants sir."

"So I am told," said James.

"My sister works there," said the driver.

"What does she do?" said Elizabeth.

"Cloakroom attendant ma'am. She's been there for two years and loves the place."

"In what way?" said Elizabeth.

"The tips she makes."

James turned to Elizabeth. "Are we to meet Dale and Georgina outside or inside the restaurant?"

"Outside, at eight o'clock."

James checked his wristwatch. "They may have to wait for a short while."

"No problem, sir, you'll be there for eight."

James smiled. "Splendid."

"You both from New York?"

"No, Scotland," said James.

"Any relatives from Scotland?" said Elizabeth. She brushed a hair off her husband's black double-breasted pin-stripe suit.

"No ma'am, just Chicago."

From Upper East Side, the taxi quickly reached Midtown. The driver manoeuvred his way through its busy streets then turned a corner and pulled up outside a well-lit establishment.

"Here we are – Vicini's."

"That was quick!" said James

Elizabeth pointed. "James, there is Georgina and Dale."

The taxi driver applied the handbrake. "One dollar ninety, sir."

James pulled out a bundle of coins from his jacket pocket and gave them to the driver. "That should cover the fare."

The driver counted them. "Thanks, sir, enjoy your evenin'."

James got out of the taxi and closed his door. He then walked to Elizabeth's side and opened her door. After she stepped onto the sidewalk, James closed the door. As he drove off, the driver waved.

"Splendid idea to book a taxi, James, it may catch on."

Georgina walked forward. "Terrific timing! Dale and I have just arrived." She kissed Elizabeth then James on the cheek.

"Good to see you again, Jim." said Dale. He shook his hand then turned to Elizabeth. "You look divine, Beth." He kissed her on the cheek.

Elizabeth smiled.

As the two couples entered the restaurant, a well-groomed gentleman in a black dinner suit greeted them.

"Good evening, do you have a reservation?"

"Carsell-Brown," said James.

The host checked a register. "Fine, sir, a lady will take your hats and coats." He pointed to the cloakroom.

The four guests walked over to the cloakroom and removed their various hats and coats. A young woman in a short shapeless pink dress took them.

"This is for you." She gave James a voucher with a number written on the front.

"I see you chose the yellow dress, Elizabeth," said Georgina.

Elizabeth turned to face her sister. "In complete contrast to your choice of light blue."

Georgina smiled. "It matches Dale's brown chalk-stripe suit."

Dale turned towards James. "That's what I like about her, Jim – she's considerate." He laughed then rubbed his hands. "Let's eat."

The host took both couples to their reserved table. A debonair waiter in a white shirt, slim black tie and dark trousers took their food and non-alcoholic drink order.

Several hours later, both couples left their table and headed for the cloakroom. The attendant took a voucher from James then returned with coats and hats.

"Terrific restaurant, James." Georgina put on her dark blue coat.

James put on his dark hat then assisted Elizabeth with her black coat.

"And also the service – sublime." Dale put on his brown fedora hat. "How about we visit a club? I could do with a proper drink!"

Georgina glanced towards Dale then at Elizabeth.

Elizabeth frowned.

Georgina took Dale's arm. "Perhaps another time."

The host approached the foursome and opened the exit door. "Hope to see you again, ladies and gentlemen, safe journey home."

Both couples departed the favourable establishment and strolled along the sidewalk. They stopped at a nearby taxi rank.

Georgina kissed Elizabeth. "Speak to you soon. Dale and I will walk home."

"Are you sure?" said Elizabeth.

"Yes, it's a lovely evening. We'll be home in about twenty minutes." Georgina whispered, "He needs the exercise."

"Hey, Beth," said Dale, "I was once an amateur boxer."

James smiled. "There are many of them on the Manhattan streets."

Dale laughed.

Elizabeth cried, "A taxi, James!" She waved her hand in the air.

The taxi stopped beside James and Elizabeth then both couples said their final goodbyes. When Elizabeth and James settled into the taxi, it drove off. Dale and Georgina waved to them.

"Let's find a club, Georgina."

"I'm tired, Dale, perhaps another time." Georgina smiled. "There is whisky in the kitchen cupboard."

Dale frowned.

"We'll soon be home. Just three more blocks to 53rd street."

"Okay, Georgina, we'll see some action next Friday night."

"You're on."

Georgina and Dale continued walking back to their apartment through the streets of Midtown. A man in a charcoal overcoat and hat came towards them. He stopped in front of Dale.

"Are you okay, fellah?" said Dale.

From inside his coat, the stranger pulled out a gun. He stood motionless and stared at Dale with cold eyes.

Dale looked at the gun. "Is it money you want?"

The stranger clicked the trigger.

"You can take all I have on me."

Three shots were fired at Dale's chest. His broad 6ft feet body slumped to the ground. The man replaced the gun into his coat pocket, walked on and over Dale, now sprawled on the sidewalk.

Georgina dropped her handbag, screamed then looked around the quiet street. "Help!" she shouted, "help us someone."

"Georgina." Dale lifted his arm.

She bent down beside her husband and held his hand. "Help will come, hang on."

People started to appear at the scene and surround Georgina and Dale. One man ran into a shop to call for medical assistance. Minutes later, a police officer on foot arrived followed by the sound of clanging bells from an approaching vehicle. It drew up at the crime scene then two men rushed out. One had a small black bag and he laid it next to Dale. He examined Dale and nodded to his colleague who went back into the vehicle. A stretcher was brought out then laid beside Dale. He was lifted onto it and taken into the ambulance. One stayed inside and the other came out then closed the rear door. He jumped into the driver's seat and the ambulance sped off.

Georgina picked up her handbag then turned to the police officer. "Will he be all right?" She took out a handkerchief from her coat pocket and wiped both eyes.

"They will do all they can, ma'am."

"I can't believe what has just happened!" Georgina shook her head. "Why?"

"Can you come down to the station, ma'am? We'll need a statement."

Georgina looked at the officer. "Now?"

"There's a gunman on the loose, ma'am. The station's not far."

A police vehicle arrived and stopped alongside Georgina and the officer. He approached it, spoke to the driver then opened the vehicle's rear door. Georgina went inside and the officer closed the door. The vehicle moved off and headed for the local Midtown precinct. When it arrived, both police officers got out and one opened the rear door.

Georgina stepped onto the sidewalk. "Thank you."

"This way please," said the officer. He led Georgina inside the building then a small room. "Have a seat ma'am, someone will be here soon to take a statement."

"Can I telephone my sister?"

The officer looked at his wristwatch. "It's late, perhaps tomorrow morning would be appropriate."

"Georgina sat down on a wooden chair.

"Coffee, ma'am?"

"Please, black no sugar."

The officer left the room and closed the door.

Georgina removed her small blue hat, shook her head then placed the hat on a wooden table. She opened her handbag, took out a small rectangular mirror and looked into it. Georgina prodded her dark blonde bobbed hair then put the mirror back into her handbag. The door opened and in walked a police officer. He had a stocky build and a grim expression.

"I'm Sergeant Johnston, ma'am."

The officer laid a cup on the table in front of Georgina and sat down opposite her. He opened a drawer and brought out a pen and piece of paper.

"Thank you." Georgina lifted the cup and took a sip of coffee.

"How do you feel?"

"Tired and weary. This has been a complete shock."

"I won't keep you long. Name?"

"Georgina Rhodes."

"Age?"

"Forty-seven."

The officer wrote on the piece of paper. "Your husband's name?"

"Dale." Georgina took another sip of coffee.

"Age?"

"Forty."

The officer looked up.

Georgina took another sip of coffee.

"Can you describe the person who shot your husband?"

"Is there any news about my husband's condition?"

"Not yet. The gunman, ma'am?"

"He wore a dark coat and hat."

"Was he tall, short, young, old, any features that stuck out?"

Georgina sipped her coffee. "Average height – around five feet eight, average build and perhaps my husband's age."

The officer wrote down the details. "Caucasian?"

"White, he had a dark moustache."

"Did he say anythin' to you or your husband? Did he demand money?"

Georgina gripped the white cup. "He didn't say a word."

"He just approached your husband and opened fire?" The officer sat back.

Georgina nodded. "He came up to Dale and shot him three times."

"What happened next?"

"I think he went down an alleyway. It all happened in an instant!"

The officer stood up. "I'll be back soon." He picked up the piece of paper, walked to the door then opened it and left the room.

Georgina laid her cup on the table.

Sergeant Johnston walked back into the room. "Two of my men will escort you home, ma'am. Still no word on your husband."

Georgina stood up and put on her hat. "This has been a long night Sergeant, can you take me to my sister's apartment in Upper East Side?"

"Yeah, no problem. Give details of her address to the driver. Also let us have a telephone number in case we need to contact you." Sergeant Johnston handed Georgina a piece of written paper. "Call the number on this if you happen to remember anythin' else about the incident."

Georgina took the piece of paper and popped it into her handbag.

Elizabeth woke up to the sound of vehicle doors being closed. She heard a man and woman's voice then the apartment doorbell.

"James." Elizabeth nudged her husband. "James!"

"What's up?"

"Someone has rung our bell."

"What time is it?" James yawned.

Elizabeth peered at the clock on the bedside table. "Just after two o'clock." She raised her head. "There it goes again."

James rose from the bed then put on his silk burgundy dressing gown and slippers. He left the apartment and went downstairs to the main door. He yawned then opened it slightly.

"Georgina!"

"Sir, there has been an incident," said a police officer.

"James," said Georgina, "Dale is in hospital."

"Hospital! What happened?" James opened the door wider."

"Goodnight, ma'am," said the police officer.

"Thank you, officer," said Georgina. She stepped inside.

"No problem, ma'am."

James closed the door. "Are you all right?"

"Sorry to wake you, James, I couldn't go home."

"Don't concern yourself." James led Georgina upstairs then into the apartment.

"What has happened!" Elizabeth stared at her sister.

"It's Dale, Elizabeth, he's been shot." Georgina fell into Elizabeth's arms.

"Shot! When?"

Georgina sighed.

Elizabeth looked at James.

"Let me have your coat, Georgina," said James.

She removed her coat and handed it to James.

He hung it on the coatstand then went into the kitchen.

Elizabeth took her sister into the living room. "Have a seat on the couch."

Georgina sat down. "What a night, Elizabeth – and on your birthday."

Elizabeth sat close to Georgina. "How did it happen and where?"

Georgina smiled. "You sound like a police officer." She wiped her eyes.

Elizabeth embraced her sister.

"We were on our way home. A man approached, brought out a gun and shot Dale three times."

James came into the living room and gave Georgina a cup of coffee.

"Thank you, James." Georgina took the cup. "Everything happened so fast."

"How is Dale?" said Elizabeth.

"They haven't revealed his condition to me."

"I will contact the hospital tomorrow," said James, "Dale would have been taken to Bellevue."

"You mean today, James," said Elizabeth.

"Yes." He glanced at the wall clock. "In the morning I will telephone the office and tell them I'm taking Saturday off."

Georgina laid her cup on the table. "I feel terrible about this."

Elizabeth put her hand on Georgina's wrist. "It's not your fault. A madman is on the loose."

"And the NYPD will catch him," said James.

Georgina's eyelids closed, opened then closed again.

Elizabeth glanced at her husband. "James, you can have the couch. Georgina will sleep with me."

"Yes, of course."

Elizabeth looked at Georgina. "Later today, we will go to the hospital."

Georgina closed her eyes.

That morning, James, Elizabeth and Georgina took the train to Bellevue Hospital situated on 1st Avenue. When they arrived at the hospital, James approached the reception desk.

"Yes, sir, how can I help?" said a young woman.

"A relative was brought here late last night – he had been shot. Can you give me information about his condition?" James looked at Georgina then the receptionist. "His wife is here and concerned."

The receptionist looked at a printed document. "His name, sir?"

"Dale Rhodes."

"After being admitted, Mr Rhodes was taken to surgery and afterwards moved to intensive care."

"How is he?"

"I'll call a doctor and he can explain." The receptionist picked up a telephone and dialled a number then placed the transmitter close to her mouth. "Dr Boninsegna?"

"Yes."

"Relatives of a person admitted yesterday evening are in reception. They would like information on the patient's condition."

"What is the patient's name?"

"Dale Rhodes."

"Which ward?"

"Ward 7."

"Won't be long, Elena."

The receptionist replaced the telephone and looked at James. "He's on his way to see you."

"Thanks." James walked over to Elizabeth and Georgina. "A doctor will be here soon." He looked at Georgina. "He will update you on Dale's condition."

A short time later, footsteps could be heard on the stone floor. As they became louder, Elizabeth and Georgina looked towards the corridor. A tall thin man with dark wavy hair and horn-rimmed spectacles approached them. He had both hands in his medium-length white coat and a stethoscope round his neck.

"I'm Dr Boninsegna."

James approached the doctor. "I am the patient's brother-in-law."

Georgina moved towards the doctor. "How is my husband?"

"He's in intensive care, ma'am. Three bullets were removed from his chest."

"His condition doctor?" said Elizabeth.

"Serious."

Georgina looked at Elizabeth.

"Thanks for your time, doctor," said James.

"Can I see my husband?"

"Not yet."

"When?" said Elizabeth.

"Give a telephone number to the receptionist and she will call you when it is convenient."

"Yes, will do." Elizabeth looked at Georgina.

"Thanks for your time," said James.

The doctor smiled then walked back along the corridor.

"James, how about a cup of coffee," said Elizabeth, "maybe there is a facility in the hospital."

James approached the reception desk.

"Yes, sir."

"Dr Boninsegna requested I give you a telephone number in the event of any developments."

The receptionist gave James a pencil and piece of paper.

He wrote his name and telephone number on the piece of white paper then handed it to the receptionist.

"Thanks."

"Do you sell coffee in the hospital?"

"There is a visitor area not far from here." She pointed. "Enter the next building and it is signposted."

James tipped his hat. "Thanks for your assistance today."

"Pleasure, sir." The Hispanic receptionist smiled.

The three hospital visitors left the main building and entered a smaller one. A board in several languages signified the respective area they sought.

"At last." Georgina sighed.

Elizabeth looked around the room. "It's busy!"

"There's a table." James led Elizabeth and Georgina to an empty table with four chairs.

Georgina sat down opposite Elizabeth and James. She stared down at the empty seat next to her.

"Dale will be fine, Georgina," said Elizabeth. She removed her hat and unbuttoned her coat.

"He's a fighter and will pull through," said James.

Georgina took off her hat and laid it on the empty chair.

"Here comes a waitress," said James. He removed his hat and placed it on the table.

The waitress arrived then stood at the front of the rectangular table. She took out a notepad from her yellow overall chest pocket then produced a pencil from behind her left ear.

"Hi, what can I get ya?"

"Three cups of coffee, please," said James.

"Do you sell tea?" said Georgina.

"Just cawfee," said the waitress, "black or white?"

"Three white coffees, please," said Elizabeth.

The waitress wrote down the order. "Cookies?" She looked at each of the three customers.

"No, thanks, just coffee," said James.

The waitress put the pencil behind her left ear and departed.

Elizabeth smiled at Georgina. "The Boston Tea Party has a lot to answer for."

Georgina cast her gaze around the room. "And also the people who popularised smoking."

James smiled. "I believe the Europeans, Georgina, after their arrival in 18th century America."

Georgina leaned forward towards Elizabeth. "That chap over there in the dark blue suit resembles Douglas Fairbanks."

Elizabeth glanced across the room, looked at Georgina and shook her head. "James looks more like Douglas Fairbanks."

"Thank you, Elizabeth." James smiled.

Several minutes later, the waitress appeared with a white tray and its contents. She lifted each white cup and saucer off the tray and put them in front of James, Elizabeth and Georgina.

Elizabeth said, "Is the facility busy most days?"

The waitress nodded. "This is normal for a Saturday, folks visitin' their relatives and friends."

"Will I pay you now?" said James.

"Pay at the counter." The waitress departed and walked towards another table where she lifted empty cups and saucers onto her tray.

Georgina lifted her cup and sipped the coffee.

"How is it?" said Elizabeth.

"I have lived here for twenty years and still miss a cup of tea!" Georgina took another sip.

"I have to admit, I prefer coffee to tea." James lifted his cup and took a sip.

"Do you miss Scotland, Elizabeth?" Georgina laid her cup on the saucer.

"Some of the time. I suppose seventeen years can be a long time." Elizabeth lifted her cup. "I don't miss the rain." She sipped her coffee.

"Manhattan has the cultural aspects of society, Elizabeth," said James, "you would miss the art galleries, museums and theatres."

Georgina smiled. "There is the Ardrishaig village hall."

James laughed. "And the harbour." He sipped his coffee.

Elizabeth laid her cup onto the saucer and sat back. "Yes, yes. I am now in my mid-forties, as you become older sentimentality creeps in." She smiled.

"You are correct, Elizabeth," said James, "I miss Docharnea."

"A beautiful house," said Georgina, "the grounds and the view over Loch Fyne."

"Now we have Central Park and the East River," said James.

Georgina laughed. "Spoiled for choice."

"If it hadn't been for that coachman who saved your life, we would not be here," said James.

Elizabeth stared at her husband. "James Carlisle."

"What became of him Elizabeth?" Georgina picked up her cup and held it with both hands.

"I'm not sure Georgina. In one of her letters, Nancy mentioned he had given up his coachman's position and gone to Edinburgh."

"Why Edinburgh?" said Georgina.

"He came from there," said Elizabeth.

"He didn't appear the type of person to participate in coachman's duties," said James.

"What do you mean, James?" said Georgina.

"He didn't appear the rough and ready type."

Georgina laughed. "Not the "hell's kitchen" type." She sipped her coffee.

"I once had a conversation with Lady Beaumont and she maintained he was well-educated," said Elizabeth.

James drank his coffee then laid the empty cup on the saucer. "I agree, Elizabeth, he had clean fingernails!"

"He must have been a gentleman," said Georgina.

"That he was," said Elizabeth.

"I speculate on what he does now." James sat back on his chair.

"Maybe on his travels somewhere?" Elizabeth smiled at her husband.

"Wherever he is – thank you. Talking about him made me laugh today." Georgina sipped her coffee.

"We'll toast him tonight," said James, "and to Dale's recovery."

"I agree, however first of all you should pay the bill." Elizabeth looked towards the crowded entrance. "People await a seat."

"Yes, let's go." Georgina drank her coffee, laid the empty cup onto the saucer then looked at Elizabeth. "Finished?"

"Yes."

On Tuesday morning, James caught his usual train for work. It was another instance of standing room only on the busy commuter train. He still had a picture in his mind of Dale being confronted by a thug and shot without mercy. If police officers had not come to his rescue, the same fate could have happened to him.

As crime increases, New York has become a dangerous place to live. Perhaps the reason why Elizabeth had sentiments about Ardrishaig. However, New York does not intimidate me but glum train conductors can at times.

"Ticket."

James handed his ticket to the conductor.

He clipped the ticket then gave it back to James.

When the train approached a station, one nearby passenger left his seat and before people boarded, James made for it. Two stations later, a well-dressed lady boarded and looked around the carriage for a spare seat.

James stood up. "You can have mine."

She smiled. "Thanks." The lady sat down, looked upward towards James and smiled once more.

Her smile is worth the effort to stand.

"Sorry, buddy." A man bumped into James.

"No problem." James straightened his hat.

"When will those guys learn to drive a train?" said the man.

"Soon I hope!" My stop, Wall Street.

The fellow passenger pulled out a New York Times from his coat pocket and read it.

James alighted from the train, walked up a stairway, reached the station exit and looked at his wristwatch.

The train may have a dodgy driver however, he has arrived on time. Since my experience with a gunman, I still feel apprehensive at this stage of the morning.

James arrived then entered his office premises and as he approached the elevator, noticed the 'out of order' sign. He took the stairs, reached his firm's floor then walked along the corridor to his office. Clara emerged from an office and spotted James.

Clara has an uneasy look about her.

"Jim, Bob is in hospital."

"Bob! What happened?"

"He was attacked last night."

"Attacked?"

"He was shot in the leg."

"Come into my office."

Clara followed a shocked James into the room. He put his briefcase down on the floor, took of his hat and coat then hung them on the wooden stand.

"Have a seat Clara."

She sat down. "The hospital called ten minutes ago – on Bob's request."

James shook his head. "The world has gone crazy!" He went behind his desk and sat down.

"Bob had just left Dresners Restaurant and apparently confronted by two men.

After an argument, a scuffle ensued then a shot was fired."

"Have the thugs been apprehended?"

"Not yet."

Dale shot on Friday evening and now Bob. "Is he in Bellevue?"

"Yes. He's in a comfortable condition."

"That is some consolation. Is he allowed any visitors?"

"No. The hospital stated not at present. You will now be in charge, Jim."

"We carry on as normal." However, I can't do Bob's work and my own.

"What about the chap who filled in for Tom last year?"

"When his wife became ill?"

"Yes, Ted."

"Ted Essen."

"Yes. Can you contact him?"

"If he has the same number and address. I'm sure he sought to live and work in Europe."

"Their employment situation is worse than ours. I reckon he'll still be in the city."

"Onto it right away." Clara stood up and walked to the door then turned around. "I sent flowers to the hospital."

James smiled.

"Tom had a nice send-off."

James nodded.

Clara closed the door.

What a start to the week!

James pulled open a drawer and took out his diary. As he browsed through it, there came a knock on the door.

Clara walked in. "Jim, a Detective McAndrew is here to see you."

"Detective McAndrew?"

"Yes, NYPD."

"Better send him in." James put his desk diary back into the drawer then closed it.

A slim middle-aged man strolled into the office. "Sorry to bother you sir. I'm Detective McAndrew."

James stood up, walked over to him then shook his hand and closed the door. "Have a seat, Detective."

"Thanks." He took off his black fedora hat and sat down.

A gruff voice indeed. "Coffee?"

"No thanks, sir, my doctor says I have to cut down."

James went behind his desk and sat down. "What can I do for you, Detective?"

He took out a packet of cigarettes, pulled one out and put it between his nicotine-stained teeth. "You don't mind, sir?"

James shook his head.

Detective McAndrew produced a box of matches from another pocket and lit the cigarette. He shoved the Craven 'A' cigarette packet and matches back into their designated pockets.

"It's about the attempted murder of your boss last night." He puffed on his cigarette.

"Your department is quick off the mark."

"We feel there could be a connection to other incidents."

"A colleague killed and the attempt on my life. Incidentally, did you apprehend the person who confronted me?"

"Not yet, no doubt he's gone to ground."

"Did anyone witness the attack on Bob?"

"A taxi driver spotted two men who both wore dark caps and jackets leave the crime scene double-quick."

"Not much to go on."

"All three partners sir – too much of a coincidence. Anybody you suspect may hold a grudge?"

"Not that I'm aware of." James sat back on his chair.

"Anyone who the firm has threatened with legal action for not settlin' their bill?"

"Due to this economic climate, clients do not settle accounts. No recent legal action has been taken against any client."

"Does any client owe a large sum of money?" The detective puffed on his cigarette.

"Not any of mine. Bob handles the major accounts."

"Could you check his portfolio to see if anythin' stuck out?"

"Of course. Do you want the information now?"

Detective McAndrew stood up and put on his hat. "Give me a call if you uncover anythin'." He laid a written card on the desk. "That's my personal number."

James stood up, grabbed a silver metal ashtray and held it in front of Detective McAndrew.

"Thanks." He stubbed out his cigarette. "Hope to hear from you soon, Mr Carsell-Brown."

James put the ashtray on his desk, walked to the door and opened it.

"I'll see myself out, sir." He smiled. "Oh, one more thing?"

"Yes?"

"You're not from here?"

"Scotland. My wife and I left seventeen years ago."

"My family originates from Scotland."

"Where about?"

"The south – a place called Dumbfrys."

James smiled. "Dumfries is pronounced Dumfreece."

"That's how you say it! I learn somethin' noo all the time."

James shook the detective's hand. A firm handshake. "Bye, Detective."

"See you, sir." He left the office.

Clara walked in and sniffed the air. "Lucky Strike?"

James shook his head. "Craven 'A'."

She smiled.

"I need details of Bob's clients over the past year."

"Will do." She smiled. "Lucky Strike cigarettes are better, they keep me slim."

As Clara departed, James lifted up his window to breathe fresh air then looked at his wristwatch. He sat down, opened the desk drawer and took out his diary. He opened it at last Friday's date – Elizabeth's birthday. It had turned out an enjoyable evening but became a forgettable one. James stared at the diary and pondered.

Dale in hospital – unlucky thirteenth day of April. I'll keep today free in order to scrutinise Bob's files. It is bad enough the firm being in financial difficulty without a possible vendetta against us.

Clara walked into the office with five files in her arms. "There is more to come Jim." She put the files down on the side of his desk. "I'll bring the rest later."

"Are there many?"

"Just another seven." Clara smiled. "When you're finished with them, give me a shout." She walked out and closed the door.

James stared at the pile of files on his desk. This will take time.

For the remainder of that day, each of Bob's files was analysed. As expected, no client had settled their account and a final demand letter had been the last piece of correspondence in each file. There came a knock on the office door and James looked up. He then glanced at his wristwatch. The door opened and Clara smiled.

"It's after five o'clock."

"I'll be here for another half hour."

"See you tomorrow."

"Goodnight."

Clara closed the door.

Just before six o'clock, James left the office, walked to the subway station and caught a train for home. He alighted from the train at Lexington Avenue and soon arrived at the apartment block. He entered his apartment and put down his briefcase.

"Is that you, James?"

"Yes."

Elizabeth came into the hall. "Did you have a good day?"

"Not particularly." James unbuttoned his coat.

"The hospital called. They want you to contact them."

James removed his hat and coat then hung them on the coat stand.

"I'll call them now." James reached for the telephone on the hall table.

Elizabeth gave him a piece of paper. "I wrote down the details."

James dialled the number then placed the receiver against his ear and the transmitter close to his mouth. He looked at Elizabeth and she moved closer to him.

"Bellevue Hospital," said a female voice.

"Nurse Fuller, please."

"Ward 7?"

"Yes."

"I'll put you through, sir."

"Thanks." James took a deep breath.

Elizabeth stared at her husband. "I hope it's not bad news."

"Nurse Fuller here."

"It's Mr Carsell-Brown. I received a message to call you."

"Its bad news. I'm sorry Mr Carsell-Brown, your brother-in-law died early this afternoon."

James stared at Elizabeth.

She gripped his arm.

"Mrs Rhodes left at two o'clock. I'm sorry."

"Thank you."

"Goodbye, sir."

James replaced the handset into its cradle and turned to Elizabeth.

She bowed her head.

James put his arms around her. "I'll call Georgina."

"No, James, we will go to her apartment."

"Yes, of course."

"Georgina will be distraught at the news." Elizabeth wiped her eyes with a handkerchief. "Poor Dale."

"This has been one hell of a day."

Elizabeth looked at James.

"I was told this morning that Bob had been attacked last night."

"Bob?"

"Yes. He is also in Bellevue Hospital."

Elizabeth put a hand to her mouth. "Good grief!"

James lifted his hat and coat off the stand. "Let's go, Elizabeth."

"Give me a couple of minutes."

The following morning, James arrived at the office tired and mentally exhausted. His brother-in-law's murder had been a traumatic experience for both Elizabeth and himself. He sat behind his desk and attempted to browse through the remainder of Bob's files.

James sighed. Let's see if there could be a link.

He picked up a file and started to read it then stopped. He looked in the direction of his office window and viewed several imposing skyscrapers.

Poor Georgina, to witness her in that terrible state of mind. It will be a blessing to have her stay with us for the foreseeable future. Elizabeth and I shall miss Dale's humour and carefree manner. After the distress of last week, at least Bob remains in a positive condition of health.

James looked away from his office window and continued reading the file. He turned over a page, then another.

Beltram Building Contractors Ltd – four hundred and thirty dollars outstanding. A workforce of fourteen employees and has been trading for eighteen years. Turnover has fallen for the last five – not a surprise given the reductions in capital budgets. Settle their fees however slow to do so. Let's try another, Allanton Plumbing Engineers. Trading for eleven years and owned by a decorated war hero. I recall Bob told me about this chap. He captured a hundred German infantry soldiers all by himself. His account – eight hundred and twelve dollars to pay? No medal from us. I note the next file has been marked with a liquidation stamp. Baymartin, a snack bar in Lower Manhattan had ceased trading ten months ago. With interest, I turned the next page of their file. The owner had been liquidated due to massive debts. To handle the administration of this business, we received a fee. Tom assisted Bob with the process of administration. What's this – a police report! NYPD had investigated the establishment on two occasions in 1927. Both instances related to a narcotics investigation. For the time being, I will put this intriguing file to one side.

Clara knocked on the door and entered. "Here is a cup of coffee, Jim." She laid the cup on the desk. "Not much space to put it!"

James smiled.

She turned to walk out the room.

"Clara?"

She stopped and looked round.

"Do you recall a business that Bob handled which went into liquidation last year?"

"Baymartin?"

"Yes."

"Bob met with police officials about the situation."

"Situation?"

"Drugs. The premises did not deal in alcohol but it had been connected to the other vice."

James lifted his cup then sipped the coffee. "How do you know this?"

Clara smiled. "My boyfriend's brother is in NYPD. The owner also had marital problems."

"Anything you can reveal?"

"I understand his wife walked out with their daughter and went to stay with another guy."

"The owner didn't have his troubles to seek."

"No doubt why he came here to remonstrate. He and Bob exchanged harsh words."

"In Bob's office?"

"Yes, I could hear everything from my office. He blamed Bob for his woes then left in a rage."

James sipped his coffee.

"A just reward for dealing in drugs."

"Was he convicted of a drugs felony?"

"He got off on a technicality."

"Thanks for the information."

Clara left the room and closed the door.

James finished his coffee and laid the cup on his desk. He reached for that particular file and studied the police report.

Interesting, Detective McAndrew's name is on this report. The chap who came here to discuss Bob. Had he been aware of the argument between Bob and the client? I'll contact the number on this report. James picked up his office telephone and dialled the number. He placed the receiver to his ear and spoke into the transmitter. "Hello, Detective McAndrew?"

"Yes this is he."

"Detective, its James Carsell-Brown from Payne and Albertson, the accountancy firm."

"A lot of names, sir. How can I be of assistance?"

"It concerns Bob Payne, senior partner in the firm."

"The gentleman shot last Monday night."

"Were you aware of a heated argument between one of our clients and Mr Payne?"

"Which client?"

"Baymartin. It no longer trades and has now been liquidated"

"Located near 'hell's kitchen' sir?"

"We have a Midtown address for the establishment." James laid out the police report.

"Yeah, it ain't a kick in the pants of it. No, I wasn't aware Mr Brown. Who heard the argument – you?"

"One of our secretaries. Mr Payne was threatened."

"What's the lady's name, sir?"

"Clara Bale."

"I'll meet with Miss Bale. Say tomorrow morning around ten?"

"That will be fine, Detective. I'll let her know."

"Bye, sir."

"Oh, Detective?"

"Yeah?"

"One of your colleagues is investigating the murder of my brother-in-law – Dale Rhodes. Do you know of any developments?"

"That'll be Mike Johnston?"

"Yes."

"Our department now deals with the case but nothin' has materialised."

"Okay, thanks." James replaced the handset into the cradle.

By five o'clock James had gone through all of Bob's files. His concern related to the business that had been liquidated. All the rest appeared in order – apart from fees owed. James looked at his wristwatch and started to yawn. He gathered a bundle of documents and put them in his briefcase then buttoned up his jacket. James took his hat and coat from the coat stand then put them on. A flicker of the late April sunlight shone through his office window. James glanced in its direction.

Next Wednesday will be the first day of May, perhaps the climate will improve – weather and economy!

James picked up his briefcase, opened wide the office doors then closed it. Due to the prompt finish of his fellow office workers, at ten minutes past five the corridor was deserted. James walked down the stairs, past the vacant reception desk and entered the bustle of Lower Manhattan. He joined the army of commuters headed for the station to catch their trains. As James turned round the block, a lady confronted him.

She looks familiar, where have I seen her?

"Excuse me, sir."

"Yes?"

"I am trying to find a restaurant located in this district."

Nice Irish lilt. "What is the name of it?"

"Conways."

"I've not heard of it. What is the address?"

The lady produced a piece of paper from her black leather handbag. "This address." She pointed to the writing.

James leaned forward and read the note. "That is not far from my office however, there is no restaurant of that name." James raised his head. "Wait a minute, the restaurant at this address is called Berkleys."

"That's strange!" The lady put the piece of paper back into her bag.

James heard a loud crash. He observed a yellow taxi had mounted the sidewalk about thirty yards from where he stood. James turned to the lady but she had disappeared. He walked in the direction of the accident. A crowd had assembled and an elderly woman retreated from the scene. She had an expression of horror on her wrinkled face.

"The cab ploughed into them!" she cried, "someone call for an ambulance."

A man rushed into the nearest shop. Cries for help and painful groans from injured parties ensured an emergency situation. A police officer arrived on the scene followed by another two. As they appealed for space around the taxi, the crowd swayed back. The elderly lady looked at James and grabbed his arm.

"There must be at least a dozen hit!"

The busy Downtown traffic had ground to a halt. Motorists popped their heads out of vehicle windows. Three ambulances drew up alongside the incident location and crews rushed out of the vehicles.

James left the tragic scene and took a short detour to the subway station. Two hours later he arrived home and after taking off his hat and coat, wandered into the kitchen. Elizabeth prepared their evening meal.

"Dinner will be in about forty minutes." She stirred a pot.

"My appetite isn't as it should be." James sat down at the kitchen table.

Elizabeth looked at her husband. "Why, what's wrong?"

"A serious accident – close to the office at rush hour."

"The morning rush hour?" Elizabeth wiped her hands with a towel.

"No, evening."

She sat down opposite James. "What happened?"

"A taxi left the sidewalk and hit a group of pedestrians. I witnessed the aftermath. A number of people had been struck by the vehicle."

"Was it travelling fast?"

"That's what taxi drivers in New York do, Elizabeth."

"I was in the vicinity of Wall Street recently and the same type of incident happened. The taxicabs should be licensed and subject to scrutiny. Anyone can drive one in the city."

"Good point."

"Something else? You have that inquisitive expression."

James sat back on the chair. "Before the incident, a lady with an Irish accent stopped me and asked directions to a restaurant."

Elizabeth moved her head forward. "And?"

"If it hadn't been for that delay, I may have been one of the victims!"

"You have a guardian angel."

"Elizabeth, it's not the first time."

"Oh?"

"Prior to your recent birthday."

"Go on."

"A gunman confronted me close to the office."

"You did not tell me this!"

James took Elizabeth's hand. "I did not want to alarm you."

"What happened?"

"Officers from NYPD arrived on the scene and the gunman ran off."

"That was incredible luck."

"Not really, they had been given a tip-off by a woman."

Elizabeth smiled. "Your lucky charm?"

"I'm not finished."

Elizabeth sat back.

"On the train home, I remembered an incident nine years ago. When I arrived home, we discussed it. Do you remember?"

"The bomb that went off in Wall Street. Many people were killed and injured."

James nodded. "That day at lunchtime I left the office ten minutes early. I had a lunch appointment with a client at our local restaurant."

"It's a couple of blocks from your office."

"The appointment had been scheduled for twelve o'clock. When I left the building, a lady stopped me for directions to an art gallery. It took a while for her to comprehend its precise location. Then the explosion occurred."

"If this lady had not asked you for directions?"

"I would have been in the vicinity of the carnage. The bomb went off outside the restaurant."

"James?"

"Yes, Elizabeth, she had an Irish accent. And I am positive it is the same person."

"Sinister."

"More than that – her appearance has not altered in nine years!"

Lucky her. "Describe this lady."

"The same height and build as yourself." James hesitated.

"Yes?"

"Maybe a tad slimmer."

Elizabeth crossed her arms. "Carry on."

"Brown eyes, jet black hair and clear white skin. She also has a beauty spot on her left cheek.

"How old would you say she is?"

James shrugged his shoulders. "Early thirties perhaps?"

Elizabeth stood up and walked to the plate cupboard.

"That beef casserole smells good."

"Hungry now are we?"

James smiled. "Yes."

"Dinner won't be long." Elizabeth took off her white apron.

James stared into space. Who is she?

Chapter 3

Hard Times

Elizabeth sat beside a window on the southbound train to Lower Manhattan. When the sun broke through the clouds and shone onto her face, she pulled down the window blind.

I hope the gallery has sold one of my paintings. Mr Arbington did say there had been an interested party. James and I could do with extra capital.

Elizabeth alighted from the train, departed the station and walked two blocks to the art gallery. She observed that since her last visit to Lower Manhattan, more people dallied around the area. Their dejected demeanour and scruffy appearance made Elizabeth feel uneasy. Some men hung around street corners; others stared into shop windows which advertised cut-price product deals. A consequence and stark reminder of what high unemployment had brought to the city. An unshaven and unsteady man wearing a shabby grey cap and coat approached Elizabeth.

The poor man looks demoralised.

The man took off his cap to reveal thinning white hair. "Excuse me, lady, can you spare a dime? I haven't eaten today."

His breath stinks of alcohol. Elizabeth opened her bag, went into a purse then brought out two coins. "Here you are." She handed them to the man.

The man bowed his head. "Thank you kind lady." He took the coins with his wrinkled shaky hand. "I wish you well." He put on his cap.

As Elizabeth walked on, she glanced behind and the same man approached another passer-by.

Poor chap, to lose his dignity and be forced to beg in full view of everyone. Unless President Hoover can provide an economic miracle, the situation will become worse. Ah! The art gallery.

Elizabeth walked up several steps to the art gallery entrance and pushed the door but it would not budge. She peered through a small glass pane within the wooden door and noticed a woman polishing a brass frame. To draw attention, Elizabeth knocked on the door. The woman turned round, put her duster on a table then came to the door. She unlocked the door then opened it.

"Sorry to keep you, madam."

Elizabeth stepped inside. "I trust you are open?"

"Yes, madam, we are. Two days ago someone tried to walk off with a painting. Mr Arbington has given strict instructions to keep the entrance door locked at all times."

"Troubled times indeed."

The sales assistant smiled. "How can I help you, madam?"

"I am here to speak with Mr Arbington. One of my paintings has a prospective buyer and I wanted to find out if it had been sold. I telephoned several days ago and left a message."

The sales assistant frowned. "We haven't sold any paintings for some time. What is your name?"

"Elizabeth Carsell-Brown."

"Which one did Mr Arbington mention madam?"

"The portrait of a coachman." Elizabeth pointed. "That one, over in the corner."

"Oh yes." The sales assistant stared at the painting. "Someone did appear interested however, they perceived the price too high."

"Can't Mr Arbington drop the price and at least achieve a sale?"

"I agree, but you know what he's like."

"Don't I just."

The sales assistant smiled. "When he returns I will tell him you called into the gallery."

"Thank you." Elizabeth walked to the entrance.

The sales assistant followed then opened the door. "It's a lovely painting. Did you know him?"

"Just for a short time, he saved my life."

"Wow! How?"

"He pushed me out of the way from a runaway horse then it hit him."

"Did he survive?"

Elizabeth nodded. "Bye."

"Bye." The sales assistant closed then locked the door.

Wow? After the horse hit him, he would have ached for weeks. Come to my rescue again James Carlisle and help me sell that painting. Time for a coffee – that place across the street will suffice.

As Elizabeth walked to towards a restaurant, the man whom she gave two dimes still hung around the vicinity. When Elizabeth stared at him, he turned away. She entered the restaurant and looked for a spare table.

A waitress came forward. "Can I help?"

"A table for one please."

"How about over by the window." The waitress pointed. "Do you mind sharin' a table? That young woman has been there for over an hour and should be about to leave."

Elizabeth nodded.

"What would you like?"

"Just a white coffee, please."

"Okay." She returned to behind the counter.

Elizabeth walked towards the table and a young woman looked up. She held a document in her hand.

She smiled. "Hi, lookin' for a seat? I've three goin' cheap." She laughed.

Elizabeth smiled, sat down opposite the young woman and unbuttoned her coat. "One will suffice." She laid her bag on the floor.

"Where are you from?" She put down her white printed document on the crimson tablecloth.

"Originally Scotland."

"Didn't think it was New York."

"I've lived in Upper East Side for seventeen years." Her bobbed curly red hair contrasts well with her long blue coat. "Do you stay in Manhattan?"

"No, Jamestown. I visit Manhattan now and then."

Elizabeth removed her beige hat. "To work?"

The young woman smiled. "I try my best." She pointed to her printed document. "I have to learn my lines by tomorrow."

"Are you an actress?"

"I wanna be one, at present I'm a model. An agent contacted me about a part in a Broadway play. One of the goils has taken ill and they need a quick replacement."

"What is the play called?"

The young woman smiled. "A Most Immoral Lady. It's on at Midtown's Cort Theatre." She laughed. "I haven't told my father yet."

"Would he not approve if you become an actress?"

"He once told me if I wanted to be one, I'll have to do it by my eighteenth birthday. He would say – it's tough out there, honey." She laughed. "I've three months to do it."

This young woman strikes me as a character. "Allow me to introduce myself. I am Elizabeth Carsell-Brown." Elizabeth held out her hand.

The young woman shook it and smiled. "Diane, Diane Belmont."

Elizabeth looked at the young woman's hand. What long red nails!

"One cawfee." The stone-faced waitress put a white cup and saucer on Elizabeth's side of the table then departed.

The young woman leaned towards Elizabeth. "She'll never make it in comedy."

Elizabeth laughed. "Maybe you could, that's the first time I've laughed for ages."

She held up the script. "This appears a serious part and could be a breakthrough."

Elizabeth lifted her cup then sipped her coffee. It tastes weak. She laid the cup on the saucer then looked at the young woman. "A sinister role?"

"If it gets me noticed, I don't care." The young woman glanced at a clock on the wall. "Oh no! I have to meet my agent at eleven."

She put the script into her red bag and a pink hairbrush fell out onto the black tiled floor. She bent down and knocked over one of the spare chairs.

Elizabeth picked up the brush. "Here you are." She handed it to the young woman.

"Thanks." She put it back into her bag.

Elizabeth replaced the chair. "Maybe comedy could be an option."

"I ain't havin' a ball." She put on a black cloche hat and tucked her long hair under it. "However, I may have to! See ya."

The young wannabe grabbed her bag, stood up and walked towards the exit. As she passed a table, her bag knocked over a glass of water and it crashed onto the floor. The young woman apologised to the table's customers who acknowledged with a rude gesture. She returned a similar one, turned round and bumped into the waitress carrying a tray of plates filled with food. After the contents splattered onto several customers, the young woman rushed out the exit door.

Elizabeth smiled. Maybe I just met a future star of the stage or screen. Mind you, she did have the potential for comedy.

From her window seat, Elizabeth noticed the man whom she gave money to. Another two men of similar appearance had joined him. She put on her beige hat, picked up her bag then went to the counter. The waitress poured coffee into a metal pot and glanced Elizabeth's way.

"Won't be a minute, honey."

Elizabeth buttoned her beige coat.

The waitress stood behind the counter opposite Elizabeth and picked up a receipt. "Ten cents."

Elizabeth opened her bag and took out a purse. She brought out a coin and handed it to the waitress. She popped the coin into a brass till, pressed a lever and the sound of a cling echoed. Elizabeth left the busy establishment and into welcome fresh air. She took a deep breath then walked on.

"Excuse me, lady?"

Elizabeth turned around. Another man who wants money.

"Spare a dime?"

"Sorry, I have no change." Elizabeth gripped her black leather bag.

He smiled. "I also accept dollars."

Elizabeth smiled. "As do New York taxi drivers, I have to catch one."

He tipped his brown cap. "Thanks for your time, lady, safe journey."

Politeness and humour in times of economic adversity – admirable. Elizabeth looked up at the large clock above a bank – twenty minutes past eleven. I must arrive at Georgina's apartment by twelve. The train will suffice – it's cheaper.

Elizabeth entered Chambers Street subway station, bought a ticket and walked down a stairway to the platform for a train to Midtown. The rumble of an approaching train inside the tunnel grew louder. Elizabeth glanced at her wristwatch and would meet Georgina on time.

James hung his hat and jacket on the hall coat stand. He loosened his tie and walked into the living room.

"What a day!"

"A swell one?" said Elizabeth.

"Not so much swell, more like hell. I need to freshen up."

James went into the bathroom, turned on the tap and filled the white ceramic sink with water. A short time later, Elizabeth could hear water draining from the sink. James dried himself with a white towel.

"I visited Georgina at lunchtime."

"How is she?"

"Can't hear you."

James popped his head round the door and buttoned up his pale blue shirt. "How is Georgina?"

"Not good."

James came into the living room and sat on the couch next to Elizabeth. "It's not a surprise given what happened."

"James, I'm not referring to a bereavement."

James stared at Elizabeth.

"Dale has left Georgina with a mountain of debt. She visited her lawyer about Dale's will and the problem surfaced."

"What about Dale's life insurance policy?"

"He surrendered it a year ago to pay off a gambling debt."

James put his arm around Elizabeth. "He did strike me as a risk-taker."

"That and more – he had a gambling addiction!"

"Was Georgina not aware of this?"

"Obviously not."

"How much debt is there?"

Elizabeth stared at James. "Six and a half thousand dollars."

"That's four times my salary! He must have been an addicted gambler for some time."

"It's a mess."

"Does Georgina have any money put aside?"

"The money mother left her all went into their apartment. How will she cope, James?"

He sighed. "It's not as if she will find a job, at present there appears none available."

"How about your firm?"

"Elizabeth, we just survive. More staff cuts may be on the way. I am not even aware of any other firms that recruit staff. Besides, Georgina has limited work experience."

"She plays the piano." Elizabeth sat upright. "She could teach music."

"To who?"

"Children of wealthy families who have large houses on Long Island. Those who go to the French Rivera for their summer vacation. Recently Georgina gave several music lessons to one of Dale's acquaintances."

"Elizabeth?"

"Yes?"

"That's a terrific idea! It won't be the solution to repay all the debt but it's a start. Georgina could place an advertisement in the New York Times."

"Make sure you tell that chap who stands at the entrance to your building."

"Lloyd?"

"Whatever his name is."

"Good idea. He could be a source to pass on information. I'll speak to him tomorrow morning."

Elizabeth clasped her well-groomed hands. "Splendid."

"Did the lawyer give an indication when Georgina has to settle the debt?"

"As soon as possible."

"It's a lot of money to pay back."

"As you say, it's a start."

James nodded.

"On a different note, what happened at work today?"

"One of the NYPD detectives interviewed Clara. He kept her for two hours."

Elizabeth raised her eyebrows. "It must have been an in-depth interview."

James smiled. "However, she likes to chat."

"Is she attractive?"

"Yes, she is."

"Maybe she should have gone into acting."

James laughed.

Acting appears a popular profession given my morning discussion with a young woman.

"If the economy doesn't pick up, she may have to."

"Did Clara discuss the interview with you?"

James shook his head. "No, she didn't mention it."

"It must have been routine."

James smiled. "How long until dinner?"

Elizabeth rose from the couch. "Soon."

When the telephone rang, James had started to read his daily newspaper. He put the newspaper down, went into the hall and picked up the black handset.

"Hello?"

"This is Mr Arbington. Can I speak with Mrs Carsell-Brown, please?"

"Hold on, please." James put a hand over the transmitter. "Elizabeth, it's a Mr Arbington."

Elizabeth wiped her hands on a towel then rushed from the kitchen into the hall.

James gave the handset to Elizabeth.

She put the receiver to her ear then spoke into the transmitter. "Mr Arbington?"

"I have good news."

Elizabeth smiled at James.

"The painting of the coachman has been sold."

"Terrific! How much?"

James looked at Elizabeth.

"Six hundred dollars, Elizabeth!" cried Mr Arbington.

"I'll come to the gallery tomorrow morning."

"Fine, see you then."

"Goodbye." Elizabeth replaced the handset into its cradle. "Six hundred!"

James raised his eyebrows. "Who bought it – Louis Mayer?"

Elizabeth smiled.

"Let's have a drink to celebrate." James held Elizabeth in his arms.

Whilst the busy morning commuter express hurtled south to Lower West Side, James stood in a carriage aisle and reflected on the previous evening.

One drink too much last night, perhaps there is a case for prohibition. I must limit my intake of whisky to a maximum of three. However it's not often Elizabeth sells one of her paintings – and for an excellent price. Someone has money to spend in this dismal economic climate.

As the train pulled into a Midtown station, several passengers rose from their seats to leave the train.

Good, an empty seat. I can't see any ladies who require one therefore I'll grab it. The previous passenger has left a morning newspaper. Since I did not have time to buy one this morning, my gratitude to a fellow passenger. An hour-long stand feels like two on this delicate morning. The front page of the New York Times – May 17. No surprise the newspaper was discarded – it is yesterday's news. However, I'll browse through the pages to pass the time. This is of interest – Douglas Fairbanks hosted the first Academy Awards ceremony in Hollywood. Elizabeth would have enjoyed that. Best film was 'Wings' and best actor award of 1928 went to Emil Jannings. No doubt he will be in demand for further roles.

James continued to read the newspaper for the remainder of his journey. When the train arrived at Wall Street station, he stood up and left the newspaper on a seat. James alighted from the train, exited the subway station and arrived at his office building. No doorman stood in the entrance to welcome staff.

Maybe Lloyd has a worse hangover than I do.

James took the elevator to his floor, stepped out and walked along the corridor. As he was about to enter his office, someone spoke.

"Jim, can I see you?"

James turned around. "Sure, Clara." James walked into the office, put down his briefcase then hung his hat on a coat stand hook.

Clara entered the office.

"What can I do for you?"

"I want to become an actress."

My goodness. "Have a seat."

Clara sat down. "I've made my decision – acting is what I want to do."

"Easier said than done, Clara. You would have to learn the profession."

"When I reached the age of eight, my parents sent me to dance classes. I can also sing and have performed in amateur plays." She smiled. "I possess other essentials."

No argument from me.

"Detective McAndrew has a contact in one of the theatres on Broadway. He has arranged an audition for me."

"What if you fail the audition?"

"I won't fail, Jim."

I believe you.

"I am sure further staff cuts will be on the cards therefore someone can retain their job."

Admirable. "I can see you have made up your mind. When do you intend to leave?"

"A week from today."

James looked at a wall calendar – Saturday the 25th.

"However, there is one drawback."

"What is that?"

"I may have to change my name."

"Why?"

"Clara Bale is similar to Clara Bow. Perhaps Claudette however, not sure about my new surname."

High aspirations indeed. "Why Claudette?"

"I was born in France then my parents came to America. My original surname is Baillin."

"Did you change it?"

"No, my mother did."

"We'll talk again soon."

Clara stood up and smiled. "Fine." She left the office and closed the door.

Good, now there is no need to tell a member of staff they no longer have a job.

Elizabeth and James strolled through Central Park on a warm sunny Sunday afternoon. They encountered many couples and families who also took advantage of the delightful weather.

"The park is popular today," said James.

"It must be the first time for weeks that Sunday has been such a glorious day. I can't remember the last time I went out without a jacket or coat."

"You still require a hat." James smiled. "That white one matches your dress."

"The brim is a tad on the wide side." Elizabeth tilted it upwards. "It stifles my view."

"Being fair-skinned you have to take precautions from the sun's rays."

Elizabeth nodded.

"Where did you arrange for us to meet Georgina?"

"The animal menagerie. I hope she turns up, James, I worry about her."

"It can't be easy for her, Elizabeth. However, the equity loan from the bank relieves any short-term financial hardship."

"At least she now has an income from teaching music, albeit a small one."

James kicked a paper packet. "Any income in this economic climate is a bonus."

Elizabeth pointed. "Look at all the paper scattered along this path – it's ridiculous! The authorities should clean up this park."

"Maybe they can't afford to." James looked across the lawn. "At least the grass has been cut."

Elizabeth adjusted her white wide-brimmed hat. "Thanks to the sheep." She pointed. "Look at them munching away."

James laughed. "At least it won't cost the authorities money."

Elizabeth held James hand. "Will they ever catch Dale's killer?"

"I hope so, and also the person responsible for Tom's death."

"How is Bob?"

"Out of hospital and at home convalescing. He may return to work next month."

"June will soon be over."

James glanced at Elizabeth. "And as yet, no glimmer of hope for the economy."

Elizabeth smiled at James. "No vacation this year then?"

"Not for many people, Elizabeth. The firm now has a skeleton staff. We've made all the cuts we can."

Elizabeth gripped her husband's hand. "What happens next?"

"I shudder to contemplate." James glanced at Elizabeth. "I meant to ask, who bought your painting?"

Elizabeth shrugged her shoulders. "When I enquired, Mr Arbington said the buyer wanted to remain anonymous."

"Strange. Mind you, six hundred dollars is a terrific price."

"James." Elizabeth pointed.

"The sprinklers?"

"No, over there." Elizabeth again pointed. "A crowd has gathered. Let's see what those cheers and handclaps are for."

James and Elizabeth wandered across the lawn to where a crowd had gathered. A young woman danced with elegance on a grey concrete-paved surface. When she finished, a young man appeared and also started to dance. When he went into a tap-dance routine, the crowd cheered. Then, he and the young woman danced together. When they finished, the crowd showed their appreciation with warm applause. After they witnessed the spectacle, James and Elizabeth continued to the animal menagerie.

James smiled. "You don't witness that every Sunday Elizabeth – fantastic!" Where have I observed that young woman before?

"The loud applause said it all." Elizabeth pointed. "There is Georgina."

"And also in white. Both of you are suitably dressed for a tennis match."

Elizabeth stared at her husband. "I prefer golf."

James smiled.

Georgina approached James and Elizabeth. "I heard a commotion."

"An impromptu dance show by a young man and woman," said Elizabeth.

James quipped, "Not us Georgina."

Georgina laughed. "What a pity, that would have been a sight."

Elizabeth smiled. "Nice to see you laugh again."

Georgina looked upwards. "Blame the warm sunshine and blue sky. However, I now feel thirsty."

"Let's go for a coffee," said Elizabeth, "there's a place next to the menagerie."

"Terrific," said Georgina.

James led both ladies into the establishment and to a white iron table with four matching chairs.

"A seat at last!" Elizabeth sat down, removed her hat and placed it on the empty chair.

Georgina placed her wide-brimmed cream hat on the table and shook her head.

"You are now a light blonde, Georgina?" said Elizabeth.

"It's all this sunshine Elizabeth." Georgina looked at James. "No straw boater this afternoon?"

"I wear a hat six days a week to work and on Sunday morning at church." James smiled. "My head deserves a breather."

"Maybe your bald patch will start to grow hair again," quipped Elizabeth.

Georgina laughed.

James rubbed the back of his head. "It's not much."

"Maybe one day men's hats will become unfashionable," said Elizabeth, "fashions tend to change."

"As the length of ladies dresses have gone from long to short," said Georgina.

"Similar to most current hair styles." Elizabeth patted her dark blonde hair.

A young waitress with dark bobbed hair and a yellow dress appeared. She looked at the three customers and smiled.

"Hi, what can I get you?"

"Three white coffees, please," said Elizabeth.

"Be back soon." The waitress departed.

Elizabeth looked towards Georgina. "James feels we could be dressed for tennis."

"I may take up tennis." Georgina smiled.

"Good luck," said James.

"Are you serious?" Elizabeth sat back on her chair.

"A girl I give piano lessons to in Long Island has parents who own a tennis club. They have invited me to come along for a game."

"You do not play tennis," said Elizabeth.

"I'll give it a go."

"That's the spirit, Georgina – just hit the ball," said James, "preferably with a tennis racket."

Elizabeth laughed.

"Ask them to give you lessons," said James, "inform them that you may be a shade rusty."

Georgina smiled. "Good idea, James, I'll pretend I once played." Georgina looked at her sister. "Do you recall when mother said that to father?"

"That was golf."

"Your mother played golf!" James took of his navy jacket and hung it over the back of his chair.

"She didn't," said Elizabeth, "and was found out."

"What happened?" said James.

"Father took mother to the local golf course in Ardrishaig," said Georgina, "when mother tried to hit a ball at the first tee, she missed and the club flew out of her hands."

Elizabeth laughed.

"Where did it end up?" said James.

"It landed in the trees," said Elizabeth.

Georgina laughed. "It took father fifteen minutes to find it."

Elizabeth laughed. "At least mother didn't lose the ball."

James laughed. "Or the club."

"Honesty is the best policy, Georgina," said Elizabeth.

Georgina smiled. "Maybe I could go into politics."

"Talking of politics," said James, "Ramsay McDonald will now have settled into his role as British Labour Prime Minister."

"He has been in office for less than a month," said Elizabeth.

"He is from Lossiemouth," said Georgina, "and will need all his highland steel and shrewdness."

"This must be a terrible period in time for any political leader, no matter what country." James loosened his tie.

"And us." Elizabeth looked towards the counter. "So much for being back soon."

"Another Scotsman has been prominent," said Georgina.

"Who?" said Elizabeth.

"A chap called John Logie Baird," said Georgina.

"Is he also a politician?"

"No, Elizabeth," said James, "an inventor."

"Can he invent a coffee-maker?" Elizabeth again looked towards the counter.

Georgina laughed. "Have you heard of a television?"

Elizabeth shook her head. "What is it?"

"A small cinema screen in our living-room, Elizabeth."

Elizabeth turned to James. "Really?"

"A broadcast took place between London and New York last year. I've heard talk that one day a television could be more popular than radio." James glanced towards the counter.

"Progress, Elizabeth," said Georgina, "technology is the buzz word."

"I'll mention a buzz term – quick customer service."

"She must have heard you, Elizabeth," said James, "here come our cups of coffee."

"Hot coffee, I hope," said Elizabeth."

Georgina laughed.

James boarded the morning commuter train and on this particular Monday, noticed many empty seats in his carriage. In the month of July, this could be due to people being on their annual summer vacation. However this time, there were more vacant seats than usual. With employees now being discarded from jobs on a regular basis, a commuter as well as an economic downturn existed. James had the luxury of a window seat and started to read the Herald Tribune newspaper. Would the current financial downturn be portrayed in a different mood of pessimism? As expected, much doom and gloom was publicised in this particular edition. However, a distinct contrast in the form of light-hearted cartoons did appear on various pages. The caption of someone who jumps off a high building to commit suicide and lands on a trailer full of manure – "now I'll have to get cleaned up!" The police officer that arrived on the scene states, "it saved us doing it." James lowered his newspaper and looked around the carriage.

I'm the sole person with a smile.

Regional news revealed the first airport hotel had been opened in Oakland, California. Passenger flights could be about to 'take off' in a big way. Since a trip from California to New York takes thirteen days, air travel would be a desirable option, especially with Hollywood being the focus of attention. James once more lowered his newspaper and looked out the window.

That's where I recognised that young woman – the one who danced in Central Park. I stood next to her on the train, around the time of Elizabeth's birthday. Maybe one day she will end up on Broadway or perhaps in Hollywood on the silver screen.

"Hey buddy, gotta light?" said a male passenger.

"Sorry, don't smoke."

He approached another passenger. "Gotta light?"

He shook his head.

The man looked at James. "Maybe I should give it up."

"Save you cash," said James.

The man nodded

An hour later the train arrived at Wall Street station. James alighted from the train then exited the subway station. He took a deep breath, smelled the air and walked quickly to his office. The confrontation of a gunman still fresh in his mind even though months had passed. James reached the office building and once inside, met a different doorman on duty.

"Mornin', sir," said the doorman.

"Morning. Is Lloyd on vacation?"

"He's left sir, I'm his replacement. I work two hours in the mornin' and one in the evenin'."

"See you later."

"Bye, sir. Oh, the name's Henry." He tipped his dark blue peaked cap.

James walked to the elevator. Not just our firm has cut costs, the building's proprietor has replaced a full-time worker with a part-timer. James entered the elevator and pressed the button for his designated floor. At least the elevator is empty therefore no cigarette smoke to contend with.

The elevator stopped at James's floor and the doors opened. He walked along a subdued corridor.

It's a deserted floor nowadays. Just myself and an office junior who has now become the bookkeeper, typist and filing clerkess.

James opened his office door, took off his hat and hung it up. He laid his briefcase on the floor then sat down. A pile of letters lay in front of him.

Maybe our clients have elected to settle their bills! How we need some cash to keep the firm solvent.

James opened the first letter and read it. The firm's bank had sent word that interest rates on overdrafts had been increased. James put the letter to one side. The next letter stated that rent for the firm's business premises was overdue.

How can we pay the proprietor if clients don't settle their accounts with us!

James put the second letter aside then opened a well-sealed one with difficulty. It contained a cheque from one of Bob's clients.

This will pay the rent.

The next letter opened also came from the firm's bank – a client's cheque had bounced. James heard a faint knock on the door and looked up.

"Mr Carsell-Brown, a Detective McAndrew is here to see you."

"Fine, Lucy, send him in."

"Will do."

"Hi Mr Carsell-Brown." Detective McAndrew walked towards James and held out his hand.

James stood up and shook it. "Have a seat, Detective." James sat down.

"Thanks." Detective McAndrew sat opposite James. "Not many people around."

"Me and the eighteen-year-old employee are all that's here. Two partners have been shot, the head clerkess has left, one typist is about to have a baby and our regular book-keeper has gone to live with her parents in Chicago."

"Why leave New York for Chicago?"

James smiled. "She misses her boyfriend."

"Save you payin' a wage."

"There is that."

Detective McAndrew took out his packet of cigarettes, put one in his mouth then replaced the packet in his grey jacket side-pocket. "Before I forget." He took out a box of matches then lit the cigarette. "Miss Bale got that part – she's doin' swell." He replaced the box of matches in his other jacket side-pocket.

"I felt she would – and so did she."

Detective McAndrew smiled.

"Any news on my brother-in-law's killer?"

"Nothin' sir. The killer would have been hired by someone else. You can hire hit-men on the cheap!"

"I believe my brother-in-law owed a lot of money."

"And no doubt warned by the lender that if he didn't pay back the money on time, he would be sorry."

"My two partners in the firm?"

"Now that's a different situation." He puffed on his cigarette. "After my chat with Miss Bale, we checked out a few leads. It turns out, the guy hired someone to put away the three of you. He held your firm responsible for the break-up of his marriage."

"The gunman?"

"Behind bars – along with your ex-client. There was another guy involved and we're tryin' to trace him." He puffed on his cigarette.

"At least some consolation for the firm but one of our partners lost his life."

Detective McAndrew stubbed out his cigarette on a desk ashtray. "It's tough on the victim's family, at least one of the killers has been caught."

James nodded.

Detective McAndrew stood up. "It's a busy time for NYPD, sir – have to leave."

"It must be, Detective." James stood up. "Economic despair no doubt invites crime."

"It sure does."

James shook the detective's hand.

"One last thing, how is your sister-in-law?"

"Fine. She keeps herself occupied."

"Accordin' to the duty officer, after such a trauma she showed little emotion."

What is he alluding to?

"After a husband's shooting, the wife is distraught."

"Georgina is a strong character."

"I'll see myself out, sir." He walked out of the office and along the corridor.

Lucy knocked on the door. "Can I see you for a moment, Mr Carsell-Brown?"

"Of course, come in and have a seat."

She entered, sat down opposite James and sniffed the air.

"Craven 'A'."

Lucy smiled then moved the desk astray sideways, crossed her legs and sat with clasped hands on her lap.

"What can I do for you?" That scarlet dress contrasts well with her short black hair.

"I feel with the extra duties, a wage increase would be appropriate."

I had a hunch that this may happen. "We remain in a difficult financial situation, Lucy. As you will be aware, not much revenue has come into the firm."

"Just a couple of employees to pay instead of seven."

Shrewd girl. "Do you have an amount in mind?" James sat back on his chair.

"What would you suggest sir?"

"How about a three per cent increase in wages."

"How about seven."

James leaned forward. "Seven! The firm has bills to pay." He held up this morning's letters.

"I now have the responsibilities of at least two employees, Mr Carsell-Brown. I deserve a respectable increase."

She is determined. "Let us say, five per cent." She doesn't look pleased. "To be reviewed in six months."

"Three months."

James smiled. "Okay, five per cent with immediate effect and a review in three months." James sat back and laid the letters on his desk.

Lucy nodded, stood up and walked to the door. "Coffee, sir?"

"Thank you, no sugar."

She departed.

If pushed, I would have gone to ten per cent. Now, let's see what the rest of these letters contain. Two from job applicants – not at this moment in time. One from our stationer – a second reminder. I'll leave that for seven days then send a cheque. Good, the last one. This is also well sealed. James slit the letter open and read the hand-written note.

"Dear sir. I am writing this letter in order to apologise for the recent actions of my father. I realise he must have caused pain, misery and distress to your firm. I can understand this letter must be of little comfort or consolation but my mother and myself are full of remorse. I would like to meet with you and convey our sincere regrets in person. Alma Allen."

James walked along North End Avenue and glanced at his wristwatch. It was ten minutes before one o'clock. After he received Alma Allen's letter, he wrote to her and agreed to meet at a suitable location. She had suggested a local Downtown restaurant called Conrad's. Ideal for James as it would be a fifteen-minute walk from his office. The majority of people he passed in business attire had a solemn look on their faces. This being the final day of July, the sun shone and a warm temperature ensued. However, this amiable climate did not chase away people's anxieties for the future. Rare smiles that James spotted came from beggars who received a dime.

I presume the person I am to meet will indeed be remorseful. I'll make this a short but dignified occasion.

Because of her father's cruel actions, one colleague lost his life and another is in convalescence.

James entered the establishment and observed two female customers. Both sat on their own and at inconspicuous far-corner tables. A blonde woman in her mid-twenties faced James and the other sat sideways. A grey-haired waitress in a purple dress came from behind the counter and walked up to James.

"Can I help, sir?"

James looked at each of the two women.

The waitress smiled. "Nice to have a choice."

The young blonde woman looked at James and smiled.

He walked to her table. "Alma Allen?"

She nodded. "Yes, that's me."

"I'm James Carsell-Brown."

"I appreciate you takin' the time to see me."

James sat down, took off his hat and laid it on the blue and white square tablecloth.

The young woman removed her black felt cloche hat from the table and placed it on a spare chair.

The waitress walked across to the table. "Can I get you anythin', sir?"

James looked at Alma Allen.

"Another black cawfee," she said.

"White coffee for me, please."

"Comin' up." She lifted the young woman's empty cup and saucer then went behind the counter.

"I'm sorry for what my father did. Since the business went into liquidation, he became depressed." She brushed a blonde hair from the shoulder of her black jacket.

What do I say? That's no excuse for the death and shooting of two men, let alone my traumatic experience.

"Do you have a family, Mr Carsell-Brown?" Alma Allen clasped her hands and gave James an icy stare.

"I have a wife."

"You don't have any children?"

Her apologetic manner has gone. "No, I don't have any children."

"Therefore you do not understand the strain that losing a business can bring?"

I feel uncomfortable.

"Do you realise what your firm has done? My mother and myself are broke."

"I or my partners in the firm did not allow the business to fail. You cannot blame us for what happened. We advised your father on how to preserve the business but he ignored us."

The waitress appeared with two cups of coffee. She laid them on the table and looked at James. "Everythin' okay?"

James nodded.

She walked to the other customer's table.

James lifted his cup and took a sip.

"Why could you not have done more to save my father's business?"

James put down his cup onto the saucer. "When we took control of the your father's business, the situation had become irreversible. He should have made contact with an accountancy firm sooner."

"It's all your fault!" she said with a stern tone, "people like you don't care."

"If there is any way to help, then I will. Maybe I could assist you to find a job. In the meantime, our firm will try to find a buyer for your father's business."

"I don't want your help." The young woman reached down to her bag, brought out a small gun and pointed it at James.

He clenched both hands. "You're about to commit a serious crime. Don't be stupid. Do you want to spend time in prison?"

"It's your fault." The gun shook in her hand.

James spotted the other customer approach with a plate in her hand. She crept up behind Alma Allen.

Stall her. "What you are about to do will not solve anything."

"I know what I'm about to do."

James stared at the gun. "What about your mother?"

"My mother! What about her?"

With a plate, the other customer knocked the gun out of Alma Allen's hand then picked it up of the floor. A well-built man grabbed the would-be killer and turned towards the counter.

"Meg, call the cops." He looked at James. "I'd returned from the storeroom and couldn't believe my eyes!"

The customer handed the gun to the male member of staff. "You take it."

The man put the gun into his pocket then escorted Alma Allen to the counter.

The customer laid the plate on a table and smiled. "That came in handy."

James sighed.

"Glad I wore my quiet soft shoes."

An Irish accent. "Wait a minute."

The customer smiled.

"You!"

"Yes, me again."

"Who are you? And how do you appear at the correct place?"

"Also at the correct time."

The waitress came to the table with two cups of fresh coffee. "You could do with this. Jerry's locked her in the back room. Police are on their way." She returned to the counter.

"Please have a seat," said James.

"Hold on."

She went back to her table and returned with her cream jacket, hat and bag then sat opposite James.

"Are you my guardian angel?"

"And an Irish one at that."

"My life insurance company is indebted to you."

She lifted up her cup and sipped the coffee.

"How are you aware of incidents about to happen?"

"If I tell, you won't believe me." She laid her cup on the saucer.

"Try me."

"I am from the future. I am aware of where and when certain incidents will happen."

"A time traveller?"

She smiled.

"Are you the daughter of HG Wells?"

She laughed. "No."

"How far have you travelled back in time?" This is incredible!

"You can ask three questions. That will be your second."

James nodded.

"For your situation, twenty years."

"My next question would be – why me? However, that would also be my final one."

She nodded. "Yes, it would."

"Can I ask your name?"

"Lori."

"I presume the next time we meet, I narrowly escape death?"

"Is that your final question?"

"No, an observation. This isn't fair, I have many questions."

"I must remain discreet."

"Why not tell people of disasters about to happen? They could be prevented."

"The authorities would lock me up! Until deemed harmless, I would be confined to an institution."

I understood her predicament.

"Besides, the future can be uncertain. Adverse events can be avoided by a stroke of good fortune."

"Like a gun that may misfire?"

She laughed. "Not on this occasion, you needed a helping hand."

"How can I repay you?"

"Carry on being yourself, that will suffice."

A time traveller, that could be why she doesn't age.

She put on her hat and jacket. "Just going somewhere." She lifted her bag and walked towards the ladies powder room.

As James drank his coffee, three police officers entered the restaurant. They went into a back room and fifteen minutes later, led out Alma Allen in handcuffs. One of them came across to where James sat.

"Hi sir, I will need a statement from yourself and the lady."

"She's gone to the powder room."

The waitress arrived and lifted one empty cup then looked at the other. "Is the lady finished?"

"No," said James, "she will be back."

"Okay."

James looked at his watch. "Mind you, she's been in there for twenty minutes."

"Ma'am, can you tell the lady a police officer would like a word?"

"Sure."

The waitress went to the counter, left a cup there and headed for the powder room. Upon her return, she had a puzzled look on her face.

"Nobody is in the powder room."

"Any other rooms?" said the police officer.

"I've checked them – she's not there either!"

"Could there be another exit from the restaurant?" said James.

The waitress shook her head. "None."

James looked at the police officer and shrugged his shoulders.

"Not a missing person as well!" The officer shook his head. "A female Houdini, that's all I need."

James left the establishment and returned to his office. He assisted Lucy in bookkeeping duties then attended to his own work. Throughout that afternoon, his mind could not dismiss the events at lunchtime.

How unbelievable to meet such a unique individual – and have a conversation over coffee about matters that can affect your destiny!

Shortly after five o'clock, James left the office and walked to the subway station. On the journey home, he gazed out the window and reflected on what happened earlier in the day. When the train arrived at his destination, James looked at his wristwatch. The journey appeared to take less time than normal. James left the station and as the Manhattan sun shone down, made his way home.

James hung his jacket and hat on the coat stand.

Elizabeth walked into the hall then kissed him on the cheek. "Did you have an enjoyable day?"

"Almost killed and met a time traveller."

Elizabeth smiled. "Apart from that."

"Just the norm."

Elizabeth went into the kitchen.

James followed.

"I met Georgina for lunch."

"How is her new enterprise faring?"

"Not bad." Elizabeth set the table."

"Does she require an accountant?"

"Not yet."

James sat down at the table.

"Hungry?"

"Just a tad drained."

"You have three partners' workload." Elizabeth chopped meat on a wooden board.

"It's not that bad Elizabeth, the workload has halved."

"Any word on when Bob may return?"

James stretched his legs. "Perhaps in two weeks. What we need is another clerkess – poor Lucy is run of her feet."

Elizabeth washed her hands then wiped them on a towel. "Don't feel guilty – she received an increase in her pay." She brushed both hands down her yellow apron.

"It's a lot cheaper than to hire another member of staff. When Bob returns, he can make the decisions."

"Georgina has met someone." Elizabeth opened a cupboard and brought out crockery.

"Who?"

"The father of a girl she teaches in Long Island."

"Is he married?"

Elizabeth turned round. "No he isn't, the chap is a widower. He has asked Georgina to dinner."

"Is it not too soon? Dale's funeral has not long passed."

"She feels it is time to move on."

James rose and stood beside Elizabeth with his arms folded. "What does he do?"

"He is a banker in the city, stays in East Williston, Long Island and younger than Georgina." Elizabeth looked at James. "Anything else?"

James smiled. "Where on Long Island is East Williston?"

"Nassau County. It's a village in the town of North Hempstead." Elizabeth smiled. "Georgina takes the subway to Penn station and catches a connection straight to East Williston."

"Why not take the ferry?"

"Have you been on one of them?"

James shook his head.

"I rest my case."

"Anyway, how long until dinner?"

Elizabeth glared at her husband. "Soon."

James smiled. "Did Georgina say much about his background?"

Elizabeth washed her hands.

James handed her a towel.

"She did mention his bank is busy buying stocks and shares for their customers. The bank is happy to loan out money." Elizabeth dried her hands then handed the towel to James.

"The share index continues to rise therefore banks view the stock market as a secure investment. The money that you received for the painting could be used to buy shares."

Elizabeth put her arms around James. "We shall discuss the matter of my capital over dinner."

Travelling to work, James read his morning newspaper and contemplated this coming week.

Elizabeth and Georgina are off to St Louis for seven days. I suppose it makes sense. Due to the sale of her painting, Elizabeth can take Georgina for a summer break. After her ordeal, the change of scenery will do Georgina good. I can't go because of the situation at work. Bob will return today and may not manage on his own. Now that Clara has gone, Bob will require me to make sure he is up to speed. Given the financial predicament of the firm, I hope his batteries have been fully recharged. As for me, I should manage to survive without Elizabeth for a week. Drat, I hate to prepare and cook my meals.

"Ticket, sir," said the conductor.

James stared at his newspaper.

"Ticket, sir!"

James looked up, took the ticket out of his jacket inside pocket and gave it to the conductor.

"A long night, sir?" The conductor examined the ticket and clipped it. "Thank you. Wall Street next stop." He smiled and handed the ticket back to James.

James smiled and put it back into his inside pocket.

The train pulled into Wall Street station a few minutes earlier than usual. James left the train, went up the stairway and reached the exit then strolled to his place of work. He entered the building and being early, did not take the elevator. When James approached his office, he spotted Bob in conversation with Lucy. James opened his office door and went in. He took off his hat, hung it up then sat down.

Lucy knocked on the door.

"Morning," said James.

"Jim, Bob would like a word at your convenience."

James stood up.

"I'll bring a couple of coffees to Bob's office." Lucy left the office.

She is a competent girl. James walked to Bob's office and knocked on his door.

"Come in, Jim."

James opened the door and walked in. Poor Bob, he has lost weight. His white buttoned-up shirt and dark blue tie now appear suited to a larger neck. His full head of silver grey hair has thinned. He looks nearer sixty than fifty-two.

"Have a seat, Jim." He coughed.

James sat down opposite Bob's dark wooden desk. "Glad to be back?"

"I should be thankful I'm here! Tom wasn't as lucky. On another note Jim, no need to tell you, we're in a bad way."

Because I had scrutinised the business finances before Bobs return, I became well aware of our situation. "Yes, we are."

"I've been in touch with our bank and can obtain funds to stay afloat however, we need to generate income."

"Lucy sent out reminders to the clients but nobody wants to pay their fees. Businesses no longer contact us to assist them in financial planning or auditing."

"I spoke with Lucy this morning." Bob sat forward. "She is a good worker."

"I gave her a pay increase."

"How much?"

"One that she deserves. The alternative being you and I do her duties."

Bob smiled. "Life is bad enough." He sat back. "What about your holiday entitlement?"

"I can take time off later, you need me here."

Bob nodded. "Thanks Jim. What about Elizabeth?"

"She and her sister left this morning for a week in St Louis."

"Why St Louis? It takes over a day to reach the place."

"Thirty-two hours from New York Central. Georgina likes blues music and Elizabeth wants a change of scenery."

"At times, New York can intimidate people. Compared to our population, St Louis is a small city."

"How small?"

"About eight hundred thousand. Since the recent movie about the city, St Louis should receive an influx of summer visitors."

"St Louis Blues?"

Bob nodded. "I prefer jazz."

"Me too."

Chapter 4

The Vacation

Elizabeth and Georgina arrived at Grand Central and headed for the ticket office. Once there they stood in a small queue, waited for several minutes then Elizabeth approached the counter.

"Yes, ma'am?" said a ticket office clerk.

"Two tickets to St Louis, please."

"Return or one-way, ma'am?"

"Return, please, plus a sleeper compartment."

"One compartment or two?"

"Just one. It does sleep two people?"

"Yes, ma'am." The clerk handed over the tickets. "Twenty-three dollars, fifty."

Elizabeth opened her handbag and gave him a bundle of dollar notes.

The clerk took the money and slotted it into a drawer. He brought out several coins then pushed them towards Elizabeth over the wooden counter.

"Platform 14," he said.

Elizabeth put the tickets and change into her handbag then turned to her sister. "Platform 14, Georgina." Elizabeth whispered, "that's cheaper than I expected!"

"We better move," said Georgina, "he may discover an error has been made."

Elizabeth smiled.

Georgina pointed. "There's the train, it's at the platform."

Elizabeth looked at her wristwatch. "The train departs in twenty minutes."

"Let's dump our cases on the train and try for a good seat. These new shoes I bought feel tight."

Elizabeth smiled. "At least it's not far for you to walk."

The two ladies picked up their respective suitcase and walked towards platform 14. Nearby, a group of men stood and hustled passengers for cash. A small skinny unshaven man approached Elizabeth. He wore a collarless grey shirt, black baggy trousers and a brown ill-fitted jacket.

Georgina whispered, "just walk on, Elizabeth."

He removed his charcoal cap.

Elizabeth stopped. An older teenager.

"Excuse me, ma'am. Can you spare a dime?"

Elizabeth opened her handbag, took out two coins then gave them to the young man."

He looked at the coins in his palm then at Elizabeth. "Gee thanks, ma'am!"

She started to walk and caught up with Georgina. "Poor chap."

"You encourage them to beg, Elizabeth." Georgina looked ahead. "At last, platform 14."

"Let's find you a seat, those poor feet must hurt."

Georgina nodded.

As Elizabeth and Georgina were about to board the train, a tall well-dressed man came forward and lifted his large beige hat. A similar individual stood behind him.

"Pardon me, ladies. Allow my friend and I to assist you with those heavy items of luggage."

"Thank you," said Georgina. She glanced at her sister.

Elizabeth and Georgina boarded the train followed by the two gentlemen who each carried a suitcase.

Later that evening, Elizabeth and Georgina had dinner in the train's restaurant carriage. Elizabeth laid her knife and fork on the half-full plate.

"A lovely meal, Elizabeth." Georgina laid her cutlery on an empty plate.

"When I travel, my appetite fails me."

Georgina leaned forward. "Because of what happened on the Titanic?"

Elizabeth shook her head. "Nowadays I'm not a good traveller. Besides, since that trip, seventeen years have passed."

"Do you still have flashbacks?"

"Through time they have diminished. However, one still haunts me."

"Which one?"

"When the ship sank. I can still hear the frantic screams of people all around me." Elizabeth paused. "I consider myself a lucky individual."

Georgina gazed out the dining carriage window. "The unsinkable Titanic."

"One gallant aspect remains from that disaster."

Georgina looked at Elizabeth.

"Musicians who continued to play on deck."

"Whilst the ship sank?"

Elizabeth nodded.

"Gallant men indeed."

Elizabeth looked around the carriage. "Not many empty seats." She turned to face her sister. "Georgina?"

"Yes?"

"Those two gentlemen who carried our bags onto the train have just sat down at the opposite end of this carriage."

Georgina turned round then faced her sister.

Elizabeth looked ahead then at Georgina. "They have left their table and are coming this way!"

"Good evenin' ladies," said one of the gentlemen, "I trust y'all had an excellent meal?"

"Yes, thank you," said Georgina.

"May my friend and I join both of you fine ladies?"

Georgina glanced at Elizabeth.

"We are about to leave and return to our compartment," said Elizabeth.

The second gentleman moved forward. "Can we gentlemen purhaps buy you coffee?"

Elizabeth glanced at Georgina.

"Ladies, how often do you have the pleasure of two genuine southern citizens?" said the first gentleman.

Georgina smiled. "Two white coffees."

A carriage steward with his distinguished white jacket, slim dark tie and trousers walked by.

"Excuse me, steward," said the first gentleman.

The steward turned to face the gentleman. "Yes, sir."

"Four coffees, if you may."

"Black or white sir?"

"Two white and two black."

"Certainly, sir." The steward departed.

"May we sit down, ladies?" said the second gentleman.

Elizabeth nodded.

A waiter arrived and removed used plates and utensils then departed. Both gentlemen took off their large hats and smiled. One sat beside Elizabeth and the other next to Georgina. They placed their hats in front of them on the dining table. Whilst Georgina remained static, Elizabeth moved closer to the carriage window. The grey moustached gentleman next to Elizabeth straightened his slim brown tie.

"Allow us to introduce ourselves. I am Mason Jennings." He put a hand to his chest.

The black moustached gentleman smiled. "I am Sam Henry." He looked sideways at Georgina, straight ahead at Elizabeth then sideways again.

"I am Georgina and this is my sister Elizabeth." Georgina smiled. Both men have a full head of hair!

"And two lovely distinguished names," said Mason Jennings.

"Which state you ladies from?" said Sam Henry.

"We are not originally from America," said Elizabeth.

"You from England?" said Sam Henry.

"Scotland," said Elizabeth.

Mason looked at Elizabeth. "Why did you come all the way to America, ma'am?"

"You both actresses by any chance?" said Sam.

"We stay in New York and on our way to St Louis," said Georgina.

"Dog gone it, you are actresses!" said Sam, "to appear in a film?"

"We are not actresses," said Elizabeth, "we are on our way to St Louis for a vacation."

"St Louis is a one horse town compared to New York," quipped Sam.

Georgina smiled. "We want a change of scenery."

Mason turned to Elizabeth then looked at Georgina. "Such a pity you a'int on the silver screen." He put his hand on his chest. "Both of you would do it a service by providin' grace and glamour."

"I agree," said Sam.

"Are all gentlemen from the south similar to yourselves?" said Georgina.

Sam smiled at Georgina. "Virginian men are a breed on their own, ma'am."

Georgina laughed.

"What do you gentlemen do?" said Elizabeth.

"Both of us are farmers," said Mason.

"Why come to New York?" said Georgina.

"To see a political and business acquaintance," said Sam.

"In Wall Street?" said Elizabeth.

Sam nodded. "Yes, ma'am."

"How long have you been in New York?" said Georgina.

"Two days," said Mason, "we stayed at the Crown Plaza."

Elizabeth smiled. "Wearing beige suits, stetsons and brown boots, both of you must have stood out in Manhattan."

Mason nodded and smiled. "We done did that."

Sam laughed. "We brought a little eccentricity to that there city."

Georgina smiled. "And charm."

Sam turned to Georgina. "Why, thank you, ma'am. I appreciate that comin' from a nice sweet lady such as yourself."

Elizabeth looked at Georgina then smiled.

The carriage steward arrived at the table with four cups of coffee on a silver tray. He smiled at Elizabeth and Georgina.

Mason leaned back.

"Four coffees, ladies and gentlemen." The steward laid four white saucers and cups of coffee on the white tablecloth.

"Take this." Mason handed the steward two dollar notes. "Keep the change."

"Thank you, sir." He put the notes into his white jacket top pocket then departed.

Elizabeth lifted her cup, sipped the coffee and laid it on the saucer. "As farmers, how do you fare in the current economic climate?"

"Bein' honest, ma'am," said Sam, "could be better."

"Because of the recession, consumer demand fur farm produce remains low hence the price we charge is comparable," said Mason.

"Also this year we suffered a bad harvest," said Sam, "it don't help."

"We got talkin' to a few guests in our hotel – businessmen like ourselves," said Mason, "they work in the car and construction industry."

"What did they say?" said Georgina.

Sam turned to Georgina. "Not good also. Demand has fallen big time! Too many automobiles and not enough buyers." Sam lifted his cup of coffee and drank it.

"Will shares in that particular industry suffer?" said Elizabeth.

Sam placed his empty cup onto the saucer. "They have but been propped up by financiers. C Mitchell bein' one of them."

"What does the 'C' stand for?" said Georgina.

Sam sat back on his seat. "Charles, I believe."

"Why were financiers involved?" said Georgina.

Mason put a thumb into each waistcoat pocket. "Avoid a crash."

"Given the state of the economy," said Georgina, "might a sharp fall in share price not happen again?"

"I'll wager Sam's Cadillac it could," said Mason.

Sam laughed. "You wager your own vehicle, old buddy."

"Glad I have no shares." said Elizabeth. She lifted her cup and took a sip.

Georgina laughed. "Or a Cadillac."

Elizabeth coughed.

Mason turned to Elizabeth. "A lot of people do possess shares and others snap up what's left! The banks are happy to give out loans fur people to buy shares."

"Can people pay back those loans?" said Elizabeth.

Sam looked at Mason. "All hats and no cattle."

Georgina giggled.

Mason nodded.

"Exuberance. No doubt in the future many people will lose." Elizabeth laid her cup onto the saucer.

"You're right ma'am but it won't be Mason and me," said Sam.

"Why?" said Elizabeth.

Mason smiled at Elizabeth. "We done sold our shares."

"Is that why you came to New York?" Georgina lifted her cup and sipped her coffee.

"No, ma'am, for another reason." Mason lifted his cup of coffee then drank it.

"A matter that involves West Virginia," said Sam, "and it's future."

Georgina turned to Sam. "Can you reveal anything to us?" She laid her cup on the saucer.

"A park," said Mason, "to revamp our part of Virginia." He laid his cup on the saucer.

"Regenerate the area?" said Elizabeth.

Mason nodded. "Utilise the unused farmland and create jobs fur the people out of work."

"An excellent solution!" said Georgina, "when does it start?"

"We hope in the foreseeable future," said Mason, "it's been on the cards fur three years."

"Maybe next year," said Sam, "if not sooner."

Mason smiled. "Them politicians need a shove now and again. Our guy in New York will lend his weight behind the project."

Elizabeth looked at Mason. "Does the park have a name?"

"The Shenandoah National. The park will encompass our Blue Ridge Mountains."

Georgina clasped her hands. "How stunning! How big will the park be?"

"We expect it to stretch around a hundred miles." Mason smiled.

Georgina raised her eyebrows. "Gosh!" Forty times the length of Central Park."

Sam nodded. "It's a big un!"

"How high are the mountains?" said Elizabeth.

"Over three thousand feet," said Mason.

Elizabeth looked at Georgina. "A 'Munro'."

Mason looked across the table to Sam then at Elizabeth.

She smiled. "A 'Munro' is a mountain in Scotland over three thousand feet."

"Are they as purty as the Blue Ridge Mountains?" said Mason.

"You and Sam should visit Scotland," said Georgina, "you will be taken aback by the scenery."

"Maybe we'll just do that." Mason looked at Sam. "What about it partner?"

"Good idea. Maybe these two ladies will show us around their purty country?"

Elizabeth glanced at Georgina then turned to Mason. "We are going back to our compartment. Thank you for the coffee."

"So soon!" said Mason, "It's still light."

"It has been a long day," said Elizabeth.

Mason stood up. "Thanks fur makin' our evenin' a done pleasant one."

Elizabeth rose and looked at Georgina.

Georgina turned to Sam. "Time for me to retire, cowboy." She stood up.

Sam stood up and smiled. "You have a long time yet before retirin'. A pleasure to have met you." He took Georgian's hand and kissed it.

Georgina smiled. "Why, thank you, sir."

113

Sam released her hand and laughed. "That's a fine southern accent! You do West Virginia proud."

Elizabeth turned to Mason. "I don't do a southern accent."

"You don't have to, ma'am. Your beauty done captivates me. It just happens Mr Henry and I will be in St Louis tomorrow evenin' and would be privileged to have the company of both you ladies."

Sam looked at Georgina. "We know a swell restaurant in the heart of St Louis."

Georgina looked at Elizabeth then at Sam. "French cuisine?"

Sam smiled. "No problem. Mason and I will escort both you ladies to the restaurant. Where in St Louis will you be stayin'?"

"The Beauville guest house," said Georgina, "I believe not far from the city centre."

"Purfect!" said Mason. He looked at Elizabeth. "We'll be there at seven."

Georgina and Elizabeth left the table and went to their compartment. The two gentlemen from West Virginia did not vacate the table. The steward approached them and smiled.

"Another two coffees, gentlemen?" He lifted the four cups and saucers onto his silver tray.

"Anythin' stronger son?" said Mason. He shoved his hat across the table.

"Any bourbon on this here train?" said Sam, "we'll make it worth your while."

The steward smiled. "I'll see what I can do gentlemen."

Elizabeth put on her pale blue jacket and hat, walked towards the bathroom door then stood next to it.

"Hurry up, Georgina, our two southern escorts will be here soon."

"I am sure they won't mind if we're not ready for seven. After all, Elizabeth?"

"Yes, a woman's prerogative."

Georgina looked into the bathroom mirror and applied her red lipstick.

"And they both appear to have a gentlemen status." Elizabeth looked out the window. "It's a nice view of the river from here. This establishment is in an excellent location."

"Handy for the railway station." Georgina stared into the mirror and brushed her blonde hair. "My hair is still lighter, Elizabeth."

"Thanks to chemicals."

Georgina smiled. "I am intrigued as to how our two gentlemen will return to Virginia. It must be a thousand miles!"

"Nearer eight hundred. I bet one of them owns a boat." Elizabeth popped into the bathroom and looked at herself in the mirror.

"Don't worry, you look fine."

"It isn't that, I feel guilty."

"Elizabeth, it's just dinner."

"What about their wives, what must they think of us?"

"They will be having a good time back in Virginia spending Mason and Sam's money."

"You won't mention this to James, will you?"

Georgina shook her head. "Mason and Sam will have left for their ranches by tomorrow."

"Are they not farmers?"

"This is America, Elizabeth, not Scotland. Here, they live in a ranch not a farm." Georgina dabbed her face with powder.

"It won't be as claustrophobic as Upper East Side."

Georgina laughed.

"Has Calvin's sister had this place long?" Elizabeth exited the bathroom.

"Five or six years. Since her divorce, she has thrown herself into the business."

"It appears spotless." Elizabeth cast her gaze around the room and dragged her finger over the surface of a bedside table. "Nice furniture and bright decor."

Georgina came out of the bathroom.

"Glad Calvin's daughter required piano lessons." Elizabeth smiled at Georgina.

"So am I." She turned round. "Did I hear a knock on the door?" Georgina returned to the bathroom.

Elizabeth walked to the door and opened it.

The lady proprietor smiled. "Two gentlemen with large hats await your company." She sniffed the air.

"Thank you, Ms West. We'll be downstairs in about five minutes." Elizabeth glanced towards the bathroom. "Perhaps ten."

"Make it fifteen!" cried Georgina.

Mrs West smiled and departed.

"She could smell your jasmine perfume."

Georgina came out of the bathroom and smiled. "She may report back to Calvin, better make sure it's not a late night."

"Is he the jealous type?"

"He married his first girlfriend."

Georgina went back into the bathroom, looked at herself in the mirror and after a couple of minutes, came out.

"Ready?" said Elizabeth.

"Yes."

Georgina put on her pink jacket and hat then the two sisters went downstairs. At reception, the gentlemen from West Virginia stood and chatted with Ms West. As Georgina and Elizabeth walked down the creaky staircase, both Sam Henry and Mason Jennings looked towards it. When the two ladies reached the bottom of the staircase, both men took off their hats.

"Ladies, your carriage awaits," said both men.

Mason and Sam led Elizabeth and Georgina outside the guest house. Two white horses and a shiny black carriage stood in all its splendour. The driver of the carriage wore a black hat, red jacket, black trousers and boots.

Elizabeth smiled at Georgina. "I am back at Docharnea!"

Georgina laughed.

"Somethin' you want to share with Mason and me, ladies?" said Sam.

Georgina smiled. "We'll explain over dinner."

Mason opened the carriage door. "After you, ladies."

"Thank you," said Elizabeth. She stepped into the carriage.

"This is terrific!" said Georgina. She stepped inside.

Sam entered and sat opposite Georgina.

Mason entered, closed the door and sat opposite Elizabeth. "That's us Luke!" he shouted.

The carriage moved off and headed for the centre of St Louis. The clip-clop sound of two horses and the rare sight of a traditional carriage ensured residents would stare in amazement.

Georgina smiled at Sam. "How did you manage to obtain this?"

"I'll explain over dinner." Sam sniffed the air. Nice perfume. "However, I can talk a cat down from a tree!"

Georgina laughed.

"The city owes us a favour," said Mason.

"Why?" said Elizabeth.

"You familiar with air travel, Elizabeth?" said Sam.

Elizabeth shook her head. "No."

"Charles Lindbergh?" said Mason.

"Two years ago he flew across the Atlantic to France," said Georgina.

"Right on," said Mason.

"What kind of involvement?" said Georgina.

Sam smiled at Georgina. "Let's just say a contribution towards the flight cost."

"Did you sponsor him?" said Elizabeth.

"Us and other businessmen," said Mason, "Sam and I believe in the future of air travel."

Georgina laughed. "Not bad for two men who live off the land."

San laughed. "You're funny." He looked at Elizabeth. "She like this all the time?"

Elizabeth nodded. "I'm afraid so."

Mason laughed. "You'll do well down West Virginia way, Georginer."

Elizabeth glanced at her sister. This evening may prove fatal.

Georgina looked at Sam and Mason. "Are you familiar with this restaurant?"

"The owner is an acquaintance," said Mason, "any time we stop by it's where we eat."

"With female company?" said Elizabeth.

"Only fine and proper ladies, ma'am." Mason lifted his hat.

Sam laughed. "That means you, Elizabeth."

"And me too I hope, Sam Henry?" said Georgina.

"Georginer!" Sam smiled. "That goes without sayin'."

Elizabeth smiled. A pair of charmers with infectious southern drawls.

"Elizabeth, I can't hold my potato," said Mason, "what or who is Dockernee?"

Georgina giggled.

"Docharnea is a small estate near the village of Ardrishaig which is in Argyll. In Scotland, that is where I once lived."

"Who did you live with?" said Sam.

"My husband, a housekeeper and a coachman."

"Like Luke drivin' this here carriage?" said Mason.

Elizabeth nodded. "And he wore a similar outfit."

"He good-lookin', Elizabeth?" said Sam, "Luke ain't no Doug Fairbanks."

Elizabeth laughed. "You're funny. In answer to your question, yes."

"Is a coach different from this here carriage?" said Sam.

Elizabeth shook her head.

"Elizabeth painted the coachman's portrait," said Georgina.

"You paint, Elizabeth!" Mason sat back on the black leather seat.

"Now and again."

"Could you paint the Blue Ridge Mountains?" said Sam.

"I don't have the time. Besides, my husband would miss me." Elizabeth glanced at Georgina.

Mason glanced at Sam.

"Here we are, ladies," said Sam, "Mason and I call it 'la bonne nuit' and more."

Georgina laughed.

Elizabeth raised her eyebrows.

Shortly before eleven o'clock, Sam, Georgina, Mason and Elizabeth left Pierre's Restaurant. As they stood outside, their transport back to the guest house appeared then came to a halt in front of them.

"How's that fur timin', ladies?" said Sam.

The driver smiled at Sam.

"Good on ya, Luke." Sam opened the carriage door.

Elizabeth stepped inside followed by Georgina who sat beside her sister. Mason entered and slumped down on the seat opposite Elizabeth. Sam entered and slammed the door then sat opposite Georgina.

"Take her away, Luke!" shouted Sam.

"How did you manage to obtain alcohol?" Elizabeth looked at Mason then Sam.

Mason smiled.

"They also owe you a favour?" said Elizabeth.

Georgina giggled.

Mason leaned forward. "You enjoy the food, Elizabeth?"

Elizabeth nodded. "Yes, the fish tasted delicious."

Mason looked at Georgina.

"Me too, Mason, the French can prepare and serve in eloquent fashion." Georgina smiled. "The dressing on the fish was superb."

"And the 'discreet' wine that was served?" said Sam, "that you drank in a furious fashion?" He smiled at Georgina.

Georgina giggled. "Fabulous."

"Down with prohibition!" cried Sam.

"I agree." Georgina burped.

"How do you gentlemen return to Virginia?" said Elizabeth.

"Not by carriage," quipped Sam.

Georgina laughed.

"My boat is tied up in the harbour," said Mason, "we leave first light."

"Do you have a crew, Mason?" Georgina burped.

"A few guys, they're on board just now."

"How long will it take for the return trip?" said Elizabeth.

Mason smiled at Elizabeth. "Long enough for Sam to get sober."

Sam laughed. "You bet." He smiled at Georgina. "My buddy looks after me."

Georgina laughed. "Just as well."

A short while later, the carriage came to a halt outside the guest house. Mason alighted from the carriage and opened the door. Elizabeth and Georgina followed then Sam.

Elizabeth smiled. "Sorry, gentlemen, we can't offer you a night-cap – rules of the house."

Mason took off his hat. "Elizabeth, it's been a pleasure." He smiled. "I won't forget you."

"Me too, ma'am," said Sam. He removed his hat.

"I'll be a few minutes, Elizabeth," said Georgina." She smiled.

"See you upstairs." Elizabeth smiled. "Goodnight gentlemen, and thank you for this evening." She walked up to the guest house, opened the front door, entered then closed it.

Mason turned to Georgina. "Ma'am, thank you. You have also graced us with your charm and endearin' personality." He put on his hat. "I'll give you and Sam some privacy." Mason looked up at the carriage driver. "Luke, take me for a spin round the block."

"Yes, sir Mr Jennings," said Luke.

Mason entered and closed the door.

Luke threw the reigns forward, whistled to both horses and the carriage moved off. Mason waved to Georgina.

Elizabeth peered out of the bedroom window. As Georgina came out of the bathroom, her sister smiled.

"Feeling better?"

"A little." Georgina sat on the bed.

"Where shall we head for first?"

"You choose sister."

"Art gallery in the afternoon then your choice this evening."

"Okay." Georgina yawned.

"Tired?" Elizabeth smiled.

"I still feel woozy and tired. Too much wine, I'm not used to it."

"You can blame prohibition."

Georgina smiled.

"No carriage on this occasion. A walk into town will make you feel better."

"Promise?"

"What did Sam and yourself talk about?"

"Not much. He would like to see me again."

"He would have to visit New York."

"No problem, he said – just give me a call Georginer."

Elizabeth laughed. "That accent is improving."

Georgina smiled. "It's infectious."

"I hope Calvin's sister did not hear your conversation with Sam."

"Sam and I whispered."

"Just as well."

"You must have gone out like a light!" Georgina yawned. "When I came into the room, you were fast asleep."

Elizabeth smiled.

After breakfast the two sisters left the Beauville and walked to the centre of St Louis. Whilst there, they stopped at a small restaurant and entered. Elizabeth spotted an empty table in the far corner.

She pointed. "Over there Georgina.

"Perfect."

They went over to the table and sat down. Georgina put a hand to her mouth and yawned.

"Do you want a strong coffee?" said Elizabeth.

Georgina nodded. "Black."

A tall dark-haired waiter with a drooping moustache approached Elizabeth and Georgina's table then gave each of them a warm smile.

"Two coffees please, one white and the other black," said Elizabeth.

"Be right back, ladies."

Elizabeth leaned towards her sister. "How does your stomach feel?"

"Unsettled. That wine last night tasted like firewater."

"You still drank it and with ease!"

Georgina smiled. "And you stuck with lime juice. Did you enjoy yourself at the restaurant last night, Elizabeth?"

"The food tasted delicious and the relaxed ambience marvellous. Lovely decor and excellent service."

"But did you enjoy yourself?"

Elizabeth sighed. "Why do you ask?"

"You've been subdued on this trip."

Elizabeth frowned.

"Sam commented to me, 'Elizabeth looks as if she's in the wrong movie!' Elizabeth, is it James?"

"No! He has a lot of problems at work but manages to keep a sense of respectability and humour."

"I am your sister, you can confide in me."

Elizabeth stared at Georgina.

"Yes?"

Elizabeth sat back. "I have started to reminisce about my time in Scotland. Since I left it has been seventeen years but feels longer."

"Do you want to return?"

"I'm not sure. I tell myself it may be because of the economic situation in New York."

"Elizabeth, it will be the same in Scotland."

"I feel claustrophobic at times."

Georgina smiled. "You're not on an estate now."

Elizabeth smiled.

"Would James return to Scotland?"

"I'm not sure. He has the firm's interests at heart and enjoys his role."

"He could try for a position with a Scottish firm, no problem."

"Maybe his former employer back in Lochgilphead?"

"You could sell your apartment and start a new life."

"Easier said than done, Georgina. Not many people buy property in troubled times – even in Upper East Side."

Georgina rubbed her hands. "I have a solution. You rent out the apartment, return to Docharnea and stay in that old coach house."

"What!" Elizabeth cried, "not that place." She raised her eyebrows. "I can still smell the horse dung."

Georgina laughed. "The smell will have gone by now."

Elizabeth shook her head. "I can still see James Carlisle clean out that stable. Poor chap, he did not strike me as someone who should be doing that task."

"Who now stays at Docharnea?"

"Relatives of James, Philip and Charlotte. They have two sons. That reminds me, I must write to Nancy."

"The housekeeper?"

"Yes, she has now retired. Nancy often spoke about James Carlisle. When Walter had to give up his coachman duties, Nancy recommended James."

"He appeared at the right place at the right time."

"If it wasn't for him, I might not be here."

Georgina thumped the table. "It's his fault you feel fed up!"

Elizabeth smiled.

The waiter shouted, "coffee coming up ladies!"

Elizabeth laughed. "That thump caught his attention."

Georgina smiled.

The waiter arrived and laid two white saucers and cups on the light blue tablecloth. He looked at both ladies and smiled.

"Sorry for the delay, enjoy your coffee."

"Merci bien."

The waiter nodded.

"Merci bien?" said Georgina.

"St Louis has a French heritage, it was founded by a Frenchman."

"I'll drink to that." Georgina lifted her cup and sipped her coffee. "Ah!"

Elizabeth lifted her cup and sipped her coffee. "It tastes strong."

"Just what I need."

Elizabeth put the cup onto the saucer. "Georgina?"

"Yes?" Georgina took another sip of her coffee.

"Is Mason married?"

"Widowed." Georgina put her cup onto the saucer. "His wife died three years ago. He has no children."

"And Sam?"

"Divorced."

Nice guys after all. Elizabeth lifted her cup, drank her coffee then placed the empty cup onto the saucer. "Georginer."

Her sister smiled. "Not bad, a bit more practice required on the accent."

The waiter appeared. "Everything all right, ladies?"

"Yes, thanks," said Elizabeth.

"If you require anything, just thump the table."

Georgina laughed.

The waiter smiled and departed.

"C'mon," said Elizabeth, "let's go to the art gallery."

Georgina lifted her cup, drank the coffee then placed it into the saucer. "Okay, ready."

The two ladies went to the cash point of the restaurant and Elizabeth paid the bill. They left and walked in the direction of the town's art gallery.

"It would be a novel idea to open a coffee shop on its own," said Elizabeth.

"Just for coffee?" said Georgina.

"Also cakes, biscuits and scones."

Georgina shook her head. "Not a chance Elizabeth. The establishment would go bust. It would have to sell food to survive."

"Maybe one day."

"I don't see the potential Elizabeth."

Elizabeth looked up to the sky. "That turned from blue to grey rather quick. Gosh! Listen to that."

"A loud thunderclap indeed." Georgina looked skywards. "The rain is about to start, I can smell it."

"Georgina, that church over there." Elizabeth pointed. "Ugh!" she cried, "it's pouring down."

"Quick," said Georgina, "head for the church."

"I'm getting soaked!" cried Elizabeth, "let's run."

People dashed for cover from the cloudburst and both sisters ran towards the church. When they reached it, a door had not been closed. Georgina pushed it forward and heard a loud squeak. The two sisters went inside and looked at each other.

"Shelter at last," said Georgina, "I'm drenched!" She shook her head.

"Phew!" said Elizabeth, "and I complain about the downpours in New York." She wiped her brow.

Georgina smiled. "You ought to see your hair."

Elizabeth stared at Georgina. "You think I'm bad!"

Georgina looked around the church. "Any mirrors?" She tugged her light blonde hair.

Elizabeth laughed.

The two ladies heard footsteps and turned round. A man dressed in black sober attire emerged from a side room.

"Good afternoon, ladies, can I be of assistance?"

Georgina glanced at Elizabeth.

The church representative smiled. "Downpours can be sudden in these parts."

"Yes," said Georgina, "we've just found out."

He smiled.

Elizabeth smiled. I should have worn my bloody hat.

The church representative turned to Elizabeth. "Yes, my dear?"

"It's, it's a lovely church." Elizabeth cast her gaze around the building.

He smiled. "The church opened twenty-one years ago. Would you care to join?"

"We are on holiday," said Georgina, "just arrived."

"From where?"

"New York," said Georgina.

The church representative clasped his hands. "The city does have a diverse population and culture." He smiled. "However, so has St Louis."

Georgina smiled. No doubt we will soon find out.

Elizabeth stared at a wall mirror.

"Do you have an interest in gothic design, madam?"

"The mirror reminds me of one I had in a coach house."

"In New York?"

"No, Scotland." Elizabeth turned round and looked up at the yellow and blue stained glass window. "The sun has come out."

The church representative smiled. "God looks kindly upon his flock."

"Thank you for your time," said Elizabeth, "we will continue on to the city centre."

"Yes, thank you," said Georgina.

"My pleasure, ladies." The church representative guided Elizabeth and Georgina to the exit door. "Come again." He opened wide the large wooden door. "I must oil this door."

Georgina smiled.

As the two ladies walked past the church representative, he smiled. Elizabeth and Georgina left the church and witnessed a glorious warm sunny St Louis afternoon.

Georgina sniffed. "I can smell the rain."

Elizabeth looked at her sister then herself. "We'll skip the art gallery."

Georgina nodded. "Let's go back to the guest house and change out of these wet clothes."

Georgina looked up to the clear blue sky then turned to Elizabeth. "Nice church."

Elizabeth glanced back. "St Francis de Sales."

That evening, both sisters walked through the centre of St Louis towards Georgina's chosen venue. Until they reached it, a couple of blocks remained.

"I can hear music," said Elizabeth.

"This is more my taste!" Georgina smiled.

"It would appear so."

When the two ladies neared their jazz venue, the music grew louder. Elizabeth and Georgina turned a corner and were dazzled by exterior lights above the venue entrance.

"I should have brought my sunglasses," said Elizabeth.

"That would look cool," said Georgina, "you may start a trend."

Elizabeth and Georgina joined a long orderly queue waiting to pay admission and sample the music.

"I did not envisage this!" said Georgina, "I don't' want to wait here all night."

"BD's jazz club appears a popular place," said Elizabeth.

A tall young African-American man in a brown suit, white shirt and tie turned round to face Elizabeth.

"Sure is, ma'am, one of the city's finest."

"Do we have your word on that?" said Georgina.

"You sure do, ma'am. Where you come from?" He looked downwards at Georgina.

She looked upwards. "New York."

"New York! Ain't you far from home."

Georgina smiled.

"You a fan of the Yankees?"

"Not really," said Georgina.

"Not the Giants? Man, last year the 'Cardinals' whooped them!"

"The Cardinal?" said Elizabeth.

"Yes, ma'am, St Louis's finest in a generation."

Georgina whispered, "baseball."

Elizabeth nodded.

"The Browns can also hold their own." The man smiled.

"Also a baseball team?" said Elizabeth.

He nodded then turned to face the front of the queue. "Be inside soon."

Elizabeth glanced behind. "A longer queue has formed!"

Georgina smiled. "We chose the correct venue."

Elizabeth glanced to the left side of the queue. "That's a tall well-built chap at the entrance."

"He's the steward, ma'am," said the man, "in case of trouble."

Elizabeth stared at Georgina. "Trouble!"

Georgina shrugged her shoulders then stood on her tiptoes. "Almost there."

Fifteen minutes later, Elizabeth and Georgina arrived at the doorway to the jazz venue. The 'large' steward in a black evening suit with blond wavy hair looked at them and smiled.

"Good evening, ladies, welcome to 'BD's'. It's the hottest spot in Missouri."

Elizabeth and Georgina entered the venue and looked around the dim-lit room. A seven-piece band played in the far corner. Similar to the steward, six wore black evening attire. The band consisted of a pianist, trombone player, saxophonist, trumpeter, guitarist, drummer and a singer. The entire band was of African-American origin with the singer being the sole female. She wore a long black evening low-cut dress and black high-heels. A bar lay in the opposite corner to where the band played. Three male bartenders who wore white shirts, black ties and dark trousers, served a long line of impatient noisy customers.

"We may have to wait a while for a drink," said Georgina.

"The place is full of smoke," said Elizabeth.

Georgina moved closer to her sister. "Can't hear you!" she shouted.

Elizabeth coughed.

Georgina nodded. Drat, the band has stopped playing.

A tall well-groomed man approached Elizabeth and Georgina. "Excuse me, ladies, would you care for a seat?"

"Where?" said Georgina.

The man pointed. "Over there."

Elizabeth looked at the table which another man occupied.

The man smiled. "He's my friend and I would be honoured if you ladies joined us."

Georgina smiled.

Elizabeth looked at her sister. Not again.

"We would be delighted to," said Georgina. She looked at Elizabeth. "My sister and I accept your invitation."

"Terrific!" said the man, "come this way." He escorted Elizabeth and Georgina to the table.

The man at the table stood up. "Good evening, ladies, I'm Les Banks."

"You're Scottish!" said Elizabeth.

"Born in Liverpool, schooled in Scotland. And you?"

Elizabeth sat down. "Born in Ardrishaig and schooled in Glasgow."

"Where in Glasgow?" said Les.

"Pollockshields," said Elizabeth, "Craigholme was the name of my school."

Georgina sat next to her sister. "I am Georgina and this is Elizabeth."

Les held his friend's arm. "This handsome man is Eddie Arnott." He sat down.

Eddie sat down at the four-seated circular table next to Georgina. "Hi." He smiled. "Are you from Scotland too?"

"I sure am."

Eddie smiled. "Are you sisters?"

Georgina nodded.

Eddie looked at Les. "We ain't brothers."

Georgina laughed.

Elizabeth turned to Les. "What has brought you to America and in particular St Louis?"

"I am a stage actor and have appeared throughout the country. As to your second question, I like this kind of music."

Georgina turned to Eddie. "And you?"

"Also a stage actor however I once acted in films then went back to my first love."

Les smiled. "He doesn't mean his wife."

Georgina laughed.

"What film did you last appear in?" said Elizabeth.

"The Misleadin' Lady." Eddie smiled at Georgina. "I've met a few of them in my time!"

Georgina raised her eyebrows and smiled. "Have you now?"

Les snapped his fingers in the air.

A nearby African-American waiter in a white suit, shirt and tie walked to the table. "Yes, sur, what can I get you?"

Les looked at Elizabeth and Georgina. "Ladies?"

Georgina turned to Eddie and whispered, "do they serve alcohol?"

He smiled. "Money talks, what would you like?"

"Gin and orange."

Les turned to Elizabeth. "What would you like?"

"A small gin with plenty of orange."

"Gentlemen?" said the waiter.

"Two whiskies," said Eddie, "on the rocks." He gave the waiter a ten-dollar note.

The waiter took it then scribbled the order on a piece of paper and put both in his top breast pocket.

"On the rocks," said Eddie.

The waiter nodded. "Yes, sur."

He removed two empty glasses from the table and put them on his silver tray then headed for the bar.

Eddie smiled at Georgina. "That should guarantee alcohol all night."

Elizabeth looked at Georgina. Another hangover beckons.

"A friend of ours may appear later," said Les, "he's also worked on the stage."

Eddie nudged Georgina. "He's now a movie actor."

"Who is he?" said Georgina.

"A guy called Stan Laurel," said Eddie.

"Has he been in talkies?" said Elizabeth.

"Yes," said Les, "he has made a couple of them."

"It's all talkies now," said Eddie, "that's the future."

"What will happen to the silent movie actors?" said Elizabeth, "they may be terrible talkers."

"They will be out of a job," said Georgina.

"That's the movie business," said Eddie, "here one day and gone the next."

Elizabeth turned to Les. "Being a stage actor appears safer."

Les laughed.

"Les!" cried Eddie, "did Stan say he had another film lined up?"

"That is correct, Eddie, with another chap as a double act."

"What's the guy called?" said Eddie.

Les looked upwards. "I think his name could be Handy."

"Handy?" said Georgina, "that's a strange surname?"

"Not if you need a quick replacement," said Eddie.

Georgina laughed.

Les snapped his fingers. "Hardy, Hardy is his name."

The waiter returned. "Your drinks, ladies and gentlemen." He laid them on the candlelit table. "Have a good evening." He smiled and departed.

"He'll be busy tonight," said Les.

Eddie lifted his glass. "Here's to American hospitality and Scottish charm."

"I'll second that." Les lifted his glass.

"Here, here," said Georgina. She raised her glass.

Eddie looked across the table at Elizabeth.

She raised her glass. "To, to good music and good company."

All clinked their glasses to one another and completed their toast. The six male members and one female member of the band resumed their places. A waiter approached Eddie.

"Same again pal," said Eddie, "make mine a double this time." He looked at Les.

Les nodded.

"Georgina," said Eddie, "a double?"

Georgina nodded and smiled.

Elizabeth looked at Georgina. She likes Eddie.

Eddie whispered, "what about your sister?"

Georgina shook her head. "A single."

Eddie nodded. He looked up to the waiter.

"Got the order, sur." He walked towards the bar.

Eddie looked up. "Terrific! The band's about to start, they have one hell of a trumpet player."

Les nodded. "Yes, he's good."

"What is his name?" said Elizabeth.

"Louis Armstrong," said Eddie.

Elizabeth woke up to the sound of magpies in a nearby tree. Due to an open bedroom window, their distinctive 'chatter' was prominent. She peered at the clock on her bedside cabinet.

"Look at the time!" she cried, "Georgina, we'll miss breakfast."

"What's the time?" said Georgina. She huddled underneath the white bedsheets.

"It's nine o'clock!"

"We've missed breakfast, go back to sleep."

"You're right, we're too late." Elizabeth sat up.

"Go back to sleep, Elizabeth."

"I'm awake." Elizabeth glared at the window. "Those magpies made sure of that."

Georgina turned towards her sister. "That was your alarm call."

"It worked." Elizabeth yawned. "However, not in time for breakfast."

Georgina sat up, stretched her arms and yawned. "We can settle for brunch."

Elizabeth yawned. "I am tired." She looked at Georgina. "Just as well men do not see you like this."

Georgina smiled. "I can't open my eyes." Her head fell back onto the white pillow.

"How much did you have to drink last night, seven, eight or nine gins?"

Georgina yawned. "Don't remember, I feel terrible."

Elizabeth smiled. "What's new?"

Georgina laughed. "Not much."

Elizabeth laughed. "You look half asleep."

"And half awake."

Elizabeth smiled.

Georgina sat up then stared at the window. "The magpies have gone quiet."

"They've gone for breakfast."

Georgina laughed then threw back the bed sheets and slipped out of bed. "I need a drink of water." She staggered to the bathroom in her short pink nightie.

Elizabeth got out of her bed and walked to the window. She adjusted her turquoise nightdress.

"Where is the tumbler?" said Georgina.

Elizabeth pulled back the burgundy bedroom curtain. "Where you left it, on top of the bathroom cabinet." She gazed out the window. Nice sunny day.

Georgina filled the tumbler with cold water then drank it. That's good.

"Better?" said Elizabeth.

Georgina emerged from the bathroom. "I can still taste the gin!" She sat on her single bed.

Elizabeth looked at Georgina. "You could do with another brisk walk. It should take away the dark shadows under your eyes."

"And a long hot bath."

Elizabeth smiled. "You and Eddie gelled well last night."

Georgina stretched her legs out on the bed. "He's a bundle of fun."

Elizabeth laughed.

Georgina looked at her sister. "What?"

"You and he would prove a formidable combination!"

Georgina laughed. Don't I know it.

"Since it's our last full day, let's go to one of the parks."

"Which one?"

"Forest Park, it's located in the west side of St Louis. Les told me it has many amenities."

Georgina hung her head. "I'm not in the mood for any sort of participation."

"There is a nearby brewery we could visit."

"The smell would make me feel sick."

"Then a walk to and around Forest Park will not harm you."

Georgina smiled. "If you insist."

A refreshed Elizabeth and a tired Georgina arrived at Forest Park on the western side of St Louis. With this afternoon being a Saturday, the location had more visitors than on a weekday. Amidst the hot August sun, both ladies wandered through the grounds.

Georgina pointed. "Look, Elizabeth, an ice cream stall." Georgina licked her lips.

"Fine," said Elizabeth, "let's go."

Georgina walked up to the stall.

"Yes, ma'am?" said the young man behind the counter, "what will it be?"

"A cone, please," said Georgina.

Elizabeth moved forward. "Same for me, please."

The young man tipped his red and white trilby hat. "Large?"

Georgina nodded.

"Small for me please," said Elizabeth.

He prepared the cones then faced Elizabeth and Georgina with one in each hand.

"How much?" said Elizabeth.

The young man smiled. "For you, lady, ninety cents."

Elizabeth went into her black handbag and took out a dollar note. "Here you are." She took her cone then handed the note to the seller. "Keep the change."

"Thanks, lady." He gave Georgina her cone then tipped his hat.

Whilst they ate their ice cream cones, the two ladies walked along the footpath through the lush green park. They came across a vacant wooden bench.

"Let's have a seat." Georgina sat down.

Elizabeth brushed a green leaf of the bench then sat down.

"This cone melts fast!" Georgina rolled her tongue around the edge of it.

"I'm almost finished," said Elizabeth.

Georgina smiled. "Wouldn't it be good if a cure for hangovers came on the market."

"Did you enjoy the club last night?"

"The music or the atmosphere?"

"Either." Elizabeth licked her cone.

"The singer had an excellent voice. Is her name Jessie Smith?"

"I am sure that's what Les said."

"I remember now, its Bessie." Georgina licked her lips. "I enjoyed two songs in particular."

"Which ones?"

"After You've Gone and Empty Bed Blues."

"What about St Louis Blues?"

Georgina shook her head.

Elizabeth finished her cone and licked both lips. "There may be a cure."

Georgina looked at her sister. "For blues music?"

"No, alcohol."

"And what may that be?"

"Alcohol in moderation."

Georgina laughed.

Elizabeth looked around the park. "This must have been a spectacle twenty-five years ago."

Georgina popped the last bit of cone wafer into her mouth. "Mmm, no doubt."

"The city and surrounding areas would have benefited from hosting the Summer Olympics."

Georgina licked her mouth. "And the ice cream sellers."

Elizabeth laughed. "With the price they charge for ice cream, fortunes must have been generated!"

"I liked the ice-cream seller's appearance. The white shirt, red bowtie and trousers matched his hat."

"Yes, a salesman." Elizabeth stood up. "Let's head on."

"Where to?" Georgina rose and adjusted her cream short sleeve dress.

"The park has an art museum, let's see what it's like."

"Can't we remain outdoors Elizabeth? After all, it's warm and sunny." Georgina smiled. "It's good for my hangover."

"How about the boating lake?"

"That's more like it, keep to the outdoors."

"Okay." Elizabeth flicked a blonde hair of her light blue dress. "Let's go."

"Maybe they will have those small paddle boats."

Elizabeth laughed. "In your condition, sea-sickness could be a possibility."

"I feel better now, must have been that ice cream cone. It did taste good."

The two sisters continued their walk through the park. The St Louis public came out in force to savour the amiable climate. When Elizabeth and Georgina reached the boating lake, a large queue had formed for pedalo hire.

Elizabeth looked at Georgina. "We should have come on a weekday."

"We will have to wait ages."

"There is also a theatre in the park. Maybe a show is scheduled."

"Let's try it."

Elizabeth and Georgina walked to the park's Municipal Theatre. When they arrived, a tall slim dark-haired man stood at the entrance. He had his hands in both trouser pockets of a charcoal-grey suit and read the billboard. He turned round and looked at the two ladies.

"The afternoon show has been cancelled! They could at least have told me."

"Are you a tourist?" said Elizabeth.

"No, I'm in the show. Are you ladies tourists?"

"Yes," said Georgina, "we're from New York."

"Could you be from England?" said Elizabeth, "I detect a slight accent."

"Yes, Bristol. I left nine years ago." The man checked his wristwatch. "Have to go ladies, nice to speak to you." He walked away.

Elizabeth looked at her sister. "Shy but suave."

Georgina folded her arms. "What now?"

"Mmm." Elizabeth looked around the area. "Hold on, what about a visit to the zoo?"

"A zoo! Here?"

"I'll ask someone in the boat queue, they will be aware of its location."

Elizabeth returned to the boating lake and approached a group of adults with children. She chatted to them and one of the adults pointed. Elizabeth walked back to Georgina.

"Is it far?" said Georgina, "my feet ache."

"No, a fifteen minute walk." Elizabeth smiled. "If you want to stretch your arms, there is a golf course nearby."

"The zoo will suffice, I'll stretch my legs."

"With this being our last day in St Louis, we must cram in as much as possible."

Georgina looked at her sister.

"I hope James has coped on his own."

"Elizabeth?"

"Yes?"

"I have something important to tell you."
Elizabeth stared at Georgina. "What about?"

Chapter 5

A Golden Age

Elizabeth and Georgina arrived at the entrance to St Louis railway station. Elizabeth put down her suitcase and faced her sister.

"Georgina, are you sure about this?"

"Yes, Elizabeth, I'm sure. Don't concern yourself, I'll be fine."

"You have just met this person, he may have a dubious past."

Georgina laughed. "All my men do."

"He is also younger." Elizabeth smiled. "I trust he isn't married?"

"Eddie told me his wife passed away two years ago."

"I wish you would reconsider."

"I'll be fine. I can distinguish good guys from the bad ones. Eddie does not appear the latter."

Elizabeth hugged Georgina. "Take care."

"When I reach California, I will write to you."

"You could telephone, it's quicker."

"I will have much to tell you. We would be on the telephone for ages!"

"Just a quick call?"

"Okay, if it makes you feel better."

"Promise?"

"Yes, I promise." Georgina looked at the station clock then at Elizabeth. "Better go or you'll miss the train."

Elizabeth lifted her suitcase.

"Give my love to James." Georgina kissed her sister on the cheek.

"Bye." Elizabeth walked on then looked back.

Georgina waved then walked to the nearby taxicab rank.

Elizabeth walked towards her departure platform.

Close to the rank, a man stood beside a stationary automobile and whistled in the direction of Georgina.

She turned round.

The man held up his left hand. "Over here!" he cried.

Georgina smiled and walked across the narrow street. "Did we not agree to meet at the guest house?"

"Couldn't wait!" He smiled.

Georgina touched the white automobile. A nice gleam. "Yours?"

"Sure is. Bought this beauty two weeks ago." He stared at the automobile. "My pride and joy."

Georgina smiled. "I can see why!" She surveyed it from front to rear.

"It's a Ford Hotrod." Eddie opened the passenger door. "Get in."

Georgina sat in the black leather passenger seat and sniffed. A strong smell of leather. "Will we be going all the way to California in your automobile?"

"You bet." Eddie closed the door then walked round to the driver's side. He opened the door, entered then closed it. "I hope you're a conversationalist Georgina, California is a long way off."

"I take it you can drive?" Georgina looked at Eddie.

He smiled at Georgina. "Don't you trust me?" He examined the controls.

Georgina sat back on her seat. "You're not sure how it starts!" she cried.

Eddie winked at his passenger then turned the ignition key. "I'll soon get the hang of it."

Georgina sighed. "Please do, Eddie."

He laughed.

The Hotrod burst into action and Eddie drove to the guest house where Georgina and her sister had stayed. He soon reached the establishment, stopped outside it and applied the handbrake.

"Won't be long," said Georgina. She stepped out.

Eddie reached over to the passenger door and closed it. "I'll keep the engine runnin'."

Georgina went into the guest house then closed the door behind her. Eddie opened a compartment under the dashboard, took out his automobile's operating manual and browsed through it. Several minutes later, Georgina appeared with her suitcase, opened the passenger door then entered. She laid her suitcase on the back seat. Eddie put his manual back into the compartment.

"You didn't take long!"

Georgina smiled. "How long will it take to Los Angeles?"

"About two days."

"You can't drive for that length of time!"

Eddie smiled. "We'll have to make stops at a motel."

"What is a motel?"

"A hotel with an area to park automobiles – motor hotel hence motel."

Georgina nodded then looked at Eddie. "How fast does it go?"

Eddie glanced at his passenger. "Let's find out!"

Georgina smiled.

James arrived at Grand Central station to meet Elizabeth and Georgina. He looked up at the large circular elevated clock then went to a newsagent's shop and bought an edition of the New York Post. He found a vacant bench, sat down and browsed through the pages. The public address system announced that the train due to arrive at platform 14 would be delayed by eighteen minutes.

Damn! Elizabeth and Georgina's train.

"Excuse me, sir," said an elderly man, "can you spare a dime?"

James put the newspaper down and looked at the man.

"I lost my job three months ago and hate to ask for cash."

James dipped into his jacket pocket and pulled out several coins. "Take these." He handed them to the man.

A police officer approached James. "Is he being a pest, sir?" The officer glared at the man.

"It's okay, officer."

The white-haired man smiled at James and walked towards the station exit.

James picked up his newspaper and glanced at the officer. "Lost his job." I am sure our paths have crossed on a previous occasion.

The officer tipped his cap and walked away.

James continued to read his newspaper and twenty-five minutes later, the public address announced the platform 14 arrival. As the train approached the platform, James stood up and walked towards the steel exit gate. The long passenger train came to a halt just short of the red platform buffers. New York arrivals started to leave the train and head for the exit gate. James spotted Elizabeth, gripped his newspaper and walked in her direction. She walked through the gate, stopped and looked around the vicinity. An opportunist young man came forward.

"Carry your suitcase, lady?" he said, "only five cents."

"She has someone to assist with luggage."

The young man turned around, grunted at James then moved off.

Elizabeth went up to her husband and hugged him. "Miss me?"

James smiled. "You bet. Where is Georgina?" James took Elizabeth's suitcase.

"I'll tell you in the taxi."

"She is okay?"

Elizabeth nodded. "What about the firm?"

"Not good."

James and Elizabeth left Grand Central and joined the queue at a taxi rank outside the station.

"Not many here," said Elizabeth.

"A sign of the times, everyone now feels the pinch. People take the subway – it's cheaper."

Elizabeth looked at James. "Back to reality, the vacation has finished."

"Here comes several taxis," said James.

People at the taxi rank entered the small fleet of yellow cabs. James opened the door, Elizabeth stepped inside then he followed with her suitcase. He put it down on the floor and sat next to Elizabeth on the rear double seat.

"Good, a seat." said Elizabeth.

James smiled. "You had a seat on the train for thirty hours!"

Elizabeth gave James a gentle nudge then wound down a window.

"Tell me about Georgina."

"She is on her way to California."

"Alone!"

"No, with a chap she met in St Louis. An actor."

"What about the banker in Long Island?"

The taxi driver turned to face the couple. "Sorry to butt in, where you folks headin' for?"

"Forgive us," said James, "Upper East Side."

"You got it."

As the taxi moved off, Elizabeth told her husband about Georgina's liaison with a former actor of the silver screen.

James raised his eyebrows. "My goodness! Does she have any plans for a return to New York?"

Elizabeth shrugged her shoulders. "I'm not sure. She asked me to look after her apartment for the foreseeable future."

"Until someone purchases it, I suppose you will have to." James looked out the window.

"What's up?" asked Elizabeth.

"I heard the screech of tyres." James pointed to across the street. "An accident."

"No accident," said the taxi driver, "the guy ran in front of the vehicle."

"Suicide!" cried Elizabeth.

James held Elizabeth's hand. "There have been a spate of them in the last week."

Elizabeth shook her head and gripped her husband's hand.

The white Ford Hotrod with distinctive black mudguards roared into the Whitley Heights district of Los Angeles. The clear blue sky, warm sunshine, tree-lined streets and Mediterranean-style villas ensured an unforgettable first impression for Georgina. The Hotrod slowed down and came to a halt outside a large property – two large metal gates barred its access. Eddie got out of his automobile, unlocked both gates and pushed them open. This revealed a driveway through a smooth green lawn, which led to the main entrance of a white villa. Eddie returned to the Hotrod then drove with caution up a grey gravel surface. Georgina gazed out her window and admired the affluent setting. Tall trees and bushes surrounded the property to portray seclusion and splendour. The Ford Hotrod stopped in front of the pristine-clean building with windows that sparkled. Birds could be heard singing in trees around the property.

Georgina stared at Eddie.

"Told you it's a nice place." Eddie smiled. "The architect who designed the properties in this district came from Spain." He got out of his automobile and closed the door.

Georgina followed and cast her gaze around the property then a white-winged butterfly landed near to where she stood.

"The property is gorgeous!"

"I have a gardener who tends the grounds and also looks after the villa."

Georgina faced the front of the villa. "Does he also clean the windows?"

"When required." Eddie walked up to the red wooden entrance door, took out a silver key from his jacket pocket and inserted it into a lock. "Come inside." Eddie turned the key and pushed the door open.

Georgina closed the Hotrod's passenger door and walked into the spacious bright hallway then looked upwards.

"My goodness!"

Eddie stood beside her. "The architect did a great job, don't you think?"

Georgina continued to look up at the ceiling's white cornice. "The light fills the room and a nice gold-coloured chandelier to match."

"I'll let you see the rest of the house."

Georgina turned to Eddie. "Who looks after the inside of your villa?"

Eddie smiled.

"Not a girlfriend!"

"The person who takes care of the inside has grey hair and sixty-four."

"Inches in height or years?"

Eddie smiled. "Years."

"Who is she?"

"My housekeeper. She also looks after Jack's property."

"Jack?"

"John Gilbert, he lives next door."

Georgina peered out of a side window. "You also may have had Greta Garbo next door!"

Eddie laughed. "It almost happened."

Georgina walked up to Eddie and put her arms around him. "I could do with a drink."

He kissed her. "Let's go into the lounge and I'll show you what's on offer."

She held Eddie. Same as the previous nights I hope.

The host led his guest into the lounge. "Have a seat."

Georgina sat on a cream-coloured couch with brown cushions, took off her white shoes and stretched out her toned legs.

"I'll fix us a drink." Eddie opened a dark wooden cabinet. "Whisky, gin, vodka, brandy, tequila or martini?"

"Tequila?"

"A Mexican drink."

"I'll settle for gin, just a small one." Georgina smiled. "It's mid-afternoon."

"I'll add a lot of orange."

"Who lives on the other side of your property?"

"Joan Crawford." Eddie poured gin into a crystal glass and added freshly squeezed orange juice. "Nice lady." He handed Georgina her drink.

She took a sip, then another and sat back. "Ah! That's better."

Eddie sat down beside Georgina. "Cheers." He drank his whisky.

Georgina looked around the bright white-walled room. "Lovely. That's a nice painting above the fireplace."

"Should be, it's a Rembrandt. Bought it three years ago."

Georgina smiled. "Do you also have a cook?"

"No, I eat out. There are plenty of restaurants Downtown. Tonight, I'll take you to a favourite one of mine."

"Perhaps you would let me prepare a meal for us. Not tonight – I can't be bothered." Georgina sipped her drink.

"Tomorrow night?"

Georgina drank the contents of her glass and laid it on the dark wooden table. "Yes, tomorrow." She snuggled up to Eddie and kissed him on the lips.

"I'll let you see upstairs." He put his glass on the table, took Georgina's hand and led her to the white wooden staircase.

That evening, Eddie and Georgina left the villa and headed for the centre of Los Angeles. The warm Californian climate made for an enjoyable drive and pleasurable evening.

"Did you book a table?"

Eddie shook his head. "Not when you become a regular." He glanced at the low neckline of Georgina's dress.

"It doesn't reveal too much. Besides, the flapper era is over." Georgina smiled at Eddie. "I like to wear blue."

"You suit that colour, matches the blonde hair and blue eyes."

Georgina picked a hair of Eddie's black suit. "One of them somehow landed on you."

Eddie laughed.

"How far to this restaurant?"

"We'll be there in about ten minutes. I don't want to drive fast, in the last few days the Hotrod has stretched itself."

Georgina looked out of the side window. "Lovely location – all those lush green trees."

"Do you like the villa?"

"It's fabulous! That en-suite bathroom is ideal."

"I gathered that. Before we left, you were in there for two hours!"

Georgina smiled. "I enjoyed the long hot bath – and the large mirror to apply my make-up. However, it only took me an hour."

Eddie looked at his passenger.

"Okay, an hour and a half. I'm not used to a lavish spacious bathroom. In my Manhattan apartment you can't swing a cat!"

Eddie smiled. "As long as you feel happy."

Georgina kissed him on the cheek. "Yes, I am."

"You may see a few celebrities here tonight. Don't feel overawed."

"I won't."

"The restaurant is round this next block."

"What is it called?"

"Antonio's."

The Ford Hotrod reached its destination and Eddie manoeuvred it into a space outside the restaurant. An array of prestigious shiny cars surrounded the red sandstone building. The sophisticated couple entered the establishment and greeted by a tall debonair gentleman. He had swish jet-black hair, short moustache and tanned complexion. A crisp white frilly shirt, black bowtie and deep red carnation in a buttonhole complemented his two-piece black dinner suit.

"Table for two, Antonio," said Eddie.

"Good to see you again, Eddie." Antonio shook Eddie's hand.

"This is a good friend of mine, Georgina."

Antonio took Georgina's hand and kissed it. "A pleasure, madam." He let go of her hand and called over a waiter. "Sandro?"

The waiter came forward and smiled at Eddie. "Good evening, Mr Arnott."

Eddie nodded and smiled.

"Table sixteen, Sandro," said Antonio. He turned to Eddie and Georgina. "Have an enjoyable evening."

The waiter led Eddie and Georgina to their table then pulled out a chair. "Madam?"

Georgina smiled at Sandro and sat down on the velvet burgundy-coloured chair.

Eddie sat opposite.

"What would you like to drink?" said Sandro. He looked at Eddie then Georgina.

"The usual for me, Sandro."

"Ginger ale, Mr Arnott?" Sandro smiled.

Eddie smiled.

"Madam?" Sandro smiled at Georgina.

She looked at Eddie.

He nodded. "Orange plus?"

Georgina frowned. "Orange plus?"

"An orange plus, Sandro," said Eddie.

"Be back soon sir." Sandro departed.

"Ginger ale, Eddie?"

"That means a brandy."

"And an orange plus?

"Gin and orange." Eddie smiled.

Georgina laughed then looked around the restaurant. "I love the decor. The floral burgundy wallpaper and furniture portrays an ambience of intimacy. Even the waiters have burgundy waistcoats on top of their white shirts and black ties." She stared. "That looks like?"

"What's up?"

Georgina whispered, "behind and to the right of you."

Eddie turned round and waved.

"You know him!"

"For sixteen years. We've worked together in several films."

Five minutes later, Sandro returned with two drinks on a gold tray and laid them on the thick white tablecloth.

"Compliments of Mr Chaplin. I will return later to take your menu order." Sandro smiled and departed.

Eddie turned round and then signalled with a raised finger to the hospitable celebrity.

The celebrity smiled.

Georgina whispered, "his date looks young!"

"But not as beautiful as mine."

The couple smiled at each other across the candlelit table, lifted their glasses then clinked them in a gentle fashion.

After a stressful Thursday, a tired and weary James finally arrived home. His regular train from Wall Street station had been cancelled thus a forty-minute delay ensued. To make matters worse, he had to stand in a congested stuffy carriage for the entire journey. James opened the apartment door and slammed it shut. He laid down his briefcase, took off his hat and jacket then hung them up.

"James?" said Elizabeth.

He walked into the living room.

Elizabeth greeted him with a kiss on the cheek then stood back. "Another bad day?"

"I'm afraid so, Elizabeth." James sat down on the couch.

Elizabeth sat next to him and held a letter in her hand. "From Georgina!"

"Nice of her to write." James loosened his tie. "What does she say?"

"She loves Los Angeles and Eddie is a nice guy."

"He must be, she's been with him for a month!"

Elizabeth tutted.

James put his arm round Elizabeth. "Sorry, it's been one of those days."

"Any good news on the business front?"

James shook his head. "The city remains depressed. Nobody is optimistic about the future."

"I went to see an agency this morning in Midtown. They will take responsibility for Georgina's apartment."

"Responsibility?"

"They will attempt to try and find a buyer. If one can't be found then the apartment will be rented out."

James nodded. "Good."

"You have that blank expression." Elizabeth sat back. "What is on your mind?"

"Detective McAndrew dropped into the office. They apprehended a thief and in return for a lighter sentence, he revealed a murderer at large."

"Go on."

"The person who shot Dale."

"Good."

"After this person was apprehended and questioned, he admitted being paid by someone to kill Dale."

"Someone paid to have him killed!"

James nodded. "He hasn't yet told officers who put up the cash."

"What happens next?"

"I'm not sure. Detective McAndrew said he would keep me informed of any developments."

Elizabeth heard three knocks and looked towards the door. "Who can that be?"

James stood up. "I'll answer it." He walked to the door and opened it.

A distinguished well-dressed gentleman stood grim-faced outside the door. He removed his grey hat.

"Can I help you?" asked James.

"Could you tell me where I may find Georgina?"

Elizabeth came to the door.

The stranger smiled. "I see the resemblance. Georgina gives music lessons to my daughter. I'm Calvin West."

"The gentleman from Long Island?" said Elizabeth.

He nodded.

"Come in," said James.

Calvin West entered the apartment and James led him into the living room. Elizabeth closed the door then followed.

"Would you like a drink?" said James.

The guest fidgeted with his hat. "No, thanks."

"Please have a seat," said Elizabeth. He looks tense.

149

Calvin West sat down on a chair and loosened the buttons of his grey pinstripe suit jacket. James and Elizabeth sat adjacent to him on the couch. He glanced around the room.

Elizabeth smiled. "It's smaller than your property."

"But tasteful." Calvin smiled.

"Georgina has not yet returned to New York," said James.

"My sister told me she left the guest house with a man. They drove off in a flashy white automobile."

James looked at Elizabeth.

"I believe the chap may be an old friend," said Elizabeth.

"When will she return? My daughter has missed her lessons. She enjoyed being taught by Georgina." Calvin fidgeted with his hat.

"She hasn't told us," said Elizabeth.

"When she returns, we will ask her to contact you," said James.

Calvin West put his hand into an inside jacket pocket and pulled out a white card. "This is my telephone number." He gave the card to James then stood up. "Thanks for your time."

James and Elizabeth rose from the couch and accompanied him to the door. He put on his hat and shook their hands.

"Did you drive here?" asked James.

"Yes, I parked my vehicle outside the building." He tipped his hat and walked along the landing then down the concrete stairs.

James closed the door. "Poor chap, it's not the music lessons being missed!"

Elizabeth walked to the window and looked at the street below. "James, what make of vehicle is that?"

James approached the window and peered over Elizabeth's shoulder.

"The cream one."

"That looks similar to a luxury Coupe Cabriolet."

Elizabeth looked at James. "How did he manage to enter the main door without a key?"

"We should have asked him. I'll go downstairs and make sure the door is secure."

"We don't want any more strangers at our apartment door."

Whilst she pondered about the future, Georgina soaked in a warm bath and sipped a glass of white wine from a crystal glass.

Why return to New York? I don't want to relinquish this lifestyle.

As Georgina took another sip of wine, she heard Eddie come upstairs then the bathroom door opened.

Eddie smiled. "The party is scheduled for tonight Georgina! Even though it's in the next property, Jack wants us there for eight."

"What's the time now?"

"Seven-thirty. He's a stickler for time."

Georgina smiled. "Ten minutes."

Eddie left the door ajar and went into the bedroom. Its ivory-coloured thick-pile carpet complemented the white bedroom furniture. He put on his deep red tie then his navy blue pinstripe jacket. Eddie looked down at his suit trousers and shiny black shoes then at himself in the mirror. He heard Georgina come out of the bath and looked at his wristwatch.

Be at Jack's party around eight-thirty – at the earliest.

Georgina came into the bedroom with a large white bath towel wrapped around her. She looked at Eddie and gave him a wide warm smile.

"Won't be long now."

"I'll be downstairs."

Eddie walked down the white wooden staircase and entered the lounge. He picked up a magazine which lay on the couch. He read it with interest – the magazine referred to a recent film made in Hollywood. A short time later, Georgina walked down the staircase and Eddie looked up.

"You were quick!" Eddie laid his magazine on the couch.

Georgina smiled. "Let's go." She looked at Eddie's jacket and plucked an ash blond hair of his shoulder. "You missed that one."

Eddie smiled and then looked towards his neighbour's property. "I can hear the guests arrive."

"Good," said Georgina, "I don't like being first to appear." She picked up Eddie's magazine and looked at the cover photograph. "Hollywood Review?"

"The film was released four months ago. Some of the stars will be at the party." Eddie flicked a hair of Georgina's short black dress. "Touché."

Georgina laughed. "Better not keep them waiting." She took Eddie's hand.

The couple left the villa and walked at a slow pace down the driveway. As they turned into the tree-lined street, they observed a long line of luxury cars on both sides. An automobile drew up alongside them and its driver tooted the horn. He turned off the engine, got out then closed the door.

"Hi Stan," said Eddie, "how are you?"

"Fine, Eddie." Stan shook Eddie's hand, smiled and looked at his dark green 1928 Elcar Coupe. "It took me for a spin."

Georgina laughed.

Eddie smiled. "Stan, meet Georgina."

"A pleasure, my dear." Stan shook Georgina's hand.

She smiled.

"I hope Ollie's arrived," said Stan, "I've great news."

"Anythin' you can share?" said Eddie.

"Not yet, Eddie, you'll hear soon enough."

Stan, Eddie and Georgina walked along to the next driveway and then up a lane. The faint sound of chatter and laughter could be heard from the owner's villa. When the three guests arrived, a tall well-groomed man with dark hair, moustache and charcoal chalk-stripe two-piece suit greeted them at the entrance.

"Stan, Eddie!" he cried, "good to see you." He embraced them then looked at Georgina. "And who may this attractive lady be?"

"Jack," said Eddie, "meet Georgina."

"A pleasure to meet you." He kissed Georgina on the cheek. "Do you stay in Los Angeles?"

"Yes, in the next property." Georgina smiled.

Jack raised his dark eyebrows. "Oh?"

"I stay with Eddie."

The host laughed. "That's the problem with our type of property, you can't see any neighbours."

"And they can't see you, Jack," quipped Stan.

Eddie laughed.

"Stan, you're a scream." Jack smiled and put his arm around the comedian. "Folks, let's go inside."

When they entered, guests stood in the large marble hallway. They chatted, laughed and drank with a wide smile on their faces. In the spacious lounge off the hallway, women in elegant dresses and men in smart suits mingled with each other. Most women had short bobbed hairstyles in a variety of colours. The gentlemen had a swish-back style with black being the predominant shade – even for 'mature' male guests. A quartet of musicians situated in the rear garden played a selection of ragtime, jazz and blues tunes. Guests would disappear for a short time then reappear to the 'main arena' – the lounge. A bar stood in the corner of the large room and it's bartender served drinks to frivolous, adventurous and ego-minded individuals. Three attractive young female waitresses in medium-length black dresses distributed glasses of alcohol to guests and removed empty ones. They carried out their duties with distinction despite amorous male actor's frequent interventions. Throughout the evening, laughter became louder and the bartender busier. Georgina and Eddie wandered into the garden and watched the band play.

"Eddie, is that the trumpet player from the club in St Louis?"

"It sure is. He moves in movie circles."

Georgina finished her drink.

Eddie took her glass. "Another gin?"

"A bit more orange, that tasted like a double."

"I'll go inside to the bar, the waitresses looks busy." Eddie walked into the lounge.

Georgina noticed a young man in a corner of the garden. He had been in conversation with an older lady but now stood by himself. Georgina recognised him, but from where? She went across to the young man.

He turned towards Georgina. "Good evening."

"Where have we met, you look familiar?"

He smiled. "I never forget a pretty face."

"Where have our paths crossed?"

"I can't remember!" The young man laughed. "Just joking, we met not long ago in St Louis."

"Where about?"

"Municipal Theatre."

Georgina put a hand to her mouth. "Of course! The play was cancelled."

"Yes, and they didn't bother to tell me!"

"Why have you come to Los Angeles?"

"I'm on tour around America. The entire cast were invited to Jack's party. I hope one day to make the silver screen."

Georgina looked around. "There is enough film industry contacts."

"I had hoped Louis Mayer would be here however I'm told he and Jack don't get on."

"Why not?"

"A contract dispute."

"Industry politics no doubt."

"Chuck Reisner is here, I may have some luck."

"Chuck Reisner?"

"He directed the film 'Hollywood Review', most of the cast have come along tonight."

Georgina glanced towards a marble statue. "Who is the dark-haired woman surrounded by a group of men?"

"Gloria Swanson."

"No, the one next to the nude male statue."

"That's Louise Brooks. She's just returned from Europe and performs in adult movies." The young man smiled.

"They must be popular!"

"Her suitors obviously approve."

Georgina laughed. "What chat-up line will they use?"

"I'm not sure, if it was me I know what I'd say."

Georgina smiled.

"I'd say to her I'm impotent, then hope she'd try to disprove it."

Georgina laughed. "You should try comedy."

"There is a glut of comedians." The young man gazed around the garden "Over at the entrance door."

Georgina stared.

"Roscoe Arbuckle, Harold Lloyd and Eddie Arnott."

"Eddie isn't a comedian?"

"He thinks he is!"

"I am his date."

"Oops! And he's coming this way."

Georgina smiled. "I won't tell."

The young man drank the contents of his glass. "Time for a refill." He glanced at a waitress. "They avoid me for some reason."

"Did you mention impotence?" Georgina smiled.

He laughed. "I hope one day we'll meet again, it's been nice talking to you."

"Before you go, what's your name?"

"Archie, Archie Leach." The young man departed.

Eddie approached Georgina and gave her a glass. "Sorry for the delay, there's many thirsty individuals at the bar and only one bartender. Also Harold Lloyd wanted to chat. " Eddie sipped his whisky. "Who was the tall dark guy?"

"Some chap called Archie Leach." Georgina smiled at Eddie. "He wants to go into films."

"Him and many others, he's no chance."

Georgina looked at two men in conversation. "That chap with Buster Keaton and Stan, he has a stern expression."

"Some guy called Karloff. He's a 'bit' actor."

"Bit?"

"Performs small parts. He's a pal of Stan."

"He looks scary. Where are the prominent Englishmen, Fairbanks and Chaplin? I imagined they would have been here."

Eddie smiled. "Politics."

Georgina rubbed her shoulder.

"Cold?"

Georgina nodded.

"Let's go inside."

Eddie and Georgina walked up the grey concrete steps from the garden then through white-frame glass veranda doors, entered the lounge. At the bar, the three waitresses received drinks from the bartender.

"At least it's not smoky near the doors," said Georgina. She drank her gin and orange. "Agh!"

"What's up?"

"How much gin did the bartender pour into the glass?" Georgina coughed.

Eddie smiled. "Enough to make you tipsy."

Georgina stared into a discreet corner of the room. "What are those two young women up to?"

Eddie whispered, "snortin' cocaine."

"Drugs! I'll stick with my strong gin."

Eddie laughed and then drank his whisky.

Georgina finished her drink and held her glass.

"I'll take that, madam," said a waitress.

Georgina handed it to her.

The waitress placed it on a gold tray and walked on.

"Eddie, where is the bathroom?"

There are two upstairs and two downstairs. The nearest should be down the hallway." He pointed.

"Be back soon."

When Georgina reached the bathroom, a queue of people stood in line. Three women at the end engaged in a conversation. One had golden bobbed hair and petite in height. Another had short dark hair and taller whilst the third had long hair in a platinum blonde shade. She had a taller and younger profile than the other two women. All three portrayed elegance, beauty and style. The subject under discussion related to sound being introduced into motion pictures. The lady with golden hair disapproved of the new technology.

"Silent films made me a star. My latest film had sound and at the release in New York, a malfunction ruined the event. In fact, it took two attempts to show the film! Talkies – they should forget about them."

"I agree, Mary," said the woman with short black hair.

The platinum blonde shook her head. "Clara, Mary and you have to embrace the future of movies. Talkies will be here to stay."

"Honey, you're young," said Mary, "I'm thirty-two and know the movie industry inside out."

"You're not thirty-two," said Clara. She's taken off five years.

"I only look thirty-two." Mary folded her arms.

"What's your speciality Carol?" asked Clara.

"I do comedy." Carol smiled. "The timing of my voice complements humour."

"Carol," said Clara, "sound will fade into the past."

Mary looked upwards to Carol. "Lombard, trust us."

"Mind you, Mary," said Clara, "you won that Oscar last year in a talkie."

"Hey, 'It girl', I should have received one long ago!"

"Were you not offered good roles?" said Carol.

"If I had adhered to the casting couch, I would have."

Georgina laughed.

As the three ladies looked at Georgina, a man came out of the bathroom and left the door ajar. Mary went into the bathroom and slammed the door shut.

Carol smiled at Georgina. "Since the ringlets were removed, she's even more feisty."

Georgina smiled. "How will she embrace television?"

"With a hammer," said Carol.

Clara giggled.

A few minutes later the cistern flushed and then tap water started to run. It stopped and the bathroom door flew open.

"The bloody hand towel is damp!" said Mary. She stormed past her fellow actresses.

Clara turned to Georgina. "You can go next. Now that Mary has gone, Carol and I can have a chat about her."

Georgina smiled and entered the white tiled bathroom. She turned the gold handle and closed the door.

"Where can Douglas be tonight?" said Carol, "it's not like Mary to come on her own to a party."

Clara folded her arms. "I bet they've had another row. Because of that Oscar, she's on her high horse."

Carol smiled. "I'll bet it's a very high one."

Clara shook her head. "It must be low, otherwise Mary could not reach the saddle."

Carol laughed.

Clara giggled.

"I hope that lady will be quick," said Carol, "I want a drink."

"So do I." Clara turned her head towards the door. "Here she comes."

"Thanks," said Georgina. She walked past Clara and Carol.

Carol turned to Clara. "I won't be long."

Georgina walked along the hallway and looked towards a painting, which hung in a squint position. She straightened the painting and stepped back to admire it.

"Rembrandt appears popular in these parts," said a male voice.

Georgina looked round.

"I'm Ollie, a pal of Eddie." He shook Georgina's hand.

She smiled. "Pleased to meet you. Earlier, Eddie introduced me to your other half."

"Have you seen him? I want to discuss an important piece of news!"

Georgina smiled. "That's what Stan said to Eddie about you."

"Did he now? Ohhh! Wait till I get my hands on him." Ollie smiled. "See you later." He marched towards the bathroom.

Georgina continued along the hallway then stopped and took off her right black high heel shoe. She rubbed her foot then replaced the shoe.

"Many guys at the party would do that for you."

Georgina looked up. "Hello, Stan. Ollie's searching for you, he passed a few minutes ago."

"I've tried to find him all night!" Stan smiled. "Have you enjoyed the party?"

"Yes, thanks. I've come from the bathroom – stuck behind Mary Pickford."

"Did someone manage to prise the two of you apart?"

Georgina laughed. "And I'm grateful."

Stan laughed. "Eddie told me you're originally from Scotland, Glasgow by any chance?"

"It's the closest city. Why?"

"I played there once and escaped with my life intact."

Georgina laughed.

Stan smiled. "And I'm not joking!"

Georgina moved closer to Stan. "You have known Eddie for some time?"

"Yes, many years."

"He does not mention his wife. What happened to her?"

"June died from an overdose of sleeping tablets."

"That's terrible."

"The coroner's report stated accidental death." Stan glanced at his wristwatch. "Must go and find Ollie."

"Stanley!" cried a man's voice.

Georgina looked down the hallway.

"Here he comes," said Stan, "I'm for it now!" He laughed.

"I better return to Eddie, he may think I have deserted him."

"Good idea, he's with Anita Page."

Who is Anita Page?

"Bye."

Georgina walked into the lounge and looked around. She observed Eddie and a young woman in conversation with each other. The young woman had hair the colour of a newly minted coin. Georgina walked up to them.

"Georgina, meet Anita Page."

"Pleased to meet you," said the young woman.

"Can I get you ladies a drink?"

"Same again for me," said Georgina.

"I'll have a tequila straight," said Anita.

"Be back soon." Eddie walked to the bar.

Georgina gazed around the room. "The waitresses must be on their break."

They have worked solid for several hours," said Anita.

A Hispanic accent. "You are not American?"

"Salvadorian. You are also not American."

Georgina smiled. "No, originally from Scotland."

"It is good to hear Eddie laugh again. Since his wife died, I have not seen much of him."

"Have you known him for some time?" She must be in her teens.

"About three years."

"Did his wife come from California?"

"Yes. Her grandfather made a fortune in the gold rush. When he died, she inherited all the money."

"What about her father?"

"The grandfather and he did not talk to each other. As Eddie would say, they did not see 'eye to eye' at any time." Anita smiled. "Have you had surgery?"

"Surgery?" What does she mean?

"Plastic."

Georgina shook her head. "No."

"I am aware of some actresses who have had treatment to make them appear younger." She smiled. "Being eighteen, I will not require treatment for some time."

"It must be dangerous. Surgery could leave nasty scars."

"If it make you look younger, I would take the chance."

Hollywood!

Anita looked towards the bar. "Good, here comes Eddie with our drinks."

Eddie handed a drink to Anita then to Georgina. "Be back soon." Eddie returned to the bar.

"I'll leave you now," said Anita, "I've spotted someone I want to meet." She looked in the direction of a certain young man.

Georgina glanced and smiled. "When I spoke to him earlier, he admitted to being impotent."

"Impotent!" Anita smiled. "I will soon find out." She walked across the room.

Eddie returned. "Where's Anita gone?"

"To chat with the young man you feel won't make the silver screen."

"Believe me Georgina, I can tell." Eddie sipped his drink.

Georgina coughed. "It's stuffy in here, let's go outside again for fresh air."

"Now that it's dark, it will be colder outside."

"Better than in here."

Eddie and Georgina left the room of cigar and cigarette-smoking guests and went into the garden. A selection of young and older guests chatted and drank in the pleasant atmosphere.

Georgina looked up to the sky. "Such a clear night! A dark blue sky and all those stars which sparkle."

Eddie glanced upwards and then sideways. "Oh, trouble! Two other stars that spark in the dark."

One woman started to argue with another guest and their voices grew louder. Other guests stopped their conversations and looked on. Insults were directed at one woman then in turn, she told her accused to go for a proper makeover. The male host intervened and the contents of a full champagne glass were thrown in his face. The perpetrator stormed off into the lounge. Jack pulled out a white handkerchief from his top jacket pocket and wiped himself.

"Poor chap," said Georgina, "he didn't deserve that."

"I could see it comin', Georgina," said Eddie, "when those two meet, its fireworks!"

Jack walked over to Eddie and Georgina. "Sorry about that. Mary and Louise Brooks together mean trouble."

Eddie smiled. "What started the row this time?"

Jack put the handkerchief back into his top jacket pocket. "Mary accused Louise of being a porn queen and then Louise said Mary would be too old for porn movies."

Eddie laughed. "That would go down like a ton of bricks."

Jack smiled. "Then one insult led to another and you witnessed the end result."

Georgina smiled. "Does it happen often?"

Jack sighed. "Yes, honey, it does. On a previous occasion, Mary grabbed Louise's cigarette holder and broke it in half!"

Georgina laughed.

Jack smiled. "I'm just glad I didn't have to separate them." He looked towards the trees.

"What's up Jack?" said Eddie.

"I thought I spotted a flash."

One of the guests ran out of the villa, down the steps and into the garden towards the trees. A scuffle occurred and the guest returned with a camera. He approached Jack and gave him the item.

"Thanks, Roscoe." Jack took the camera and laid it on a step.

"I spotted someone from the front window going from tree to tree then came a flash. He's now lost a camera and gained a bloody nose." Roscoe took out a black comb from inside his brown jacket and swept back his fair-coloured hair. "He won't bother you again.""

"Thanks, pal," said Jack.

Roscoe straightened his fawn tie and walked back into the lounge.

Eddie whispered, "I didn't realise he could run!"

The host smiled. "I'm glad he can, saved me the bother."

Georgina giggled. "Hic!" She put her hand on her chest. "Sorry."

"Too much orange, Georgina?" said Eddie.

"I'm off to the bathroom again," said Georgina, "excuse me." She walked into the lounge.

Jack looked at Eddie. "Have you much invested in the stock market?"

"No, why?" Eddie sipped his whisky.

"I hear shares may soon start to plummet. A few of the film directors have sold whatever they had." Jack moved closer. "If you know anyone with shares, advise them to sell, and fast!"

Eddie finished his drink.

"A refill?"

"No, thanks, Jack, I've had enough. I'll wait for Georgina and then head home."

"Okay pal." The host took Eddie's empty glass and went into the lounge.

Eddie stood on the steps and viewed the garden. As all guests had gone inside, the vicinity remained peaceful. He observed one of the waitresses with a tray. She picked up empty glasses which had been left around the garden. The slim dark-haired teenager observed Eddie and walked over to him.

"A drink, sir?" She held a tray full of empty spirit and champagne glasses.

Eddie smiled. A waitress, just when you don't need one. "No, thanks, I'm about to leave."

She smiled.

"Has the evenin' been busy for you?"

The waitress laid her tray on a nearby table. "It sure has! Two of us had to do the work of three."

"Why?"

"Bett had to go home, she took ill."

"How unfortunate." Eddie looked at his gold wristwatch. "What time do you finish?"

"Mr Gilbert pays us till one."

Eddie smiled. "Not long left."

The waitress sighed. "Thank goodness."

"Do you have to work in the morning?"

The waitress shook her head. "Still at school – my final year."

"When you leave, what's your intentions?"

She smiled. "An actress or dancer in the movies."

"It's tough to break into movies."

"I have an special talent."

"What kind?"

The waitress composed herself then did a tap-dance routine that lasted for several minutes. She finished her act with a courtesy.

Eddie clapped. "You do have a chance."

"Mr Gilbert said he could arrange an audition." The waitress picked up her tray. "Must resume my duties." She smiled. "I have to impress him!"

Smart girl. "What's your name, young lady?"

"Eleanor, Eleanor Powell." The waitress walked with grace into the lounge.

Georgina passed her and approached Eddie. "Did I hear someone clap?"

"Ready?"

Georgina yawned and nodded.

"I've said our goodbyes to Jack. We can take a short cut round the garden."

Eddie and Georgina walked down the steps, onto the garden then around the rear of the villa. As they walked towards the front driveway, a young man and woman kissed. They stopped and the young man smiled at Georgina.

"Goodnight," said Georgina.

"Goodnight," said the young man.

"Night, Anita," said Eddie.

"Night, Eddie."

Eddie whispered, "still don't think he'll make it."

Georgina smiled. He may tonight.

Eddie awoke and looked at the bedside clock. He slipped out of bed, put on his white cotton dressing gown and went downstairs into the kitchen. He opened a cabinet, took out a glass and filled it with tap water. He opened the refrigerator door and took out an ice cube from a tray. Eddie put the cube into the glass of water then drank it. He refilled his glass with water and walked with caution up the stairs. Eddie entered the bedroom and laid his glass on the bedside cabinet. He went to the window and pulled back the cream curtains.

Georgina turned towards him. "Mmm, what time is it?"

"Three in the afternoon."

She raised her head and opened her eyes. "What!"

Eddie smiled. "Ten past ten." He handed Georgina the glass of water.

"Any headache tablets?" She took the glass and drank it. "Ugh! I can taste gin."

Eddie took the empty glass.

Georgina laid her head back onto the white and gold patterned pillow then turned her head towards Eddie. "I didn't notice your other neighbour at the party."

"Joan is on location at present. She and Bob Montgomery have been signed for a 'talkie' with Universal."

"Is that her first?"

Eddie nodded.

"That may be the way forward for actors and actresses."

"You bet."

Georgina smiled. "Mary Pickford would disagree."

Eddie laughed. "She would disagree today is Saturday!"

"Stan and Ollie are funny."

"The word goin' around is that they could be bigger with the advent of sound."

"They have a chemistry in their make-up."

Eddie smiled. "Appropriate for the movie business."

She laughed.

Eddie bent down then kissed Georgina on the cheek. "I'll get cleaned up." He took the empty glass into the bathroom.

Georgina sat up and cast her gaze around the bedroom. A few minutes later, she threw back the white sheets and went over to the window. She tried to open it without success therefore the stubborn window received a thump. As the window opened, an intake of fresh air made Georgina feel better. She stood and admired the well-maintained garden below.

Eddie came out of the bathroom. "You okay? I heard a loud noise."

Georgina turned round. "The window wouldn't open so I gave it a thump."

"Thought you had fallen out of bed." Eddie wiped shaving cream of his face with a towel.

"Finished?"

Eddie smiled. "It doesn't take me long."

Georgina walked up to Eddie and kissed him on the cheek.

"Georgina, there's something I need to tell you."

"Me too, but later." Georgina walked into the bathroom.

Chapter 6

The Crash

James departed for work with a heavy weight on his shoulders. Last Friday, Bob revealed the firm's cash flow dilemma was critical. This did not come as a shock to James given his recent analysis of the firm's financial affairs. The junior clerkess now worked on a part-time basis and further cost-cutting measures would follow. As James reached the station entrance, a group of men had congregated and pestered commuters for cash. They consisted of both young and old that had not only lost their income but also personal dignity. Affluent Upper East Side now became a target for beggars seeking a cash handout however James ignored them and entered the station. He purchased a ticket then walked down the stairway to his platform. Since the previous month of September, passenger numbers had dwindled. Familiar faces that caught the same commuter train no longer appeared at their regular platform space. This being the consequence of not only men but also women discarded by employers. Fortunate commuters who waited for the train still had a look of despair. Would they survive the next 'cull' and remain in employment until the end of October? No doubt this and other factors of a deep recession played on their minds. The train came through the long dark tunnel on time, which at least provided a good start to Monday. After the train stopped and doors opened, commuters boarded then went into various carriages. Most of them dashed for a seat then started to read a magazine or newspaper. A possible indication that nobody was receptive to a cordial chat with a fellow passenger. Shortly after the train departed, a young woman looked through her white bag and then at the carriage floor. A male passenger next to her asked if he could be of assistance.

"My purse has gone!" she cried.

The male passenger looked around her vicinity. "Nothin' here," he said.

"When I left home, the purse was in my bag," she said. Once more the young woman looked in her bag.

An older woman who sat opposite leaned forward. "Did anyone outside the station bump into you by any chance?"

"An unshaven man in a scruffy coat and cap." She put her hand against her mouth. "It must have been him!"

The older woman opened her handbag. "How much do you need?"

The young woman wiped a tear from her eye. "It's my mother's birthday tomorrow." She sniffed. "I planned to buy her a present today."

The woman handed her a five-dollar note. "I also planned to buy a birthday gift today – for my five-year old grandson. His birthday is not till Wednesday therefore I can buy his present later."

The young woman took the note and put it in her bag. "Thanks."

Before the next stop, a conductor came into the carriage to check tickets. The young woman stood up and walked to the far end exit door. The conductor looked her way.

"Excuse me!" he cried. The conductor walked towards the young woman.

As the train stopped and carriage doors opened, the young woman jumped off. She edged past passengers who tried to board the train then ran up the stairway. The conductor stood at the open carriage doorway and shook his head. The door closed and he returned to check passengers' tickets. The man who had sat next to the young woman looked at the conductor.

"She had her purse stolen."

The conductor clipped the man's ticket. "That person is a known con-artist on the rail network. She tells a sad story to obtain cash from passengers. A favourite is her father's fiftieth birthday and the money she had to buy a present has been stolen."

"This time it was the mother!" said the charitable woman.

The conductor shook his head. "I'm sorry, ma'am."

She sighed. "Me also."

The carriage had a quiet despondent atmosphere with no passenger in need of a conversation. Even the actions of a con-artist did not encourage discussion! James read his New York Times with unease. The forecast for financial week commencing Monday 28th October foretold of drama plus trauma within the stock market. Last Thursday, the value of shares had eleven per cent wiped from them. The press referred to that day as 'Black Thursday', a fateful day on Wall Street.

To reflect, James put the newspaper down on his lap and gazed out the carriage window.

"Excuse me, could that be your pen?" said a lady. She pointed to the floor.

James looked down at the stylish black fountain pen. "No."

The lady picked up the pen and put it into her handbag. "At least that's one gain today."

James smiled. Given the economic prediction, a gain in share price may not occur for some time. After the weekend break, how will the financial markets fare today?

As the next stop was Wall Street station, James put the newspaper into his briefcase. When the train pulled into the station, it came to an abrupt halt. Passengers, who stood at the door, were thrown off balance. After the train came to a halt, carriage doors opened and people transferred onto the platform. They observed a crowd which had gathered at the front of the train. A railway employee arrived on the scene and the train driver vacated his compartment. He ushered commuters back and was soon joined by the conductor.

"The guy jumped in front of the train!" said a male onlooker.

"Suicide," said a woman.

An older woman gasped.

Another man nodded and then stared at the body sprawled over the track. "Was hit straight on, look at the amount of blood."

"Ugh!" The older woman vomited on the rail track.

James vacated the scene and reached the station exit. When he bent down to view a pen on the carriage floor, observed his black shoes required a polish. He spotted a shoeshine boy on the opposite street corner, crossed over then went up to the juvenile.

He tipped his brown cap. "Have a seat sir."

James sat on the dark wooden chair and laid his briefcase next to it.

The boy applied polish to James's shoes. "Do you play the market, sir?"

"Not in today's climate."

The boy stared upwards. "A storm's a comin' sir."

"You may be correct."

He used a second brush and produced a shine on both shoes. He stepped back and nodded at James.

"Finished?"

"That's me, sir." The boy smiled. "Ten cents please."

James stood up, went into his coat pocket and pulled out a bundle of coins. He picked out two and put the remainder into his pocket.

"Here's twenty."

The boy took the two coins and tipped his cap. "Have a good one, sir."

James picked up his briefcase and walked on. Let's hope so.

He continued along Wall Street and passed many individuals who wore anxious expressions as well as overcoats to combat the late October winds. James entered his place of employment – for how much longer? With the elevator being out of order, he walked up several flights of stairs then along the corridor to his office. Once there, James noticed the small wastepaper basket had not been emptied and the room had not been dusted. A tired and bedraggled Bob entered the office.

"Hi, Bob." He has not shaved this morning.

"Jim, I had a hell of a night."

James put his hat and coat on the stand. "What's up?"

Bob rubbed his stomach. "I hope it's not an ulcer. I'm off to visit my doctor on the chance he can see me."

"You don't have an appointment?"

Bob shook his head. "When I called earlier, the receptionist admitted that appointments could not be arranged until Thursday."

"Did she reveal why?"

"Medical staff are booked – no doubt to deal with people who have depressive symptoms. However, I need an appointment now."

"If you need attention, they won't turn you away." James stared at the wastepaper basket.

"Had to dispose of the cleaner. See you later."

Bob left and went back to his office. He put on his grey hat and coat then walked towards the stairway.

James sat down and looked around the room. For all a cleaner would cost! He sat back on his chair. After seventeen years in America, could it be my business career is about to end? James booted the wastepaper basket and the contents emptied onto the floor.

"Morning, Jim."

James looked up and then at his wristwatch. "It's not eleven o'clock yet." He retrieved the wastepaper basket and put the scattered bits of paper into it.

"I came in an hour before my start time to tidy the offices."

How admirable. She may lose her job yet prepared to do additional duties. James walked to his filing cabinet and wiped his finger across the top. "Could you start in here?"

"Give me five minutes." Lucy went into her bag and brought out a rolled-up yellow item of clothing.

"An overall?"

Lucy nodded.

"Bob has gone to visit his doctor. I don't expect him back today therefore I'll go into his office."

"Then I'll start with your office."

As Lucy went into a toilet to change, James picked up his files then moved into Bob's office. He laid the files on Bob's desk then sat on the vacant black leather chair. He looked out of the window and observed passers-by in the street below. The telephone rang therefore James picked up the handset and placed the receiver against his ear.

"Payne?" said a male voice.

"No this is Jim, an associate in the firm."

"When will Payne be back?"

"I'm not sure. He is off work. Can I help?"

"What's his home number?"

"We don't give out home telephone numbers."

"This is urgent!"

James sat back on the chair. "Give me your name and if he contacts the office then I'll pass on the message."

"Tell him to call Joe Mancini and quick!" The caller hung up.

Not the polite type. James replaced the handset into its cradle.

Lucy knocked on the door. "Your office now looks habitable."

"You're quick!" James vacated Bob's chair and picked up his files from the desk.

Lucy laid a grey duster on Bob's desk, took out a handkerchief from her overall pocket and sneezed.

"Dusty?"

"A bit." She blew her nose.

"I'll let you carry on." James left the office and returned to his own.

A short time later, his telephone rang. James put down a client's file, picked up the handset and placed the receiver to his ear.

"Jim?"

"Yes?"

"Jim?"

James put his mouth close to the transmitter. "Yes, Bob."

"I have to visit hospital for further examination. I won't be back today."

"A Joe Mancini called, he wanted a word with you."

"If he calls back, tell him I've gone to Michigan on business."

"It sounded urgent."

"Stall him."

"He doesn't appear the type who takes to being stalled."

"I'll contact him in due course."

"Okay."

"Jim."

"Yes?"

"I'm in a bar and the radio is on. Since this morning, shares have dropped another five per cent."

"How worse can the economy get!"

"Have to go, I'll be in touch."

"Bye." James replaced the handset into the cradle. He glanced at his wristwatch, stood up and walked to Lucy's office."

"I've started my other duties." She sat at a typewriter.

"I'll buy lunch, you deserve a treat."

"Five minutes? Have this letter to finish."

"Whenever you're ready."

James and Lucy left the building and walked along busy Wall Street. Men in pin-stripe suits moved with energetic strides towards the Stock Exchange. One such person bumped into a woman and did not bother to stop or apologise.

"Watch where you're going!" the woman shouted.

The two colleagues continued for another two blocks and before they reached the restaurant, a beggar approached them. When James gave him a dime, the beggar raised his grey cap and bowed. When James and Lucy entered the establishment, a waitress came forward.

"A table for two," said James.

The waitress smiled. "Take your pick, you are only our second customer."

James nodded. "By the window?"

"Sure." The waitress led her two customers to the table with four chairs.

Since no coat stand existed, Lucy took off her beige coat and hat, laid them on a spare chair then sat down. James took off his grey hat and coat and placed them on the other spare chair then sat down.

"What would you like to drink?" said the waitress.

"Orange juice, please," said Lucy.

"A soda water for me, please," said James.

"Back soon." She walked towards the counter.

"Six months ago you would have to wait for a table." James glanced round the empty restaurant. "It's dead!"

"Maybe that's why the waitress wears a black blouse and skirt."

James smiled.

Lucy patted her short brown hair. "I overheard a conversation this morning on the train that homeless people have set up a refuge in Central Park."

James sat back on his chair.

"They have built small shacks."

"If the economic situation becomes worse, Central Park will inherit more residents."

"And the need for soup kitchens." Lucy looked towards the counter. "Here comes our drinks."

The waitress laid both drinks on the white tablecloth. "Ready to order?"

"A few minutes?" said James.

"Sure." The waitress returned to the counter and turned on a radio.

James smiled. "Drinks were brought on a silver tray, now it's by hand. The owner must have sold the tray."

"Plus the coat stand."

James laughed and read the menu.

Lucy read her menu, lifted her drink then sipped it.

The waitress returned and held her pad and pencil.

"Beef casserole please," said Lucy. She laid her glass on the table.

"Same for me please," said James.

The waitress wrote down the order, lifted the two menus and departed.

James looked towards the counter. "What news on the market? When she returns, I must ask."

"I'd rather listen to music at lunchtime."

James smiled. "That's because you are sixteen. People my age listen to business and current affairs – especially today." James lifted his glass and took a sip.

Lucy smiled.

"What would you like to do in the future?" James took another sip of his drink.

"Have my own company."

James raised his eyebrows. "What type of business?" He laid his glass on the table.

"One which caters for household parties."

"There appears many of them – nobody can afford to socialise in the city."

"Finger foods such as shrimp patties and oyster cocktails served with alcohol. I believe an opportunity may exist for a particular type of tray in which to serve them. One that is distinctive and would encourage people to purchase for their own home."

Smart young lady. However, with a surname of Wise, it's not a surprise.

"Until this recession ends, I'll have to wait."

That could be a long time.

"Jim, what would a recession be called if it deepens?"

"One newspaper article mentioned the term 'depression'."

"How would we escape it?"

"The Government could implement projects such as infrastructures around America funded by public money."

"Infrastructure?"

"Roads, buildings and schools. People would be employed to complete them and in turn spend their wages on goods to regenerate the economy. Also private investment could help to regenerate the economy. A project will start in January to build New York's tallest building."

"What type of building?" Lucy lifted her glass and drank the contents.

"I believe a hotel, in Midtown."

Lucy laid her glass on the table. "Who can afford to stay there?"

"There will be some people, not everyone is broke."

"That's good news, they can purchase my future product."

The waitress appeared. "Sorry for the delay, another drink?"

James looked at Lucy.

She nodded.

"Same again please."

The waitress walked back to the counter.

"Delay?" said Lucy, "it's not as if the restaurant is busy."

James smiled. "Has Bob mentioned a Joe Mancini to you?"

Lucy shook her head. "No." She looked upwards. "Wait a minute! About a week ago, I filed documents in Bob's office and his telephone rang. He answered it and mentioned someone called Joe. Bob signalled for me to leave the room and when I left, he closed the door. Who is he?"

"I'm not sure."

"Bob did appear tense."

Interesting.

Lucy looked towards the counter. "Food at last."

The waitress brought over a white tray which contained two meals and laid it on the table. She removed the plates from the tray then started to walk away.

James looked at her. "And another fork please?"

"Oh sorry, be right back."

The waitress walked back to the counter with her empty tray and put it on a shelf. She picked up a fork from a container and returned to the table.

"Apologies." She gave the silver fork to James.

"Thanks." He took it. "What news on the radio?"

Lucy reached for her silver cutlery.

"The market's down nine per cent." The waitress departed.

"This will be a long stressful day, Lucy."

"It won't affect my appetite."

James smiled.

At five o'clock, James left his office building and walked to the subway. People on the sidewalk had expressions of disbelief and disappointment. James reached the station, made his way down the stairway and joined other northbound commuters on the platform. A man read an evening edition of the New York Herald Tribune. A well-groomed lady approached him and he turned to face her.

"It's a special edition on the crisis." He pointed to the front-page headline printed in large bold letters. "Black Monday".

She moved closer. "What's the latest?"

"Down twelve per cent."

"I heard fourteen," said another man.

A well-dressed commuter came down the stairway with a cigarette in his mouth. He edged his way towards the front of the busy platform then lit the cigarette. The same lady turned to face the late arrival.

"Are you a stockbroker by any chance?"

The man nodded then puffed on his cigarette.

"What's the latest?"

"Down eleven."

James leaned forward. "Down eleven!"

"The Stock Exchange resembles a madhouse! Brokers scream and shout at each other – and it's not finished yet."

"What do you mean?" said the lady.

"The word goin' around is tomorrow could be as bad!" He puffed on his cigarette.

Gasps then chatter ensued around the immediate platform vicinity. The rumble of a train which approached, interrupted intense discussions. The train stopped, carriage doors sprung open and people boarded. Once inside, James observed and overheard regular passengers speak to each other about the financial predicament. Individuals, who kept to themselves on the homeward journey, now conversed with fellow passengers. As everyone would be affected, the crisis had created a bond between commuters. They discovered solace in each other's financial woes. The conductor entered the carriage and checked tickets. Halfway along the carriage, he approached a short man in his twenties. He wore no hat or coat and his dark jacket had a tear at the side pocket.

"Ticket, please?" said the conductor.

"I don't have one."

"Why don't you have a ticket?" The conductor leaned forward.

"A thief robbed me." The man rubbed his red cheek.

"Okay, get that cheek seen to." The conductor walked on.

As the train approached his station, the man stood up. He walked to the exit door and waited. He hid his face from public view due to the embarrassment of today's incident. The train stopped and carriage double-doors opened. The man jumped onto the platform then rushed up the stairway out of sight. After people boarded, the train moved off and James picked up a newspaper that had been left by a fellow passenger. As James read the front page, an elderly lady who sat next to him leaned over.

"If this is 'Black Monday', what will tomorrow be called?"

James turned to her. "I hope it's not 'Blacker Tuesday'!"

The lady smiled. "With this current situation, you have to keep a sense of humour."

"When you lose your job and livelihood," said a well-dressed man who sat opposite, "it's not easy, ma'am."

The lady looked at the gentleman in a camel coat and hat. "Are you out of work?"

The gentleman stared at her.

"You don't look it."

"My firm sacked me today. I now have to go home and explain to my wife why no money will come into our household. I'm forty-four years old, how am I going to find another job? Bills still have to be paid." The gentleman looked downwards and shook his head.

James looked at the man. As he is younger than I am, what chance would I have?

The train rolled through Manhattan and arrived at James's stop. He picked up his briefcase, alighted from the carriage and walked up the stairway. Whilst he made his way home, an ambulance sped past. On the sidewalk a man in a long black coat and hat watched. He lifted his hat to reveal silver grey hair and then turned to James.

"I hope it's not another attempted suicide. Lennox Hill and other hospitals could be busy over the next few days."

"Let us hope not," said James.

"Terrible times." The man put his hat back on his head.

James continued his journey and could perceive demoralisation in the air. The street outside his home had an unusual eerie silence. He approached the main entrance, opened the door with his pass key and gently closed it. James walked slowly up the stairs and along the landing. He started to feel anxious and began to sweat. James unbuttoned his coat then took out the apartment key from his pocket. Suddenly, a pain gripped his chest. He dropped his briefcase and it clattered to the ground. A moment later, the door opened and Elizabeth rushed towards her husband.

"James! What's wrong?" Elizabeth held his arm.

He steadied himself. "I'm okay." James put the key back into his coat pocket.

Elizabeth picked up the briefcase, led James inside and closed the door.

He took a deep breath then stood up straight. "I'm fine, I'm okay."

Elizabeth laid his briefcase next to the coat stand.

James removed his hat and coat.

Elizabeth took both items and hung them on the coat stand. "You should sit down." She followed him into the living room.

James sat down and sighed. He unbuttoned his suit jacket and looked towards the elevated radio on a sideboard. "What programme is that?"

"Never mind the radio, what happened?" Elizabeth sat next to James.

"It must have been an anxiety attack of some sort, I'm okay."

"You almost collapsed!"

James looked at Elizabeth.

"It's a warning."

James hugged Elizabeth and smiled. "As a precaution, I'll make an appointment to visit a doctor."

"Promise?"

James nodded then looked at the radio.

"It's an extended news bulletin on the crisis."

"What's the latest?"

"The market has ended for the day thirteen per cent down. My ears have been glued to the radio all afternoon."

"Stockbrokers must feel worse than me."

Elizabeth rose, walked over to the radio then turned it off.

James looked at her.

She sat down next to James. "How do you feel now?"

James held her hand. "This cold weather does not help." He smiled. "Or the beef casserole I had for lunch."

Elizabeth smiled.

"I'll contact a doctor's surgery tomorrow morning."

"I received another letter from Georgina."

"And?"

"She loves Los Angeles and plans to stay for the foreseeable future."

"Good for her, the quality of life will be better than here."

"I'll tell you about her stories over dinner."

James raised his grey eyebrows. "I can't wait. What's for dinner?"

Elizabeth smiled. "Beef casserole."

James sat at his desk on Tuesday morning and read the New York Times. It predicted further falls in the value of stocks and shares. Coverage of the financial crisis dominated the newspaper. An article that was highlighted involved a former U.S. Interior Secretary by the name of Albert B Fall. He received a conviction for bribery and sent to prison. James turned to the next page and came across International Affairs. The Government of Aristide Briand in France had fallen. Given what happened in America, a new French Government could experience a financial backlash in their country. The French may need formidable and shrewd ministers to cope with austere monetary measures.

"Good morning, Jim," said Lucy.

James looked up. "After yesterday, it's not such a good one."

Lucy smiled. "The situation can only improve." She removed her cream hat and shook her brown hair.

That's optimistic. "Let us hope so."

"How is Bob?"

"He hasn't contacted me, I'll give him a call at lunchtime."

Lucy held up a letter. "Maybe a large cheque has arrived from a client."

James smiled. "That would be a welcome change."

"See you later." Lucy walked towards her office.

James put the newspaper aside then picked up a client's file. He opened it and checked the amount due for professional fees.

$1285.00, they have had two reminders. I'll give them a call.

James reached for his telephone, lifted the handset and dialled the number. He sat back and put the receiver hard against his ear. As there was no dial tone, he put the handset into the cradle.

Lucy knocked on the door.

James looked her way.

She held a document in her hand. "Jim, this statement has come from our bank – the previous one is missing. I've looked but can't find it."

James stood up then approached Lucy.

She handed the statement to him. "A large discrepancy exists between this statement and the previous one."

"The debt amount is lower than I would have anticipated."

"A cheque for a substantial amount must have been paid into our account. It should be on the missing statement."

"I have no recollection of a large cheque from a client and Bob did not mention such an amount being received."

"The one place I have not checked is Bob's desk but it's locked."

James raised his eyebrows. "I have a spare key." He went to his desk, opened the top drawer and took out a small silver key.

Lucy accompanied James to Bob's office. James inserted the key into Bob's desk drawer and turned it anti-clockwise. He opened the drawer and it contained several documents. James removed them and looked at each one. He glanced at Lucy, held up a solitary bank statement then handed it to her.

"Is that it?" said James.

"Yes, this is the missing statement." Lucy pointed. "Look at that amount!" She handed the statement to James.

He took the statement and read it. "Just the one credit transaction. No single client owes the firm that amount. I'll contact Bob to clarify the situation."

James returned to his office and telephoned his associate's private number. The telephone continued to ring therefore James hung up. A short time later, he tried again but still no answer.

Lucy walked into James's office. "Any luck, Jim?"

James shook his head.

"I called the bank about the transaction."

"And?"

"Bob paid in the money."

"Bob!"

Lucy nodded.

"I'll take a trip up to Midtown and pay Bob a visit. It's not like him to remain anonymous and he can enlighten me about the money paid into our bank."

"Where in Midtown does he stay?"

"32nd street. There is a subway station on 33rd street. It shouldn't take long from here."

"I believe they now have a 'soup kitchen' near Times Square."

James smiled. "If I am hungry, I'll try it out."

Lucy laughed. "See you later." She walked back to her office.

James went to the coat stand, lifted off his grey hat and coat then put them on. He walked along the corridor then made his way down the stairs. As he left the building and entered Wall Street, an uneasy atmosphere existed. Most people on the sidewalk had a cigarette in their mouth and automobile horns were frequently heard. A probable consequence of public anxiety and frustration in the midst of misery. James arrived at Wall Street station and approached the ticket office.

A dark blue uniformed employee stood behind the open wooden shutter. "Yes, sir?"

"A return ticket to 33rd Street please."

"One dollar twenty, sir."

James handed him two dollar notes.

The employee took the money then gave James his ticket and change.

"Thanks."

"Thank you, sir."

James picked up his ticket and change then put both in his coat pocket. He walked down the stairway and waited on the northbound platform. He noticed a well-dressed woman with a newspaper who turned the pages in a frantic manner. James moved closer to the platform's edge. A man followed and stopped beside him.

"Don't do it, Mac," said the man.

James turned to face the grey-bearded stocky man. "I heard a noise in the tunnel and wanted to see if the train may be about to arrive."

The man smiled. "Yesterday a guy committed suicide in this very spot."

James nodded. "I'm okay." He moved closer to a woman reading her newspaper. "What's the latest?"

She sighed. "Still on the slide."

A few minutes later, the woman put her newspaper into a shopping bag and laid it on the ground. As she adjusted her black cloche hat, a man grabbed the bag. He made for the stairway but was chased then caught by another man. The thief took a swipe at the man but missed. The man dodged a second punch then threw a right hook and knocked the thief out cold.

The woman walked up to the chivalrous individual and he handed over her bag.

"Thanks," she said.

"No problem, lady."

"You know how to avoid punches and dish one out!"

The man smiled.

"What's your name?"

"Benny Leonard."

"The former world lightweight champion?"

He nodded. "Won the title here in Manhattan twelve years ago."

"My husband is a boxing fan, wait till he hears about this!"

The thief regained consciousness and the former boxing champion stared at him lying dazed and horizontal. He turned to the woman and smiled.

"His jaw will be sore for some time."

"Got what he deserved," she said, "his groans tell it all."

As the train approached, a rumble echoed inside the tunnel. When the train arrived and came to a halt, passengers converged upon it. The carriage doors opened then passengers boarded. James spotted a vacant window seat and sat down. The train departed Wall Street station amidst passenger conversations on the financial situation. One of them confirmed what Lucy had revealed – a charitable food unit. However, not in the vicinity of Times Square but at Central Park. Another conversation related to the world's tallest structure earmarked for Midtown. The discussion being that it would give work to the needy and help New York's economy. A stylish lady who sat next to James browsed through a brochure on refrigerators and toasters. She laid it down on her lap then read a magazine on new cars. After studying the Essex and Plymouth Sedans, she turned a page to reveal the exclusive Sedan Cadillac. This lady would not come under the category of a 'needy' New Yorker. Two men speculated on how the plummet of shares could affect other countries. One suggested reverberations for Europe and beyond.

"It won't just be America who suffers," said one of the men.

His acquaintance nodded. "It's grim for everyone, even thieves have less to steal!"

The other man laughed. "We could try California."

A woman passenger looked at both men.

"Just kiddin', ma'am," said both men.

The train pulled into a station and the lady next to James rose from her seat then went to the exit doors. The train stopped, doors opened and she stepped onto the platform. Since she had left her automobile magazine, James picked it up. He browsed through it with interest.

Nice automobiles but will anyone buy them in this current economic downturn? James laid the magazine on the empty seat next to him.

A teenager on the opposite seat leaned forward. "Mind if I take that?"

"No." James handed the magazine to him.

He took it. "Thanks, bud."

A short time later, the train slowed down inside a tunnel then stopped. Whilst it lay stationary, curious passengers looked out of their respective windows but viewed only darkness. One elderly woman appeared agitated. She shuffled her feet, stood up and sat down then became breathless. A man who sat nearby stood up and sat next to her

"I am a doctor." He removed his hat and put it on his lap. "Take slow deep breaths."

The lady breathed in and out. She repeated this process a further nine times. "Thank you, I feel better." She sighed.

The teenager who sat opposite James put down the magazine and rose from his seat. He stood in the carriage passageway near the woman who had a panic attack. Intrigued passengers stared at him. He cleared his throat then went into a rendition of 'California Here I Come'. When he finished, the passengers applauded. He then turned towards the elderly woman and sang 'It Had To Be You' with sincerity. As he finished, this time the passengers cheered and clapped.

An African-American man shouted, "any Alger Alexander?"

The teenager shook his head.

"How about Sam Collins?"

He shook his head.

"Leroy Carr?"

The teenager smiled. "How about Al Jolson!"

The passengers cheered then he sang 'Sonny Boy' and 'Bye Bye Blackbird'. When he stopped, they gave him loud applause and whistles. A conductor entered the carriage and looked at the teenager.

"Did I hear someone sing?" The conductor smiled. "What's your name son?"

The teenager removed his white cap and straightened his spectacles. "Phil Silver, sir."

"What an appropriate name." The conductor gave him two dimes.

The teenager took them, put both coins in his pocket and sat down.

"Sorry for the delay, folks." The conductor walked through the carriage.

The train started to move and passengers cheered. Not just for the resumption of their journey but also the welcome impromptu in-house entertainment.

The elderly woman leaned towards the teenager. "Have you ever been on the stage?"

He smiled. "Sort of, ma'am, I once worked in a cinema. When the film reel was stuck, I would walk onto the stage and sing till it was fixed." He picked up the automobile magazine, adjusted his spectacles and started to read.

When the train arrived at 33rd Street station, James left his seat and went to the exit doors. As they sprung open, he stepped off then walked up the stairway. James reached the exit and spotted a newspaper-seller.

"Get the latest news on the 'Crash', read all about it!" he shouted.

"Newspaper, please," said James.

The boy handed James a newspaper.

James gave him five cents.

"Thanks, sir."

185

James walked towards 32nd Street then stopped to have a quick read of his newspaper. The front-page headline of 'Wall Street Crash' appeared in large thick letters. James read the page then continued towards Bob's apartment. Upon his arrival, he walked up eight steps to the main entrance door and looked at names against each apartment bell.

"Mr Payne, good to see ya."

James turned round.

"I've been here for some time," said a tall well-built man, "what kept ya?" He chewed gum.

"I'm not Mr Payne."

"Oh yes you are. You fit his description and my associate followed you here."

He looked at his wristwatch. "Left your office over an hour ago."

James looked at the other man. He's shorter but also built like the side of a house. "My name is James Carsell-Brown, a colleague of Mr Payne."

The tall man moved forward and faced James.

"You have the wrong person."

The other man also moved closer to James.

The tall man smiled. "My associate has a gun pointed at you, don't mess with us."

"I don't intend to. What is this about?" James looked at the two men wearing dark overcoats and hats.

"We want the money you borrowed plus interest."

The money paid into our account.

"The person who loaned you the money wants it repaid, and now!" said the short man.

"Let me speak to this person and the matter can be resolved." James clenched his hands.

"The talkin' is over Payne, you've stalled before, no more chances."

A click came from the pocket of the other man's coat pocket. James stared at both men.

"We can sort out the confusion. If Mr Payne is in his apartment then he will confirm who I am."

"Nice try," said the tall man, "we rang the bell earlier."

James glanced behind the two men.

They both turned round and spotted three police officers. The two men turned to face James and two shots were fired at him. The thugs ran off and James slumped to the ground. Whilst one officer knelt down beside James, the other two gave chase. A male passer-by appeared and the officer looked up.

"Please, call an ambulance."

The passer-by ran along the sidewalk and into a shop.

"Ahh! My stomach aches."

"Keep still, sir." The police officer removed his black coat and laid it under James's head.

The passer-by returned. "An ambulance is on its way."

A crowd gathered and the officer looked around the vicinity. A lady came forward and stood beside the officer.

"I am a nurse, can I be of any assistance?" She glanced towards James.

"He's badly hurt – two bullets in the stomach."

"I will tend to him."

The officer looked at the enlarged crowd. "I'll give you some room." He stood up and ushered the crowd away from James.

The lady knelt down, took James's hand and held it.

James blinked then gazed at her.

She smiled.

"Why could you not prevent this?" James coughed then smiled. "You left it a bit late."

The lady caressed his hand. It is your time.

"Did you alert the police?"

"No, it must have been someone else."

"Then why are you here?"

"To ensure you're not alone."

"Why now?" James coughed.

Lori took a handkerchief from her handbag and wiped James's mouth.

"Elizabeth, what about Elizabeth?" James looked at Lori.

"She will be fine."

"Promise?"

Lori smiled. "I promise."

James blinked. "I ache all over."

Lori wiped a tear from her eye then looked behind her. "Is that the ambulance?"

"Yes."

"What has my life been worth?" James looked at Lori.

"Today you will make a contribution to the future welfare of New York citizens. Because of what has happened, a person in this crowd will be influenced to reduce street crime."

James smiled at Lori.

She wiped his mouth.

"Promise me again Elizabeth will be fine."

"I promise." Lori kissed James on the cheek.

He closed his eyes and let go of her hand.

Two men with a stretcher came out of the ambulance. One had a black bag and he attended to James. He examined him and looked at his colleague.

"Quick! The stretcher."

The two men lifted James onto the stretcher and took him into the ambulance. As it drove away the crowd dispersed. The solitary police officer looked around the immediate vicinity. Another police officer arrived on the scene and approached his colleague.

"What's up Len, you look puzzled?"

"The broad with an Irish accent, the nurse."

"What about her?"

"Where did she go?" The officer stared at the blood on the sidewalk. "She was just here!" He tipped up his cap.

On Wednesday morning following Black Tuesday, Detective McAndrew entered the building where James Carsell-Brown had worked. He walked up several flights of stairs then along the corridor. He stopped at the office that James had occupied then heard the sound of a typewriter from another office. Detective McAndrew approached it and knocked on the door.

Lucy looked up. "You startled me!"

"Sorry miss, I'm Detective McAndrew." He showed Lucy an ID. "Is Mr Payne around?"

"No, yesterday Mr Carsell-Brown tried to contact him by telephone but without success. He then left here to visit Mr Payne's apartment but did not return." Lucy glanced at her wristwatch. "Mr Carsell-Brown is late but should arrive soon and will give you an update on Mr Payne."

"I have bad news."

Lucy stared at Detective McAndrew.

"Mr Carsell-Brown was shot yesterday in 33rd Street."

"Shot!"

"He passed away not long after."

Lucy put a hand to her mouth. "Oh no!"

"I'm sorry to have to tell you, however I want to locate Mr Payne."

Lucy wiped her eyes with a handkerchief.

"You okay, miss?"

Lucy nodded then opened her desk drawer and took out a sheet of paper. "This is his address and telephone number." She handed it to Detective McAndrew.

He took the sheet of paper and read it then looked at Lucy. "Miss, you be okay?"

Lucy nodded.

Detective McAndrew put the sheet of paper into his coat pocket.

"Detective?"

"Yeah?"

Lucy handed a bank statement to Detective McAndrew. "This is why Jim wanted to speak with Mr Payne."

Detective McAndrew took the bank statement.

"The amount which has been highlighted with a pencil."

Detective McAndrew read the statement.

"Mr Payne paid that amount into the bank. Jim believed Mr Payne received the money from a Joe Mancini."

Detective McAndrew stared at Lucy. "That means trouble. Does Mr Payne resemble Mr Carsell-Brown?"

"When they wear a hat and coat." Lucy wiped her eyes.

"What about build?"

"About the same."

"Can I keep this statement?"

"The firm needs it for record purposes. Should you have to contact our bank, here is a note of the details." Lucy handed a piece of written paper to Detective McAndrew.

He took the piece of paper and put it into his coat pocket."

"Here's the bank statement." He gave it to Lucy.

She took the statement and replaced it into her desk drawer.

Detective McAndrew adjusted his hat. "Will you be okay here on your own?"

Lucy nodded. "I can deal with the administration side of the business. Because of the economic situation, client business has stopped. They can't pay fees owed to us."

"Yeah, desperate times. That's when I'm at my busiest."

Lucy smiled, sniffed and dabbed her eyes. "What about Mr Carsell-Brown's wife?"

"She was informed of his death last night."

Lucy dabbed her eyes.

"Bye, miss."

"Bye."

Detective McAndrew departed Lucy's office, walked along the corridor and down the stairs. As he left the building, a young man ran towards him with a red handbag under his arm.

"Stop thief!" shouted a woman.

When the thief was about to run past him, Detective McAndrew put out a leg. The thief tripped and crashed to the ground. As the woman caught up, Detective McAndrew lifted her handbag off the ground and gave it to her.

"Thanks," she said."

"Pleasure, ma'am." Detective McAndrew looked downwards at the injured dejected thief. "You're done."

Detective McAndrew sat in his office and read the New York Times. He lit a cigarette and loosened his tie. A short while later came a knock on his door.

"Yeah?" he said.

A police officer entered the room. "Detective, we've discovered Joe Mancini's whereabouts."

Detective McAndrew put down his newspaper. "Where?"

"He boarded a train from Grand Central to Chicago yesterday morning."

"Any luck on who killed the English guy?"

"Not yet, sir. Was he not from Scotland?"

Detective McAndrew nodded. "Yeah, that's right. Did you trace the Irish broad?"

"Not yet. When the ambulance arrived, she disappeared."

"Whilst she tended to Mr Carsell-Brown, he may have revealed who shot him."

"Possibly."

"Any news on Bob Payne?

"A neighbour spotted him three days ago with a suitcase but we've no leads. He's the brother of Will Payne."

"The investor?"

"That's the one."

"Keep me posted. A Republican Senator was at the murder scene and has spoken to our Chief of Police. The Senator isn't pleased a homicide took place on a respectable New York street at mid-day."

"Will do, sir."

"What's the latest on the Park?"

"More shacks have sprung up."

"How many now?"

"Fourteen, three appeared last weekend. People have a nickname for the site."

"A nickname?"

The officer smiled. "They call it 'Hooverville', sir."

Detective McAndrew stubbed out his cigarette. "At least someone has a sense of humour."

The officer smiled.

"What of the other districts?"

"The lower east and west sides report no significant increase in crime." The officer laughed. "Maybe the 'crash' has hindered them."

Detective McAndrew sat back on his brown leather chair. "Give them time. I feel a backlash aimed at our Stock Exchange could be on the cards with stockbrokers being targeted. The public has lost a lot of cash and will face hardship or even ruin. Some individuals and families won't be able to adapt and may vent their anger."

"Then we could be in for a busy time, sir."

"Let's hope not."

The officer walked towards the door.

"Is Sergeant Johnston around?"

"Yes, sir."

"Mention I want to see him."

"Will do, sir." The officer walked out and closed the door.

Detective McAndrew picked up his newspaper and started to read. Financial predicaments dominated the newspaper coverage and would do so for the foreseeable future. Then came three knocks on the door. Detective McAndrew again put down his newspaper and laid it on the desk. The door opened and Sergeant Johnston walked in.

"Bill, take a seat."

Sergeant Johnston sat opposite Detective McAndrew.

"What's the latest on the Dale Rhodes case?"

"We've interviewed the banker but don't have enough evidence to charge him."

"Mrs Rhodes has not yet returned to New York?"

Sergeant Johnston nodded. "We discovered her affair with the banker began over a year ago. When we first questioned the banker, he stated six months but later changed his story. Dale Rhodes had severe financial problems and lived outwith his means for some time."

"Then he wasn't killed for his money."

Sergeant Johnston smiled. "No, sir."

"Then perhaps to remove an obstacle?"

"Could be, sir, but no hard evidence as yet."

Detective McAndrew sat back on his chair. "You heard Rhodes brother-in-law was murdered?"

Sergeant Johnston nodded.

"I'm goin' to pay his widow a visit. I want the murderer caught."

"We're on it. It could have been a case of mistaken identity."

Detective McAndrew nodded.

Sergeant Johnston stood up, walked to the door and opened it then turned round. "Sir?"

"Yeah, Bill?"

"The banker, his bank has closed."

"More will no doubt follow."

Sergeant Johnston closed the door behind him.

Chapter 7

Alone

On a cold grey November morning, Detective McAndrew arrived at Elizabeth Carsell-Brown's apartment block in Upper East Side. Since the death of her husband, Elizabeth had suffered nine long days of depression. Before he pressed the apartment doorbell, Detective McAndrew glanced at his wristwatch. He had made it on time for the eleven o'clock appointment. The door opened and Detective McAndrew found himself confronted by a young woman. She smiled, breezed past him and down the steps. He entered the building, closed the door, and walked up the stairs then along the white walled landing. A lady with a pale complexion stood outside a door.

"Mrs Carsell-Brown?"

Elizabeth nodded. "Come in, Detective."

Detective McAndrew removed his dark fedora hat and entered the apartment hallway.

Elizabeth closed the door. "Please, go into the living room, it's straight ahead."

"Thanks, ma'am." Detective McAndrew walked into the room and looked around.

"Have a seat. Would you like a coffee?"

"No thanks, ma'am." Detective McAndrew sat down on the couch and laid his hat next to him.

Elizabeth sat down on a chair opposite Detective McAndrew. "You are punctual."

"I try my best, ma'am."

Elizabeth smiled.

"My condolences, ma'am. I met your husband several times – a genuine guy."

"Thank you, Detective. Many attended the funeral." Elizabeth clasped her hands. "How can I be of assistance?"

"Did your husband, sorry late husband, ever mention a Joe Mancini?"

"No, I don't recollect that name."

"Did he ever mention being intimidated by anyone?"

"He was held up one morning about seven months ago."

"That was connected to a previous client of his firm. He didn't discuss anythin' troublin' him?"

"He would discuss the firm – not many clients tended to settle their accounts."

"Nothin' else, ma'am?"

Elizabeth shook her head. "Sorry, Detective."

Detective McAndrew reached for his hat and stood up. "Okay, ma'am, I won't keep you. If you remember anythin' give me a call." He produced a card from his coat pocket and handed it to Elizabeth.

She took the card and read it. "I will."

"How are you shapin' up?"

"I am fine, Detective. It has been a shock and I miss James. He would want me to remain dignified and move on with my life."

"Do you have any plans?"

"I will return to Scotland. My sister who stayed in Manhattan has moved to Los Angeles. She suggested I join her." Elizabeth smiled. "An earthquake would not make her leave Los Angeles. After the funeral, she stayed for a few days then went back."

Detective McAndrew smiled. "I'm like that with New York, ma'am – in with the bricks."

"You love your job?"

"Yes, ma'am. Every day can be different, that's the way I like it."

Elizabeth smiled. "I'll show you out." She escorted Detective McAndrew to the door and opened it.

"Does your sister not feel isolated in Los Angeles?"

"She has met someone."

"What about your apartment, ma'am? If you leave it empty, squatters could move in."

"I have signed it over to our bank. When the apartment is sold, proceeds will go towards paying off the firm's debt."

"What about yourself?"

"For the time being, money from James's life insurance policy should be sufficient."

Detective McAndrew put on his hat. "By the way, ma'am."

"Yes?"

"A Senator found himself at the scene of the incident and was appalled. I have it on good authority he will introduce reforms to combat street crime and make our city safer. Your husband did not die in vain."

"That would please James." Elizabeth shook Detective McAndrew's hand. "Thank you."

"Bye, ma'am."

Elizabeth closed the door.

Detective McAndrew walked along the landing, down the stairs and opened the main door. He looked behind and closed it.

Elizabeth went into the living room, sat down on her chair and wept.

Two days later, Elizabeth caught the train for Downtown Manhattan. She had telephoned Mr Arbington and wanted to discuss her paintings. Elizabeth arrived at the art gallery on time for her twelve o'clock appointment. She adjusted her navy-coloured cloche hat and knocked on the door. A lady opened it and smiled.

"Come in, Mrs Carsell-Brown."

Elizabeth entered the premises.

"Mr Arbington will be with you in a few minutes."

The lady left Elizabeth and walked over to a display. She rearranged a number of large and small paintings. Elizabeth cast her gaze around the room.

Since my last visit, it does not appear any paintings have been sold.

Mr Arbington approached Elizabeth. "My condolences, Elizabeth."

"Thank you, Mr Arbington."

He led Elizabeth to a two-seater burgundy couch. "Have a seat."

Elizabeth sat down and laid her black handbag on the floor.

Mr Arbington sat next to her. "How can I help you?"

"I presume none of my other paintings have been sold?"

"I'm afraid that is the case, Elizabeth." Mr Arbington glanced at the lady assistant. "In fact since your last visit, no paintings have been sold." He sighed. "I don't envisage much business in the foreseeable future."

"I am returning to Scotland, Mr Arbington. If and when the paintings that remain do sell, could you forward the money?"

"Of course, my dear. Where shall I send it to?"

Elizabeth lifted her handbag off the floor, opened it and took out a folded piece of white paper. "Send the money to this address." She handed the piece of paper to Mr Arbington.

He took it. "I will do as you request."

Elizabeth closed her handbag and stood up. "Thank you for all you have done, Mr Arbington." She shook his hand.

"I will miss you, Elizabeth. You are a talented artist."

Elizabeth smiled.

Mr Arbington led her to the door.

Elizabeth looked at the lady assistant polishing a brass frame. "What became of the younger assistant?"

Mr Arbington smiled. "She's gone to Hollywood in search fame and fortune." He opened the door. "Bye, my dear."

Elizabeth walked out of the gallery and onto the sidewalk then looked at Mr Arbington.

He waved then closed the door.

"Spare a dime, lady?" A beggar confronted Elizabeth.

She opened her handbag and brought out a bunch of dollar notes. "Take these, I won't need them."

The beggar took them. "Thanks, lady!" He looked up to the grey sky and smiled.

Elizabeth observed the traffic on the street. As a yellow taxi came round a block, she stepped off the sidewalk. A person grabbed her arm.

Elizabeth turned round.

"Please move back onto the sidewalk."

Elizabeth stepped back.

When the yellow taxi passed her, it's driver pumped his horn. The driver of a van behind the taxi also pumped his horn.

Elizabeth shook her head then turned round to face the lady. "I must have been in a daze!"

"It could have been your final one."

"Thank you."

"Are you all right?" The lady held Elizabeth's arm.

Elizabeth nodded.

The lady looked across to the other side of the street. "Let's go into that place over there and have a coffee."

"I gave all my money to a beggar."

"My treat."

Elizabeth smiled.

"However, I insist we cross at the proper place." The lady smiled.

Both ladies walked to the end of the block and used the pedestrian crossing. Then they headed for the nearby restaurant and entered.

A waitress came forward. "Hi."

"We would like to order coffee," said the lady.

The waitress smiled. "Take your pick of the tables, you're our first today."

The lady pointed. "That one in the corner."

"I'll bring the cawfees over," said the waitress, "black or white?"

"Black for me," said Elizabeth.

"White for me," said the lady.

Both customers walked over to the corner table and sat down. They removed their hats and placed them plus handbags on the table.

"Are you from Ireland?" said Elizabeth.

The lady nodded then unbuttoned her cream coat, opened her handbag and took out a small handkerchief.

"You seem familiar." Elizabeth unbuttoned her navy blue coat.

"Whenever you cross a main street in New York, be cautious at all times."

"At present, I am not myself."

"Can I ask why?"

"I have just lost my husband." Elizabeth fidgeted with the top button of her coat.

"I'm sure he would want you to have a long and pleasant future."

Elizabeth stared. "What makes you say that?"

"You remain a person with time on her side."

"I'm forty-five."

"You do not look it."

"Today, I feel my age and more."

The lady smiled. "We all have off-days. Tomorrow is a new one therefore embrace it."

"After what happened, I will."

The waitress came over to the table with two cups of coffee. She laid them on the red tablecloth then her left hand knocked over the Irish lady's handbag and several items fell out.

"Oh!" she cried, "clumsy me."

"It's okay," said the Irish lady.

The waitress walked towards the counter.

She put the items back into her handbag.

Elizabeth reached down to the floor and picked up a small object. "I trust this also fell out of your handbag?" She examined the object. "This looks odd."

"I found it on a sidewalk."

Elizabeth held the object in her right hand. "It's similar to a pencil or a fountain pen." She touched its sphere-like point with her finger. "Ink!" Elizabeth took a train ticket out of her handbag and placed it flat on the tablecloth. She dragged the point across the ticket. "An implement that has ink stored inside it! This will render the fountain pen redundant." Elizabeth stared at her companion. "Where did you find this?"

"Not far from here."

Elizabeth handed over the writing instrument.

"Thanks." She put it into her handbag.

"That's a nice ring." Elizabeth looked closely at the lady's hand. Unusual.

"It belonged to my great-grandmother."

A two-crossover pearl diamond ring. "Victorian?"

"Yes." The lady looked at her wristwatch. "Please excuse me, I will be back soon." She stood up, lifted her handbag and walked toward the toilet.

Elizabeth lifted her cup and sipped her coffee.

Twenty minutes later, the waitress came back to the table and stared at a full cup of coffee which lay opposite Elizabeth.

"Cawfee okay, hon?"

"Yes. The lady I am with went to the toilet but has been gone for some time. She could be unwell."

"I'll check to make sure she's okay." The waitress looked at the full cup on the table. "It ain't the cawfee, she hasn't touched it."

The waitress departed then headed for the toilet. She opened the door, went inside then came out and approached Elizabeth.

Elizabeth looked up.

"It's empty!"

"She walked towards the toilet."

"She didn't pass me at the counter."

Elizabeth sat back on her chair. "Where could she have gone!"

The waitress shrugged her shoulders. "Search me, hon, there's been a lotta strange occurrences these past few months."

Elizabeth reached over the table and picked up a brown cloche hat. "At least I didn't imagine her."

The waitress lifted the full cold cup of coffee. "Would you like a fresh one?"

Elizabeth nodded.

The waitress departed.

Elizabeth closed both suitcases, put on her hat and coat then stared into the mirror. She lifted both suitcases, walked to the door and turned around for a final look at the apartment. Seventeen years in Manhattan had provided James and herself with many memories. Elizabeth opened the door, lifted her two suitcases and entered the landing. As she turned to close the door, a neighbour appeared.

"Recovered from last night, Beth?"

"I only had one drink, Molly."

"What time do you sail?"

"Thirty minutes past eleven." Elizabeth glanced at her wristwatch. "Just three and a bit hours left in New York."

"When do you arrive in England?"

Elizabeth smiled. "Scotland."

"Sorry Beth, I get them mixed up."

"I sail to Ireland then catch a connection to Scotland. The journey takes four days therefore I should be home on Friday."

"Is this not your home?"

"Manhattan has been my home for seventeen years however, it's time to return to Scotland."

Molly kissed Elizabeth on the cheek. "I wish you well." She smiled. "Over there it'll soon be Christmas."

And I will be on my own.

"When you reach Scotland, then what?"

"I'll stay with a relative."

"Remember to write." Molly smiled, hugged Elizabeth then walked along the landing to her apartment.

Elizabeth closed the door and locked it, picked up her suitcases then went downstairs to the main door. When she opened it, a taxi driver greeted her.

"Mornin', lady, give them to me." The taxi driver took both suitcases, put them in the boot then opened the passenger door.

"Thank you." Elizabeth got into the taxi.

The driver closed the door then entered his cab. "Where to, lady?"

"54th Street then to the docks."

"Gotcha."

As the taxi moved off, Elizabeth took a final look at the apartment block. She reminisced about her time with James in New York. After twenty-five minutes the taxi pulled up outside an estate agent's office. Elizabeth rushed out, went into the building and returned a few minutes later. She got back into the taxi and adjusted her hat.

"Okay, lady?" said the driver.

"Yes, that's the apartment taken care of."

"You rentin' it out?"

"The agency will try and sell my apartment but if not, they will rent it out."

"You goin' on a long vacation?"

"No, I am leaving New York and America."

"Where you off to?"

"Scotland."

The taxi sped towards New York docks and before the Aquitania's departure, arrived with an hour to spare. The driver got out of his cab, opened the boot and brought out Elizabeth's suitcases. He opened the passenger door, Elizabeth stepped out then closed it.

"Thank you." Elizabeth opened her handbag and gave the taxi driver a handful of dollars.

He took them and smiled.

"I trust that covers the fare?"

The driver pushed up his cap. "Lady, that amounts to double the fare! Have a safe journey." He returned to his cab, smiled and drove off.

Elizabeth picked up her suitcases. *Given my 'Titanic' experience, let us hope my return journey to Scotland will be trouble-free.*

"Can I help you, ma'am?" said a naval uniformed gentleman.

"I am here to board the Aquitania."

The gentleman smiled. "One of our finest ocean liners." He pointed. "That is it down there, the ship with four funnels."

"Thank you."

"Pleasure, ma'am." The uniformed gentleman walked on in the opposite direction.

"Carry your bags. lady?"

Elizabeth turned round. A helper at the right moment.

"A dime a bag, lady," said the young man.

"It's a deal." Elizabeth laid her suitcases on the ground.

He picked them up and smiled. "Cash on delivery."

Elizabeth and her helper soon reached the Cunard Company premises. She handed over three dimes and he wished her well. At the departure desk, Elizabeth paid for her passage then received travel documentation. She proceeded to the Aquitania, showed her pass to a ship's clerk then boarded the liner. A short time later, Elizabeth arrived at her cabin. She took off her hat and coat, hung them in a wardrobe then started to unpack one of her suitcases. She took out a framed photograph of James, smiled and laid it on the single bed with crisp white sheets. A timetable for breakfast, lunch and dinner had been left on a dark wooden bedside cabinet. Elizabeth looked at the document and read it. She put it down on the bed, picked up her photograph of James and placed it in an upright position on the cabinet.

On a cold damp December morning, the Aquitania left New York harbour amidst a flotilla of small boats. Elizabeth stood and gazed out of her cabin porthole. As the liner headed out to sea, the Statue of Liberty became smaller. Then came a knock on the cabin door. Elizabeth walked towards the door and opened it. A gentleman in a white jacket with a dark tie and trousers smiled.

"I am your steward, madam, Arthur is my name. Will you be having lunch?"

"Yes."

"It will be served in the dining room at one o'clock."

"Thanks. You're Scottish?"

The steward smiled. "Yes, madam, me and this ship. I am from Fraserburgh and the Aquitania was built at John Brown's shipyard in Clydebank. Have you heard of Clydebank, madam?"

Elizabeth smiled. "I am also from Scotland."

"Where about madam?"

"Ardrishaig. I've stayed in New York for seventeen years."

"Your accent is more American than Scottish, madam. Are you heading to Scotland for a holiday?"

"No, not a vacation. I'm going back for good."

"You'll no doubt have missed the highlands and lochs." The steward smiled.

"And other aspects of my past." Elizabeth looked down to the ground.

"If you need anything, madam, give me a shout."

Elizabeth smiled and nodded.

The steward walked along the corridor and knocked on the next cabin door.

Elizabeth closed her cabin door and continued to unpack. She came across her address book and opened it.

I hope Nancy will by now have received my letter about James. When I reach Ardrishaig, I can speak to her in person.

After dinner on her penultimate evening of the voyage, Elizabeth went for a walk along the ship's deck. The cold windy Atlantic evening ensured a coat and tight hat being worn. Elizabeth stood in front of the solid white barrier and gazed out to sea. As she raised her head, the wind blew into Elizabeth's face. She held on to her black cloche hat.

"Careful you are not blown overboard."

Elizabeth turned round.

"The Atlantic can be stormy at this time of year."

Elizabeth smiled.

"Allow me to introduce myself, I am John Watson, Chief Officer of the Aquitania."

"I have seen you in and around the ship on several occasions."

The officer smiled. "I do an assortment of duties to make sure the ship runs smoothly."

"Are you ever out of uniform?"

"When I am ashore on leave."

"The Aquitania is a wonderful ship. The amenities, food and service are of a high standard. Also, I haven't slept as well for a long time."

"The sea air can be good for you."

"How long have you been at sea?"

"From the age of nineteen, twenty-seven years ago."

"You don't look that age."

The officer smiled.

"Don't tell me, it's the sea air."

He laughed.

"How many passengers are aboard?"

"Just under three thousand. The capacity is three thousand two hundred."

"And should the ship sink, there are enough lifeboats?"

"Oh yes, that situation won't happen again."

Elizabeth smiled.

"Have you visited any of our libraries?"

"Yes, the one I visited had an excellent selection of fiction and crime novels."

"We try to cater for all our passengers."

"Even a supply of rugs for deckchairs!"

The officer smiled. "December can be chilly."

Elizabeth laughed. She looked down at the small waves. "How fast does the ship travel?"

The officer looked over the side. "Twenty-three knots." He looked at Elizabeth. "Are you bound for England?"

"Ireland, then I will catch a connection to Scotland."

"Which port?"

"Ardrishaig. I left the village seventeen years ago."

The officer looked up to the stars in the clear dark sky. "In seventeen years from now, passengers may well fly across the Atlantic."

"The aeroplane journey won't take four days."

The officer laughed. "No, but it also won't be as luxurious." He smiled. "You will not be able to go for a walk in the fresh air."

Elizabeth nodded. "Agreed." She shivered. An aeroplane won't be as cold.

"A rug?"

"No, I'll head inside, a hot drink will suffice."

A seaman approached the Chief Officer and saluted. "Excuse me sir, could you report to Captain Wilks?"

"Now?"

"Yes, sir."

The Chief Officer turned to Elizabeth. "Please excuse me."

As the two men left, Elizabeth walked along the deck and then into the garden room. The decor and furniture resembled a luxurious period garden. Elizabeth sat at a white table with two matching wicker chairs then a waiter appeared with a pleasant smile.

"Can I get you a refreshment, madam?"

"A small white coffee, please."

"Have that on me, ma'am." A tall distinguished man with grey wavy hair and moustache stood next to the waiter. He gave him several dollar notes. "Make mine a cognac."

"Special or ordinary, sir?"

The man smiled. "I only drink special cognac."

"Of course, sir." The waiter departed.

The man sat down. "Hi, I'm Casper Todd."

Pushy.

"You don't mind, do you?" He coughed.

"You didn't give me much choice!"

"I apologise, ma'am. When I notice a lady on her own, I have this urge to befriend her."

"Maybe I'm with someone?"

The man smiled. "Not before I arrived."

Nice cream three-piece suit.

"You like the suit? I buy all my clothes from a tailor in London."

"Is that the reason for this trip?"

"No, I'm on the lookout for new talent."

"What kind of talent?"

"Actors and actresses. I'm a movie director with Paramount."

"Why London? There must be an abundance of talent in America."

Casper Todd stretched out his long legs and then crossed them. "With the advent of talkies, the sound of a voice has become influential." He smiled. "There have been disasters and careers ruined for American silent movie stars who appeared in talkies."

"Have director's careers also been ruined, Mr Todd?"

He laughed. "Not yet, ma'am."

Elizabeth smiled.

"I want people with a distinguished voice who can project themselves on the screen. I've been told London could be the place to find them."

"There will be enough theatre plays in progress."

Casper Todd nodded.

"Any individuals you plan to see perform?"

From his inside jacket pocket, Casper Todd pulled out a folded piece of paper then opened it.

"Let me see." He peered at the piece of paper. "Yeah, here we are." He coughed. "Basil Rathbone, Eric Portman and William Lawson.. Also a couple of ladies called Greer Garson and Celia Johnson."

"How long will you be in London?"

"Ten days. By then, I'll have cast my eyes over them." He smiled. "Whilst there, I could show you a good time."

Oh no you won't.

The waiter appeared with a tray and laid a white saucer and cup on the table in front of Elizabeth. He then laid a glass of cognac in front of Casper Todd.

"Thanks, son," said Casper.

"Pleasure, sir." The waiter departed.

Elizabeth lifted the small cup and drank some coffee then laid it on the saucer. "Thanks for the coffee, Mr Todd, I am now off to the pool for a swim."

"Now!"

"Yes, now."

"Can I join you?"

"I swim alone."

"We could meet up later."

"I'm having an early night." Elizabeth stood up.

Casper Todd stood up. "Nice to have met you, ma'am."

Elizabeth shook his hand then left.

Casper Todd sat down, picked up his glass of cognac and drank it. He put down his empty glass on the table.

The waiter appeared. "Another cognac, sir?"

"May as well."

The waiter lifted the saucer and half-empty cup onto his tray.

Casper handed him the empty cognac glass.

"Thank you, sir." The waiter took the glass, put it on the tray and departed.

Casper looked at his gold watch. Tonight it looks like the ship's smokin' room instead of a bedroom.

When she disembarked from the Aquitania, Elizabeth looked around Cobh pier for transport into the town. As the connection to Ardrishaig did not coincide with the Aquitania's arrival in Ireland, accommodation at a local hotel had been booked in advance. Elizabeth spotted a white horse and small black carriage that appeared then came to a halt. The driver sat motionless in his grey cap, jacket and charcoal trousers. Elizabeth approached him with her two suitcases.

"Excuse me, can you take me to the Marina Hotel?"

The man looked at Elizabeth and smiled. "Of course, m'dear." He came down from his carriage seat, opened the door and took Elizabeth's suitcases then put them on the seat.

"Thank you." Elizabeth stepped into the coach and sat next to her suitcases.

The driver closed the door, climbed into his black leather seat, released the handbrake lever and threw forward the horse's reigns. As the coach moved off, Elizabeth pulled down her black cloche hat and put up the collar of her dark blue coat.

The driver glanced back. "Are you cold, m'dear?"

"A bit, it's windy."

"Comes straight off the Atlantic. We'll soon be t'ere, just round t'e waterfront." He glanced back. "Did you have a good trip?"

"Yes, a smooth sail from New York."

"No choppy ocean?"

"No, glad to say." And no iceberg either.

The horse and carriage approached an isolated building which looked onto the waterfront. Its brilliant-white coloured frontage gleamed from intermittent sunshine and the gold-coloured nameplate sparkled. The driver stopped outside the entrance then applied the handbrake. He vacated his seat then opened the carriage door.

Elizabeth stepped out. "Thank you."

The driver reached for Elizabeth's two suitcases, lifted them out and laid them in front of her.

Elizabeth opened her purse, brought out several coins and held them in her hand.

The driver smiled.

"Will that cover the cost?" Elizabeth handed several coins to the driver.

He took the coins. "More t'an enough, m'dear." He tipped his cap.

The horse moved its head up and down.

"Barnaby agrees." said the driver, "do you want me to take t'e suitcases insoide?"

Elizabeth smiled. "I'll manage."

The driver returned to his seat and pushed forward the handbrake lever. "It was once an old coach house and t'e owner built a large extension. Bye, m'dear."

As the horse and carriage departed, Elizabeth picked up her two suitcases. When she reached the hotel entrance, a door opened. A man wearing a green sweater and dark trousers smiled.

"Let me take them." He lifted up the suitcases. "This way, miss."

Elizabeth followed the grey-haired gentleman into a burgundy- carpeted foyer. He laid both suitcases at the front of a dark-wooden reception desk then walked behind it.

Elizabeth removed her hat and shook her head.

The gentleman brought out a large black book and opened it. "Could you sign in, please?" He turned the book around and gave Elizabeth a pencil.

She wrote her name and then looked up. "Are you the owner?"

The gentleman nodded. "Dermot." He turned the book around and looked at the page. "No address, Mrs Carsell-Brown?"

Elizabeth handed the pencil to him. "No, I have left America and tomorrow will sail to Scotland. At this present time, I don't have a permanent address."

The owner nodded.

"Can I book a call for tomorrow morning?"

"Yes, that can be arranged. When do you sail?"

"Tomorrow morning at nine-thirty."

"Seven o'clock for your call?"

Elizabeth nodded.

The owner turned around and lifted off a brass key from a hook behind the reception desk. He left the desk then picked up Elizabeth's suitcases.

"Thanks."

"Room number sixteen, two floors up."

Thank goodness I don't have to carry my suitcases.

Elizabeth followed the owner up the narrow dark wooden staircase. She observed framed prints of the town's pier and local landscapes on the white walls. When he reached Elizabeth's room, Dermot laid both suitcases outside the door. He unlocked it, lifted the suitcases and deposited them near a wardrobe.

Elizabeth smiled. "Thanks."

"This room has the best view of the seafront."

"Dinner?"

"Seven to eight-thirty."

After the owner left, Elizabeth walked over to the window and looked out. A scenic view of the waterfront greeted her and she opened the window to smell sea air. A few minutes later, the light wind suddenly became a gale and battered the window. Waves crashed against the waterfront barrier wall and seawater spilled onto the street. The dark green window curtains blew towards Elizabeth and the room door slammed shut. She closed the window however as a rattle ensued, latched it tight.

Phew! Before tomorrow's sail to Ardrishaig, I hope this wind eases.

Eileen set each guest's dining room table for breakfast then returned to assist her husband in the kitchen.

"That didn't take long?" said Dermot.

"Dermot, we only have three guests!"

He smiled. "Business should pick up when the festive celebrations begin. Our function room has been booked for next weekend and until early January."

"Just as well."

"Don't worry." He prepared pots of coffee and tea.

"Where's Lorraine?"

"She must be in her room."

Eileen removed her white patterned apron. "I will make sure she's okay and go upstairs to her room. Maybe the poor soul has suffered another nightmare."

"Hold on." Dermot looked at the kitchen ceiling. "I can hear her footsteps, she could be on her way downstairs."

A young teenage girl with long black hair came into the kitchen and looked at Dermot then at Eileen.

"Sorry."

"Another sleepless night?" said Eileen.

The teenage girl nodded.

"Never mind, after a cup of your uncle's tea you'll be right as rain."

She smiled.

Eileen pulled out a chair from the kitchen table. "You have a seat and I will take the guest's orders." She walked into the dining room.

The teenage girl sat down on the wooden chair.

Dermot put a cup of tea in front of her. "Something to eat?"

She lifted the white cup and sipped her tea. "No thanks, uncle."

"A nightmare, Lorraine?"

"Yes, and vivid."

Dermot sat down opposite his niece. "What was it about?"

The teenager took another sip of tea. "A boat in a storm and in difficulty." She stared at her uncle. "It appeared to sink with people on board."

"A large boat?"

"A small one. I could hear screams from passengers."

"Many?"

Lorraine shook her head. "No."

"What happened next?"

"I woke up." She sipped her tea.

Eileen came into the kitchen. "One bacon and poached egg plus white coffee."

Dermot stood up. "Right away."

Eileen stood over Lorraine. "How do you feel now?"

"Better."

Eileen smiled. "Good, you can take coffee to the lady at table sixteen."

Lorraine laid her cup on the wooden table then rose.

Dermot put a small white pot of coffee on a brown tray. "Bacon and egg will be a few minutes."

"I'll take this to the lady now." Lorraine lifted up the tray and left the kitchen.

"The colour in her cheeks have returned."

Dermot smiled. "Next will be her appetite."

Lorraine came into the kitchen with an empty tray and sat down.

Eileen stared at her. "You've gone white again, like you've seen a banshee!"

Lorraine looked up at her uncle. "She was in my nightmare!"

"The lady guest?" said Eileen.

"In Lorraine's nightmare," said Dermot, "a passenger boat had been caught in a storm and about to sink."

Eileen stared at Dermot. "That lady sails to Ardrishaig this morning."

Dermot looked out the window. "The sea remains calm. Last night's gale has gone."

"I could see a storm in my nightmare," said Lorraine.

Eileen looked at her husband. "What time does the boat leave for Ardrishaig?"

Dermot glance at the wall clock. "In just under two hours."

"Dermot, what's the weather forecast for today?" said Eileen.

"According to the radio this morning, fine."

"What's fine, Dermot?"

"Calm with a bit of light wind later."

Eileen folded her arms. "Those radio weather forecasters have mince for brains. They predicted a 'bit of light wind' yesterday. Four roof slates flew off last night!"

Dermot shrugged his shoulders.

Eileen sat down opposite Lorraine. "You foresaw that recent collision between two boats outside Cork harbour. Is this as vivid?"

Lorraine nodded. "Yes, auntie, more so."

Eileen stood up. "I'll mention to the lady a storm is on its way. She can catch tomorrow's sailing and stay the extra night for free."

"Here's her breakfast." Dermot put the plate of bacon and poached egg on a tray.

Eileen picked it up and left the kitchen.

Dermot smiled at his niece. "I would bet on you being correct."

Lorraine smiled.

Eileen entered the kitchen. "That's fine, better safe than sorry she said." Eileen looked at Lorraine. "The other guest has appeared in the dining room. Can you give me a hand?"

Lorraine smiled. "Will do."

After breakfast, Elizabeth handed in her room key at reception then took a walk along the waterfront to Cobh's local shipping office. She entered the small wooden hut, walked up to the closed wooden shutter and knocked on it. A minute later the shutter was raised.

"Hello again, m'dear. What can oi do for you?"

Elizabeth smiled. "You have changed outfits!"

"Dark blue jacket for t'is role and grey for outdoors." He smiled.

"I would like to cancel my sail to Ardrishaig and travel tomorrow."

The shipping clerk looked at a clock on his office wall. "Your cuttin' it foine, t'e boat leaves in t'irty minutes."

"I don't feel too good, the journey would make me worse."

"Since it's you. Give me your ticket and oi will replace it."

Elizabeth opened her black leather handbag, took out the ticket and handed it to the clerk.

He took the ticket, stamped it and gave it back to Elizabeth. "Valid for tomorrow, m'dear."

Elizabeth popped the ticket into her handbag.

"T'e forecast is calm for today."

"I don't want to take a chance." Elizabeth touched her stomach. "A bit queezy."

The clerk smiled. "Fresh sea air would cure it."

Elizabeth smiled. "See you tomorrow morning."

"Bye, m'dear."

Elizabeth left the premises and walked back towards the hotel. As a man and dog approached, a gust of wind blew in her face.

"Good morning," said Elizabeth.

"So far," said the man, "you stayin' at t'e hotel?"

Another grey-bearded man with a grey cap. "Yes."

"You an American?"

"I'm Scottish. I lived in New York for seventeen years."

As a dog in the distance barked, the man turned around. His own black and white collie sat motionless.

"The two dogs look similar," said Elizabeth."

The man looked at his dog. "From t'e same litter."

Elizabeth stared in the distance. "It must be lonely for her, I've not seen any other teenagers."

The man looked in the distance towards the teenager. "She's similar to her great-grandmot'er."

"In appearance?"

"She could foretell disasters."

"Disasters?"

The man turned to Elizabeth. "Oh aye, she could tell if somethin' was about to happen."

"What kind of disasters?" Elizabeth put up the collar of her coat.

"People say she spoke of our food famine years before it hit us."

"Her great-grandmother must have been young. The famine began in 1845."

The man looked towards the teenager. "Same age as Lorraine is now. Her great-grandmot'er also foretold of incidents at sea."

"The Titanic?"

The man shook his head. "She'd passed on by t'at time."

Elizabeth looked at the man's collie. "It is well-behaved."

He smiled. "Well trained is she." He glanced at his dog.

Elizabeth looked along the waterfront. "I met her at breakfast this morning. She appears to enjoy helping her parents in the hotel."

"Her parents passed on year's back. Her uncle and aunt own t'e hotel. After t'e war, moved here from England."

Elizabeth held on to her hat. "This wind is getting up!"

The man smiled. "T'e radio said today would be calm." He looked upwards. "T'e sky has turned from blue to grey."

Elizabeth stared out to sea. Thank goodness I cancelled.

"Anyway, must go."

"Bye."

The man walked on and the collie followed. Elizabeth continued her walk back along the waterfront to the hotel. She observed a church on the hill and headed in its direction. Elizabeth walked up a grey gravel path and soon reached the building. At the church entrance, one of the two large wooden doors had been left ajar. She pushed the door wide open and entered then closed it. The church appeared empty therefore Elizabeth ventured inside. It had a calm aura, which eased her tensions. As she walked down the aisle, her footsteps on the wooden floor echoed. Elizabeth reached the front wooden pew and sat down. She took off her hat, stared straight ahead at a large cross on the wall, bowed her head and closed both eyes. A short time later, she opened them and looked up.

"Did I disturb you?"

Elizabeth stared at the small white-haired man in his black attire and white collar. He had a warm smile.

"I am Father O'Shea. What is your name?"

Elizabeth, Elizabeth Carsell-Brown."

"I trust you have not come all the way from America to this place of worship?"

"I'm on my way to Scotland."

"Scotland?"

Elizabeth nodded.

"For a holiday?"

"My roots are there. I have left America and am going home to stay for good."

"Did you not enjoy America?"

"My husband died a short time ago and I am now alone."

Father O'Shea sat down close to Elizabeth. "Do you not have any children or close family?"

"My sister lives in America, I have an aunt however we are not close." Elizabeth brought out a white handkerchief from her coat pocket.

"When you return to Scotland, a pretty lady such as yourself will not be alone for too long." Father O'Shea smiled.

Elizabeth sniffed then smiled.

"I believe a wonderful new life could unfold. There is goodness in you."

"Father, I did a terrible deed a long time ago for which I regret." Elizabeth wiped her eyes.

"What kind of deed?"

Elizabeth's voice grew raspy. "I rejected a loved one."

"How old were you?"

"Eighteen."

"You had not grown into an adult."

"I can't forgive myself. I've put it to the back of my mind for many years, I now feel remorse."

"Maybe one day you'll be together again. Does this person live in Scotland?"

"I'm not sure." Elizabeth gripped her handkerchief.

"Elizabeth, our Lord works in mysterious ways. Have faith."

"I will try."

Father O'Shea smiled, stood up and walked to the end of the pew.

Elizabeth rose, put on her hat and approached Father O'Shea. "Can I make a contribution to the church?"

Father O'Shea walked to the altar and returned with a copper plate.

Elizabeth went into her coat pocket, brought out coins and put them on the plate.

"Thank you."

"My pleasure."

Father O'Shea escorted his guest to the exit door. "Have a safe journey home, Elizabeth." He opened one of the doors.

"Thank you, Father." Elizabeth moved away from the doorway and grabbed her hat.

"Goodness me! The wind has got up."

Elizabeth turned to face Father O'Shea, held her hat and smiled.

"Goodbye, Elizabeth, take care and embrace the future."

"I will."

Elizabeth left the church and walked with force against a strong wind towards the Marina Hotel. She came across a grey stone memorial over twelve feet in height. Whilst she held on to her hat, Elizabeth read the inscription carved on the base. 'Seven hundred and sixty-one people killed.'

I remember the outcry in New York. The Lusitania, a passenger ship with Americans on board sunk by a German submarine. How quickly fourteen years have passed.

A man's cap flew past Elizabeth and the owner ran past her to retrieve his precious head garment.

"It's a windy one today!" cried the man. He pursued the cap.

Elizabeth looked towards the choppy sea. I hope the fishing boats are tied up in the harbour.

Elizabeth closed the door, picked up her two suitcases and walked downstairs to the reception desk. When she arrived, laid both suitcases on the floor.

"Enjoyed your stay, Mrs Carsell-Brown?" said Dermot.

"Yes and thank you for the extra night." Elizabeth smiled.

"Our pleasure. We've arranged transport to the harbour for you." Dermot looked at the circular dark-wooden wall clock. "Be here in ten minutes."

"That is excellent. Before the boat sails, I'll arrive there in good time."

Eileen entered the reception area. "Off at last, Mrs Carsell-Brown?"

"I may come back. It's a lovely tranquil location. This place reminds me of my younger days in Ardrishaig."

"New York must have been a shock to the system," said Eileen.

Elizabeth laughed. "Yes, without a doubt. However, I managed to survive for seventeen years."

Eileen laughed.

Lorraine entered the reception area. "Aunt Eileen, there is no marmalade left. A guest has requested it for his toast."

"Which guest?"

"Room four, Mr Griffith."

"Explain to him that our supplier has no stock of marmalade."

"Okay." Lorraine went into the dining room."

Eileen smiled. "Marmalade, we're lucky to have butter! Doesn't he realise there's a squeeze on?"

Dermot laughed.

"That's a lovely ring your niece has." It's familiar.

"A family heirloom," said Eileen, "it belonged to her great-grandmother."

Dermot looked towards the hotel's entrance door. "Your transport has arrived, Mrs Carsell-Brown."

Elizabeth turned around. "Same as before."

Dermot came from behind the desk and lifted Elizabeth's two suitcases. "I'll take these to the carriage for you."

"Thank you for your hospitality" said Elizabeth.

"Our pleasure, Mrs Carsell-Brown," said Eileen. She kissed Elizabeth on the cheek.

Elizabeth walked out of the hotel and approached the carriage. "Hello."

"Hi there, m'dear," said the driver.

"I see you've changed again." Elizabeth smiled.

"Aye, and when oi drop you off oi will have to change again!"

Dermot opened the carriage door and put the suitcases on the seat.

Elizabeth got into the carriage and sat down.

Dermot closed the door. "Have a good trip."

Elizabeth smiled.

The driver released the handbrake lever, threw forward the horse's black reigns and the carriage moved off. The proprietor waved at Elizabeth.

"It's calm today, m'dear."

"The local radio station reported yesterday would be calm."

"Oi can't feel it in me bones today. When t'e weather is unsettled, me legs ache all over."

"The storm has gone but a chill exists therefore I have taken precautions."

The driver glanced back.

Elizabeth held up her black leather gloved hands.

"Ideal for December, m'dear."

Elizabeth smiled. "Are many people booked to travel this morning?"

"Not too many. A fair share of t'e passengers are businessmen."

"Businessmen?" Elizabeth tucked a loose hair inside her hat.

"T'ey represent our local area."

"Sales people?"

The driver glanced round. "Hoteliers who want to promote t'eir establishments. Dermot travelled to Scotland last week."

"We're in winter, who would take their vacation now?"

He glanced back. "Not now – next summer. Make people aware of t'e hotel, get t'em to put down a deposit and time to pay t'eir balance."

"Many people right now won't be able to afford a vacation."

"T'at's why our hotel's proices remain low. Hotels also subsidoise fares from Scotland."

"Has there been much business done?"

"T'is is t'e foirst year it's been troied."

"Who came up with the idea?"

"Dermot, all hoteliers have followed."

"The other hotels may take away his customers."

The driver glanced back. "T'ey have formed an association and help each ot'er out."

"Admirable."

"Here we are, m'dear." The carriage stopped and the driver pulled back the handbrake lever. He came down from his seat then opened the carriage door.

"Thank you." Elizabeth stepped out.

The driver collected Elizabeth's suitcases, laid them beside her then closed the door.

Elizabeth opened her handbag and took out her purse.

"No charge, m'dear." He tipped his cap and smiled. "Have to go now and change for my ot'er role."

Elizabeth smiled. "See you soon."

He walked towards the shipping office and entered through a side door.

Nice Irish hospitality.

After she reappeared from the shipping office, Elizabeth popped the journey ticket into her handbag. A gentleman in a brown hat and coat came forward.

"Can I be of assistance and carry those heavy suitcases?"

Elizabeth looked at the gentleman. "Why yes, thank you."

"Is your boat the one headed for Scotland?"

"Yes, it is."

"Me too." The gentleman lifted both suitcases. "That's the boat coming this way."

Elizabeth looked across the harbour.

"Let's go."

Both passengers walked along the pier and awaited their boat's arrival. A queue of men and women had gathered.

The gentleman smiled. "Unlike yesterday, the sea is calm."

"I cancelled yesterday's trip."

"Just as well!"

"What happened?"

"The boat sank in a storm near the Mull of Kintyre."

Elizabeth stared at the gentleman.

"Two passengers and a crewman are missing."

My goodness!

"You're a lucky person."

As the boat arrived, a small number of passengers disembarked then those on the pier boarded. When Elizabeth reached the deck, she received her suitcases.

Elizabeth smiled.

The gentleman lifted his hat.

"What's your name?"

"Archie, Archie Kinnell."

"Thank you, Archie."

"A pleasure." He replaced his hat, smiled and departed.

Elizabeth put her handbag under her arm, lifted both suitcases then walked into the boat's sitting area. She put down her suitcases and sat next to a long rectangular window. Elizabeth removed both gloves, opened her handbag and brought out a small mirror then looked into it. She put the mirror back into her handbag and then took off her left shoe. As Elizabeth massaged her toes, an elderly lady watched and smiled.

Elizabeth smiled at her. "My foot aches."

"Those narrow high-heeled shoes won't help."

Elizabeth nodded.

"You are American?"

"I was born in Scotland and later moved to America."

"I am also from Scotland and moved to Ireland."

"Why did you leave Scotland?"

"I met someone from Ireland and left Scotland to stay with him."

Elizabeth glanced at the lady's wedding ring.

"He died fourteen months ago." The lady looked downwards.

"I'm sorry."

The lady looked at Elizabeth. "Are you off to visit family in Scotland?"

Elizabeth paused. "I have an aunt and plan to visit her."

"Which part of Scotland are you headed for?" The lady tightened her black scarf. "You must excuse me, the cold bites."

Elizabeth smiled. "It is December."

The lady nodded. "Isn't it just."

"I'm headed for Ardrishaig."

"So am I! One of my old friends has invited me to celebrate Christmas and New Year with her." She smiled. "My friend lives in a large house and has plenty of space."

"What's her name?"

"Lydia Beaumont. Lady Lydia Beaumont to give her the proper title. I am just plain Mary Butler."

Elizabeth smiled. "And I am plain Elizabeth Carsell-Brown."

"You don't strike me as being plain my dear."

"Thanks."

"Lydia's son was killed in the war and she still grieves his loss." The lady looked downwards and then at Elizabeth. "However, she has a wonderful grand-daughter."

"How old is she?"

"Lydia?"

"Her grand-daughter."

The lady looked upwards. "Let me see, fourteen, fifteen oh I lose track of the time nowadays." She smiled. "The years fly past!"

"I stayed in New York for seventeen years."

"When you left Scotland, what age were you?"

"Twenty-eight."

The lady touched Elizabeth's arm. "Nature has been kind to you, my dear."

Elizabeth manoeuvred her shoe back on. "I wish nature had been kind to my feet."

The lady laughed. "Have you missed Scotland?"

Elizabeth nodded. "I loved to paint scenes around Loch Fyne. I even did a portrait of our coachman."

"He must have been pleased."

Elizabeth laughed. "I don't believe so."

"A local man?"

Elizabeth shook her head. "He came from Edinburgh."

"Where in Ardrishaig did you stay?"

"Docharnea, a property just outside Ardrishaig."

"I once met the coachman from that property. He came to Lydia's home to collect the owner."

"Mary Carsell-Brown?"

"Yes, she and her husband left Scotland to live in Africa."

"A long distance from Scotland."

"Yes it is. Where was I? Oh yes, the coachman. He appeared a pleasant chap, about the same age as myself."

"The same age?"

The lady nodded. "When I met him in 1896, two months earlier I had celebrated my fortieth birthday. I'm now seventy-three." She looked at Elizabeth. "You're surprised? I've not been old all my life!"

"When he worked for us, I would have put his age at around forty."

"What year would that be?"

"1912."

The lady laughed. "Nature has been kind to both of you."

Elizabeth smiled and put on her black gloves.

"Does your husband live in America? I don't mean to pry but you wear a wedding ring."

"He died a short time ago."

"Oh I am sorry to hear that."

Elizabeth looked out the window. "The sea appears calm."

"Yes, yes it does."

Chapter 8

Return Of The Coachman

I opened both eyes and lifted my head of the wooden floor. I stood up, steadied myself then checked my wristwatch – it had stopped again. The coachman's quarters felt colder than usual. I gazed around the room and it appeared different from my visit to 1967. In that year, this room required a fresh coat of paint. However, in this timeline the room is presentable. Before I passed out, the painting I stared at had vanished. I went over to the window and looked out onto the garden. The trees were in place but without any leaves. An autumnal appearance existed within the garden. Pity the poor chap who has to gather up all those dead leaves which fell from the trees. I walked down the wooden staircase and turned the black door handle. As it would not budge, I went into my trouser pocket and took out my own coach house key. I inserted the key into the lock, turned it then opened the door. Glad I made the decision to carry it with me at all times. I stepped out into the courtyard then locked the door. A grassy surface greeted me and I observed tyre marks alongside the main house. When I reappeared in 1938, a surface of grey gravel filled the courtyard therefore this era could be earlier. As the trees are fully-grown, this timeline would be after 1926. I remember them being planted in 1896! I wandered around the property with discretion and did not detect evidence of anybody at home. At least on this occasion, the housekeeper from my last visit isn't around to 'interrogate' me. I stared down the familiar driveway, which led onto the main road. This road had been covered with tarmac therefore maybe used by vehicles on a regular basis. I could hear one approach the property. As it passed by, my timeline estimate would not be too far off the mark. The chassis had advanced from 1912 but less streamlined than 1938. How much money do I have? I went into my trouser pocket and pulled out the cash contents. I counted the pound notes and coins – my cash from 1967 will be worth a lot more now. One advantage of going back in time as opposed to going forward! On another note, although it looks sunny, I am not warm. As in previous occasions, a stroll into Ardrishaig will enlighten me of the date. Since there may be no public transport in this timeline, I will have to walk. Why would I have been sent back to this era? After my initial journey to 1896, on each time shift I had travelled forward. I walked to the bottom of the driveway and reached the road. I turned left and headed for the village. A woman with a small black dog on a brown leash came towards me.

"Hello," she said.

"Hello."

"Are you a stranger? I've not noticed you around these parts." She looked at her dog. "Sit, Ben!"

"I popped into Docharnea, nobody was about." I looked at the dog.

"The family have gone on holiday to Inverness."

"That's a pity."

"When they return, I can give Philip and Charlotte a message."

"I'll be back this way in the near future."

The woman smiled. "Okay."

"Thanks anyway."

"You're welcome." She stared at me. "Have we met before?"

"No." I shook my head.

"Oh well, enjoy your day."

The young woman walked on with the dog at her side. As the dog barked she looked at it and smiled.

"Yes Ben, his clothes are a tad strange."

I have met that young woman before, not in the past but in the future. In 1938 and 1940 accompanied by her daughter, Abigail Anderson. I continued towards Ardrishaig and after twenty minutes, reached the main street. It looks more run-down than in 1938! Most of the shops are closed and the remainder have exteriors for the uninspired – drab is a term that would describe them. On my previous visit in 1967, I witnessed a marketing revolution for this small rural village. Now I observe a complete reversal! The main street is quiet and lacklustre. One other aspect I notice – men wear scruffy double-breasted jackets. My smart mid-sixties three-button single breast jacket receives intriguing stares along with narrow and no turn-up trousers. However, my first task is to find out the date of this timeline. I went into the street's general store and bought a Daily Express. I handed over a threepenny piece and received two coins in change. I walked to the exit door and stared at my broadsheet newspaper's front page. It stated the 22nd of October 1929. My historical knowledge revealed two days remained until the infamous Black Thursday. A day when more than ten per cent was wiped off the value of shares held on New York's stock market in Wall Street. It is outwith my control to prevent that occurrence therefore why am I here? I spotted a tearoom and crossed the street. As Nancy is now retired, maybe our paths will cross at some point in the village. When I entered the tearoom, a bell rang. That particular shop contraption still takes me by surprise. I sat next to the window and glanced at my wristwatch. It had started to work thus I observed the wall clock and set my wristwatch to the correct time. As this remains an era for pocket watches in rural Argyll, I took off my wristwatch and put it into my jacket side-pocket. Since I will purchase it nine years from now, this wristwatch is ahead of its time and could attract unwanted attention. A black-outfitted waitress approached and glanced at my jacket.

"Yes sir, what can I get you?"

"Do you have coffee?"

The waitress shook her head.

"A cup of tea, please, and do you have ginger cake?"

She nodded and smiled. "One or two?"

"Two please."

"Be back soon."

As the waitress departed, I picked up my newspaper and read the front page. No surprise that the main article referred to the crisis on Wall Street. 'A Financial Catastrophe For The Western World Nears' is the headline in bold capital letters. It would not take a genius to work that out given the financial turbulence encountered over previous months. What happens two days from now will have repercussions for years to come – even in rural Ardrishaig. I turned the pages and extended financial articles with a negative slant dominated. Ramsay MacDonald at the helm of a hung Parliament faced more economic challenges ahead. The British people would endure austerity for another thirty years and have to participate in another war. I turned to the sports section and read about Glasgow Rangers strong start to the football season. The sportswriter expected them to retain the first division title. In the round up of second division news, Leith Athletic had shown good early form. The columnist added, "this Edinburgh side who play at Leith Links could be a contender for promotion to the top division." If Leith Athletic were promoted, their supporters would have a short walk to watch the away fixture with Hibs at nearby Easter Road. A potential derby match in Leith? It's a possibility provided Hibs don't end up being relegated. Cinema received a good amount of coverage even though talkies had not yet reached Scotland. The silent films of this era remain a necessity, albeit temporary refuge for people to forget about dismal times. Films such as 'The Streets of London' directed by Norman Lee and 'The Woman in White' starring Blanche Sweet appeared popular amongst cinema critics.

"Excuse me, sir, your tea and cakes."

I looked up.

"Any good news?" said the waitress.

I put down my newspaper. "Not really."

The waitress smiled.

Wait until Thursday.

"If you require any more tea, give me a wave."

"Thanks."

The waitress left and attended to another table occupied by two ladies. She took their order and departed then both ladies glanced in my direction. Yes, the clothes I wear do look strange. After all, they do come from the 1960's. Buttoned-down collars on shirts plus narrow ties and jacket lapels reigned supreme. I picked up my newspaper, lifted my cup and sipped the tea. Let's try the crossword puzzle and test my 1929 vocabulary.

Twenty minutes later, I paid the waitress and departed the tearoom. After shutting the glass door, I observed the waitress examine the coins given to her. My first task was to find accommodation and fast. I want to keep what cash is in my possession for essentials. Even if I could hide in the coach house, this autumn climate would be chilly. To light a fire in the living quarters may help but smoke from the chimney would draw attention. Further along the main street, I spotted a woman who wore a jacket over her nurse's uniform. The hospital at nearby Lochgilphead! It could be an ideal refuge, however I'm not going to badly injure myself for the sake of a bed. Maybe the hospital requires someone to carry out manual labour duties. Nothing ventured nothing gained therefore I'll head to the hospital and find out. On my way there, I approached the office of MacMillan Solicitors. Look at the mess you've got me into. The sun-kissed city of Nice feels like a lifetime ago. In fact, it's akin to several lifetimes ago! I left Ardrishaig village and thirty-five minutes later arrived at the town of Lochgilphead. Glad I've not lost my zest for walking however my feet ache in those narrow shoes I'm wearing. I passed the office where Elizabeth's husband once worked as an accountant. My coachman journey from Docharnea to here still fresh in my mind. I reached the hospital entrance and went inside. Since my visit in 1912, it had not changed. I recall the young patient who arrived with a minor leg injury accompanied by his mother. He now has a gold medal for his performance in a race event at the 1924 summer Olympics held in France.

"Can I help you?"

I turned round.

"Have you come here for an examination?" said a nurse.

"I was informed you may have a vacancy for a porter." This era can be a precarious one to seek employment.

"Wait here, please." She walked down the corridor and into a room.

A few minutes later, a thin middle-aged man wearing a long grey overall and dark trousers came out of the room then walked towards me.

"Hi, I'm Roy Stone. What's yours?"

"James Carlisle."

"Any hospital experience?"

I nodded. Here, seventeen years ago.

"Good, come this way." He walked down the corridor.

I walked alongside.

He stopped and pointed. "In here."

I entered the small sparse room which consisted of a tall grey metal cabinet, a wooden table and four chairs.

"You've come at the right time, we've a man off sick." Roy opened the cabinet, pulled out a grey overall and handed it to me. "Try that for size."

I put on the overall.

"It's a bit loose on you however, I've seen worse." He looked at the wooden wall clock. "I'm going on my break. Report to Matron and introduce yourself to her."

"Where will I find her?"

Roy went into the corridor. "This way."

I followed.

He pointed. "That's her office, second on the left."

"Is there accommodation I can use in the hospital?"

Roy nodded. "We have a spare room if required. What's the problem?"

"My own accommodation is being renovated."

"Later today, I'll show you where the room is. I'm off on an errand." He headed for the hospital exit door.

Thank goodness stringent employment practices don't exist in 1929. Now, where is Matron? Let's hope she is not the same person I met in 1912. If so, I hope her memory has faded.

"Excuse me."

I looked sideways.

"I need your assistance."

"Sure." The nurse I spoke to earlier.

"This way, a patient is due in theatre."

"Excuse me, nurse, I have just started today. Where is the theatre?"

"I'll escort you and the patient to the theatre."

"Thanks."

"This patient suffers from extreme anxiety." The nurse whispered, "an ulcer will be removed."

"Unfortunate."

"Over the last few weeks, there have been several patients admitted for stress-related illnesses."

Given the current financial predicament, it is not a surprise.

"Just here." The nurse took me into a ward.

Several hours later when my duties finished, I retired to my spartan accommodation. Roy mentioned the room was not in a four-star category, how about minus two. The small compact room consisted of a single bed, wooden wardrobe and a cracked white ceramic sink. Not even a bedside table or lamp. The coachman's quarters in the coach house now appear extravagant! Ah well, at least the room is warm and I do have a paid job. For October 1929, that could be perceived as a comfortable existence. However, my main focus of thought – why am I in this period of time? I have encountered Philip and Charlotte in the past therefore why again? I folded my grey overall and put it inside the wardrobe. The overall is not a fashion item but it does cover my controversial 1967 attire. I will make a return visit to the village charity shop for a change of clothes appropriate for this era. With the absence of a chair. I sat on one side of my bed and stared at the bare window. Since nobody can look into this room, a curtain is not required but it would give the interior an impression of being habitable.

Maybe one of the hospital staff could provide me with a spare curtain. That reminds me, is Doctor Campbell still here? After my collision with a horse, he attended to me in 1912. If our paths cross, would he have any immediate recollection? Fortunately, it is a different matron from my previous visit. As I have not changed physically in seventeen years, what would the good doctor's medical diagnosis be? A surprising aspect of time travel is that it does not produce side effects. I have travelled six times and my appearance remains unchanged. I no longer suffer giddiness experienced at the start of my travels and hope this won't be a premature analysis. An advantage of this role as opposed to a coachman – no mucky stinky stable full of horse dung to clean out. I heard three distinct knocks on my door and answered it.

"James, please fill in this form for the personnel records." Roy handed me a white document.

I took the form and glanced over it.

"No rush, tomorrow morning will do." He smiled. "Give the completed form to Gabrielle."

"Gabrielle?"

Roy nodded. "She works in the reception office."

"Will do." I looked behind me. "Sorry I can't offer you any hospitality."

Roy laughed. "I'll check if there is any spare furniture."

"With a few items, it could look comfortable."

"Six o'clock start tomorrow, James."

"Six o'clock?" That's early.

Roy nodded then departed.

I closed the door and looked at the form. Name, address, age, place of birth and previous employment. I suppose being a coachman comes under the service sector and there is my marketing experience. Given that concept does not exist, it could raise Gabrielle's level of intrigue. Due to my early start tomorrow morning, I will complete this form now. It makes good sense to add details being fully awake.

Not fully awake, I walked in a sluggish manner from my room to the reception desk situated in another part of the building. Early dark and cold mornings do not complement me. However with winter soon to commence, being able to work indoors has a favourable appeal. As nobody stood at the desk, I picked up a small brass bell and shook it. A man in a dark blue uniform and white peaked cap appeared from a back room.

"One ring is sufficient," he said.

"Can you give this form to Gabrielle, please?" I handed the folded form to him.

"I'm a security guard not a message boy. However, as she won't be in for another two hours, I'll pass it on." He took the form.

"Thanks." And have a grumpy day.

I headed for Ward A where my duties would commence. As I approached the ward, a nurse came out of a room. She looked similar to the nurse I had met yesterday – dark, curvy and of medium height. Her blue uniform matched the colour of her eyes.

"Good morning, ready and able?"

I nodded. "At this deathly hour, yes." Perhaps 'deathly' is not the most appropriate word to use in a hospital.

"I am Nurse Robertson."

"James."

"Careful what you say, James." She smiled. "Come this way." She led me into a room. "This is the staff quarters."

I looked around the compact and tidy room. I noticed a couple of elegant flower-patterned armchairs, a polished dark-wooden table and a radio that had been placed on it. Upon observing a dignified grandfather clock in the corner, I smiled at Nurse Robertson.

"A donation from one of our former doctors. Two years ago he moved to Glasgow and gave us those items for the rest room."

"Admirable."

"Doctor Campbell enjoyed his time at the hospital hence the gesture."

"Splendid." Good, now I won't have to explain why my appearance has not changed.

"That's a word I've not heard around here."

"A relative uses it often in his vocabulary."

"You are not from around here?"

I shook my head. "My origins are in the east – Edinburgh."

"You're a long way from home! Why come to Argyll?"

That could take a long time to explain and you wouldn't believe me. "I enjoy the scenery."

She smiled. "Let us hope you enjoy the hospital scenery, it can be stressful."

Similar to when you travel through time. "I'm sure I will." I must, this hospital could be my home for the foreseeable future.

After the completion of my initial morning duties, I took my lunchtime break. I sat alone in the staff rest room and read this morning's newspaper. Predictions in large letters of 'Financial Armageddon' will not be exaggerated. As they happen, it feels strange to read about known pivotal events in history. When you are aware of the negative consequences, a personal sadness ensues. The door opened and Nurse Robertson breezed into the room.

"James, Gabby would like a word."

I put down the newspaper. "Now?"

"When it is suitable."

"I'll go right away."

"Fine."

I departed the rest room and walked along the white polished floor to reception. Upon my arrival, I knocked on the closed side door. I heard footsteps approach the door and it opened. A young woman with long auburn hair and a short turquoise dress smiled.

"Gabrielle?" I said.

"Yes, come in."

I entered the light-coloured bright office. I could smell roses but did not observe any flowers.

She closed the door. "Have a seat."

I sat down on a wooden chair.

Gabrielle went behind her desk, sat down and held a white document in her hand. "I have your details, James." She picked up a pencil and looked towards me. "Place of birth?"

"Edinburgh."

She wrote on the form.

"Can I ask a question?"

She looked up and smiled. "Of course."

"How much is the weekly wage for a porter? Roy did not mention the amount."

"That is because your role is voluntary."

Voluntary! What little cash I have from 1967 will soon run out.

"I believe you have a room within the hospital?"

I nodded.

"Your room and meals are free of charge. If you want to earn cash then we can offer additional work."

"What kind of work?"

"You can maintain the hospital grounds."

I could take time off from my duties.

Gabrielle smiled. "Once the porter's shift has been completed then you could work in the grounds. No time off I'm afraid."

I nodded. "Okay." I'll have to try and make my money last. I rose from my chair.

She stood up, went to the door and opened it. "Due to a lack of funds, we work to a tight budget. Roy is the only porter who receives a wage."

"I understand." I departed.

"Bye." Gabrielle closed the door.

I returned to Ward A which consisted of adult female patients. They had finished their lunch and due to the sunny October afternoon, requested to sit in an adjacent lounge. Nurse Robertson agreed and seven patients affiliated to the warm sunny room. As I took a senior citizen in a wheelchair to the lounge, she looked at me.

"Are you new to here, son?" said the elderly patient.

I nodded.

"Are you part of the ambulance crew?"

"No, I'm the new porter."

"What's your name?"

"James. What's yours?"

"Greer, son. I was named after my grandmother."

I wheeled the lady into the bright sunny room and placed her near a window. My 'wheelchair skills' improve with each shift.

Greer looked at me. "Trinny tae?"

"Trinny?"

"Yes, Trinny Boswall."

Nurse Robertson approached Greer. "Trinny has decided to have a lie down. She feels tired."

"It's all that talkin' she does." Greer looked at Nurse Robertson. "I forgot my pill tin."

"When you return, it will still be there." Nurse Robertson smiled. "I'll make sure of that."

"Thank you."

I left the lounge and walked to the rest room – time for another read of my newspaper. A tall lean gentleman with wavy dark hair wearing a white medical coat approached then smiled.

"You're new here?"

I nodded.

"You don't repair vehicles by any chance?"

I shook my head.

"Pity." He walked on.

I entered the rest room and looked around for the newspaper.

"Looking for this?"

I turned around. Roy held it in his hand. "Had a quick read in the dining room." He handed the newspaper to me.

"Thanks." I took it.

"That was Doctor Grant-Owen. He has problems with his motor car – blames it whenever he's late for work."

I smiled. "Does Ward A cater for any particular type of patient?"

"For burns or related problems. There is a sign outside the hospital entrance – Ward A Burn Admissions."

Following an uncomfortable sleepless night, I dragged myself out of bed on this cold dark Thursday morning. Today would be forever spoken about as 'Black Thursday' in a historical context. I dressed for work with a heavy heart. The despair about to unfold for people around the globe will bring austerity for decades to come.

At my morning break, I went into the bright sparse patient's lounge to admire the view. Whilst working and living in the hospital, at times I experienced claustrophobia. The large wide window looked onto the well-maintained hospital garden. After my collision with a horse, I sat there in 1912. Apart from a selection of shrubs and bushes, the garden has remained unchanged. As I reminisced about bygone days, a chap entered the warm comfortable lounge. He wore a brown dressing gown over light blue pyjamas plus dark blue and green tartan slippers. I would put his age at around fifty years.

"Hello," he said, "terrific view."

I nodded. "All the fallen leaves have been cleared."

"Roy and another chap tided up the grounds. You're new here?"

"Yes, I started this week."

He held out his hand. "I'm Adam Fraser."

I shook his hand. "James Carlisle."

He smiled. "I detect a foreign accent."

"East coast."

"This is the first time I've been allowed out of my bed. Nurse Robertson runs a strict regime however Matron is worse!"

I laughed. "What are you in for?"

"I had an ulcer removed." He smiled. "Must be the pressure of my business."

"What type of business do you have?"

"Antiques. I also sell paintings."

I had not come across this type of outlet in Ardrishaig. "Where is your business located?"

"Here in Lochgilphead."

"How long have you been trading for?"

236

He looked upwards. "Nineteen years, yes nineteen. This year will be a write-off."

"As with many others."

Adam nodded. "How worse can it get!"

You will find out in tomorrow morning's newspapers and financial problems won't be restricted to Lochgilphead. "Why did you venture into antiques?"

"Our family have stayed in a small estate outside Lochgilphead for the best part of two centuries. My grandfather stored all the old furniture and momentums. He then gave them to my father and when he passed away, I inherited the items."

"Do you live on the estate?"

"The property was sold off to repay my father's debts. I stay in a modest property above the shop."

Nurse Robertson came into the lounge.

Adam turned round and smiled. "About to go back nurse."

Nurse Robertson nodded.

Adam looked towards me. "Bye." He departed.

"Nice chap."

She whispered, "his business could be in trouble."

"He told me. However, most businesses in the area will be in a similar position."

"I believe he still has to settle his father's debts."

"The father must have accumulated a lot of debt! Adam told me the estate was sold off."

"His father became addicted to gambling and made the family destitute. Adam managed to retain a stockpile of old furniture. Apart from those items and debts, that's all the father left him."

"Has he no other family?"

"He is an only child. At the age of ten, his mother died of cholera."

"Does he have a partner?"

Nurse Robertson stared. "A partner?"

Remember this is not the twenty-first century. "A wife?"

She shook her head. "He had been engaged but it didn't work out. He suffered a broken heart and has remained single."

I observed the brass clock on the wall. "Break time over."

Nurse Robertson smiled. "I need equipment transferred from Ward C to Ward B."

"Lead the way."

As we walked along the corridor to Ward C, a junior nurse approached Nurse Robertson.

"The ambulance has arrived with a young woman. She was knocked down by a motor car near Inveraray."

"Another one! What is her condition?"

"Bruising to one of her legs."

"Is she in shock?"

"She appears composed."

"We can put her in Ward B for the time being." Nurse Robertson looked at me. "The equipment can wait, James."

I arrived at the hospital entrance where two ambulance crewmembers had prepared a young woman for transfer into the hospital. Given her traumatic circumstances, she looked calm. As I transported her along the corridor, she stared at me then smiled. I took the young woman into Ward B where two nurses attended to her. When I left, they closed the white curtain that surrounded the bed. I went into the rest room to have a read of my newspaper. The junior nurse I observed earlier looked up from her seated position then put down a magazine.

"Hello, I'm James."

"I'm Maria."

I sat down on the opposite chair. "Are there many admissions as a result of motor car accidents?"

She nodded. "Oh yes."

"Was the young woman in the motor car?"

"No, a pedestrian. The motor car skidded of the road and hit her. The driver must have lost control. In fact, too many of them lose control of their vehicles. There should be a proficiency test for drivers."

I nodded. "It will come." From next year, a driving test will commence for some vehicle owners and full implementation four years later.

"I hope sooner rather than later." She looked at the wall clock. "Back to work."

"Do you cover the four wards?"

Maria stood up and placed a blue nurse's cap on top of her short blonde hair. "Just A and B." She smiled. "Two is enough! Nurse Shaw covers C plus D and Nurse Robertson is in charge of the four wards."

"What about Matron?"

"She has overall responsibility for patient care."

"What if yourself or Nurse Shaw is unavailable or off sick?"

"Nurse Robertson steps in." Maria adjusted her uniform and departed.

I stood up and switched on the radio. I looked at the wall clock – three minutes before the hour. Let us hear what the BBC Home Service has to say on this eventful day.

The next day I observed members of staff throughout the hospital in conversation with each other. Their expressions did not appear positive and one of them being Nurse Shaw. She was in discussion with Nurse Robertson, spotted me then approached.

"James, a chair in one of my wards has broken and requires a replacement armrest. Can you take it to the storage room?"

"Yes, of course."

She led me into Ward D and I picked up the damaged armchair then took it along to the storage room. When I entered, other items of small damaged furniture had been placed to one side of the room. Roy had informed me that a firm in nearby Ardrishaig repaired any damaged furniture free of charge. A person called Angus, who due to his charitable work, received praise from Roy. The same person I encountered many years ago that mended his ways and started a family business. Now he also mends furniture for the local hospital. I put the damaged chair with other items, shut the door and walked back along the corridor. A lady with an infant girl came up to me.

Sorry to bother you, there is nobody at the reception desk. My little girl has scraped her leg."

"Hold on, I'll find a nurse." I walked further along the corridor and spotted Nurse Shaw. "Nurse!" I shouted.

She looked round and walked towards me.

"There is a young patient with a grazed leg near reception."

Nurse Shaw looked along the corridor. "Let's see how she is."

We walked to the mother and daughter. The little girl had long fair hair and wore a rusty-coloured coat. Nurse Shaw crouched down and examined the infant girl's leg.

"Does it hurt?"

The little girl nodded.

Nurse Shaw smiled. "Oh well, we better put on a bandage and make it better."

The infant girl smiled.

Nurse Shaw looked at her mother. "Just a flesh wound. I'll be right back with ointment and a bandage." She entered a nearby storeroom and returned with a first aid kit.

I noticed a chair in the corridor and brought it to Nurse Shaw.

She smiled at the girl. "What's your name?"

"Jennifer Jackson," she whispered, "and I'm four years old."

"If you sit on this chair, I'll make your leg better."

She perched herself on the chair.

"I'll return to my duties," I said.

"James, mention to Nurse Robertson I'll be ten minutes late."

The mother smiled at me. "Thank you."

"My pleasure." I walked away then stubbed my toe on a disjointed floor tile. "Ouch!"

The infant girl laughed.

Nurse Shaw looked round. "Not another patient!"

"Bye," said the infant girl.

Nurse Shaw said, "don't forget to tell Nurse Robertson."

"I won't forget." I limped along the corridor. This toe hurts.

"Casualty in the opposite direction."

I looked to the side. "Hi, how are you?"

"Better than you by the sight of that limp," said Adam Fraser.

"I stubbed my toe on a damn tile."

"At least it happened in the ideal place for treatment."

I laughed.

Adam frowned. "What's happened in America?"

"The stock market has crashed."

"That happened several months ago and the banks intervened to avert disaster."

How do you tell a businessman who is here to recover from illness that the world economy will enter a state of depression? "They will no doubt try again." However this time the banks will fail to halt the slide.

"You look as worried as I feel!"

"Don't be. You have to recover and return to a normal life."

"You're correct, we'll chat later." Adam headed for the lounge.

Nurse Maria Bradley approached me. "James, you listen to the radio, what is the latest about the stock market?"

"I'm on my way to find out."

"Let's both go."

We went into the rest room and found two doctors and Gabrielle had arrived there first. As they huddled around the radio, no sound apart from the male broadcaster through a crackle could be heard.

"What's the latest?" asked Maria.

Dr Grant-Owen looked at her. "A continuous fall. Down at least ten per cent on yesterday." He glanced at the clock on the wall and departed.

Maria stared at me. "Further stress-related cases could be imminent."

I nodded. And an influx of hospital staff needed to cope. This medical establishment is at present stretched to the limit.

Matron entered the room.

I whispered to Maria, "back to work."

"Me too," she whispered.

I continued my duties and finished a tiresome shift at six o'clock. I went for an evening meal in the hospital dining room then returned to my accommodation. Since I had no chair, the side of my bed sufficed. So much for items of additional furniture being provided! If I go along to the staff rest room, it may be filled with anxious people and conversations to match. I will venture outside the hospital for some respite.

When I left the hospital grounds, as a time-traveller I experienced external early evening darkness for the first time. My previous visits had been in late spring or summer months of the year. The dim sparse streetlights of Lochgilphead did not provide adequate artificial daylight. It is of no surprise why motor vehicle accidents remain a frequent occurrence at night. I walked along the street pavement with caution and considered an about turn. Then I spotted a licensed establishment with a bright light above a nameplate. I walked towards the Commercial Inn and upon my arrival, peered through the exterior window. Not much in the way of commerce – it's empty. I entered and went up to the polished wooden bar then looked around this compact outlet. Not much furniture, no other customers and no barman! Could it be self-service? That would be a novelty for 1929. Then a tall hairless man in a white collarless shirt, brown waistcoat and long white apron appeared from a rear room.

He smiled. "I was about to close."

"A quiet evening?"

He nodded his bald head. "Oh yes, and it's been like this for the previous three nights."

And for the foreseeable future. "Do you have 70/- ale?"

He laughed. "I've barrels of it in the cellar, how many do you want?"

I smiled. "Just a glass."

He went to a font on top of the bar, pulled on its wooden handle and poured my beer into a large glass. "That'll be five pennies, sir."

I pulled out several coins from my trouser pocket.

He laid the glass on the bar counter.

I gave him two threepenny pieces. "Keep the change."

"Thanks, sir." He pressed a metal lever on the till and a bell rang then the drawer opened. He put my two threepenny pieces into the till drawer. He turned round and smiled. "It still works."

I laughed. At least the pub has a barman with a sense of humour. I took a sip of my beer. Ugh! I've tasted better.

"Beer okay, sir?"

"Yes, fine thanks. Who brews the beer?"

"A company in Alloa. The delivery is once a fortnight. If business remains like this, every six weeks would suffice."

"What other licensed outlets exist in Lochgilphead?"

"There's a hotel further along the main street and another close by" The barman smiled. "Their beers don't taste as good as ours."

Must be bad. "What time do you close?" I sipped my beer and looked at the wooden clock on the brown-coloured wall.

He also looked at the clock. "No rush, sir, you have ten minutes."

"Have you been in the trade for long?"

"Eighteen years. After I finished my studies at Glasgow University, didn't know what to do. My mother bought me this pub and it has been my livelihood ever since."

"Do you enjoy it?"

"It has ups and downs. At least I will be in a job given the radio predictions."

I nodded. "Yes, grim."

He wiped the bar top with a white cloth.

"Does your mother stay in the town?"

"No, in Ardrishaig. The family has lived there for close on fifty years."

They may know of my family. "She must have met the Carsell-Browns?"

"Oh yes. In fact a relative married James Carsell-Brown."

My namesake.

"They live in America, New York."

Elizabeth. Does she still paint? In 1912 I was older than her, now she is the elder of us. "New York will be a place of anxiety and in particular, Wall Street."

The barman nodded.

I finished my beer and laid the empty glass on the bar.

"Another?"

"No, thanks."

"Have you just moved into the area?"

"Yes. I work at the hospital." I noticed the barman had viewed my jacket on several occasions. I touched my thin lapel. "This is from America, a present from my aunt."

"I haven't observed a jacket like it."

"Goodnight, hope tomorrow is busier."

"Me too, sir, goodnight."

I left the establishment and headed back to the hospital. As the temperature had dipped, I turned up my jacket collar. If I am to venture outside, I'll require a coat. I shivered then gazed up at the dark sky full of bright stars. Why me?

Saturday arrived and my first week at the hospital complete apart from one shift. Since Roy Stone would be on Sunday duty, I looked forward to that day. I do not anticipate an early morning rise on the Sabbath. However, Roy did state I would do the Sunday shift next weekend.

When I started my Saturday shift, Nurse Robertson asked me to visit the hospital chef. After a cordial handshake, he asked if I could assist in an administration capacity. I enquired what this involved and he smiled.

"Unload the delivery lorry and bring the boxes into the food store."

I unloaded the final box then our delivery driver gave me an itinerary note. I checked that it tallied with our new stock in the food store.

"Could you sign it?" He gave me a pencil.

I applied my name and returned his pencil.

He took it. "You're an efficient one, this is the first time it's been scrutinised!"

The delivery driver entered the lorry, started the engine and drove out of the hospital rear entrance. I went into the kitchen and handed the itinerary note to chef.

"Thanks." He glanced at the note. "You signed it!"

"Don't you check the delivery?"

Chef shook his head.

I returned to my normal duties and wheeled a patient from Ward C into the lounge. The room had become a popular spot for patients to meet and chat. The main topic of conversation being dramatic events in New York. Because of radio, news could be revealed to the public within a short period of time. The nurses would have passed on Wall Street updates to interested patients. I departed the busy lounge, entered the corridor and bumped into a young woman. She resembled the person admitted several days ago with a leg injury.

"Oh! Sorry," she said.

"No harm done. How is your leg?"

"I've been discharged."

"Safe journey."

She laughed. "I hope so."

"Bye."

"Bye." The young woman walked towards the hospital entrance.

Nurse Robertson approached me. "People come here to heal their injuries, not receive them."

I smiled and looked along the corridor. "Does she stay local?"

"Inveraray. Not far from where the accident happened. Evelyn is her name."

She looks familiar. I glanced at Nurse Robertson. "Must return to work."

Nurse Robertson nodded.

Roy had given me time off to visit a charity shop in Lochgilphead. He understood I required a coat for the inclement seasonal months ahead. A jacket would not be sufficient to combat the bitter cold winter gales and snow which lay ahead. I left the hospital and walked towards the main street. When I reached the charity shop, my legs ached.

I'm glad it's not the charity shop in Ardrishaig which is a longer distance! I entered the shop and observed several sectioned areas. One for ornaments and pictures, another with small items of furniture and my requirement – clothing. I browsed through the clothes on display but could not find any coat. The lady assistant came over to me with a warm friendly smile.

"Is there a particular item you want?"

"A coat. No particular type but one to keep me warm throughout the cold winter months."

"I may have what you require." The grey-haired lady went into a rear room and returned with a long black garment. "I believe this was once worn by a coachman."

Not me, I wore a red coat.

She held it against me. "It suits you."

"A local coachman?"

"Yes. A lady from Ardrishaig brought it into the shop."

"How long ago?"

"Last week. The coat may be around twenty years old but you wouldn't presume so. It looks like new!"

I studied the coat.

"That's an unusual jacket you have on?"

"A gift from America."

The lady smiled.

"How much for the coat?"

"You appear in need of this garment therefore it will cost a mere ten shillings."

I noticed a solitary hat to match the coat on a nearby shelf. "Could you include that hat?"

She looked towards it, nodded then picked it up.

I tried on the coat.

"A perfect fit." She flicked a bit of fluff from my left shoulder.

It's a good fit. "I'll take it."

She handed me the hat.

I put it on. "Also a good fit."

"Splendid. I have a second-hand gentleman's umbrella in the back room, how about that as well?"

246

"No, thanks." I hate carrying a brolly.

The lady went behind the small wooden counter.

I gave her a pound note.

"Do you want the garments wrapped?"

I looked out the shop window and then at her. "I'll keep them on."

"It does look bitter outside."

The lady gave me a ten-shilling note. "Thank you and good luck."

I departed the shop and walked back to the hospital. Since it is 1929, hats remain fashionable therefore my uneasiness to wear one will be tolerated. What did she mean by 'good luck'? However, back to the hospital and resume my Saturday afternoon duties. I went into my jacket pocket, looked around the immediate vicinity and brought out my wristwatch. I checked the time – 3.40pm. In my normal timeline it is half time in rugby and five minutes remain for football's first half. Will I ever experience normality again? I put the wristwatch back into my pocket, buttoned my coat and walked on. I came across a general store and entered to purchase personal essentials. After I left, it started to rain therefore my legs moved faster. As the rain became heavier, my hat and coat became wetter. Maybe I should have also purchased the brolly.

I entered the hospital and made haste for my room. After drying off, I went to the rest room for some Saturday early evening entertainment – at least there is a radio. To discover what programmes will be broadcast, I hope a current copy of the Radio Times exists. How I miss my wide-screen colour television and to make matters worse, not even a cinema for many a mile.

Chapter 9

Wind of Change

November's dark shadow fell upon Lochgilphead in this fateful year of 1929. The first Monday of this month heralded a stark reality in which people now found themselves. With recent events in New York's Wall Street highlighted and publicised, a gloomy economic forecast spread like a virus around the town. What happened in America would ultimately affect the local community. This despair made November more miserable than usual.

To avoid earlier rises and constant sensitive wet shaves, I let my face grow long and grew a beard. I won't take an electric razor for granted ever again. Nurse Robertson had mentioned that Adam Fraser would be discharged today. On my mid-morning break I went along to his ward. When I arrived, he had vacated the ward. A male patient came over to me.

"He's in the lounge – likes the view."

I walked along the corridor then into the lounge. I spotted Adam at the window and went over to speak with him. He turned around and smiled.

"It won't be long until I can experience this view from outside."

"Are you a hill-walker?"

"A former girlfriend and I often climbed those hills." He looked out the window.

"I heard that you were being discharged today."

Adam turned round. "You heard correct, however, the hospital can first serve me lunch."

Smart chap.

He whispered, "as I don't like to cook, the meal will keep me going till this evening."

He and I think alike.

"James, pop into the shop, there may be a painting you like." He nudged my arm. "Give you a discount."

"Okay, I'll pop along in a few days."

"Terrific." He shook my hand in the manner I would expect from a brother.

I left the room and resumed my porter's duties. This role had become a way of life. I settled into a weekly routine and enjoyed it, even though the pay remained non-existent! However, I am fed and have a warm room.

As mid-day approached, I returned from the operating theatre with a groggy patient and took him into a small recovery ward. Nurses took over and I left the vicinity. Whilst near reception, I spotted a familiar face. I recognised the person as Andrew, Angus's son who I met in 1912. I recall he had left school and started an apprenticeship within his father's firm. Will he remember me from our conversation seventeen years ago? With my new beard, probably not. Nevertheless, I shall keep out his way to avoid any chance of being recognised. I went into my pocket, took out my wristwatch and checked the time. Good, it's lunchtime therefore I will head for the rest room and turn on the radio. A few minutes later, Maria came in and sat down. She removed a shoe and rubbed her foot.

"This one aches."

"Too many long shifts."

"Not enough breaks."

I laughed.

She stared. "Has the price of razor blades increased?"

I smiled.

"Not sure if you suit a beard."

"Did someone attend to the chap in reception?"

"That's Andrew, he collects damaged furniture and fixes them for us." Maria smiled. "Free of charge."

I know.

Nurse Shaw rushed into the room. "Emergency! An attempted suicide."

Maria shoved her shoe back on.

I accompanied Nurse Shaw to the hospital entrance where the ambulance had halted. Two ambulance crewmembers lifted a man on a stretcher out of the vehicle then onto a trolley. The man appeared unconscious and blood seeped through the white cloth that covered him. Accompanied by Nurse Shaw, I wheeled the patient into an emergency room where Maria waited. As a doctor appeared, I departed and returned to the rest room. This can be a traumatic role at times. Having a business background does not prepare me for this type of medical emergency.

Two hours later, I went to the dining room and noticed Nurse Shaw alone at a table. She had removed her blue cap to reveal bobbed auburn-coloured hair. I received my mince and potatoes plus a cup of tea from the meal counter assistant then laid them on a wooden tray. I collected my silver cutlery, went over to her table and sat down.

"How are you?"

"I've been better."

"How is the patient admitted earlier?"

"In a serious condition." She shook her head. "In his early thirties."

"Terrible."

She lifted her cup of tea then took a sip.

"Does he stay in the town?"

"No, Ardrishaig." Nurse Shaw drank her tea and put the empty cup aside. "I gather he owns a pub in the village."

"It would not have much trade in this economic climate." I ate my lunch.

"He had been drinking and later shot himself."

I choked then coughed. I lifted my cup of tea and took a large sip.

"Sorry, James, I should have waited until you swallowed."

I cleared my throat and took another sip of tea. "It's okay." I laid my cup on the table.

Nurse Shaw leaned forward. "I suspect you're unfamiliar with hospital work."

I chewed and swallowed.

"Don't worry, you will become used to it."

I looked around the dining room. "A popular place for visitors."

"After the late morning visit, people tend to congregate here." She smiled. "The tea and biscuits are sold to visitors at a reasonable price."

"A source of income for the hospital."

Nurse Shaw sat back on her chair and sighed. "I feel we may receive more fatal admissions."

"It's a depressed time for all and we will have to endure it for decades."

She stared at me. "Can you tell the future?"

Careful. "Just what I have heard on the radio."

Nurse Shaw looked at the circular dark-wooden clock on the pale white wall. She reached for her cap and put it on.

"Back to my wards or Nurse Robertson will give me a rude stare." She rose and stared at my plate. "Does your mince taste okay?"

"I've tasted better."

"See you later. Oh, two volunteer nurses start on Monday."

As Nurse Shaw departed, I finished my lunch. I picked up my cup, drank some tea then laid it on the table. My cup of tea doesn't taste good either! I left the dining room and walked along the corridor. A lady and young boy waited at reception. The lady looked towards me and waved her black gloved hand. I stopped then walked towards her.

"Excuse me, my son has injured his leg."

My goodness! A younger Charlotte Carsell-Brown and with my great-uncle William.

"Are you all right? You appear dazed."

"It's been a hectic day." What a coincidence!

She smiled. "I take it the person on reception has also had a similar one."

I smiled and knocked on the reception door.

"I've tried – no answer."

"The lady will be at lunch."

"My son is in pain." Charlotte glanced at William.

"I will contact a nurse for you."

"Thank you."

I went along the corridor and noticed Nurse Robertson with a patient. I raised my hand to catch her attention. She spotted me and moments later came across.

"There is a lady with her teenage son at reception. He has injured his leg and appears in pain."

"I'll attend to them." She walked towards reception.

In a visit to 1938, I met Charlotte Carsell-Brown. At that period in time, I was clean-shaven. Because of my current facial growth, she did not recollect me nine years from now. Her photographic memory became legendary within our family however my beard prevented a possible future dilemma. A close unshave.

For the next few weeks, a steady stream of people with stress-related conditions were admitted to the hospital. I overheard Nurse Robertson comment that excessive alcohol could be a contributory factor and whisky being the main culprit. At least there had been no further admissions for someone who wanted to end their life. Two volunteer nurses lessened the workload and made life a tad easier for Maria and Nurse Shaw. Roy Stone revealed the two volunteer nurses, Isabel and Kate, had once worked at the hospital. Due to cost-cutting measures, they had been relieved of their duties. However as both ladies lived locally, they volunteered their professional medical expertise to assist the hospital. I did not recall them from my previous stay.

St Andrews Day drew closer and also the community of this small rural town. In the depths of financial hardship for many, I observed genuine warmth between its citizens. Not just family and friends would visit related patients in hospital but also other townsfolk. When visiting time ended, the nurses had to cajole and usher non-patients out of the wards. Being the bell-ringer for time-up made me an unpopular figure. No doubt the reason why Roy delegated this thrice-daily duty to me. From the wards, they would exit then congregate in the hospital dining room to blether with each other. Visitors served a dual purpose as they interrupted a patient's mundane spell in hospital and occupied an unemployed person who had time to kill. A practice which benefited the area's community amidst a difficult period of time.

At lunchtime, I forfeited my normal visit to the dining room and headed to Adam Fraser's shop in the town. Much as I like the dining room, it helps to break the usual routine. Also, his shop is a short distance from the hospital and today remains sunny although cold. The coat I purchased from a charity shop is warm and comfortable and without it, I would freeze. I arrived at the shop and entered the compact outlet. I shut the door and Adam appeared from a back room.

"James! Good to see you." He shook my hand. "Can I offer you a drink?"

"No, thanks, I don't drink until evening."

"Why is that?"

"One drink during the day has me sozzled!"

Adam laughed. "You won't fit in around here."

Spot on Adam, I can smell your breath. "How is business?"

"Just the usual."

I cast my gaze around the room. "A lot of picturesque scenes." I observed many of the local area.

Adam led me to a particular painting. "This is a favourite of mine."

I moved closer to the painting. It resembled a scene of Loch Fyne. The painting had a signature – L Traquair.

"Do you like it?"

I nodded. "The colours capture the loch's beauty. It must have been a sunny day."

"Yes, James, a beautiful day."

Adam left and went into the back room then returned with a piece of white paper. He handed it to me. I looked at the piece of paper – a poem that consisted of eight lines written with elegance. I read the poem then gave it back to him. He had love and affection for a certain lady.

"Thanks."

"I'll wager you won't sell the painting."

He smiled and nodded.

"What is the time, Adam?"

He looked at his brass pocket-watch. "Forty minutes past twelve."

"Better rush back or Roy will send Nurse Robertson or even worse, Matron to retrieve me."

Adam laughed and opened the exit door.

"Take care, I'll pop in again." I departed.

"Bye, James." Adam closed the door.

As I walked back to the hospital, my mind focused on that poem and Adam's demeanour. I would imagine the writer had been Adam's former girlfriend whom he had wanted to marry. Where have I seen that style of handwriting?

I arrived back in time to observe the 'congregation' of visitors leave the hospital grounds. Since they appeared happy, the tea must have improved. As a teenage girl wearing a red coat walked by, she dropped a white handkerchief. I picked it up of the tiled floor.

She put a hand into her coat pocket and stopped.

"Here it is."

The teenage girl with long black hair turned round.

I held the handkerchief in my hand.

She approached me, smiled and took it. "Thank you."

"My pleasure."

I carried on walking along the corridor and spotted Nurse Shaw looking at me from outside a ward.

"Always the gentleman."

"I try my best."

Nurse Shaw looked towards the hospital exit. "Nice girl, stays in Ardrishaig. She visits her mother's aunt once a week."

"She must enjoy a walk!"

"It's good exercise and it will take her mind of other matters."

"Other matters?"

"She lost her father in the war and Mrs Beaumont doesn't keep well."

Surely not. "Mrs Beaumont?"

"Yes, you just met her daughter – Olivia."

My great-aunt and I cross paths again.

Nurse Shaw smiled. "A penny for them."

I spotted Matron. "Back to work."

"Me too."

A new volunteer porter started in the hospital and this allowed me to have additional spare time. I would now only have to work five days per week instead of six. A local chap called Craig Hall had worked for a firm in the town which repaired small boats. Due to a lack of demand for this service, he had lost his job. As Craig could not find paid work within the district, he elected to participate in voluntary work. In the meantime, his family had to supplement limited benefit income with what little savings they possessed. This would now be the norm for people in a similar situation throughout the country. However, a kindred spirit existed in the area to combat individual family hardship. Relatives helped family members in whatever way possible and neighbours acted in a similar manner.

As St Andrew's Day fell on a Saturday, I would participate in a celebration to mark the occasion. The final day of November will be a joyful one – to heck with doom and gloom. No porter duty tomorrow and my monetary funds should allow me this infrequent pleasure. I am sure Adam would welcome a jovial drinking companion on the special night. I checked my wristwatch – fifteen minutes past two. I will visit his shop and find out if he is in agreement.

When I arrived at Adam's premises, the door was locked. I peered through the front window but did not witness any activity. I went to the rear and knocked on the door but no response. I turned the handle however this door had also been locked. I tried to look into a window but it was too high. I spotted a grey metal bucket and placed it against the wall beneath the window. I stepped onto the bucket and could now look inside a small room. What I witnessed disturbed me – a body lay slumped on the floor. I heard a noise behind me and turned round. A man with a sturdy physique and a curious expression stared at me.

"What are you up to?" he said.

"There has been an accident. I believe the shop owner has injured himself and both doors to the premises are locked. One of them must be forced open." I stepped off the bucket.

"You won't be able to, but I can." The man moved towards the door then moved back and prepared to ram it.

"Wait!"

He looked at me. "What's up?"

I pointed to a flowerpot on a narrow ridge above the door. "The vibration could topple it." I stepped onto the bucket, grabbed the flowerpot then stepped down. "On you go."

The man rammed the door but it remained closed. He wiped his brow then looked towards me.

"This time," he said.

"Go for it."

He took several steps back and a deep breath then threw himself against the door. There was a loud thud and the door burst wide open. I entered the property with apprehension and anxiety. A man's body lay face-up and motionless on a bloodstained floor. I knelt down beside Adam and checked his pulse.

"How is he?" said the man.

"Unconscious but still alive." I turned to face him. "Can you ask someone to telephone the hospital?"

"Will do." The man rushed out of the property.

It appeared Adam had attempted to take his life. Both wrists had been slashed and not just the floor was covered in blood but also his clothes. I observed a bloodstained razor on the floor beside Adam's right arm with its destructive blade wide-open. The man returned and took a deep breath.

"Phew! The ambulance is on its way."

"Thank you."

I found a small cushion and put it under Adam's head. I then took off my coat and spread it over his body in order to keep him warm.

The man walked to the door. "Here's the ambulance."

A vehicle screeched to a halt outside the shop followed by footsteps approaching the rear entrance. I looked round and two ambulance personnel entered the room with a stretcher. One of them examined Adam then nodded to his colleague. He gave me back my coat and I put it on. They lifted Adam onto the stretcher then took him to their ambulance. The vehicle sped off towards the hospital.

"At least it's no' far," said the man.

"Just as well."

He smiled and nodded.

I went to the damaged door and examined it.

"I can fix it for you, I'm a joiner to trade."

"Thanks."

"I'll get my tools, I just stay two minutes from here."

He departed and I surveyed the traumatic scene. A part-full bottle of whisky and an empty glass lay on a nearby table. A note had been placed next to the glass. I picked up the note and glanced over it. I also observed the painting he had mentioned on my recent visit. Adam had not replaced this item on the wall. The painting had been positioned against a chair in the rear room. Whilst staring at it, had he reminisced about the past? The man returned and fixed the damaged door. I offered to compensate him but he refused.

"Won't hear of it." He put his tools into a brown bag and departed.

I mopped the tiled floor and secured the premises. Before leaving, I replaced the flowerpot above the door.

After my arrival at the hospital, I contacted Nurse Robertson to enquire about Adam Fraser's state of health.

"He remains in a stable condition," she said, "I will let you know if there is any change."

"Thanks."

"He is fortunate you visited the shop at that particular time. Any later and his condition would not have been stable."

"Praise must go to the ambulance crew," I said, "they arrived in a jiffy."

Nurse Robertson smiled and nodded. She then looked towards the wall clock. "Visiting time will soon be over. I hope the new chap rings that bell louder than this morning. When we ushered the visitors out, they stated no bell had been rung."

That ruddy bell.

The bell rang and visitors emerged from each of the four wards. I spotted Olivia, my future great-aunt. She walked past Nurse Robertson then me and smiled.

"Do you know her?" said Nurse Robertson.

"On a recent visit, she dropped a handkerchief and I returned it to her."

"She has started going out with one of the Carsell-Brown boys. Whilst William attended casualty as an out-patient, Olivia visited her relative and their paths crossed." Nurse Robertson smiled. "Fate."

Maybe a handkerchief played a part in their fateful meeting.

On St Andrew's Night, I went to the public house visited several weeks ago. Let us hope the Commercial Inn's atmosphere has taken a turn for the better and its bar till can therefore ring on a regular basis. As I approached the outlet, loud cheers could be heard. I entered the noisy establishment and edged forward towards the wooden bar. The owner came forward with a wide smile.

"Three cheers for St Andrew!"

"I agree. I'll have a glass of pale ale."

From a font he poured the contents into a glass and pushed it in front of me.

"To you, sir, three pennies."

I gave him a shilling and picked up my glass. The barman put the silver coin into his till then gave me nine bronze pennies. I put them into my coat pocket, took a sip of ale then laid my glass on the bar.

"Excuse me, son," said a small man with white hair.

I moved sideways. "It's busy tonight!"

The man looked up at me. "A rare occurrence."

I cast my gaze around this small bar filled with locals. There would be around twenty-five men in the bar and not much spare room in which to stand. Tobacco smoke filled the bar and the smell evident. This would ensure my stay would not be a prolonged one. A chap who sat on one of the few wooden chairs stood up and started to play an accordion. People cheered and whistled to a melody of Scottish tunes. I finished my drink and this time ordered a bottle of ale. The draught ale I sampled was as vile as on my previous visit. The owner laid one on the bar and I gave him two pennies. At least a bottle is cheaper albeit only half the content. Maybe just as well given the taste. How I long for the taste of future draught beer – chemicals and all.

"Thanks," he said. He poured the bottle into a glass.

I lifted the glass and took a sip.

"Have you met my mother yet?"

I put down my glass on the bar and moved closer to him. "Did you say your mother?"

"Yes, Isabel," he shouted, "a nurse."

One of the volunteer nurses. "I will see her on Monday."

"Excuse me," said a tall man.

I moved away from the bar and listened to the accordion player. He had a full repertoire of songs, which he played with enthusiasm. I finished my drink, put the empty glass on a nearby table then left the premises. My ears rang and my coat smelled of tobacco. Not sure if I like the establishment when it is busy – the consequences can be negative. As the sound of music and laughter emanated from the establishment, I walked back to the hospital. The current economic downturn will bring unprecedented hardship for many people. A touch of light relief that customers experience tonight can provide a tonic, albeit temporary. Happy St Andrew celebrations.

Whilst on my Monday mid-morning break, a lady with silver hair under her nurse's cap came into the rest room.

"Hello," she said, "I'm Isabel."

"I'm James."

"Nice to meet you."

"I visited your son's pub on Saturday evening."

"Yes, he mentioned that to me."

"Very busy."

Isabel smiled. "About time too."

"How is Adam Fraser?"

"Better, he will be here for a while yet. Poor chap."

"Have you known him for some time?"

"Ever since he was engaged to my niece."

Elizabeth!

"Six months before the wedding, she called it off. I don't believe Adam has recovered."

From what I observed, he hadn't.

"Lucky for Adam you visited his shop."

Don't I know it.

"However, Elizabeth has also been scarred."

"What happened?"

"Her husband was shot and died in a Manhattan street."

Poor Elizabeth, and James. My namesake was a good and decent chap.

"You look shocked, are you okay?"

"What about your niece?"

"She is on her way back to Ardrishaig."

"Much different from New York."

Isabel nodded. "Are you going to the meeting tonight?"

"Meeting?"

"In the Town Hall at 7.30. The Local Authority will outline its plans for next year."

"That will be of interest to many people."

Isabel laughed then departed.

I completed my duties for the day, had an evening meal then went along to the meeting being held in Lochgilphead. Before I entered the hall, I read a public information notice on a corridor wall. It stated that local councillors from Labour, Liberal and Conservative would be in attendance. I observed the name of Alan Lambton who would represent the Conservatives. In time, he will become the local MP for this area and as I witnessed in 1938, had an egg thrown at him. Hopefully tonight's meeting will be less boisterous than that future public gathering. I went into the hall, spotted Isabel and found a seat beside her. I would estimate two hundred people, with the majority being middle-aged men and women. Whilst people waited for the meeting to start, conversation amongst groups of locals ensued. As three male councillors and a male chairperson walked onto the wooden stage, chatter in the packed hall diminished. They received polite applause from the local inhabitants. The chairperson introduced each of the guests and then sat down. The Labour councillor, John Douglas stood up and outlined plans for the following year. They included increased benefits for the unemployed, more rural houses built, an increase in widows' benefits and pensions plus higher compensation for car accident victims. Cheers of approval echoed from the floor. John Douglas then added that more funds would go towards Public Work projects in order to get short and long-term unemployed people back into work. Also people who do not seek work will not have their benefit cut. A louder cheer came from the floor. A well-dressed lady wearing a fur coat, black hat and gloves raised her hand.

"Yes?" said the chairperson.

She stood up. "Who is to pay for all those benefits? It cannot be the Government, they're broke!"

Several men and women voiced a polite agreement with the lady. The well-spoken lady then sat down on her creaky wooden chair.

John Douglas looked at the lady. "Some taxes will be increased."

"Can you enlighten us on what type of tax?" said the lady.

"Higher-earners and businesses."

The same people who had shown polite agreement now groaned. One of them, a gentleman in a dark blue overcoat, directed a comment at the Labour councillor.

"You are in power because of being first past the post. Is this how you treat professional people."

A lady beside him said, "Why should we subsidise layabouts who do not want to work?"

Boos and hisses came from non-professional and unemployed members of the audience. The chairperson asked for calm. The same lady addressed the Conservative member.

"What is your take on these plans, Mr Lambton?"

He straightened his tie. "It is unfair to impose a wealth tax on decent honest individuals who work hard and put in long hours to attain a certain credible standard of living. Those astute entrepreneurs may even employ people and thus give them an income that they would otherwise not have. This is helpful to the Government as it keeps down benefit costs. If Government expenditure is reduced then personal income tax will be less therefore more money available for each family."

I smiled. Eloquent as ever.

Isabel looked at me. "Why are you smiling?"

"I'll tell you later."

A man who sat two rows in front of me raised his hand and caught the chairperson's attention.

"Yes?" said the chairperson.

The man stood up. "I have a relative who stays in Germany. He told me that Britain and America gave Germany a large sum of money to help regenerate their economy. When Britain is at present in dire straits, how can we afford to hand out money to another country?" He sat down.

The Liberal representative said, "America gave Germany the money – not us."

Alan Lambton added, "it was a loan and Germany will have to repay it."

The man stood up. "I trust if another war breaks out then Germany will be on our side." He sat down.

Laughter came from sections of the audience. Alan Lambton had a wide grin on his face. Once more, he straightened his tie and looked at the man.

"I would expect that would be the case, a gentleman's agreement."

As the hilarity diminished, a young woman in the front row raised her dark blue gloved hand.

"Yes, miss?" said the chairperson.

"How can Germany pay back such a loan? Are they not also skint?"

Scattered applause came from the audience and silence from the guest speakers. When Adolf Hitler became German Chancellor in 1933, he ignored America's demands to repay the loan. No doubt spare German resources had been distributed to armament production.

"Excuse me." A dark-haired young man raised his hand.

The chairperson nodded.

"What is the Local Authority doing to promote this area?"

I observed blank expressions on each of the three councillors. The chairperson glanced at his three guest speakers then at the young man.

"Can you elaborate?" said the chairperson.

"Entice visitors to sample our area, we have a beautiful scenic location."

"We will look into that aspect," said the Labour councillor.

"Can you elaborate?" said the young man with a grin.

"I will get back to you on that question," said the Labour councillor.

I smiled.

"I will look forward to it," said the young man.

He made a valid point given the scenic countryside, shipping links and retailers in need of trade. An influx of visitors would be beneficial for all parties concerned.

The meeting ended thirty minutes earlier than the specified time and also on a quiet subdued note. On this occasion, no person threw an egg at any of the guests. Maybe because eggs had become a precious item and not for wasteful disposal! The meeting did not appear to raise people's hopes for a better future – only doubts. I bid Isabel farewell and walked in the hospital's direction. As I passed Adam Fraser's shop, I heard the sound of a faint crash. I looked in the front window – no activity. I walked round to the rear and heard someone run off. I spotted someone climb over a nearby wall then disappear. As he wore dark clothes and a cap to match, identification was difficult. I checked the back door and it remained secure. I noticed the pieces of a broken flowerpot scattered on the concrete surface. I looked upwards to an empty ridge above the rear door. When the intruder attempted to burst their way in, the vibration must have toppled the flowerpot onto the ground. It would have just missed the person's head. I picked up the broken pieces, put them into a nearby bucket then continued my walk back to the hospital.

As my shift did not commence until mid-day, I lay in bed for extra sleep. I woke up to a knock on the door and looked at my bedside clock – six-thirty. I stood up, made myself respectable then opened the door.

"James, I need you for the early morning shift."

"Now?" I yawned.

"Can I come in?"

I let Roy in and closed the door. He had a worried expression and put both hands into his overall pockets.

"What's up, Roy?"

"Our new volunteer porter has been relieved of his duties."

"Why?"

"Theft. Valuables and money disappeared from patient's belongings. Nurse Robertson caught him red-handed."

"Not good."

Roy nodded. "Can you start right away? I have to visit the local police station at Lochnell Street and make a statement."

"Yes, give me fifteen minutes."

"Terrific."

I opened the door. "Have all the valuables and money been recovered?"

Roy shook his head and closed the door.

I prepared for a re-arranged shift and left my accommodation still half-awake. Nurse Shaw approached and smiled.

"Back to the grind."

I nodded.

"He was caught last night."

"Early or late?"

"Around eight, when patients gathered in the lounge for an evening cup of tea. I believe Nurse Robertson had her suspicions and managed to catch him."

As a consequence of the economic depression, crime will increase to unprecedented levels – even in a hospital!

"Patients' personal items had vanished over the past week."

Glad I kept my door locked at all times.

"Other matters came to light."

"Oh?"

"Roy had warned him on several occasions about being late for work and not to take time off without permission. He went off duty two nights ago much to our annoyance. Craig told Roy he had visited a sick relative."

"What time?" The meeting at the Town Hall took place on that particular evening.

"Around nine-thirty. I spotted him enter the hospital and then informed Roy."

"Can you recall what he wore that evening?"

"Roy?"

"No, Craig."

"Dark jacket and trousers. Oh, and a black cap. Why?"

The person he had gone to visit was indeed unwell but in hospital – Adam Fraser. An ideal opportunity to rob someone's property.

"I also remember he had a limp."

As he made his escape over the wall, he must have fell and injured his leg.

"Back to work."

"How is Adam Fraser?"

"His condition has improved."

"Good."

"I have to transfer a patient to another ward."

"Lead on."

"This way."

After my morning shift had finished, I departed the hospital and headed for the main street. I required a woollen jumper to wear during the cold winter months. At times within the hospital, early December felt chilly. At least there had not been any major snowfalls in the area but they would no doubt soon arrive. The charity shop closed at one o'clock until two o'clock for lunch. This practice existed for all the town's shops and its two banks. As I approached the charity shop, a man brushed past me and I staggered.

"Sorry." He walked on.

I stared at him.

The stocky unshaven man moved towards a petite well-dressed lady then grabbed her black handbag. The man ran off and the lady shouted for help. I noticed Roy up ahead and as the thief ran past him, he put out a leg. The thief crashed onto the pavement and a couple of local men held him down. Two policemen soon appeared on the scene. The lady retrieved her handbag and glared down at the helpless robber. Roy walked over to where I stood.

"How is that for timing! I had just left the police station."

"I would say perfect."

"I've not seen him in the town, he must be an outsider."

"An outsider?"

"Strangers from the neighbouring areas – they come here to steal."

I looked towards the charity shop. "I need a jumper."

Roy smiled. "I understand – your quarters can sometimes be cold. See you later." He departed.

Sometimes? Most of the time! I entered the shop.

"Hello again," said the lady assistant, "wasn't that terrible!" She gazed out the window.

"Glad he was caught."

The lady shook her head. "It also happened last week, not what you expect around here."

"Changing times."

She shook her head. "No excuse for that kind of behaviour."

I better not get on her wrong side.

"What can I sell you this time?"

"A jumper to keep me warm."

She came from behind the counter, walked over to a pile of bags and from one of them, pulled out a bulky item.

"What about this?" She held up a knitted brown crewneck jumper.

"It looks fine."

She brought the jumper across and held it against my chest. "Perfect!"

"How much?"

"To you, one shilling."

"Thank you." Another bargain.

She wrapped the jumper in an old newspaper and gave it to me. I went into my trouser pocket, brought out a shilling and handed it to her.

"Does the coat keep out the elements?"

"Yes, an excellent garment "

"See you again some time." She smiled.

After leaving the shop, I put a hand inside my coat pocket to bring out my wristwatch and check the time. Where is it? I tried the other pocket – it's not there either! Drat, it must have been that thief. When he brushed against me, no doubt picked my pocket. However, the police apprehended him therefore my wristwatch should be in their possession. I will visit the police station tomorrow at lunchtime. I looked at the Town Hall clock – time to make haste for the hospital. Just five minutes until my shift resumes. I hope the police officers don't look to close at my wristwatch. Given that I purchased it as new in 1938, I could be asked questions which may be difficult to explain.

Since I had the previous Saturday evening off, this upcoming Saturday will confine me to porter duties. If only Roy would recruit another porter and free up more spare time for myself. However, I have tonight off and will venture along to the Commercial Inn. This first Friday evening in December was a chilly and frosty one. The pavements could be icy later tonight and therefore slippery. As a precaution, I will limit my intake of alcohol to avoid unsteadiness.

When I approached the outlet, no boisterous behaviour could be heard. I entered and walked up to the bar. I looked around and could count the customers on one hand. The barman smiled.

"Good evening, sir, a bottle of ale?"

"Could I have draught?"

The barman nodded, pulled on the font and poured my ale into a glass. "There you are, sir." He laid the full glass on the counter. "Four pennies please."

"Thanks." I gave him the money.

The barman put the coins into the till.

I lifted my glass. Not much of a froth on top. I took a sip then laid my glass on the bar counter. Oh for a lager.

"My cousin has arrived from America," said the barman, "she arrived yesterday."

"How is she?"

"Subdued."

"Her life has changed dramatically."

The barman nodded. "Manhattan is not Lochgilphead!"

And she has lost her husband. I lifted my glass and sipped some beer.

"It can be tough." He wiped the bar counter with a cloth.

Again I cast my gaze around the establishment. This place requires some kind of enticement to attract people. Last week I could not move in here – the music did lend to a joyful evening. A one-armed bandit machine in thirty years from now could attract additional customers. Thereafter draught Tennent's Lager to complement the selection of beers on offer. A pool table in the corner and a wall-mounted jukebox would also bring in extra revenue. I finished my beer and put the empty glass on the counter.

"Another one, sir?"

"No, thanks. Have you ever considered serving food?"

"Instead of beer?"

I smiled. "As well as beer."

"What kind of food?"

"Pie and beans. You may lure customers to come in at lunchtime."

"If business does not improve at lunchtime, I will open only in the evening."

"Try the pie and beans."

"Will do.

"Why not ask the accordion player to perform on Friday and Saturday evening?"

The barman nodded. "I need more customers therefore I'll try that as well."

I bid him farewell and left the outlet. As I headed back to the hospital, two men were a short distance in front of me. Both of them carried a black bag and walked with quick steps along the white frosty pavement. One of them slipped and his bag fell onto the ground. As it landed sideways, the contents fell out – items of silver gleamed under a nearby streetlight. The man crouched and put the goods back into his bag. Both men surveyed the vicinity, spotted me and dashed off. They slipped, fell and got up then fell again. As they eventually made off round a corner, I had to laugh. I returned to the Commercial Inn, used the owner's telephone and called the local police station. I gave a description of the two men and their last location – close to the police station! I thanked the owner and continued my journey back to Lochgilphead Hospital.

The next day, a police officer arrived at the hospital and asked to speak with me. Officer Urquhart explained that the two men I reported were apprehended close to a bank in Portaloch Street. As they had been caught with stolen valuables in their possession, both admitted to breaking into several houses within the local area. Fortunately, the stolen goods would be returned to their owners.

Officer Urquhart smiled. "Both burglars had bruises probably from several falls on slippery pavements. It slowed down their means of escape."

"Have there been many burglaries in the area?"

"As money becomes scarcer, this type of crime has increased and dark winter nights assist the burglars. There exists much hardship in the area, not just because of high unemployment but also cuts in benefit. Crime will not diminish within the foreseeable future."

I nodded.

"If you could come down to the station and complete a statement, sir."

"Sure."

"Thanks."

"I had an item of value stolen several days ago. The thief was apprehended for an additional crime."

"A bag-snatcher in the main street?"

"Yes."

"He had several valuables on him. At the station, you can identify which item belongs to you."

"Will do."

The officer left my quarters and headed for the hospital exit. I speculated on what police personnel in the station would have made of a wristwatch from 1938. As they have more important matters to deal with, perhaps nothing at all.

"I hope you're not in any trouble, James?" said Maria. She walked into my quarters.

"Not on this occasion."

Maria laughed.

"How is Adam Fraser?"

"Much better however he received a nasty scare."

"Any word of an additional porter?"

"When Roy interviews candidates from now on, he has been instructed to carry out background checks. Matron is adamant that no more undesirables will be in her wards!"

"I can understand her point of view."

"Catch you later." Marie departed.

Chapter 10

Licensed To Fail

The Burgess Hotel is one of three licensed hotels within Inveraray and according to its owner, the most prestigious. The hotel consists of fifteen bedrooms, public and lounge bars, a function suite and dining room. Due to the popularity of motor vehicle ownership after the war, a parking area now exists for guests next to the hotel. Tarmac and grey chipping stones cover the once muddy waste area. As guests approach the hotel frontage, they are met with a public bar entrance to the left and a lounge bar entrance on the right. Between them is the hotel's main doorway, which leads into a foyer complete with reception desk. The dining room and combined function suite entrance is situated at the hotel's rear. All bedrooms and bathrooms are situated on the upstairs floor. As a consequence of the adverse economic climate, this prestigious hotel has experienced a period of difficult trading conditions. Savage staff cutbacks have reduced costs but the future appears bleak for the hotel's very own existence. However, the other two hotels in the town face similar financial hardship.

A hotel employee stood behind the reception desk and flicked through a register book. Then, an elegant well-groomed lady in a beige coat, black hat, handbag and gloves entered the hotel. She walked up to reception and the hotel employee looked up.

"Can I help you?" said the employee.

"Do you by any chance serve coffee?"

"Coffee?"

The lady nodded. "Yes, coffee."

"I'll just check."

The employee went through to a back room and the lady cast her gaze around the immediate vicinity.

"Mr Burgess, there is a lady at reception."

A man in a jaded brown suit looked up from his desk and raised his grey eyebrows. "Oh?"

"She has asked for coffee."

"This is Scotland not America. Tell her we don't stock it."

The employee returned to reception and observed the lady stare at a painting on one of the reception walls. She turned round to face the young woman employee.

"A lovely painting."

"That is Loch Shira, not far from here."

The lady peered at the painting. "Is Evelyn a local painter?"

"I am Evelyn."

The lady turned around. "You painted this!"

The young woman smiled and nodded. "I paint in my spare time."

"You have a talent for someone so young. Why not paint all the time?"

"I need a regular income."

"Have you sold many paintings?"

"That is the only painting I have displayed."

"I like it."

The young woman smiled.

"How many paintings do you have?"

"Three, two local scenes and one of Loch Fyne."

"Does an art dealer exist in the area?"

"There is one in Lochgilphead but it doesn't do much business."

"They don't do much in New York either!"

"Is that where you come from?"

"I stayed there for seventeen years but I'm from Scotland."

"Are you here for the festive season?"

"Yes, and maybe longer."

The owner appeared from his office.

"Good morning," said the lady. That suit looks scruffy and too big, it hangs on him.

"Are you on holiday?" said the owner.

"Yes, for how long I'm not sure." He has not shaved.

The owner sneezed then returned to his office.

The lady whispered, "he requires a new suit."

The young woman smiled. "I'm sorry, we do not have any coffee but have excellent tea."

"Fine, a small pot will suffice."

"If you take a seat in the dining room, I will bring it to you."

"Thanks."

The lady went into the dining room and sat down at a table. She laid her handbag on the floor then took off her gloves. A short time later the young woman came into the room with a silver tray. She put the tray and its contents on the lady's table. She laid a silver pot of tea, small white jug of milk, white sugar bowl and matching cup and saucer onto the pale blue tablecloth.

"Teaspoon?" said the lady.

"Sorry, I'll bring you one."

The young woman departed and returned with a silver teaspoon. She handed it to the lady then flicked off a blonde hair from her short navy dress.

"Is this room ever used?" It's cold and dated.

"No."

"I trust you're the receptionist?"

"Yes, and more." The young woman smiled. "I carry out a variety of duties."

"You won't have time to paint."

"I can't complain – I have free accommodation and meals."

"You stay here?"

"Yes. I am an only child and my parents are dead."

"I see." The lady took off her small black hat and patted her short dark blonde hair. "Do many people visit the hotel?" She put her hat back on.

"Not as often as the owner would like. We don't receive many visitors and local people have a limited amount of money to spend. Most of our business comes from public bar income at the weekend."

"What about Christmas and Hogmanay celebrations? Christmas is two weeks on Wednesday."

"We have two festive functions arranged but nothing else for the foreseeable future."

"That's a pity."

"Do you stay in the town?"

"No, Ardrishaig."

"How did you travel?"

"I used the local motor coach."

"A regular service?"

"It depends on the weather. Many years ago, I stayed outside Ardrishaig. Our means of transport in and around the area was by a coach and two horses. I must admit, New York came as a shock with an abundance of automobiles, buses and trains."

"You must find it strange being back in Argyll?"

"In New York, technology is advanced. The telephone is a good example."

"In what way?"

"The transmitter and receiver are on one handset – it's less cumbersome. Also, you can contact the receiver direct."

"How?"

"The telephone has a device which allows you to dial their number." The lady smiled. "No need to speak with abrupt switchboard operators."

The young woman smiled. "Can I pour the tea for you?"

"I'll do it."

"I better return to the desk, the owner will start to prowl."

The lady laughed. "I understand, how old is he?"

"Thirty-eight."

He has gone grey before his time.

As the young woman departed, the lady poured tea from the small pot into a cup, added milk and used the teaspoon to stir. She lifted the cup, took a sip then looked around the lifeless dining room. No cutlery or crockery was displayed on any of the fifteen tables. Scratched wooden furniture had seen many better days. The dark blue carpet which covered the floor, appeared tatty and discoloured. The lady took another sip of tea then laid the half-empty cup on the saucer. She lifted her handbag off the floor, put on her gloves and went through to reception. Since nobody was there, she opened her handbag, brought out several coins and laid them on the reception desk then departed.

The lady caught the return motor coach from Inveraray to Lochgilphead. She searched for the outlet which dealt with art and eventually found it. The shop had a white exterior and a large glass window that was in desperate need of a clean. The lady observed several paintings in the window and went to enter the premises. As she tried to open the door, the brown handle would not turn. A small man in a grey jacket and cap with blue dungarees approached the shop.

"He's no' in," said the man.

The lady turned round.

"He's in the hospital, tried to kill himsel'."

"The owner?"

"Aye." The man shook his head then walked on.

The lady walked along Lochgilphead's main street to the nearest bank. She entered the Bank of Scotland premises and approached the counter. A male employee sat at a desk with his back to the counter and collated documents. The lady knocked three times on the wooden counter. The male employee looked round, rose from his chair and went to the counter.

"Can I help you, madam?"

"I would like to see the manager."

"What about?"

"Personal finance."

"I will check if he is available."

"Thanks."

"Your name?"

"Elizabeth Carsell-Brown."

The Burgess Hotel's owner sat in his office and opened a letter marked 'URGENT' then read it with apprehension. It came from his bank and did not raise hope for the establishment's future prospects. The hotel's overdraft facility would be suspended if Jeremy Burgess missed further payment deadlines. Due to lack of revenue, it would be difficult for him to comply with this assertive demand. His family had built and run the hotel for eighty-one years. It had been passed down from generation to generation and if the business failed, Jeremy faced humiliation. His family on three previous occasions had injected money into the business to stop it from going bust. This made Jeremy Burgess's position within his family shameful and intolerable. On a more personal note, two ex-wives accentuated his adverse situation. A rumour exists that after leaving the hotel one evening, he knocked down a young teenage girl then drove off. His alcohol intake had become excessive and Jeremy now lived on the edge. He did however recognise that Evelyn, a dedicated employee held the hotel together. This astute young woman of twenty-three mature years had become his saviour. Jeremy sat back on his black leather chair and sighed. He stood up and went to a wall-cupboard then opened the white double-doors. A bottle of whisky stored there had disappeared. He closed both doors then hurried to the reception desk.

"Evelyn!"

She turned round.

"What happened to the bottle of whisky in my cupboard?"

"You disposed of it, Mr Burgess."

"Threw it out!"

"The bottle was empty."

"Can you take one from the spirit cupboard?"

Evelyn pulled open a drawer under the reception desk and took out a key. She went downstairs to the cellar and opened a cupboard which contained tonic wine and spirits. Both commodities had become depleted due to cash-flow problems apart from a certain brand of the owner's favourite tipple. Evelyn lifted a bottle from a shelf, closed the door and locked it. She observed the two barrels of ale in a corner of the cellar.

Ale flowed from each barrel through a pipe up to the public and lounge bars. Since not much ale had been sold, the two barrels had remained static for weeks. When Evelyn arrived back at reception, Jeremy turned pages of the booking register.

"Nothing for next year?"

"The other two hotels will be in the same situation." Evelyn handed over a bottle of Grouse whisky.

He took it. "How busy was the lounge bar last weekend?"

"Seven people on Friday evening and six on Saturday evening."

Jeremy shook his head.

"They are regulars."

"Did they spend much?"

"It amounted to a couple of drinks for each customer."

"Close the lounge altogether, it will cut our heating bill."

The hotel doesn't pay bills.

"We'll just keep the public bar open."

"They may not want to drink in the public bar."

"What's wrong with the public bar?"

"Men use offensive language therefore it's not suitable for couples who are our weekend customers."

"Then they will have to become used to it."

"They may go elsewhere."

"Too bad."

"Do you want the lounge stock transferred to the public bar."

"Why do that?"

"It will save you a spirit order for next week."

The owner smiled. "Yes, Evelyn."

"Will I ask Iain to disconnect the lounge barrel and connect it to the second public beer pipe?"

The owner nodded. "What time is he due in?"

"He starts at seven-thirty."

"Fine." The hotel owner picked up a poster on the reception desk and studied it.

"I'll put it up in the public bar to advertise the Christmas and Hogmanay functions."

Jeremy handed the poster to Evelyn then went into his office and closed the door. Evelyn laid the poster on her desk. She picked up four brass tacks, the poster and went into the public bar to find a suitable site. Jeremy picked up the black candlestick-style telephone from his desk. He removed the small circular receiver with his right hand and then placed it against his right ear. He put the voice transmitter speaker close to his mouth.

"Can I help you?" said the operator.

"Argyll 343." He sighed.

"Hold on, I will connect you."

"Hello?" said a voice.

"Jack?"

"Is that you Jeremy?"

"Yes, about our conversation at my house last week."

"What about it?"

"Hold on."

Jeremy laid the telephone arm and receiver on his desk then went to the door. He opened it, looked around then closed it. He returned to his desk and picked up the receiver. He placed it against his ear and spoke into the voice transmitter speaker.

"Still there?"

"What's up?"

"I've been going over what we spoke about."

"And?"

"The receptionist has a bedroom in the hotel."

"So?"

"She may get caught up in the blaze."

"Do you want me to set fire to the building or not? It's the only way out for you."

"I am aware of that but do not want the young woman harmed."

"You can't have your cake and eat it!"

"Give me a couple of days."

"The second day of January is not far away, be quick or find someone else."

As the line went dead, Jeremy put the receiver back into the arm. Then came a knock on the door and he rose from his chair to answer it.

"That's the poster up in the bar Mr Burgess. I've put it where everyone can view it."

"Thanks, Evelyn."

"Can I take my break now? It's early but I've finished my duties and the weather is sunny outside."

"Are you going out to paint?"

Evelyn smiled.

Jeremy nodded.

"Thanks."

As Evelyn departed, Jeremy went to the wall-cupboard and opened the doors. He pulled out the bottle of whisky and an empty unwashed crystal glass. He took off the bottle cap, poured a full glass of whisky then drank it.

At lunchtime, I sat in the hospital dining room and read Saturday's Daily Express. Being the weekend, children's voices could be heard loud and clear. Maria came into the dining room and spotted me. She collected her silver cutlery, a plate of mince, potatoes, and peas plus a cup of tea. Maria put them on a white tray, walked over to the table and sat opposite me.

"Any good news?" said Maria.

I shook my head. "Not in today's edition."

Maria glanced around the dining room. "You can hear excitement in the children's voices."

"Less than ten days to Christmas."

"Could you pass me the salt please?"

I reached across the table and handed the salt dish to Maria.

"Thanks." She took the small white holder, sprinkled it over her food then placed it on the white tablecloth.

"You take a lot of salt!"

"The salt gives the mince a credible taste." She smiled.

I looked around the room. "Whenever children visit, they appear well-behaved."

"Around here, parents can be strict with their children."

"I have noticed."

"Any plans for Christmas?"

I laid my newspaper down on the table. "Just Christmas Day off therefore not enough time to visit my family in Edinburgh."

"That's a pity."

"Since Roy has been unable to recruit another porter, spare time is now in short supply."

An infant child left his mother and came across to Maria. Then the boy looked at me in an inquisitive manner.

"Are you the ghostly coachman?" said the boy.

"No, I'm the ghostly porter!"

Maria laughed.

The boy laughed then returned to his mother.

She smiled.

"Ghostly coachman?" I looked at Maria.

Maria put down her knife and fork, lifted the cup of tea and took a sip. "There is a Victorian property outside Ardrishaig. A legend exists that the former coachman who disappeared, now reappears on particular nights to haunt its coach house."

I smiled. "Is this for real?"

"As children, the current owner's two sons started the rumour."

"How long has the rumour existed?" As if I didn't know.

Maria took another sip of tea. "About thirty years."

Thirty-three. I first vanished in 1896.

Maria laid her cup on the table.

"Why did the boy come over to me?"

"You are the sole male in the dining room."

Or maybe the boy is a future psychic!

"Do you like our Christmas tree?"

"When you enter the hospital, it strikes you. Who supplied the tree?"

"It is a gift from Lady Beaumont."

"Admirable."

"She lives in Ardrishaig."

I have been in her large house on many occasions, albeit thirty-three years ago. "That is a kind gesture, it's an impressive tree."

"I would say twelve feet."

"Does she supply it every year?"

"Since 1914."

"When the war started."

"Her only son died in that terrible conflict."

Edward, Olivia's father. How he enjoyed our conversations about Edinburgh in the nineteenth century. Just as well my history knowledge for that particular period did not desert me.

"You appear as if you're in another world."

"No, another time!"

Maria laughed.

"Are you working on Christmas Day?"

"Yes, but off on New Year's Day. What about you?"

"Roy is working over Christmas and I have the New Year shift."

"Lucky you, I prefer to have Christmas off."

I looked at the wall clock. "Time to resume my duties."

"Oh, Adam Fraser is being discharged today."

"I'll pay him a visit."

"Can I have your newspaper?"

I gave the newspaper to Maria. "See you later."

"Bye."

As I left, Maria ate her meal. Since Adam Fraser would soon be discharged, I entered his ward for a quick chat.

"Hello James, I'm off once more."

"How do you feel?"

"A lot better. That will not happen again. I feel such a fool."

"I'll call into the shop."

"Yes, please do."

We shook hands, Adam departed and walked along the corridor to the hospital exit door.

"He's a lucky man," said an elderly patient.

I nodded.

"At least now he will be aware of it."

"Let us hope so."

"Can you take me into the lounge, son?"

"Sure."

I assisted the patient into a wheelchair then took him to his desired location. As the weather remained bright and sunny, other patients had gathered in this room. When I left, Isabel spotted me in the corridor.

"Adam appears less tense," she said.

"I will visit him in a few days."

"The hospital should appoint a person to counsel patients who have suffered depression."

A commendable solution. "I agree."

"Do you have any plans for Christmas?"

I shook my head. "What about yourself?"

"My niece and I will celebrate Christmas together. Her parents, my sister and brother-in-law have passed on therefore it's just the two of us."

"At least you're not on duty."

"When I started my volunteer shifts, I made that clear."

I laughed.

Isabel whispered, "here comes Matron.

"Back to work."

"See you later."

On a dull December afternoon, Jeremy Burgess drove to his bank in Lochgilphead. A stern letter from the manager had prompted him to make an appointment and discuss the future of his hotel. He parked his vehicle outside the Bank of Scotland building and entered the premises. A lady seated behind the polished wooden counter looked up and smiled.

"I have an appointment with Mr Macdonald."

"Your name, sir?"

"Jeremy Burgess."

"What time was the appointment for, sir?"

"Two o'clock."

The lady looked at the clock on the wall. "Hold on, I will check if Mr Macdonald is free." She approached an office door, knocked on it then entered.

Jeremy glanced at the clock. Damn, ten minutes late.

The lady returned to the counter and lifted a hatch. "He will see you now, Mr Burgess."

Jeremy walked through the passageway to Mr Macdonald's office and knocked on the door. He took a deep breath.

"Come in."

Jeremy entered and took off his hat.

"Have a seat, Mr Burgess," said Mr Macdonald.

Jeremy sat down on a wooden chair then coughed several times.

This is a cold office, I'll keep my overcoat on.

"Would you like a glass of water?"

Jeremy shook his head. "No." My hand will shake.

Mr Macdonald sat back on his chair, took off his brass horn-rimmed spectacles and cleaned them with his white handkerchief. "You are ten minutes late."

"My apologies. I had to wait until my receptionist returned from lunch."

"Does she take a late lunch?" Mr Macdonald put his spectacles back onto his bald head then shoved the handkerchief into his grey-suited trouser pocket.

Jeremy nodded.

"Very well." Mr Macdonald studied the white printed document on his desk then looked at his client. "It doesn't make for good reading, Mr Burgess."

Jeremy tightened his clasped grip. "I have cut back on staff as much as possible. The receptionist carries out a variety of roles. One of the bars has been closed and we no longer use a stocktaker to calculate our trading account."

"Who undertakes the stocktaking?"

"The receptionist."

"Do you work as hard as the receptionist, Mr Burgess?"

"I do whatever is required."

Mr Macdonald sat upright on his black leather chair. "Unless turnover increases, you will not have a hotel. You are well behind on your overdraft payments."

"The hotel has functions organised for the festive season and these will generate income."

"What about next year?"

"Myself and the receptionist will work on that."

"Have you any rooms booked for next year?"

"One." Evelyn's accommodation.

"How do you promote the hotel?"

"Word of mouth."

"You will have to devise other ways, word of mouth is not enough."

"The receptionist has designed a poster for the hotel. I will use this to publicise my establishment."

Mr Macdonald sighed. "It's a start however more must be done."

He reminds me of my maths schoolteacher.

"Your receptionist appears an astute person – pick her brains. She may have other ideas."

Jeremy nodded.

Mr Macdonald stood up. "We shall talk again later – after New Year."

Jeremy stood up. "Fine."

"What is the name of your receptionist?"

"Evelyn White."

"A valuable asset to your business."

Jeremy nodded then sneezed.

Mr Macdonald led his beleaguered client to the door and shook his clammy hand. When Jeremy left the building, he took a long deep breath and put on his hat.

"Miss Guthrie, can you bring me the files for the town's other two hotels?"

"Will do, Mr Macdonald. Right now?"

"Yes, please." Mr Macdonald returned to his office.

Jeremy Burgess entered his vehicle, started the engine and drove off. He headed back to the hotel and upon his arrival, parked his black Ford four-door saloon in the designated area for guests. He got out, slammed the driver's door then entered the hotel. The receptionist looked up from her desk.

"Mr Burgess?"

"Yes?"

"Have additional staff been hired for the Christmas and Hogmanay functions?"

The hotel owner shook his head. "Can you arrange it?"

"I will contact the local Unemployment Office."

"Thanks."

Jeremy sneezed twice then went into his office. Evelyn followed and sat next to the telephone. She removed the small circular receiver with her left hand and then placed it against her left ear. She moved her head close to the voice transmitter.

"Yes?" said the operator.

"Argyll 250, please."

"Hold on, I will connect you."

"Thank you."

"Hello?" said a male voice.

"This is the Burgess Hotel Inveraray, we require temporary bar staff."

"How many?"

Evelyn looked at Mr Burgess. "Four?"

Mr Burgess shook his head.

"Three?"

He shook his head.

"Two," said Evelyn.

"I will send four and you can choose two that will be suited for the role."

"Thank you. Can you send them right away?"

"I'll do my best. If not then tomorrow."

"Goodbye."

"Goodbye."

Evelyn replaced the receiver back into the arm then looked at Mr Burgess. "The candidates will be here today or tomorrow."

"Good."

"Would you like me to contact the local Rotary Club?"

"Rotary Club?"

"We could invite them to use the function suite for their monthly meeting and supply snacks along with refreshments."

"They use a specified venue."

"The Town Hall does not supply alcohol. The Rotary Club Secretary is in the public bar on a Friday evening therefore I could have a word with him."

"Okay."

"It's worth a try." Evelyn returned to the reception desk.

The next morning, a man entered the hotel and walked up to reception. Evelyn put down her pencil and closed the ledger book. The man appeared unshaven and his grey coat had a stain on the lapel.

"I've come aboot the job."

"Your name, sir?" His breath smells of alcohol. Evelyn picked up a piece of white paper and her pencil.

"Frank."

"Have you any experience of bar work?"

"Yeh, my last job."

"Where did you work?"

"The Grey Gull in Ardrishaig."

"How long ago?" Evelyn wrote on the piece of paper.

"A while back."

"How long back?"

"Aboot two years, I think."

"Why did you leave?"

"A disagreement with the owner. He accused me of stealin' whisky."

"Did you?"

"I borrowed some bottles but was goin' to pay for them later."

"How much whisky did you borrow?"

"Just one case."

"How many bottles did the case contain?"

"Twelve."

"I will contact the Unemployment Office and they can inform you of our decision."

"Is the job mine?"

"Other candidates have still to be interviewed."

"Okay, see ya."

As the man left the hotel, Evelyn crumpled up the piece of paper. She threw it into a small wastepaper basket under the reception desk.

"Mornin'," said a male voice.

Evelyn looked up. "I did not hear you enter the hotel."

The man smiled. "I once worked as a cat burglar."

Evelyn laughed.

"I've come about the vacant job."

"What recent work have you done?" Evelyn picked up another piece of writing paper and laid it on top of the reception desk.

"I haven't worked for three years."

"Why not?"

"I've been inside."

"Inside?"

"Yes, prison."

"The hotel will contact the Unemployment Office and they can inform you of our decision."

"Bye."

When the man departed, Evelyn put the unwritten piece of paper aside. She heard the entrance door open and a well-dressed middle-aged man walked up to reception. He was clean-shaven and sported a black hat and coat.

"Good morning," said Evelyn.

The man removed his hat. "I have come about the vacant position."

Evelyn reached for the piece of paper and picked up her pencil. "Your name, sir?"

"Charles McSorley."

Evelyn wrote his name on the piece of paper.

"Any relevant bar experience?"

"I once owned three pubs and also assisted with bar work."

"Once?"

"I sold my pubs to a brewery."

"Why do you want this job?"

"I miss the banter with customers." He smiled. "Because I enjoy bar work and comfortably off, you do not have to pay me."

"The role is just for the festive season."

"That is fine. I can give you my residential telephone number in order to contact me."

"I will contact the Unemployment Office."

"I have not been sent by them – I am not registered."

How did you learn of this vacancy?"

"Word of mouth my dear – the quickest form of communication!"

Evelyn smiled. "Your number?"

"Argyll 285."

Evelyn wrote it on the piece of paper and looked up. "Thank you."

"My pleasure." The gentleman put on his hat and walked out of the hotel.

Evelyn then attended to clerical duties at her desk. She heard a person sneeze and looked up. A boy approached the reception desk. He took off his blue cap and smiled.

"Can I help you?" said Evelyn.

"Hi, I've come about the vacant job."

"How old are you?"

"Almost sixteen."

"You are too young for bar work."

"Are there any other tasks I could do around the hotel, it's big enough. I can do book-keeping and other clerical duties."

Evelyn smiled. "That is what I do."

"If I did them, you would have time to carry out urgent duties that may arise."

Persistent.

"I am a hard worker."

"Are you sure?"

The teenage boy nodded. "Since last September, I have been at college. When I'm older, I want to run and own a hotel. If you let me work here then I can gain valuable experience."

He's astute for a sixteen-year-old. "What do you study at college?"

"Accountancy and Business Management."

"What about your course?"

"I'm on holiday for four weeks. I do not return to college till mid-January."

"The owner can only pay for bar employees."

"Are you not the owner?"

"No, I am the receptionist."

"Can I please speak to the owner?"

"He is busy and has delegated this task to me." Who does this upstart think he is!

"I am prepared to undertake work on a voluntary basis. I have come a fair distance, just outside Ardrishaig."

Admirable.

"You're not old enough to serve alcohol but if any other hotel duties arise that could be appropriate, I will contact you."

"Great!" The teenager went into his blue jacket pocket, pulled out a small white card and gave it to Evelyn. "My name, list of qualifications and telephone number."

"Your parent's telephone number?"

"Yes."

Evelyn laid the card on the desk. "If anything does arise, I will be in touch."

"Promise?"

Evelyn nodded.

The teenage boy put on his cap. "Thank you."

Evelyn smiled.

As the teenager left the hotel, Evelyn noticed he had a slight limp. She picked up her pencil and ticked the boy's card. She opened a drawer underneath her desk and placed the card into it.

"Good morning," said a petite well-groomed middle-aged woman.

Evelyn looked up. "Good morning, can I help you?" She laid her pencil on the desk.

"I have come about the job vacancy."

"The bar vacancy?" Surely not.

"Yes." The lady nodded.

"Have you done bar work in the past?"

"Oh yes, my father worked for a brewery in Glasgow and ran one of their pubs. I assisted him in the evening."

"Which part of Glasgow?"

"The West End, the bar was in Byres Road."

"What did you do in the bar?"

"Pamper the customers then serve them."

Evelyn smiled. "Our customers may be different from those in Glasgow's West End."

"Believe me, they will be no different. Some need a shoulder to cry on, others require a refuge and the remainder enjoy a good swally!"

Evelyn laughed.

"I can put more business the hotel's way."

"Oh?"

"My brother is Secretary for the local golf club and I am on the committee of Inveraray and District Bowling Club." The woman smiled.

"Why do you want the job?"

"I miss the banter with customers."

"It is part-time over the festive period."

"That's fine."

"Can you give me a name and telephone number?" Evelyn grabbed a sheet of paper and picked up her pencil.

"Vivien Daly. My number is Argyll 094."

Evelyn wrote down the woman's details on the sheet of paper. "I'll be in touch."

"Thank you."

As the job candidate departed, Evelyn wrote golf and bowling club next to the woman's name.

"I forgot to mention."

Evelyn looked up.

"My uncle is President of Inveraray and District Rotary Club."

Evelyn smiled.

"See you later."

When Vivien Daly departed, the rear office door opened and Jeremy Burgess emerged. A strong smell of whisky infiltrated the reception area.

"Any good candidates?" He sneezed.

"Two who would benefit the hotel." Evelyn laid down two sheets of paper. "Those two."

Jeremy picked up both sheets and looked at them. "One is a woman!"

"They are the best candidates so far."

"Okay, we'll go with those two."

"A teenage boy came to enquire about the vacancy."

"A teenager?"

"Yes."

"Too young."

"He enquired about possible voluntary work."

"He must be keen!"

Evelyn smiled then opened her desk drawer. "He left a card." She took the card out of t the drawer and handed it to Jeremy.

He took the card and read it. "William Carsell-Brown." Jeremy shook his head and gave the card back to Evelyn.

"Do you want me to contact the two successful candidates this afternoon?"

"Let them wait a bit, leave it until tomorrow."

Another well-groomed woman entered the hotel and approached reception. The owner gazed at her.

"Good morning, madam, nice to see you again," said Evelyn.

"Morning coffee?" said Elizabeth.

"It is still morning tea," said Evelyn.

"Good morning," said the owner. He coughed then went into his office.

"Can I have a seat in the lounge?" said Elizabeth.

"The lounge will be cold, it has been closed for business."

"Then I will settle for the same as before." It is also cold.

Elizabeth went into the dining room, sat down at a bare scratched wooden table and looked around the drab vicinity. She removed her black gloves then placed them on a nearby chair. She laid her black handbag on the floor then opened the buttons of her red overcoat. Evelyn appeared with a white tablecloth and spread it over the table then smoothed the cloth with both hands.

"Thank you," said Elizabeth.

"Back soon."

When Evelyn departed, Elizabeth lifted the handbag and put it on her lap. She opened it, brought out a small mirror and looked into it. She rolled her tongue round both lips then put the mirror back into her handbag. Evelyn came into the room with a tray and laid it on Elizabeth's table. She lifted the matching blue and white crockery and silver teaspoon onto the table.

"Would you like me to pour?"

"Please."

Evelyn poured from the small silver teapot into the cup.

"That's fine, thanks."

Evelyn lifted a plate of ginger snap biscuits from the tray.

"I've not had those for a while!"

"Do you like them? If not there are digestive biscuits."

"Which type?"

"Plain."

"The ginger snaps will suffice." Elizabeth shivered. "Has the heating been turned off in here as well?"

"We put it on at certain times of the day. The public bar is worse!"

"I hate to imagine what it must be like, I'll keep my hat on." Elizabeth glanced around the room. "Does the hotel have a cleaner?"

"She is off sick. Mr Burgess asked if I could carry out her duties."

"I trust you refused."

"I suggested we contact the Unemployment Office for a replacement cleaner."

"And?"

"He made no comment."

Elizabeth lifted her cup of tea and sipped it. "I need more milk." She laid her cup onto the saucer.

"I will be right back."

As Evelyn left the room, Elizabeth leaned forward to the next table and wiped her finger over the top then flicked off dust. Evelyn returned with a small silver jug of milk and laid it on Elizabeth's table.

"Thanks."

Elizabeth poured milk into her cup, put the jug aside, lifted her cup and took a sip.

Evelyn smiled.

Elizabeth took another sip. "Do you expect many to attend the festive events?"

"I hope so."

"Have you distributed any leaflets or advertised in the press?"

"The owner is reluctant to spend money – even to publicise the hotel!"

"A recipe for failure."

Evelyn nodded.

"Have you painted recently?"

"A bit, however I don't have the time. Perhaps after next month, the hotel will be less busy."

"Less busy!"

Evelyn laughed.

"Do you have a boyfriend?"

Evelyn nodded.

"Have you known him for long?"

"We met last Christmas."

"How romantic."

Evelyn smiled.

"What age is he?"

"Twenty-nine."

"What does he do?"

She is inquisitive. "A pharmacist."

"Where does he work?"

"Glasgow, in Duke Street close to the centre. The company supplies him with accommodation."

"Lucky him!"

"He enjoys the city's vibrant atmosphere."

293

"Does he come to visit at weekends?"

"Sometimes, I have to work most weekends. His family stay in Lochgilphead therefore when he visits them, we meet up."

"I trust he does not use the motor coach? It would take an eternity from Glasgow."

Evelyn laughed.

Elizabeth laid her cup on the saucer. "Time to brave the elements once more."

Evelyn glanced out the window. "The sun is shining."

Elizabeth put on her gloves. "Yes but it's cold. It won't be long 'til the snow arrives."

"Were the winters in New York severe?"

"Just as cold as here with plenty of snow." Elizabeth reached for her handbag, opened it then took out a black purse. "Here you are." She opened the purse, took out a silver florin then handed it to Evelyn.

She took it. "I will bring you the change."

Elizabeth placed her handbag on the table. "Don't bother, the hotel needs the cash."

Evelyn nodded.

Elizabeth looked around the function suite. "How often is the room used?"

"Not often, our functions are few and far between."

"Why not turn it into a billiards room?"

"Billiards?"

"Yes, the British army soldiers enjoy a game of billiards. Due to its popularity in New York, competitions take place between districts."

Evelyn looked around the function suite. "Interesting."

"There must be a number of ex-soldiers in the district."

"Yes, there are."

"All you need is a cloth-base table with six pockets and a couple of cues. A nominal price could be charged for each game."

"And we could sell beer to the players."

"The hotel will therefore make use of an empty room and bring in much-needed revenue."

Evelyn smiled. "I like that idea."

"As it becomes popular, more people will participate. The recreation is popular throughout America."

"I will put the idea to Mr Burgess."

"Don't tell him the idea came from me, you take the credit." Elizabeth buttoned up her coat, stood up and lifted her handbag. "We must meet for a painting session."

"I would like that."

"When you won't be busy."

Evelyn laughed.

"Time to catch the motor coach home, see you later."

"I will look forward to it." Evelyn glanced out of a window. "It's dark, maybe the snow is about to fall."

Elizabeth adjusted her hat. "It won't compare to New York."

Evelyn laughed.

As Elizabeth departed the function suite, Evelyn put the used crockery, teapot and milk jug onto the wooden tray. She went into the hotel kitchen and laid the tray on a tabletop. Jeremy Burgess came into the kitchen and washed a whisky glass. He turned the glass upside-down then laid it beside the cracked white marble sink.

Evelyn gave Mr Burgess a florin. "For the tea and biscuits."

"Thanks." He shoved the silver coin into his trouser pocket.

Similar to when he empties the bar till at the end of each evening.

Later that day, Evelyn heard a knock on the door of her room. She put down her novel to answer the door. When she operand it, Mr Burgess stood with a solemn expression.

"Iain has not yet appeared. Can you stand in for him?"

"This is the third time in two weeks."

"I will speak to him about his poor timekeeping."

"Give me five minutes."

"Thanks."

Evelyn closed the door, went to her wooden wardrobe and brought out a casual black dress. She changed into it, applied red lipstick and looked at her bedside clock. As opening time approached, she vacated her room, locked the door and rushed downstairs. When she arrived at the bar, Iain had turned up for his shift. He was in the process of adding a liquid to the part-full bottles of whisky and gin.

"What are you doing!" Evelyn cried.

Iain looked round.

"You can't do that!"

"Mr Burgess told me to."

"How long have you been doing this?"

"Six months."

Evelyn shook her head. "This could be a reason why customers have deserted the hotel bars."

Iain placed a full bottle of diluted whisky on the counter then put on the cap. "Customers can't tell the difference."

"What if a Customs and Excise Officer arrives to test the spirits? The hotel could lose its license to sell alcohol."

Mr Burgess walked into the bar. "You can return to your room, Evelyn."

When Evelyn departed, the owner went to the bar entrance door and unlocked it. He returned to the bar counter and handed over the key to Iain. He went upstairs to Evelyn's room, took a deep breath then knocked on her door. When it opened, the owner was met with an icy stare.

"I'm sorry you had to witness what Iain has been doing. It's not his fault – I gave him instructions to water the whisky."

"The hotel could lose its license."

"I am aware of that but I have to reduce costs."

"I understand the situation appears grim, Mr Burgess, but to cheat customers is unfair. Where would you be without them?"

The owner hung his head. "I will instruct Iain to stop the practice."

Evelyn crossed her arms. "Can I make a suggestion?"

Mr Burgess stared at Evelyn.

"Iain spruces up his appearance. The white shirt he has on is filthy."

"I'll speak to him and insist that when behind the bar, he must wear a clean shirt."

Evelyn smiled. "A tie would not go amiss either."

"I agree."

"I will see you tomorrow morning, Mr Burgess."

He nodded.

After Evelyn closed her room door, the owner took another deep breath. He went downstairs to his office then shut the door behind him. Jeremy walked over to the wooden cupboard, opened both doors and took out his bottle of whisky plus a glass. He removed the bottle cap, poured a full glass and laid the bottle on his desk. Jeremy took a large swig then stared into his office mirror. He consumed the remainder and once more filled up his glass. The dejected owner of a once prestigious hotel sat down on his chair. He put the glass on his desk and started to weep. Then came a knock on the door. Jeremy dragged himself out of the chair and wiped his eyes.

"Mr Burgess?"

Jeremy opened his office door.

"I require some change for the till."

"How much do you need?" Jeremy sniffed.

"Two pounds in change. Half-crowns, florins, shillings, sixpences and threepenny bits."

"What about pennies, halfpennies and farthings?"

"There is ample in the till."

Jeremy opened his office drawer. "I have one florin, three sixpences and two threepenny bits."

"I don't expect the bar will be busy tonight."

Jeremy turned round. "Why do you say that?"

"It has started to snow."

The owner took the coins out of the drawer and handed them to Iain.

"Whilst I'm here, can I have my wages for last week?"

"Last week?"

"Yes, you asked me to wait for an additional week."

"Can we discuss this tomorrow?"

"Okay, Mr Burgess."

As Iain left the office, Jeremy closed the door. He picked up his full glass of whisky, gulped it down then reached for the half-empty bottle. He poured another glass and laid the bottle back on his desk. Jeremy's temperature started to rise, he loosened his necktie then became breathless. Suddenly, he held his chest and slouched into the chair. The glass of whisky slipped from his grasp onto the floor.

Chapter 11

Oh Come All Ye Faithful

On a chilly mid-December morning, Evelyn alighted from the motor coach in Ardrishaig's main street. She walked in a brisk manner to the office of Macmillan Solicitors and soon reached it. Once inside, Evelyn observed a lady at a desk typing a document. The lady stopped, looked towards Evelyn then smiled.

"Good morning," she said, "can I help you?"

"I have an appointment with Mr Macmillan at eleven o'clock."

The lady glanced at the clock hung on a wall. "You are fifteen minutes early, please take a seat." She pointed to a wooden chair. "I will inform Mr Macmillan you have arrived."

"Thank you."

As Evelyn sat down, the lady left her desk then walked to a nearby office. She knocked on the closed door and entered. Evelyn turned round to look out the window at passers-by. Most people wore scarves, hats, gloves and coats for protection against the bitter cold weather. The lady came out of the office, closed the door behind her and returned to her desk. As she resumed work on her black typewriter, Evelyn cast her gaze around the uninspiring room. Furniture consisted of a dark wooden desk and two chairs plus an olive green filing cabinet. The dark wooden floor looked in need of a polish and the exterior window a good scrub. One bright aspect being the small green-fir Christmas tree with white tinsel in a corner. A short thin man in a grey three-piece suit with silver hair appeared from an office. He walked over to the lady, gave her a file then approached Evelyn.

"Miss White, I am Mr Macmillan."

Evelyn stood up.

"Good to meet you." Mr Macmillan shook Evelyn's, hand. "Please come this way."

Evelyn followed Mr Macmillan into his office. He placed a wooden chair opposite his desk and she sat down. Mr Macmillan closed the door, went behind his desk and sat down. He took off his brass horn-rimmed spectacles, rubbed one of his eyes and put the spectacles back on.

"Why did you ask to see me?" said Evelyn.

"Well, Miss White, you are the new owner of the Burgess Hotel, Inveraray. In his will, Jeremy Burgess bequeathed the property to you."

"Me!"

"Yes, you Miss White."

"Why?"

"You must have made an excellent impression on Mr Burgess."

"What about his own family?"

"Mr Burgess had no dependants and he did not choose to leave the hotel to either of his two ex-wives. I believe he had fallen out with other members of the Burgess clan."

"I met the two ex-wives at the funeral."

Mr Macmillan coughed. "Yes, I spotted them."

"How much is the hotel worth, Mr Macmillan?"

He sighed. "Therein lies a problem. The hotel is valued at just under £28,000 however, much debt exists. You should contact the bank to obtain an accurate assessment of the situation."

Evelyn nodded.

"The person responsible for the hotel's account is a Mr Macdonald. He is based at the Bank of Scotland in Lochgilphead." Mr Macmillan smiled. "Keep on his good side."

"Will I have to make an appointment?"

"I would expect so."

Evelyn stood up. "No time like the present."

"Splendid." Mr Macmillan stood up, went to his office door and opened it. "Good luck."

Evelyn shook his hand.

"If you want to discuss any aspect which relates to the hotel, do not hesitate to telephone my office."

"Thank you."

"My pleasure."

The new owner of Inveraray's Burgess Hotel decided she would contact Mr Macdonald without delay. A short time later, Evelyn arrived at the Bank of Scotland premises. Several people stood in a queue for the solitary bank assistant to serve them. After fifteen minutes, the assistant acknowledged Evelyn and she moved towards a polished wooden counter.

"Can I speak with Mr Macdonald, please? It is urgent."

"What is it in connection with?"

"I have taken over the ownership of the Burgess Hotel."

"In Inveraray?"

"Yes."

"Your name?"

"Evelyn White."

"Hold on, please."

The assistant left the counter and approached an office. He knocked on the door and entered. After a few minutes, he returned to the counter and smiled.

"Yes?" said Evelyn.

"Mr Macdonald will see you now." The assistant opened a hatch.

"Thank you." Evelyn walked up to the manager's office door.

"Come in," said an authoritative voice.

She pushed the door wide open and walked in.

A tall bald-headed man in a black double-breasted pinstripe suit stood in front of a large desk. He smiled and held out his hand.

"I am Mr Macdonald."

Evelyn shook it.

"Please have a seat." Mr Macdonald closed the door then sat behind his desk.

Evelyn sat on the visitor's brown wooden chair opposite Mr Macdonald's desk. She unbuttoned her cream coat, removed her brown cloche hat and patted her short blonde hair. The top two buttons of her dark blouse had been left open and revealed a cleavage.

"How did you know I was outside your door?"

Mr Macdonald smiled. "I heard your shoes on the tiled floor."

Evelyn glanced down at her black high-heel shoes.

"How can I help you Miss White?"

"I am the new owner of the Burgess Hotel, Inveraray, and would like to know its financial situation."

"Not good. Mr Burgess had debts comparable to the value of his hotel. Sooner rather than later it would have been put up for sale."

"Then I am the owner of a debt-ridden establishment."

"I am afraid that is the situation. Mr Burgess signed all his assets over to the bank."

"If run in a proper manner, the hotel has potential."

"Can you elaborate?"

"There are three bars of which one is being used. I can fulfil each bar's potential."

"How would you do that?"

"First of all I would reduce the prices in all of the bars. Other hotels in the area have cheaper prices. This would make us competitive."

"That would result in less income for the hotel."

Evelyn shook her head. "It should attract more customers and increase turnover."

"Continue."

"At present, the public bar is the only one used. I would encourage men to bring their wives and girlfriends to the lounge. The function suite could be utilised for other matters. All three bars would earn revenue."

"All good in theory, Miss White, how would you achieve this?"

"We have one barman and if he doesn't smarten up his appearance and manner then he will be dismissed. I have interviewed a number of candidates for bar work and from those, two individuals stood out.

"In what way?"

"Their attitude and experience. Also one of them has promised she will encourage friends and family to frequent the hotel."

"How?"

"She has contacts through a variety of local clubs, committees and associations. The lounge would be perfect for meetings."

"What about the function suite?"

"We have a Christmas Eve dance next week and a Hogmany dance seven days later. I have distributed posters around the area to promote each event."

"And after the festive season has ended, what would you do with the function suite?"

Evelyn smiled. "A pocket billiards suite!"

"Billiards?"

Evelyn nodded. "Men like to play billiards. I have been informed that during the war, a popular pastime with soldiers was to have a game of billiards. Many former servicemen live in the area – they will flock to the hotel."

That's a novel idea.

"I run the hotel and am therefore aware of its potential. Strengths can be maximised, weaknesses minimised, threats eliminated and opportunities explored. A plan will be devised in order to take the business forward and make it profitable. I am honest and trustworthy – all cash will be recorded."

Mr Macdonald smiled. "What do you intend to do about the bedrooms?"

"I will ask the Local Authority to assist me with a view to promote the hotel further afield. This could encourage visitors to spend their weekly summer vacation within the district. Also motor car ownership is on the increase thus people from Glasgow could sample a short weekend break."

"The local area is also accessible by sea."

"If the hotel is run efficiently and promoted effectively, it will be a success. This will not be done overnight but the hotel can achieve its full potential."

"And you appear the right person to do that Miss White. The bank will continue the overdraft facility therefore trading can continue. We will support you in every way possible."

Evelyn smiled.

"Are you aware of suppliers who have not been paid?"

"No, who are they?"

"The brewery and a local electricity company. Mr Burgess had been sent two warning letters. Don't worry, I will contact those companies and advise them the hotel is under new ownership."

"Thank you."

Mr Macdonald stood up. "I better not waste any more of your valuable time, Miss White." He walked up to Evelyn. "A pleasure to have met you."

"And you too." Evelyn rose, put on her hat and buttoned her coat.

Mr Macdonald shook Eleven's hand. "Goodbye." He opened the door.

Evelyn left the bank with a spring in her step and a determination to make the business a successful one.

James entered the hospital dining room for a welcome seat and a bite to eat. Being the Saturday before Christmas, many visitors and staff filled the room. Due to the appearance of festive decorations, a joyful vibrant atmosphere existed. James collected a plate of mince and potatoes plus his usual cup of tea then put them on a tray. He spotted Maria at a table and went across to her. As he sat down, James looked around the vicinity.

"Christmas is upon us." Maria smiled.

"The hospital cashier will be delighted!"

Maria laughed.

"The decorations make a difference however, it took a while to put them up."

"Why?"

"A shaky stepladder, not stable enough for the task."

"At least you're here in one piece."

I lifted my cup of tea and took a sip. "Just!"

Maria smiled then glanced around the dining room. "Who supplied all the red balloons?"

"Lady Beaumont, she also gave us the silver and gold tinsel."

"As well as the hospital Christmas tree."

I nodded and laid my cup on the table.

"Have you any plans for Christmas Eve?"

I shook my head. "Nothing as yet." I picked up a knife and fork.

"There is a Christmas Eve dance at the Burgess Hotel in Inveraray."

I chewed my food.

"The Argyllshire Standard publicised it."

I swallowed. "It is too far away."

"The hotel has organised coaches for guests who stay in Ardrishaig and Lochgilphead."

I lifted my cup. "For free?"

"The advert stated 'subsidised by the hotel' therefore it should be cheaper than a normal fare."

"A nice gesture."

"Why don't you go and also take Adam along?"

"Adam?"

Maria nodded. "To go out and meet people would do him no harm."

"That's a good idea, Maria. Can we pay at the door or is admission by ticket only?"

"The advertisement did not state you required a ticket therefore I would presume pay at the door is acceptable."

"Good."

"Besides, the hotel will be grateful for business."

"Why is that?"

"I heard it could have gone out of business. I believe it is now under new ownership."

"If Adam is hesitant then I will drag him along to the dance and give the new owner our support." I sipped my cup of tea then laid it on the table.

Maria smiled. "Terrific."

As I continued to eat my meal, Maria stared at the clock on the wall then stood up and dashed out of the room. I smiled and shook my head. Nurse Shaw entered, collected a cup of tea then came over to the table.

"Hello." I put my plate and cutlery aside.

"Hi." Nurse Shaw sat down and laid her cup on the table.

"Have you lost your appetite?"

"Today I don't have time for one! It's the usual hectic schedule that precedes Christmas." Nurse Shaw lifted her cup, took a sip then laid it on the table. "Are you going to the Burgess Hotel on Christmas Eve?"

"The dance?"

"Yes."

I nodded and lifted my cup. "What about you?" I drank my tea and laid the empty cup on the table.

"Oh yes, plus four of my friends. Gabrielle may also join us"

"Splendid."

"She is doing her best to have Christmas off. Also two of the doctors have threatened to attend!"

"Maybe Matron will attend."

"Let's hope not – she'll scrutinise our behaviour!"

I laughed. "I believe transport from Ardrishaig and Lochgilphead to the hotel has been organised.

"Yes, from both main streets. One of my friends has her own transport."

"Does she drink alcohol?" No drink driving contravention in this era.

"Maybe the odd glass of gin."

"What about yourself?"

"The odd half-bottle."

I laughed.

"Thank goodness I am off on Christmas day."

Just as well. I stood up. "You will have to excuse me, time to resume work."

"See you later."

I took my empty plate, cutlery and cup to the counter then placed them on a table. Pity the person who has to wash all those dirty dishes and cutlery. I left the room and walked down the corridor.

"Hello, James."

I turned round. "Hi, Isabel."

"What are your plans for Christmas?"

"I am off on Christmas Day therefore will be out on Christmas Eve."

"Me too, going anywhere special?"

"The Burgess Hotel, Inveraray. The hotel has put on a coach which leaves from Lochgilphead's main street."

"Also Ardrishaig's main street. Let us hope there will be enough room for everyone."

"We'll all have to squeeze in."

Isabel laughed.

"Are you going with a group of people?"

"Just Elizabeth. I want her to meet new friends."

"Good idea."

"I can introduce you to her."

Now that I have a beard and seventeen years have passed, would Elizabeth recognise me? I have not aged and still have the same eyes. When she painted my portrait in 1912, no doubt she paid careful attention to them.

"Both of you are of a similar age."

"How old is she?"

"How old are you?"

"Forty-two."

"Elizabeth is a tad younger."

Oh no she isn't! Elizabeth will be forty-five. "I'll look forward to meeting her."

"Good." Isabel glanced along the corridor. "Time to go."

As Isabel departed, Nurse Robertson approached. She had a stern look on her face and I awaited my fate.

"James, I need you to change a bulb on the Christmas tree. As it is near the top, you will require the stepladder."

Not the damn stepladder again. "Will do."

Evelyn stood behind the reception desk and studied the hotel's trading journal. She turned to the next page, heard footsteps and looked up. A gentleman in a dark blue overcoat and hat approached the desk.

"Good afternoon." The gentleman removed his hat.

Evelyn smiled. "Good afternoon, can I help you, sir?"

"I noticed your advertisement board outside the hotel. Do you perhaps hire out the function room?"

"Yes, we can if no function has been booked. For what purpose would the room be used?"

"Choir practice for a Christmas Eve service."

"Choir practice?"

The gentleman smiled. "Our local church is being renovated for the Christmas Service. Urgent repairs are required and our singers cannot concentrate on harmonies. The workmen will be at the church for the foreseeable future."

"The function suite is available until Christmas Eve."

"Splendid. How much will it cost for two days?"

"How many hours per day do you require?"

"From one o'clock until four in the afternoon, tomorrow and Monday."

"I will just take a payment for Monday, my Christmas gift to your church. The price is £1 and ten shillings."

"Thank you. Can I pay on Monday?"

Evelyn nodded and opened the hotel booking register. "Your name, sir?" She picked up a pencil."

"Struthers, Alan Struthers. I am one of the Elders."

As Evelyn wrote, the gentleman looked around the reception area. He stared at a painting on one of the walls.

"Do you have any leaflets about the hotel's facilities?"

Evelyn looked up and smiled. "They are being printed as we speak."

"Keep one for me. I have colleagues in Glasgow who would enjoy a short break in this area."

"What is it you do, sir?"

"I am a psychologist. My colleagues and I tend to participate in hill-walking and rock-climbing."

"Then this location will be ideal."

The gentleman nodded.

"There is a discount for block bookings."

"Splendid."

"And we have fifteen excellent bedrooms." Evelyn put down her pencil and closed the register. "That is it arranged for tomorrow and Monday."

"Thank you." The gentleman put on his hat. "Are you prepared for the Christmas Eve celebration?"

"Yes, extra staff and a band have been organised."

"See you tomorrow."

"How many of the congregation will attend each rehearsal?"

"About thirty." The gentleman glanced out of the reception window. "The snow is back on again." He smiled. "Bye."

"Bye, sir."

When the gentleman reached the hotel exit, he stopped to read a poster. It publicised a billiards amenity within the hotel. After he departed the building, Evelyn opened her diary and searched for the Unemployment Office telephone number. She flicked through the pages and found it then went into her office and sat down next to the telephone. She removed the receiver and put it against her ear.

"Hello, can I help you?" said the woman operator.

Evelyn put her mouth close to the voice transmitter. "Argyll 250 please."

"I will connect you."

"Hello," said a male voice.

"This is the new owner of the Burgess Hotel."

"How can I help you?"

"I require a general helper to assist me in the hotel."

"An assistant manager?"

"No, someone to clean and cook."

"A cleaner/cook?"

"Yes, do you have someone who can fill the vacancy?"

"Hold on, I will check my file."

In the background, Evelyn could hear the sound of papers rustle. She lifted up a pencil with her right hand and started to doodle on a spare piece of paper.

"Here's one."

"Can you ask her to come straight away?"

"Yes, will do. The lady is a Mrs Abaletti, spelt with a double 't'."

"Abaletti?"

"Yes, she is Italian."

"Thank you, bye."

"Goodbye."

Evelyn replaced the receiver onto the telephone arm, stood up and returned to reception.

On Sunday afternoon, a large group of people entered the foyer. One of them approached the reception desk, removed his hat and smiled at Evelyn.

"Well, here we all are," said the gentleman.

"Just go through, Mr Struthers," said Evelyn, "it's all yours."

"Thank you." He replaced his hat.

"I uncovered a piano in the spare room next to the suite. It was in amongst old items of hotel furniture."

"Splendid."

"I am unsure as to its performance quality."

"Leave that to Doris, my dear, she plays the piano."

The choir went into the function suite and took off their coats, scarves and hats then laid them on a set of bare tables. A grey-haired lady walked across the room to the piano, pulled a chair towards it then sat down. She lifted up the scratched wooden piano lid to reveal black and white ivory keys. Alan Struthers approached the lady and leaned forward.

"Good luck, Doris."

Doris looked up at him and smiled. "Has the piano been in use?"

"Not for a while."

Doris stared down at the rusty metal piano pedals. "By the looks of it, a long while!"

The choir gathered around the piano and waited with anticipation. Doris placed her nimble white fingers on a selection of keys and pressed down. She then played a selection of notes, looked down at her feet and stopped.

"What is the matter?" asked Alan Struthers.

"One of the pedals appears faulty." She looked at him and smiled. "The piano is otherwise fine."

"Splendid," said Alan Struthers. He distributed carol song sheets to the choir.

"What's first, Alan?" said Doris.

"O Come All Ye Faithful, then Once in Royal David's City, followed by Hark the Herald Angels Sing. Let us see how those three sound then we can progress with the next selection."

The choir stood in three rows, which consisted of nine men and women for each row. Alan Struthers acted as conductor and the choir sang in harmony with the piano. After six Christmas carols had been sung, the choir smiled at each other.

"Excellent," said the conductor, "let's try something softer."

The choir sang Silent Night then Away in a Manger followed by When Shepherds Watched Their Flocks.

"How about Ave Maria, Alan?" asked a lady choir member.

"We'll give it a go."

The conductor guided the attentive choir's singing with his hands and tender facial expressions. As they finished the rendition of Ave Maria, Evelyn entered the suite. Alan Struthers looked at her and smiled.

"Do we deserve pass marks?"

"High pass marks. My father's favourite was God Rest Ye Merry Gentlemen. Could you sing that one?"

"We don't have that one scheduled."

"I'll sing it, Alan."

"Okay, Jack," said Alan, "on you go." He glanced at the piano player. "Ready, Doris?"

"Ready, Alan."

The soloist sang it beautifully and in complete harmony with the piano player. As he finished, Evelyn applauded.

"Perfect tone, Jack," said the conductor, "we will finish off today's practice with The First Noel and The Twelve Days of Christmas."

When the practice session ended, the men and women retrieved their winter garments. As he gathered the song sheets, Alan Struthers was approached by Evelyn.

"Mr Struthers?"

"Yes?"

"As it is Sunday, could the choir sing outside for a short while?"

"Outside?"

"Yes, it will promote the spirit of Christmas to passers-by."

"Passers-by?"

"With the choir in fine voice, it would promote your church's festive service."

"You're a smart lady, my dear." He nodded. "We will do it."

Whilst the choir put on their scarves, coats and hats, Alan Struthers announced Evelyn's suggestion. They all agreed, went outside and stood in their choir formation. At the hotel entrance, Alan Struthers conducted the Christian choir in a selection of carols. Vehicles which passed, slowed down and came to a halt at the roadside. People out for a Sunday stroll stopped to watch and listen. It did not take long for a crowd to gather and witness the pre-Christmas spectacle. During an interlude, a lady wearing a fur coat and wide-brimmed hat came up to Alan Struthers.

"Excuse me, can I make a donation?"

"A donation, madam?"

"Yes, to your church. I believe repairs are required."

"We are doing this as a pre-Christmas gesture."

"But your church could do with extra funds?"

"Yes."

"Well then, take this donation. The singing is inspirational for the season of goodwill."

Alan Struthers took the ten-shilling note. "Thank you, madam."

"My pleasure."

After the lady departed, a gentleman in a camel coat and hat appeared. He gave a silver half-crown coin to Alan Struthers and his thanks. As the crowd grew larger, the donations became more frequent. When the carol singing ended, Alan Struthers entered the Burgess Hotel and went to speak with Evelyn.

"Your idea has given our church much-needed funds to help pay for repairs." He smiled.

"My pleasure, see you tomorrow."

When he departed, the latest recruit to the hotel's staff appeared. Mrs Abaletti wiped her brow and laid a duster on the reception desk.

"I need more polish," she said.

"Would you prefer a cup of tea? You've been cleaning for the best part of four hours."

Mrs Abaletti laughed. "The place needs a good scrub."

Evelyn nodded.

"Did you have a cleaner?"

"Some of the time – she would not turn up every day."

"Did the previous owner not deal with the situation?"

Evelyn shook her head. "Have a seat and I'll make us tea."

"Thanks."

As Evelyn left the reception area, Mrs Abaletti lifted her duster of the desk and sat down at a small dark wooden table with two chairs. She wiped the table with her duster and observed various paintings on the walls. She loosened her fawn-coloured apron and took a deep breath. A few minutes later, Evelyn returned and handed Mrs Abaletti a cup and saucer. Evelyn sat down next to her and laid a cup and saucer on the table.

"Thank you." Mrs Abaletti lifted the cup, took a sip then laid the cup and saucer on the table. "That's better."

"Are you from Scotland?"

Mrs Abaletti nodded. "I left Inveraray in 1907 to start a new job in the south of Italy."

"Why Italy?"

"Plenty of sun and a warmer climate – unlike here."

Evelyn laughed. "Being dark, you are fortunate. Too much sun and I turn red!"

"The problem with fair skin."

"What type of job was it?"

"A children's nanny, in Sorrento."

Evelyn lifted her cup of tea and took a sip.

"I had been a nanny to a family in Inveraray. I found out about the job which would be based in Italy, applied for it and was successful."

"Terrific." Evelyn laid her cup on the saucer.

"The family I worked for provided excellent references and I had also studied languages at university."

"What languages did you study?"

"French and Italian." Mrs Abaletti lifted the cup and sipped her tea.

"Have you sought any current similar positions?"

"None." Mrs Abaletti laid her cup into the saucer.

"Why did you return to Scotland?"

"Not long after I moved to Sorrento, I met a handsome Italian gentleman full of charm. A year later we were married and lived a happy life until the war started. My husband enlisted in the Italian army and not long after, was injured in a fierce battle on the Swiss border. He recovered from physical wounds but his mental wounds did not heal. He could not relax and suffered anxiety attacks. Gino lived for a further eleven years then passed away fourteen months ago."

"How awful."

"He suffered a massive heart attack."

"Do you have any children?"

Mrs Abaletti shook her head.

"You then made the decision to return home?"

"Yes, my sister lives here. I left Italy four months ago, just before the Wall Street Crash. Also because Italy has changed."

"In what way?"

"Politically. The country is run by a dictator – Mussolini. The Fascist Party now run Italy and dictate economic and social policies. Any opposition is crushed."

"Crushed?"

"There have been rumours of violence being used against people who object to their ideology."

"What about the police?"

"The Fascist Party control the authorities."

"My goodness!"

"I have heard the Fascist Party in Germany are similar."

"It appears change is happening across Europe. The Labour Party in power is a further example."

"I am uncertain they can improve our country's economic situation."

"I agree, it's a mammoth task."

Two women entered the hotel and walked towards the reception desk.

Evelyn stood up and went behind the desk. Mrs Abaletti picked up the two cups and saucers then made her way to the kitchen.

"Good afternoon, can I help you?"

"We would like afternoon tea?" said the older woman.

"That can be arranged."

"Oh good," said the other woman.

"If you care to go into the dining room, I will bring tea and biscuits to your table."

"Can we sit in here?" said the older woman, "beside the log fire?"

"I will be back in a few minutes."

As Evelyn departed to the kitchen, both women sat down and smiled at each other. The younger of the two laid a black leather handbag on the floor and then adjusted her scarlet hat. When Evelyn entered the kitchen, Mrs Abaletti polished a brass door handle.

"Do you know those women, Evelyn?"

"No, I have not seen them before."

"The oldest is Nora Banks and the other is Julia, her daughter. Mrs Banks owns the Imperial and Manor House hotels in Inveraray. My sister worked in the Imperial but left a couple of months ago."

"Why did she leave?"

Mrs Abaletti smiled. "A difference of opinion."

"Maybe they are here to observe the competition."

"Since Nora Banks owns the towns two other hotels, you are their only competition."

Evelyn smiled. "We must therefore ensure our standards remain high."

Mrs Abaletti nodded. "Precisely."

A few minutes later, Evelyn took a silver tray which contained white crockery, pot of tea, jug of milk, bowl of sugar and a plate of assorted biscuits into the reception area. She laid the tray on a table where the two women sat.

"Thank you," said the older woman.

"Would you like me to pour?" said Evelyn.

"We will manage," said the younger woman.

"Can we have a word with you later?" said the older woman.

"In twenty minutes?" said Evelyn.

"Fine," said the younger woman.

Evelyn returned to the kitchen and had a cup of tea plus several ginger snap biscuits. She sat down and read a copy of the Sunday Post. Mrs Abaletti took out the contents of the larder, cleaned it and then put them back. Evelyn finished her newspaper and returned to the reception area. Two empty cups and a plate with several shortcake biscuits lay on the table. A teapot, milk jug and sugar bowl lay on the tray.

"Would you care for anything else?"

"No, thanks," said the younger woman.

"Tell me," said the older woman, "would you consider selling this hotel?"

"I have just taken ownership!"

"If I made you a good offer, would you accept? After all, these are difficult times for this type of business."

"I enjoy a challenge."

"You won't sell?"

Evelyn shook her head.

"Are you positive?"

"Yes I am."

"I haven't told you how much I am prepared to offer."

"Keep your offer."

"How much do I owe you for the tea and biscuits?"

"Two shillings please."

"Pay her, Julia."

The younger woman picked up her bag, took out a small black purse and opened it. She gave a silver florin to Evelyn, closed the purse and then popped it into her handbag. Both women stood up then departed the reception area. Evelyn put the florin onto the tray along with a biscuit plate plus two cups and saucers. As she lifted it up, the hotel exit door slammed shut. The two women walked toward a black Rover saloon parked outside the hotel. A stocky man wearing a dark hat and overcoat opened both rear passenger doors. When the two women entered and sat down, he closed their respective doors. He returned to the driver's seat and shut the door.

"Don't drive away yet, Bert," said Nora Banks.

"How did it go?" said Bert.

"She is not for selling," said Julia.

"Give it time, Julia," said Nora Banks, "in a month she will be desperate to sell."

"And if she isn't?" said Julia.

"Then we can start to apply pressure," said Nora Banks, "similar to what we did with the previous owner."

"He did not sell the hotel," said Bert.

"In another month he would have," said Nora Banks, "he could not pay bills."

"His personal life was in tatters," said Julia.

"It is of no surprise he suffered a heart attack," said Bert.

"Do you feel sorry for him?" said Julia.

Bert shook his head.

"This is business," said Julia, "there will be casualties."

"Quite correct, Julia," said Nora Banks, "we have to eliminate any competition our hotels face."

"What's the next move?" said Bert.

"You can dig into her past, Bert," said Julia, "see what dirt you can find."

"There may not be any," said Bert, "she's a young woman."

Nora Banks looked at Julia.

"With Burgess, it was what to leave out!" Bert laughed.

"We had a dossier full of incidents," said Nora Banks, "the main one being that motor car accident which involved a girl."

"It's a miracle he survived for so long!" said Bert.

"We got him in the end," said Julia.

Nora Banks turned to Julia. "But not the hotel."

"We'll get it," said Julia.

"Do you want me to attend their Christmas Eve dance?" said Bert.

"Why?" said Nora Banks.

"See if I can find out anythin'."

"You will attend our festive evening!" Julia stared at Bert.

Bert nodded.

"Let's head for home, Bert," said Julia, "you have to decorate the Christmas tree."

Bert turned the ignition key and released the handbrake.

"It's cold," said Nora Banks.

"Soon be home, mother." Julia wiped the rear window.

The black four-door saloon moved off over the thin layer of snow then onto a main road. As it sped away, Julia looked out of the small rear window at the Burgess Hotel.

Mrs Abaletti polished the brass fitting of the hotel's main door. She then dusted paintings, fixtures and fittings in the reception area. Evelyn looked up from behind her desk.

"Would you care for a cup of tea, Mrs Abaletti?"

She took a deep breath. "Yes, thank you."

Evelyn went through to the kitchen and Mrs Abaletti started to sweep the floor. She picked up loose tinsel, which had fallen from the Christmas tree and put it into a waste bag. Evelyn returned with a tray, which consisted of two cups of tea, a small plate of rich tea biscuits plus a newspaper. As Evelyn laid the tray on a table, Mrs Abaletti turned round and put down her brush. Both hotel staff sat down then Evelyn lifted up the newspaper and browsed through it.

"Last night a customer mentioned an article had appeared about our hotel in Monday's edition of the Argyllshire Standard."

"What kind of article?"

"They didn't elaborate." Evelyn turned another page. "I hope it's positive."

Mrs Abaletti picked up her cup of tea and took a sip.

"Here it is, under the 'readers comments' section."

"What does the article say?"

Evelyn smiled. "It's a letter written by a J Smith. The letter states that this person visited the Burgess Hotel, Inveraray. Since their previous visit, they could not believe the transformation in such a short period of time. The polite efficient staff, high standards of hygiene and warm friendly atmosphere were a joy and pleasure to experience."

Mrs Abaletti smiled. "Well done, J Smith." She laid her cup on the saucer.

"Well done indeed. Who is he?"

"Maybe it's a woman."

Evelyn put down the newspaper, lifted her cup of tea, and took a sip then laid it on the saucer. "Well whoever the person is, good on them. If the article attracts more customers, terrific!"

"Did yesterday's second choir rehearsal go well?"

"Yes, they sang outside the hotel and drew another good crowd. I believe Mr Struthers will make this an annual event. The public turn up in the cold weather."

"Their performances enhance the festive spirit."

Evelyn nodded.

"Tonight's dance could prove a welcome distraction for people. They can put aside any woes and enjoy themselves."

"All three bars are stocked and staff ready to go. However, another helper may be required."

"I could ask my sister, she has experience of bar work."

"Please do, that would be terrific. I don't want customers to wait longer than necessary for service." Evelyn smiled. "It's money lost."

Mrs Abaletti laughed. "I will give you Louisa's telephone number."

"I'll contact her and explain the situation."

"What about the band?"

"They play in and around Glasgow, however a friend at the city's university has persuaded them to perform here. They will receive free accommodation and drinks."

Mrs Abaletti smiled.

"The income from tonight will provide much-needed finance. The New Year's Eve dance plus regular function suite bookings for next year should put us on a sound footing. Oh come all ye faithful!"

Mrs Abaletti laughed. "It all goes well then?"

Evelyn sighed. "It will be hard work."

"And worth it."

Evelyn nodded, picked up her cup, drank the contents and laid it on the saucer. "I better phone the supplier and make sure the food will be here on time for tonight's dance."

"Food?"

"Yes, I call it a 'finger selection' – light snacks."

"Will the food not diminish this evening's profits?"

Evelyn smiled. "It's included in the admission price."

Mrs Abaletti picked up a rich tea biscuit from the plate and ate it. As Evelyn went into the office, Mrs Abaletti finished her cup of tea. She took the tray and its contents through to the kitchen. Evelyn sat down next to the telephone, picked up a small card and looked at it. She lifted the receiver, placed it against her ear and moved closer to the transmitter.

"Can I help you?" said the operator.

"Argyll 195, please."

"I will connect you."

"Hello, Charlotte Carsell-Brown speaking."

"Can I speak with William please?"

"Is that you Olivia?"

"No, my name is Evelyn."

"He has a girlfriend."

"William came to see me at my hotel concerning a part-time job."

"Here he is, you can explain the situation to him."

"Hello, William here."

"It's Evelyn from the Burgess Hotel. Could you be here tonight from 7.30 until 10.30?"

"What will I be doing?"

"Managing the cloakroom. You will receive guests garments, give them a ticket and when they return make sure the correct items are given back. You can board the subsidised hotel motor coach from Ardrishaig and it will also take you home. I will pay for your time."

"I am going out tonight for a Christmas Eve dinner with my parents."

He is not interested. "Goodbye."

"Goodbye."

Evelyn replaced the receiver into the arm.

"Evelyn?" said Mrs Abaletti.

"Yes?" She popped her head out of the office.

"The vegetables have not arrived yet and cannot envisage a delivery on Christmas Day."

"I will contact them, maybe deliveries are behind schedule."

"We also require washing-up liquid, a box of salt and two bottles of detergent."

"When I speak to the supplier, I will ask them to add those items to our order. We may not receive them today – it may be Boxing Day before they arrive."

"Do they deliver on Boxing Day?"

"The suppliers are grateful for the business."

Mrs Abaletti looked out of the kitchen window. "It's snowing again."

Several minutes later a man walked into the foyer, removed his hat then shook it. He looked in Mrs Abaletti direction and took a deep breath.

"Refuge at last!"

Mrs Abaletti smiled.

Evelyn went behind her desk. "Would you care for a cup of tea?"

"It's not a cup of tea I need but a job." The white-haired man turned down his coat collar. "Do you require someone to assist in any kind of work?"

"We can't offer you any work," said Evelyn, "however we can offer you tea."

"I have no money."

"It's our treat."

"Thank you," said the man, "can I sit down?" He looked at a nearby table with two chairs.

"Of course," said Evelyn.

"I'll prepare the tea," said Mrs Abaletti. She departed to the kitchen.

The man sat down. "Ah! That's good." He smiled at Evelyn. "I've been out of work for twelve months and have been searching for a job ever since."

"Around Inveraray?"

"No, Ardrishaig, Lochgilphead and further afield. Since there was no work there, I decided to try my luck here."

"Did you travel by motor coach?"

The man shook his head. "I can't afford the fare but managed to hitch a lift in a workman's van."

"What are your plans for Christmas Eve?"

"I don't have any."

"We have a dance and require a cloakroom attendant."

"I'll do it!"

"Where do you stay?"

"Just outside Ardrishaig."

"Can you walk to Ardrishaig's main street?"

"Yes, it's not far."

"A bus will leave there for our hotel at 7.15. Do you have a clean white shirt and dark tie?"

"Yes."

"Wear them and preferably dark trousers."

The man nodded.

Evelyn went through to her office and opened a desk drawer. She took out several silver coins then returned to reception. She approached the man and gave him the coins. He took them and looked at Evelyn.

"That is for your fare home and to pay the coach driver tonight."

Mrs Abaletti entered the reception area and laid a shiny silver tray plus its contents on the guest's table.

"I trust you take ginger snaps with your tea?"

"I do and thank you."

Chapter 12

The Main Event

Evelyn looked into the mirror and admired her bobbed blonde hair. She noticed a hair on her medium-length black dress and flicked it off. Evelyn applied more red lipstick then adjusted the white pearls round her neck. Before leaving the room, she switched off the light then closed the door and locked it. She walked downstairs to reception and glanced at the wall clock. It was 6.30, ten minutes until the bar staff would arrive. She went to the hotel entrance door and unlocked it. When she opened the door, a small group of people stood outside. They consisted of Iain, Charles McSorley, Vivian Daly and Mrs Abaletti's sister Louisa. Evelyn led them to the kitchen where they put their coats, scarves and hats in a small cloakroom. Evelyn smiled – everyone had adhered to Christmas Eve dress protocol. Both men wore a white collared shirt, black bowtie and dark trousers whilst the women dressed in a white blouse and black skirt. The four staff members went to their designated place of service. Iain to the public bar, Louisa the lounge bar and Charles plus Vivien in the function suite. Evelyn entered her office and removed money from the safe. She deposited a specific amount of silver and bronze coins into each bar's cash register drawer. Iain and Louisa opened their respective public and lounge bar doors. Evelyn opened the function suite double-door then positioned herself inside it. She placed a small wooden table by her side and on this lay a grey metal box to deposit admission money. When each

Christmas Eve dance revellers appeared they would pay their entry fee and receive a white numbered ticket.

A man approached Evelyn and removed his hat. "Ready for cloakroom duties."

"Just in time." Evelyn gave him two identical blue ticket books.

He took them.

"When guests hand over garments, give them a ticket then attach the same ticket from the second book onto their hanger."

"Will do." He departed to the cloakroom.

Evelyn glanced at the function room clock. 7.35, Mrs Abaletti should have been here by now to organise the finger buffet and the band has not yet turned up.

As revellers came through the function suite double-door, they stood in line to pay their admission money. The first customer was a young woman.

"Thank you for the subsidised transport." She handed over her admission money.

Evelyn took her money and put it in the metal box. "Did you come here in the Ardrishaig coach?"

She nodded. "The Lochgilphead coach has just arrived, we beat them to it!"

Evelyn laughed.

"It's okay for you Fiona, we had to stand," said a man behind the young woman.

"You had to stand!" Evelyn stared at the man.

He nodded. "Me and another twelve people." The man handed money to Evelyn.

Evelyn put his money into the metal box and gave him a ticket.

"It's goin' tae be a busy night," said his friend, "hope there's enough room for us all."

Evelyn smiled.

He handed money to her.

She put it into the box, gave him change and a ticket.

"Thanks." He took both.

A short time later, Mrs Abaletti walked into the function suite and approached Evelyn. A group of young men and women objected.

"Hey!" said a man, "wait your turn like the rest of us."

Evelyn looked at him. "This lady will arrange snacks for tonight."

"That's different then," said the brash man.

"Sorry for being late Evelyn, I'll prepare the food."

"The spare table at the far end of the suite can be used to lay out food and plates."

"Fine," said Mrs Abaletti.

"Make sure guests only have one snack," whispered Evelyn, "take their ticket once they have been served."

Mrs Abaletti nodded.

As she departed to the kitchen, a young man stepped forward with his admission money. He handed it to Evelyn and smiled.

"What time does the bar close?"

"When the drink runs out!" cried his friend.

"We have a special license to consume alcohol until 10.30," said Evelyn, "an additional thirty minutes."

Both men and several others behind them in the queue cheered. Whilst Evelyn continued to take money, she once more glanced at the function room clock. The band had not turned up. Then five young men in long unbuttoned dark coats and hats, black suits, white shirts and dark neckties carrying instruments appeared. They stopped in front of Evelyn and one member raised his hat.

"Apologies, our transport broke down."

"Can you start at eight."

"No problem, we'll set ourselves up right now."

"Terrific!"

The bandleader looked towards the stage. "I see the piano is in place."

Evelyn nodded.

Band members took their instruments plus a drum kit to the function suite stage situated adjacent to the bar. Whilst they awaited customers, Vivien and Charles looked on. The five musicians removed their coats and hats then placed them in a neat pile on a chair.

"They appear on the young side," said Charles.

One member opened his case, took out a guitar then placed it against a chair. He stood back and stumbled over the case. Another member grabbed him and prevented a fall.

"One of them appears a bit unsteady," said Charles.

"I bet he's had a skinful," said Vivien.

Charles laughed.

"He would fit into a Laurel and Hardy sketch," quipped Vivien.

The drummer positioned his kit, pulled over a chair to sit on then bumped into the cymbals. As they crashed to the ground, revellers laughed and whistled.

"Is this the cabaret or a band?" said Vivien.

"A bit of both," said Charles, "pre-dance entertainment."

"That and more." Vivien shook her head.

Revellers who infiltrated the function suite approached the bar and a queue formed. The first customer looked at the band and then Vivien.

"At least the piano can't be knocked over."

"Don't hold your breath," said Vivien.

The customer laughed.

After they bought a drink, revellers would head for tables and chairs in which to sit. The band began their preparations to entertain them. The pianist, trumpeter, drummer, bass and clarinet player familiarised themselves with their individual instrument of music.

A young woman moved forward and handed money to Evelyn. "What time does the band start?"

"Soon. They play until 8.45 then a break for thirty minutes when snacks will be served."

"One session?"

"Two, the band will resume at 9.15 until 10.15." Evelyn handed her a ticket.

"Thanks." The young woman took the ticket.

"Are the snacks free?" said her friend.

Evelyn nodded.

"What do they consist of?"

"Sandwiches and sausage rolls."

"Don't lose your ticket Doreen." She nudged her friend.

Evelyn looked at the metal cash box full of money. She spotted a nearby empty bucket a short distance from where she sat. An observant guest in the queue approached Evelyn.

"Would you like me to fetch it for you?"

Evelyn smiled. "Please."

The young gentleman walked over to the bucket, picked it up and carried it to where Evelyn sat.

"There you are." He placed the bucket at Evelyn's side.

Evelyn smiled. "I'm grateful."

"Do I get in for free?"

"No, but you will receive food free of charge."

He laughed and handed Evelyn his admission money.

Evelyn took his money and dropped it into the bucket. "Next please."

"Busy evening?" said a lady.

"Hello, nice to see you again."

The lady glanced at her acquaintance. "This is my aunt, she persuaded me to come along."

Her aunt stepped forward. "I am Isabel, Elizabeth has told me a lot about you."

Evelyn smiled. "I hope you will enjoy tonight."

Elizabeth handed over money then glanced around the room. "Not many spare chairs left."

"We will squeeze in somewhere Elizabeth," said Isabel.

Evelyn gave Elizabeth two tickets. "Have a terrific evening."

"Thanks." Elizabeth took the tickets. "When does the band start?"

"Soon."

"Let us find a seat Elizabeth and also a table."

As Isabel and Elizabeth wandered off, Evelyn welcomed more revellers to the popular event. A queue stood outside the function room entrance and only a few vacant chairs remained. A group of young men approached Evelyn. The tallest cast his gaze around the room.

"We are short on chairs," said Evelyn.

"We don't need them, we'll stand."

"Are you sure?"

"We're sure," said the smallest member of the group.

"If shorty says it's okay, miss," said the tallest member, "that's fine by us."

Evelyn handed him the last five tickets and the group followed the leader to the bar. She looked around the suite then at the queue. The empty ticket book was laid on the table.

"Sorry, we're full up."

"Can you not let us stand around the floor?" said a young man.

"No. However, there is room in the other two bars."

Men and women made for both lounge and public bar entrances. Evelyn lifted the heavy bucket and metal box onto a small trolley then wheeled it into her office. She opened the safe, put the admission money into it, locked the door and placed the key in a discreet place.

Revellers sat on every available chair and those who did not, stood around the dance floor. The band commenced at 8.05 and soon the sound of laughter and chatter diminished. They played a selection of melodic good-time tunes and revellers tapped their fingers on tabletops.

"That band sound good," said Elizabeth.

"It is all new to me this jazz stuff."

"I went to a club in St Louis and witnessed something similar. However, the American musicians had a professional background whereas these guys will be part-time."

"Oh look Elizabeth! It's James." Isabel pointed.

"James?"

"Yes, from the hospital."

"The porter?"

Isabel nodded. "The chap in a dark suit."

"Most of them have dark suits."

"The chap with the beard. Next to the small guy in the queue."

"Yes, I see him."

"I will introduce you."

"I'm not desperate Isabel!"

"He isn't that bad."

Elizabeth smiled. "I didn't mean that, I'm not in a rush to meet someone."

"No time like the present."

Elizabeth sipped her glass of martini. "Who is he with?"

"Let us wait and see where he returns to from the bar."

"We may have to wait a while, it's a long queue."

Isabel smiled. "Patience is a virtue." She sipped her gin and orange.

Elizabeth stared at Isabel's drink. "In Manhattan, that plus my martini would be known as a 'Bronx' drink."

"Why is it called that?"

"I did not find out but if you consume more than two, the next day can be tiresome and weary."

"In Manhattan, you would not be allowed to consume alcohol."

Elizabeth smiled. "However, house parties exist to accommodate a tipple."

Isabel laughed.

A young man approached Elizabeth. "Would you care to dance miss?"

"No, thanks."

"Perhaps later?"

"I doubt it."

He departed.

Elizabeth took another sip of her drink.

"He must be half your age," said Isabel.

"That would be accurate."

"Would you care for a seat ladies?" said a well-dressed man, "we have two spare at our table."

"Thank you," said Isabel.

"This way," said the man.

"My feet hurt," whispered Isabel to Elizabeth.

The man in a dinner suit led Isabel and Elizabeth to a table with five people. Two women and three men shared a conversation. When they arrived at the table, the man pulled out two chairs. When Isabel and Elizabeth sat down, he sat next to them. The table's other festive dwellers continued to chat and drink. Several empty glasses lay on the white tablecloth along with several alcohol stains.

"Would you care for another drink ladies?" said the man.

Elizabeth looked at Isabel and then at the man. "I am fine."

"Me also," said Isabel.

"What part of America are you from?" said the man.

"East coast, New York."

He moved his chair closer to Elizabeth. "Are you on holiday?"

"No, I've returned for good." His breath stinks of whisky.

"You have been here on a previous occasion?"

"I was born here." Elizabeth sipped her drink.

The man whispered, "is that your mother next to you?"

Elizabeth stared at him. "No, it is not!"

He picked up his drink and finished it. "I'm off for another double, sure you don't want something?" He burped.

"No, thanks." Elizabeth looked at Isabel.

The man stood up and steadied himself. He moved several steps forward then bumped into another man.

"That must have been a strong drink!" said Isabel.

"He's no doubt had a few," said Elizabeth, "let's go."

As the two ladies stood up, one of the men who had his arm round a woman's waist looked at Elizabeth.

"Leaving so soon?"

"You got it," said Elizabeth.

James and Adam sat at a table close to the bar. For twenty-five minutes the band played a selection of tunes however, only a few couples ventured onto the dance floor. James observed men and women around the function suite chatting and drinking.

"When the alcohol consumption takes effect, there won't be a space on the dance floor!"

Adam laughed and sipped his whisky.

James looked towards the bar. "That was close!"

Adam turned round. "What happened?"

"A chap in a dinner suit just about barged into a women with a tray of drinks."

"That young woman near the front of the bar queue looks familiar."

"It's Nurse Shaw! She looks different without her uniform."

"Her bobbed hair and stylish dress gives her a modern look."

"Just about every lady at the dance has a black dress whereas she wears red."

"It complements her jet black hair."

"That young man appears to agree with you Adam, he has approached her." James smiled. "Nurse Shaw has just shaken her head."

"Did he ask her to dance?"

"Maybe." James drank his whisky. "Do you want another?"

"Okay."

James rose from his wooden chair. "I may be a while, it's a long queue therefore I'll buy doubles."

"Good idea."

When James joined the queue, he could hear an exchange of voices which emanated from the front.

"How come it takes so long to get served?" said a man.

"Because I only have one pair of hands!" said Vivien.

"Why just two behind the bar? You need another three at least."

Vivien poured whisky into a glass.

"Make it a double, I won't have to return for a while."

Promise? Vivien poured another whisky then gave him the glass.

The man handed over a florin. "Keep the change, it's a tip."

And I have several for you. Vivien took the coin and put it into the till. "Next please."

As another customer moved forward to the bar counter, Evelyn entered the rear door and approached Charles.

"How is everything?"

"Too many customers! We are short of glasses."

"I will go and collect the empty ones, clean them and bring them to you."

"Great."

After Evelyn left the bar, Charles wiped his brow then served the next customer.

Nora Banks, Julia and Bert sat together at a table in the Manor House Hotel, Inveraray. Due to a lack of customers, the dining room did not provide the usual Christmas Eve atmosphere. Julia cast her sinister gaze around the room.

"Where is everyone?"

"There is a deep recession, Julia," said Nora Banks.

"There was a long queue for entry to the Burgess Hotel," said Bert.

"How do you know?" said Nora Banks.

"On my way here, I drove past the hotel. Two coaches were in the vehicle parking area and many motor cars."

"We cannot stand for this!" cried Julia.

"Advertise, that's what their new owner did."

"Bert, we will not compete with that young upstart," said Nora Banks.

"What then?" said Julia.

"We will put her out of business."

"How do you plan to do that?" said Julia.

"Who was the woman that had a fling with Mr Macdonald?"

"Shelly Pratt."

"I'll compose a letter to our 'over-amorous' bank manager and state that if he does not cancel the Burgess Hotel's overdraft, his wife will be informed of his affair."

"Will he do it?" said Julia.

"If he doesn't, his marriage and job will be in tatters. Don't worry Julia, the Burgess Hotel will cease to be a threat. Just after New Year, the letter will arrive on Mr Macdonald's desk. If he does not have a hangover from New Year celebrations then after he reads my letter, one will ensue."

Julia laughed.

At another table in the empty dining room, a mother, father and two teenage boys were having a discussion.

"Mother, why is the hotel not busy on Christmas Eve?"

"Most families will celebrate tomorrow, Geoffrey."

"This hotel was busy last year." Geoffrey turned to his brother. "Do you agree William?"

William nodded.

"Families do not have as much money this year, Geoffrey," said his father.

"Everyone has gone to the Burgess," said William, "people in the district have been talking about it for over a week."

"What have they been saying?" said the father.

"More action!" William smiled.

The mother glanced at her husband. "Action?"

"The hotel has a band playing tonight," said William.

"Both of you are not old enough to attend that type of celebration," said the father.

William looked at his brother. "I can't wait till I'm older!"

"Me too!" said Geoffrey.

The mother looked across the table at her husband and raised her eyebrows. He gave his wife a wry smile.

At the end of their first session, the band received a good round of applause from the Christmas Eve attendees albeit not many couples had infringed upon the polished wooden dance floor. Mrs Abaletti laid out a white-clothed table with plates, white paper napkins, sandwiches and sausage rolls. Revellers who wanted a finger snack handed over their ticket to Mrs Abaletti. Due to the large number of tickets sold, a refill of food at the table appeared probable.

Ten minutes later and carrying a tray of used drinking glasses, Evelyn approached Mrs Abaletti at the table.

"We have too much food, the guests would rather consume alcohol!"

Evelyn laughed. "Tomorrow we can use what remains therefore the food won't be wasted."

Mrs Abaletti nodded.

Evelyn went into the kitchen and placed the tray next to the sink. She washed the glasses, dried them and placed them back on the tray. Mrs Abaletti brought in a tray of sandwiches and sausage rolls then stored it in a food cupboard. Evelyn took a tray full of clean glasses through to the function bar and laid them on a table.

"We have sold all our whisky and gin," said Vivien.

"I will fetch bottles from the cellar," said Evelyn, "what about rum?"

"There is an ample amount at present. Do you have any wine in stock?"

"Wine?"

"Three young women have asked me for red wine," said Charles. He served a customer.

"I must keep tabs on red wine," said Evelyn, " maybe it's the start of a trend."

"No red wine for me, just two glasses of ale," said the male customer, "I want to get plastered!"

"Try red wine," said Vivien, "you'll be plastered quicker."

"Hic! Maybe next time." He handed over money to Charles, picked up his glasses of ale and staggered off.

Vivien glanced at Charles. "If he survives that long!" She served a refined male customer.

"I have waited in this queue for fifteen minutes." The man pointed to his gold pocket watch. "Can't you serve customers faster?"

Here we go again. "I do my best, sir."

"Do you have Pimm's No 3?"

"We don't have 1, 2 or 3, sir."

"How about Benedictine?"

Vivien shook her head. "Sorry, no." This isn't a monastery.

"A snowball?"

Try outside.

"It consists of advocaat and lemonade."

"The advocaat is finished."

"I will settle for a sherry, I trust you have some in stock?"

"Yes, we do, sir."

"Hit me with two large glasses if you please."

Don't tempt me. "Certainly, sir." Vivien picked up the full bottle of sherry, poured two glasses and handed them to the customer.

He gave her a silver half-crown.

"That will cover it."

"Thank you, sir."

Vivien took the coin from the customer, went to the till then put the half-crown into a drawer. As she returned to the bar counter, she heard loud cheers and applause. The band had re-appeared and took their places on the stage. When they started to play, couples drifted onto the dance floor. It soon became crowded with men and women engrossed in the Christmas Eve party atmosphere. Two over-zealous dancers almost knocked over the eight-foot tall Christmas tree which stood nearby. They then restricted their movements to the floor and not beyond. Next came the popular Charleston with an abundance of younger revellers taking centre stage and displaying modern dance prowess. The band expanded their musical repertoire and adaptability by next performing the Tango. This dance was embraced by a selection of mature revellers. The introduction of the Can-Can increased energy levels once more and the dance floor was taken over by the fitter element of reveller.

"Yes, sir, what will it be?" said Charles.

"Two double whiskies please."

As the barman poured whisky into two separate glasses, James turned round and looked at the enthusiastic partygoers on the dance floor.

What will they make of the Jitterbug, Jive and the Twist in years to come? House Music could be an eye-opener!

"Your drinks, sir," said the barman.

"Thanks." James handed over a florin.

"Thank you, sir." The barman went to the till, opened it and deposited the silver coin into a drawer.

James picked up the two full glasses of whisky and manoeuvred his way through people standing within the bar's vicinity. When back at the table, he laid both drinks in front of Adam.

"I must pay a visit to the toilet."

"See you later." Adam picked up a glass, took a small sip then a larger one.

James edged past people who stood close to the dance floor and in between tables. As he approached the toilet, Isabel and another lady stood in his path.

Elizabeth!

Isabel smiled.

He walked towards them.

"Good evening, James, having a nice time?"

"Yes thanks."

"This is my niece, Elizabeth."

"Hello, good to meet you." After seventeen years.

Elizabeth hesitated then smiled.

Do you remember me Elizabeth?

He looks familiar.

James turned to Isabel. "Have you been up to dance yet?"

"It is too busy."

Elizabeth's stare is making me feel self-conscious.

"Have you been on the dance floor?" said Elizabeth.

The accent has changed but her beauty remains. James touched his leg. "I bumped into a trolley at the hospital and have to take it easy."

"Pity." Probably doesn't know the steps.

"However, I've had an enjoyable evening." James looked towards the toilet entrance door. "I will have to leave you."

Isabel smiled. "We understand."

As James walked towards the gentleman's toilet, Elizabeth looked at Isabel and then sipped her martini.

"He is not that bad, Elizabeth!"

"Perhaps charming."

"Did you not like him?"

"He has an educated voice, not what I would expect from a hospital porter." I have heard it before and those eyes, there is a familiarity about them. "Not sure about the beard." Elizabeth drank her martini. "Let's go to the bar for a refill."

"You're too fussy."

Both ladies walked round a busy dance floor and eventually reached the bar. They joined a line of women and men in the queue. A man near the front became agitated – his body moved from side to side then the head bobbed up and down.

"Get a move on!" cried the man, "if you were ma wife you wouldna be slow."

Vivien served a woman customer, popped her head over the counter and looked sideways towards the irate impatient man.

"What's keepin' ye," said the man.

"I'm not your wife and no way would I be! Any more cheek and you'll be refused service. Okay, buddy?"

The man groaned then nodded.

"We could be in this queue for a while, Elizabeth, I am off to the ladies room."

"Okay."

When a group of men and women standing beside a table went onto the dance floor, a gap appeared. Elizabeth observed a man on his own sitting at the table. As another customer was served, she moved forward in the queue then stared at the man. He looked towards the bar and noticed Elizabeth. She left the queue, walked over to his table and sat beside him. The man blinked and Elizabeth gave him a warm smile.

"Elizabeth!" he whispered.

She hugged him.

After a visit to the toilet, James walked back to his table. He observed Elizabeth and Adam in each other's arms. James diverted to the bar and joined a queue. The man in front of him turned round.

"It takes ages to be served, you'll be here for a while."

That's the reason why I'm here.

"Hello."

James turned round. "Hi Isabel."

She looked in the direction of Elizabeth and Adam. "After all those years!"

"Reunited."

Isabel smiled.

"I have spotted Nurse Shaw and she's had a skinful." James pointed.

Isabel looked. "The loud giggles tell it all."

"And six empty glasses beside her!"

A man with a full tray of drinks left the bar counter and stopped where Isabel and James stood.

"That's the beer finished."

As he walked with caution across the edge of the dance floor, a shout came from the bar.

"Last orders, ten minutes to drink up!" Vivien served the next customer.

James looked towards the bar. "Not much of a rush to buy a final drink."

"Everyone has had their fill."

James laughed.

Once the band finished their current tune, the pianist made an announcement. He said the next dance would be the final one. Elizabeth and Adam stood up from their chairs and walked onto the floor.

"It would appear I have another guest for tomorrow's Christmas dinner," said Isabel.

James smiled.

"What are your plans for tomorrow, James?"

"Christmas with the patients."

"At Christmas, they can be in fine fettle."

James looked towards the dance floor. "Elizabeth looks happy."

"Yes, she does."

James felt a tap on his shoulder and turned round. There stood Nurse Shaw with a wide grin.

"C'mon James, let's dance."

As the two hospital colleagues took to the floor, a tall grey-haired gentleman wearing a kilt and dinner jacket asked Isabel to dance. She accepted and accompanied him onto the floor. Nurse Shaw stumbled and stood on James's foot.

"Sorry, James, are you all right?"

"If I require attention, I'm with the appropriate person."

Nurse Shaw giggled. "You have to excuse me, I've had too much gin."

"Incidentally, what is your first name?"

"Victoria."

"Lucky you, not having to work tomorrow."

She smiled. "With what I've had to drink, it's just as well!"

James laughed.

Whilst the last waltz continued, Evelyn, Vivien and Charles went round the function suite tables and collected glasses. The majority contained little or no alcohol.

As the final revellers departed, a fresh fall of snow began. Evelyn stood at the function suite exit, wished them a safe journey home then closed the door and locked it. Mrs Abaletti dried the remaining glasses then stacked them in a cupboard. Evelyn walked into the kitchen and sat on a chair.

"Phew! What a night."

Mrs Abaletti smiled. "A successful one?"

Evelyn nodded. "I have counted most of this evening's cash. The amount is more than what I had anticipated therefore the bank manager will be pleased." She laughed. "However, not much beer remains and the whisky stock has been depleted."

"When the hotel opens for business, what will you do?"

"We may be fine for a couple of days."

"Then what will you do?"

"I'll contact the brewery on Friday and ask them for an emergency delivery. I'm sure they will oblige."

"Let's hope so."

"They will be delighted to gain extra business."

"Where are the band members?"

"Upstairs in their beds. It has been a long day for them and they are off to Glasgow early tomorrow morning."

"Their music provided a terrific atmosphere."

Evelyn smiled. "It certainly did and they almost didn't make it!"

"What happened?"

"A mechanical fault with their transport. Fortunately a passing vehicle stopped and the driver was a motor mechanic."

"That was lucky."

"For them and me!"

"Has Vivien, Charles and Iain left?"

"Yes, all looked as if they had put in two shifts instead of one. They earned their money this evening."

"And the cloakroom attendant?"

"He caught the return coach to Ardrishaig – wanted home before midnight."

"In case he turns into a pumpkin?"

Evelyn laughed. "He had to prepare for Christmas morning."

"Prepare?"

Evelyn shrugged her shoulders. "He didn't elaborate."

"How did he fare?"

"He was rushed off his feet taking and organising hats and coats but when guests retrieved them, they gave him a tip."

"He must have been pleased!"

"The tips plus money I they gave him will ensure he has an enjoyable Christmas."

"Where is Louisa?" Mrs Abaletti glanced at the kitchen clock. "She is giving me a lift home."

"Clearing the snow of her vehicle's windscreen."

Mrs Abaletti put on her red coat and white woollen scarf. "What are your plans for Christmas Day?"

"As soon as the band leaves and the hotel is secured, I'm off to my boyfriend's parents. After the Christmas meal, we will listen to the King's Christmas message."

Mrs Abaletti buttoned her coat.

"I hope you have a Merry Christmas."

"You too."

"Oh! Almost forgot."

Evelyn rushed out of the kitchen, went into her office then came back with a Christmas card.

"For me?"

Evelyn gave Mrs Abaletti the card.

She took it. "Thank you."

341

"My pleasure."

Evelyn accompanied her colleague to the main exit door and opened it. Mrs Abaletti stepped outside and gazed at the snow-filled surroundings then a vehicle drew up alongside her.

"Evelyn?"

"Yes?"

"I forgot to ask, what is the cloakroom attendant's name?"

"Nicholas."

Mrs Abaletti entered the vehicle and before it drove off, she waved. Evelyn closed the main door and locked it. She went into the function suite with its abundance of coloured balloons and silver tinsel strewn over tables and across the dance floor. Evelyn smiled and switched off the lights.

Chapter 13

The Gift

Three days into the new decade, Evelyn went to the Bank of Scotland office in Lochgilphead. Yesterday, she had received a telephone call from Mr Macdonald requesting an urgent meeting with her. Evelyn would reveal the success of both events held at the hotel over Christmas and New Year. She alighted from the local motor coach at a stop close to the bank and trudged along the snowy pavement. Evelyn entered the premises, wiped her feet on a mat then approached the counter.

"Morning," said a male employee.

"I am here to see Mr Macdonald."

"Just go through to his office, he is expecting you."

"Thank you."

The bank employee went to the end of the counter and lifted up the shiny wooden hatch. Evelyn walked through the passageway, approached Mr Macdonald's door and knocked twice. He asked her to enter therefore she went in and closed the door.

"Please, Miss White, have a seat."

Evelyn sat down and smiled. "I have good news."

"Yes?"

"Both festive events proved successful." Evelyn took off her cream hat.

"Excellent."

"Why did you ask to see me?"

"Would you care for a cup of tea?"

"No, thanks." He appears glum and sheepish.

"It's your overdraft."

"What about it?"

"We have to cancel it."

"Cancel it! Why?"

"The bank is short of funds therefore only priority customers will continue to receive support."

"The hotel is busy and will thrive. You cannot cut me off now!"

"I am sorry, Miss White, my hands are tied."

"Then I will take my business to another bank who can support me."

"You will discover that other banks are in a similar situation. The state of our economy has caused this harsh measure."

"Then what am I to do?"

"Sell the hotel."

"Nobody can afford to buy in this deep recession."

"I am aware of one party."

"I won't sell my hotel to that old witch! If that was to happen, no competition would exist in the district."

"I agree, Miss White, however, no other option exists."

Evelyn put on her hat and stood up. "I will find one."

Mr Macdonald rose from his chair, walked round his desk and stood in front of his client.

"Goodbye." Mr Macdonald held out his hand.

Angry and frustrated, Evelyn turned round, opened the door and walked out of the office. Mr Macdonald closed the door, went behind his desk and stared out of the small window. He looked down at his wastepaper bin on the floor and kicked it. Due to a personal misdemeanour, he had betrayed a client.

Evelyn departed the building and headed for another bank within the town. She entered the Clydesdale Bank premises and stomped her feet on a thick doormat. She walked up to the polished wooden counter and waited. A man in a black chalk-stripe suit sat behind a desk and scribbled on a piece of white paper. He looked up over his horn-rimmed spectacles, laid his black fountain pen horizontal on a sheet of blotting paper then stood up.

Evelyn smiled.

The bank employee approached the counter. "Yes, what do you want?"

"A loan."

"You will be lucky in this current economic climate. How much do you seek?"

"£28,000."

The bank employee removed his spectacles. "How much!"

"It is a lot of money however, I can repay the loan."

"Are you sure?"

"I own the Burgess Hotel in Inveraray and business has picked up. The hotel is twice as busy from this time last year."

"Admirable young lady, the problem is we do not have sufficient funds to give you."

"This is a bank?"

"Our funds remain low. Savers do not deposit money into their accounts as they once did."

"What am I to do?" Evelyn frowned.

"I understand your predicament." The bank employee put his spectacles back on. "You are not alone in this type of situation."

"Can I speak to the manager, maybe he can suggest a way to obtain money?"

"I am the manager." He smiled.

"Where are your staff?" Evelyn looked around the vicinity.

"Similar to every other business in the area, I had to cut costs. With regard to a loan, most banks will be in a similar position."

"I had financial backing with another bank but it has been withdrawn."

"Withdrawn?"

Evelyn nodded.

"Did you fail to maintain repayments?"

"On the contrary, I can increase them!"

"That is an unusual measure for your bank to take."

Evelyn sighed. "Thanks for your time."

"Do not lose heart young lady, a new decade may bring good fortune."

"I hope so."

"Good luck." He shook Evelyn's hand.

"Thank you."

"Goodbye."

As Evelyn departed the premises, the bank manager went back to his desk and picked up his fountain pen. He dipped the copper nib into a small circular ink container on his desk then started to write.

Evelyn walked to the nearest motor coach stop and joined a long queue of people wrapped in scarves, hats and coats. A woman turned round and shook her head.

"I've been here for ages!" She lifted up the collar of her long black coat. "The coach must have broken down."

Evelyn shivered.

"I'm freezin' hangin' aroond here," said another woman. She tightened her grey scarf.

"Here it comes!" shouted a man.

"Aboot time," said the woman, "I'll give the driver a tellin' off."

"It may not be his fault," said Evelyn, "perhaps the snow is to blame."

"Too bad, hen," said the woman, "he's goin' tae get it!"

When the motor coach arrived, people crammed into it and voiced their annoyance at the blue uniformed driver. Evelyn spotted a vacant seat grabbed it then a lady sat next to her. After the coach moved off, Evelyn stared out of the window. A few minutes later, a voice interrupted her train of thought.

"A penny for them."

Evelyn turned to face the lady who sat beside her. The wrinkles on her white face suggested a person who had lived a long life.

"I could do with a lorry-load."

"Why don't you make a wish?"

Evelyn smiled.

"What have you got to lose?" The elderly lady looked out the window. "My stop, good luck."

"I hope so."

The lady stood up. "Have a good New Year, 1930 could be special."

"Bye."

When the motor coach halted, she alighted and waited at the stop. As the coach moved away, the lady waved and smiled at Evelyn.

After breakfast, Elizabeth assisted her aunt in the kitchen to wash and dry plates, cups and cutlery.

"Yesterday in the general store, the owner revealed that fake coins had been discovered in several shops," said Isabel

"Fake coins!"

"Yes, they had dates on them years from now."

"How many coins?"

"A handful."

"Why would anyone go to the bother of making a handful of fake coins? It doesn't add up."

"Maybe there are more coins in circulation throughout other parts of Argyll. From what I heard, the only difference is the date."

Isabel heard a letter being popped through her letterbox and went to the front door. Elizabeth placed the blue-patterned crockery in a cupboard and put the silver cutlery into a drawer. She removed her mauve cotton apron, laid it on a wooden chair then went into the living room. Isabel came into the room and smiled.

"A letter for you Elizabeth." Isabel looked on the reverse side. "From America!"

"America?"

As Elizabeth sat down on the soft three-seater couch, Isabel handed over the letter. Elizabeth took it and looked at her aunt.

"It can't be from Georgina, I've received her recent letter and card." Elizabeth opened it.

"Who is it from?"

Elizabeth unfolded a piece of paper. "Somerville and Brookes, a law firm in Virginia."

"Virginia!" Isabel sat down next to Elizabeth.

347

"It is dated 10th November 1929."

"Almost two months ago." Isabel moved closer to Elizabeth. "What is that attached to the letter?"

Elizabeth removed a paper clip. "It's a cheque."

"A cheque?"

"Oh my goodness!" Elizabeth put a hand to her mouth.

"What?"

"$50,000!"

"How much is that in pounds?"

Elizabeth looked upwards.

"Yes?"

"Around £35,000."

"Gosh."

Elizabeth laid the cheque on the couch then read her letter. Isabel looked on with intense curiosity.

"The letter is from a Virginia law firm who represent a client – Mason Jennings. How did they trace me?"

"Who is he?"

Elizabeth continued to read the typewritten letter then put it down next to the cheque. She stared at her aunt and sighed.

"What is it?"

"On a train bound for St Louis, Georgina and I met two farmers from Virginia. It happened after Georgina lost her husband and I felt she could do with a vacation. We had a brief encounter with them."

"A brief encounter?"

"Dinner, nothing else."

"Why the cheque?"

Elizabeth picked up the cheque. "He passed away and left me this in his will." She retrieved the letter and read it. "They state I made an everlasting impression on their client and this cheque is a token of the affection he had for a lovely lady."

"What was he like?"

"A fine southern gentleman."

"And a rich one!"

Elizabeth stared at her aunt. "The poor man has passed away."

"He could not have been poor and you need the money."

"No mention of his ranch?"

Isabel laughed.

Elizabeth smiled.

"What will you do with the money?"

"First of all, I will deposit the cheque in a bank."

"Now that Adam and yourself are together again, will you tell him? It is a lot of money Elizabeth."

"I trust Adam therefore I will tell him. I may even give him money to assist his business."

"To repay a debt?"

Elizabeth nodded.

"Will the money compensate for what you did?"

Elizabeth shook her head.

James carried a stepladder from the hospital workshop to reception. Since the festive celebrations had passed, the Christmas tree could now be removed from this area. After he removed all the tinsel, baubles and lights, James stored them in a large cardboard box. Gabrielle came out of her office and approached James.

"Do you have to take it down?" She smiled. "It cheered everyone up!"

"Orders from above."

"Disregard Matron's command, James."

"At my peril."

Gabrielle laughed.

"Besides, Twelfth Night has passed."

Gabrielle crossed her arms. "I suppose so."

"There have been a lot of elderly admissions this week."

"A flu bug is going around the district."

I looked towards the entrance door. "This cold winter weather doesn't help."

"Or the current hardship people endure."

"Maybe 1930 will be a better year."

"Let us hope so." She looked down the corridor. "Here's Roy coming this way."

I turned round. "Good, I will need an extra pair of hands to shift this tree."

"I'll leave you two men to it."

As Gabrielle returned to her office, Roy smiled and pushed a metal trolley in my direction.

"A trolley is not just used to transport patients."

"It would have been some task carrying this tree to the waste disposal."

Roy and I managed to place the large tree onto the trolley then wheeled it along the corridor. Given the weight and size, it is difficult to comprehend how the tree was put in place.

A short time later, I took my lunch break and went to Adam's premises. When I arrived, he was polishing a brass frame. Adam looked round and smiled.

"Hard at work?" I closed the door.

"The frames are in need of a good clean. I have let the shop display deteriorate."

"Better late than never, Adam."

"I agree."

"You appear happy." There is a glow about Adam.

"Elizabeth has come into my life again."

"I am pleased for you."

"She would like to start painting again."

"And you can provide the ideal outlet to display her work."

Adam nodded. "Spot on."

"Must return to my chores."

"Thanks for popping in."

"You should start to market the business."

"Market?"

"Promote, distribute leaflets around the area."

"Now that I feel enthusiastic, I will make the effort."

I opened the door. "Take care."

"You too."

As I closed the door, Adam waved. I walked through the slushy pavements back to the hospital. In the main corridor, I observed Isabel exit one of the wards. She spotted me and came across.

"I have good news."

"I have just visited Adam and he appears rejuvenated."

"And Elizabeth."

"It all goes well for the future."

Isabel nodded. "Yes, it does." She glanced along the corridor. "Time to resume my duties."

I turned round. Nurse Robertson beckoned.

After Isabel departed, Nurse Robertson approached me with an authoritative expression.

"The Christmas tree has been dumped at the rear of the hospital."

"Roy said to leave it there in the meantime."

"Why not cut it up and use it for firewood to stoke the hospital boiler?"

Good idea. "I will do it now."

"After you have done that, I have another job."

"Be back shortly."

"Good."

Holiday time has ended.

Nurse Robertson marched off into a nearby ward and I walked towards the waste disposal area.

Elizabeth entered the Burgess Hotel and walked towards reception. Evelyn looked up and closed the hotel's accounts ledger.

"What a pity the tree and decorations have gone." Elizabeth glanced around the foyer. "They enhanced the festive period."

"The snow is still here."

Elizabeth smiled. "How are you today?"

"All right." Evelyn laid her pencil next to the black ledger.

"Just all right! After the success of Christmas and New Year, are you not elated?"

"Yes, a financial success however, I have a dispute with my bank."

"What kind of dispute?"

"An overdraft dispute – it is being cancelled."

"Did you try the Clydesdale?"

"Yes, their funds remain stretched and therefore will not give credit to any new customer. I have contacted other banks and received the same answer."

"Why did the bank stop your credit?"

"Funds have been depleted and being a new customer, my account took preference for disposal."

"If the payments are being met, it's a strange business practice your bank has adopted."

Evelyn shrugged her shoulders.

"What will you do?"

"Right now, I will make a pot of tea for us."

Elizabeth smiled.

As Evelyn left reception, Elizabeth sat down at a table with four chairs. She took of her pale blue hat, scarf and black gloves then laid them on one of the chairs. Elizabeth stood up and viewed Evelyn's paintings on the wall. After a short while, Evelyn returned.

"Why not sell your paintings?"

Evelyn laid the wooden tray on the table. "They're not that good."

Elizabeth turned round. "Oh yes they are!" She pointed. "This one would not look out of place in a Manhattan gallery."

Evelyn smiled. "New York is too far."

"How about Glasgow or Edinburgh?"

"Or the one in Lochgilphead?"

"I will speak to Adam."

Evelyn sat down and lifted the small shiny metal pot of tea from the tray. She poured tea into two cups then replaced the pot onto the tray.

Elizabeth sat opposite. "Any functions booked for this year?" She lifted a small jug, poured milk into her cup then laid it on the tray.

"There is a dance arranged for the final Saturday of each month."

"Would it be the same band as at Christmas Eve and Hogmany?" Elizabeth lifted her cup and sipped her tea.

Evelyn nodded. "Yes, they are now our resident band." She lifted up her cup. "They are also paid by me at the end of their performance."

Elizabeth laughed and then put her cup down on the saucer. "That's a bonus in this economic climate!"

"And not to mention free bed and breakfast thrown in."

"Lucky them."

"It makes them play better." She sipped her tea and replaced the cup onto the saucer.

Elizabeth laughed. "Another bonus – for the guests."

Evelyn sighed. "If a buyer cannot be found, the hotel will have to close."

"That buyer may not run the hotel as you do. I noticed many young people at the festive events. Everyone appeared to enjoy themselves. A new owner could undo the recent upturn in trade."

"The hotel will end up similar to The Manor House."

"If she buys this hotel, you can depend on it. That woman lives in the past and does not take customer's preferences into consideration, just her own."

"She may be the sole person to put in an offer."

"What is the price?"

"I'm not sure of the exact price, why do you ask?"

"I may have an interested party."

"Can you reveal who the person is?"

"Not at this stage, however, they would have the Burgess Hotel's best interests at heart." Elizabeth lifted her cup, drank some tea then laid it on the saucer. "Must go." She put on her hat, scarf and gloves then stood up. "What bank is it?"

"The Bank of Scotland in Lochgilphead, a Mr Macdonald is the manager."

Elizabeth bent down and kissed Evelyn on the cheek. "Speak to you soon."

When Elizabeth departed, Evelyn lifted her cup of tea, took a small sip then replaced it into the saucer. She put all crockery onto the tray then took it into the kitchen.

Isabel and Elizabeth sat in the living room and relaxed with a cup of hot chocolate. A roaring coal fire kept January's winter chill at bay.

"A vast difference from Docharnea?" said Isabel. She sipped her cup of hot chocolate.

"Our living room did not feel as warm."

"That room was double the size!"

"Fortunately, with many trees we had an abundance of firewood. However, we suffered cold winters at Docharnea." Elizabeth picked up her cup of hot chocolate and sipped it.

"Since returning from America, do you feel settled?"

Elizabeth put her cup onto the saucer. "I'm glad to be back."

Isabel sipped her cup of hot chocolate.

"Are you aware of Nancy's whereabouts?"

"Nancy?"

"Our housekeeper at Docharnea. I have been to her house several times but she is never around."

"She takes regular trips to England, Bournemouth I believe."

"Her sister lives there. Now that Nancy is retired, she will have much spare time on her hands."

"I am surprised she can make such a journey."

"Nancy was an active person."

"I'm not referring to her fitness, Elizabeth."

Elizabeth stared at her aunt.

"It's her memory."

"What about it?"

"She has difficulty relating to when events happened."

"Therefore she may perceive I left Scotland for America seven years rather than seventeen?"

Isabel nodded.

"Poor Nancy. I remember her as a strong individual and any problem she has won't deter her from a normal life."

Isabel took another sip of hot chocolate.

Elizabeth smiled at her aunt. "I have an idea what I'll do with the money."

"What have you decided?" Isabel laid her cup down onto the saucer.

"I am to become a partner in the Burgess Hotel and will start my own interior design business."

"My goodness!" Isabel sat back on the couch.

"Part of my capital will be invested in the hotel. I have discussed it with Evelyn, the manager of her bank and a local solicitor."

"Mr Macmillan?"

Elizabeth nodded. "The bank appeared delighted that I came forward with cash."

"Given the financial situation, I can understand why."

"The bank manager gave me the impression that I would be a suitable investor."

"Suitable?"

Elizabeth smiled. "I would have the best interests of the hotel at heart as opposed to another potential buyer."

"Will Evelyn be your employee?"

"In a certain way. She will continue to run the hotel, receive a wage but also become a junior partner."

That is appropriate.

"What do you think?"

"Terrific, and the other business?"

"I have discussed it with Adam. To begin with, he and I will share his business premises."

"Is his studio not too small for both of you?"

"We can share costs and if business improves, build an extension or seek new premises. As the bank manager said, it is prudent. I will no doubt be a treasured client."

Isabel laughed. "Because you have money, it is a rare commodity."

Elizabeth nodded. "And plenty of it!"

"Why interior design, Elizabeth?"

"Auntie, it is big in America – Art Deco being the term."

"What does that mean?"

"Buildings and products – architecture plus furniture with different types of design. Bold patterns, vibrant colours, geometric shapes, intense lighting – it's fantastic!"

"You are enthusiastic about it and do possess artistic skills."

"Art Deco will be ideal for me – even in a cash-strapped economy. Anyone who has property will be a potential client."

Isabel smiled. "A new dawn beckons."

Mrs Abaletti dusted tables and chairs in the hotel's foyer. Evelyn stood at the desk and analysed yesterday's trading figures. Mrs Abaletti approached the reception desk with a duster.

Evelyn looked up.

"I require more polish, Evelyn."

"Hold on, I will be right back."

Whilst Evelyn went to the storeroom, two women and a man entered the hotel. They came towards reception and Mrs Abaletti turned round.

"The owner will not be long," said Mrs Abaletti, "would you like to have a seat?" She looked in the direction of a table and four chairs.

"Thanks," said the man.

As the three guests sat down, Evelyn returned with a bottle of polish. She looked their way then handed the bottle to Mrs Abaletti. The black ledger book was closed and put in a drawer under the reception desk counter.

"Can I help you?" said Evelyn.

"We would like a word," said Nora Banks.

Evelyn came out from behind the reception desk and walked up to her guest's table. All three had a grim expression.

"Please sit down," said Nora Banks, "I get nervous when I look up to people."

Evelyn sat down.

"I want to make you an exceptional offer for the hotel. You can still work here and stay in private accommodation."

"The hotel is not for sale."

"It soon will be."

"Why do you say that?"

"Because I am aware of certain instances that occur in this area, my dear. I have important contacts in high places."

"I would review your contacts."

"This hotel is a financial burden to your bank. The overdraft will soon be terminated."

"I no longer have an overdraft, the debt has been cleared."

"Cleared!" cried Julia, "how?"

"That is my business, not yours."

Julia looked at her mother.

Evelyn stood up. "Any other business you wish to discuss?"

The three guests stood up and walked out of the hotel with stern expressions. Evelyn rearranged the chairs then returned to her desk. Mrs Abaletti appeared from the function suite.

"They did not stay long!"

Evelyn smiled. "No, and they left with their tails between their legs."

Mrs Abaletti laughed.

Nora Banks and Julia got into the back of the car. Bert closed both doors then sat in the front seat.

"What now?" said Julia.

Bert closed his door.

"Where did she get the money to pay off the hotel's debt?" said Nora Banks.

"Maybe a Christmas present from Santa Claus." Bert laughed.

"I don't pay you to make jokes."

"Sorry, Mrs Banks."

"Take us home, I'll have to devise another way to capture that hotel."

"Or put it out of business?" said Julia.

"Yes, there are ways." Nora Banks looked straight ahead. "Home, Bert, mind the icy roads."

"Yes, Mrs Banks."

"We don't want anybody hurt."

"Yes, Mrs Banks."

As the motor car drove away from the hotel, Elizabeth arrived then entered the main door. Mrs Abaletti polished a table top and looked up.

"Good afternoon," said Elizabeth.

"Good afternoon," said Mrs Abaletti, "is it still cold outside?"

"Let's say I'm glad to have on a warm coat, scarf and gloves."

Mrs Abaletti smiled. "And a hat to match."

"You bet." She looked towards the reception desk.

"Good afternoon," said Evelyn, "tea?"

"Yes, please."

Whilst Evelyn went through to the kitchen, Elizabeth sat at down at a table. She removed her hat, scarf and gloves then patted her blonde hair. Mrs Abaletti polished the main door brass handle and looked towards Elizabeth. Evelyn appeared with a tray.

"Not having tea?" said Elizabeth.

"Not just now. In case you are hungry, I also brought through a plate of digestive biscuits."

"As I came into the hotel, Nora Banks and her two accomplices drove off."

"They enquired about the hotel."

Elizabeth picked up the small metal pot and poured tea into her cup. "And?" She replaced the pot onto the wooden tray.

Evelyn smiled. "They left stone-faced."

"You mean more stone-faced than usual."

Evelyn laughed.

"Nora Banks can try all she wants to buy this place. The bank is now on our side – money talks."

Evelyn nodded.

"I've decided to start an interior design business."

"Terrific."

"Art Deco!"

"That's interesting. I believe it is prominent in parts of Europe."

"And in America. In Manhattan, I observed its popularity. I could introduce my own blend of ideas into the hotel."

"Great! It needs a fresh look. I would imagine the hotel decor has remained static for years."

Elizabeth smiled. "Perhaps decades. We are in agreement?"

Evelyn nodded. "Oh yes."

"Good."

"The hotel could become a showpiece for your work."

"And also improve the footfall for the hotel – a win-win situation."

"Effective business practice."

The two business partners carried on their conversation about the hotel's new image. After an hour, Elizabeth prepared herself for the outside chilly winter weather and departed the hotel. When Evelyn picked up the wooden tray, Mrs Abaletti came into the reception area.

"That is everything nice and clean."

"The hotel is to have a makeover. I am not sure at this stage how much however, it will be welcome."

"That is good news."

"We are fortunate to have Elizabeth on board."

"Both she and yourself are similar."

"Similar?"

"Yes, in manner and appearance."

Evelyn took the tray through to the kitchen and Mrs Abaletti stared at a painting on one of the walls. She moved closer to study it.

When February arrived, the temperature dipped bringing more falls of heavy snow. The hospital had no spare beds due to an influx of people who suffered from flu and related symptoms. The elder residents of the local area were hardest hit. A virus had spread throughout the community and caused misery. Doctors and nurses within the hospital worked long and demanding hours attending to patients. After he took a patient back to Ward B, James pushed an empty trolley in the direction of Ward C. In the corridor he spotted a familiar face walking towards him. The man smiled and acknowledged James.

"You appear well, Adam."

"I don't have the flu!"

"Are you here to visit a patient?"

Adam nodded.

"How is Elizabeth?"

"Fine, James. She is about to start an interior design business."

"Splendid. Does she have premises?"

"She will use mine. The property is suitable for both of us."

"I hope the two of you don't fall out."

Adam laughed. "It happened many years ago however, not this time."

"Must return to work."

"See you later."

I pushed the trolley forward. "Ahhh!"

"What's wrong James?"

"A pain shot up my back. It happens now and again."

"You are in the perfect place to receive medical attention."

I nodded.

"This severe cold weather can cause back ailments."

I slowly stood upright. "I was knocked over by a runaway horse eighteen years ago and the injury still plagues me."

"Where did it happen?"

"Ardrishaig."

"I wasn't aware that you had previously been in the area."

"Just for a short time."

"How unfortunate to suffer that sort of injury in your 20s. Does it hinder you in any way?"

I shook my head. "I will have to ensure not too much hard work."

Adam laughed.

"See you later."

"Bye, James."

I gently pushed the trolley forward and noticed Roy in the corridor. He spotted me and came over.

"Hi Roy."

"I need you to collect furniture from a property near Ardrishaig."

"Collect furniture?"

"You can use my van."

With the way my back feels I hope the items of furniture are small and light.

"Just a few odds and ends for the hospital charity shop."

"What is the address of the property?"

"It has a name – Docharnea. It's on the main road to Inveraray, you can't miss it."

I do and very much. However now I've been given a chance to return home! At the property, I will seek an opportunity to enter the coach house and attempt a return to my own timeline.

Roy took out a set of keys from his overall pocket. "You have driven before?"

"Yes." I started five decades from now.

"Do you know how to start the engine on a Ford van?"

Start the engine?

"You look puzzled, I'll show you how it's done."

Whilst Roy led me to his van, we discussed how to start it. I entered the van, inserted a key into the ignition, and turned it then pulled out the choke. Next, Roy instructed me on the van's controls. There were only two forward gears instead of four. No gearstick – just pedals used in conjunction with the handbrake. When pushed forward, the handbrake acted as an accelerator. Roy picked up a crank lever that lay on the floor, went to the front of his van and put it into a slot below the engine.

"If you don't do this properly, you could end up with a broken wrist."

With a particular hand motion, Roy turned the crank twice but the engine did not start. He did it again and this time the engine started.

"There should be enough petrol in the fuel tank but when you leave the property, check it."

I looked at the dashboard for a fuel indicator. A speedometer, choke knob and ignition lock existed but nothing else. Roy appeared at the driver's door and pointed.

"It's at the rear of the van. Screw off the cap which is on the floor and use the dipstick."

Dipstick!

"It's next to the cap."

I looked behind. "I see it."

Roy handed me the crank. "Take care on the roads, there is a lot of ice around."

"Will do." I took the crank and laid it on the floor.

I closed the door and drove out of the hospital's exit gate. A layer of snow covered the road therefore I drove with caution. I soon acquainted myself with the 'vintage' controls and prayed the vehicle would not stall. Give me a modern car any day, it's less hassle.

After a slow drive along the main rural road, I arrived at Docharnea. I drove up the snow-filled driveway and stopped outside the main building. As I will meet Philip and Charlotte nine years from now, my beard is an excellent cover to protect my true identity. A dark-haired gentleman came out of the house and walked towards the van. I turned the ignition key to switch off the engine, got out and closed the driver's door.

"Good-day," said the owner.

"I believe you have items of furniture for the hospital?"

He shook my hand. "I am Philip Carsell-Brown."

"James Carlisle."

"Come this way, James, the furniture is stored in an old coach house."

I walked with my great grandfather towards the familiar black and white building. Philip took a key out of his trouser pocket and opened the stable door.

"This part of the building once had two horses."

I tended them – Cole and Char.

"Pity the person who had to clean out this place."

I can still smell the dung!

Philip pointed. "That's the items."

"Splendid."

"Do you want me to give you a hand?"

I shook my head. "As they are small items, I will manage."

"There are also a couple of chairs in an upstairs room. I will take you there."

Philip unlocked the door which led to the coachman's quarters then led me upstairs to that particular room.

"When my two sons were younger, they used this as a playroom. A rumour exists that it is haunted."

"Haunted?"

Philip nodded. "By the former coachman."

"Have you seen him?"

Philip shook his head. "I don't believe in ghosts."

How about time travellers.

Philip looked down the stairs. "My wife calls, no doubt a fault with the radio again." He turned to me. "Can I leave you?"

"Yes, I'll manage."

As my great-grandfather walked down the wooden staircase, I cast my gaze around the familiar room. Now I have an opportunity to return home. I composed myself then stared into the gothic mirror which hung on the wall – it has a lot to answer for. Please this time, take me back to my own timeline.

Charlotte walked into the living room and observed Philip at work with the radio. She went up to him and smiled.

"Any luck?"

"Not yet, I don't understand what the problem is." Philip turned the knob back and forward.

Charlotte stood next to the radio and with a clenched fist, thumped the top of it. As the crackled sound of jazz music was heard, she looked at her husband.

"Well done, Charlotte!" cried Philip.

"That method usually works." Charlotte looked out of the window. "The chap from the hospital is taking his time."

Philip looked at the clock on a sideboard. "I'll go and check on him."

"I hope he hasn't had an accident. The coach house staircase is steep."

Philip left the house, walked across the courtyard and into the coach house. He looked in the downstairs and upstairs rooms then returned. He entered the living room and shook his head.

"Is he finished, Philip?"

"All the furniture is still there."

"What is wrong?"

"He has vanished!"

"You will have to telephone the hospital. Not only do they have furniture to collect but also a van!"

Elizabeth and Adam attended the Burgess Hotel for a Friday evening meal. Elizabeth sipped a glass of red wine, laid it on the white tablecloth then looked around the dining room.

"It's busier than last week, Elizabeth." Adam sipped his glass of wine.

"Yes, Adam, but I feel we could attract more people. St Valentine's Day is one week away therefore we have an ideal opportunity. Maybe the hotel should adopt a different method of advertising."

Adam laid his glass on the tablecloth. "If James had been around I could have sought his advice."

Elizabeth looked at Adam. "He appeared familiar." She picked up her glass and took a sip.

"Familiar?"

"When Isabel introduced me to him at the Christmas Eve dance, I felt we had met on a previous occasion." Elizabeth laid her glass on the tablecloth. "What could have become of him?"

"I heard he went to where you once lived to collect furniture for the hospital then disappeared."

"How can someone just disappear?"

"It has now been six days."

"Strange."

"Maybe another horse has knocked him down and he is badly injured." Adam lifted his glass of wine and drank it.

"Another horse?"

"The last time I spoke to James, he had a problem with his back. When I enquired, he told me a horse had once knocked him over. Because of the accident, he would suffer the occasional backache." Adam laid his empty glass on the tablecloth.

"Adam, did James say when this happened?"

"Eighteen years ago."

1912. "What is James surname? Is it Carlisle?"

"Why do you ask?"

"Before I moved to America, I missed being killed by a whisker. The coachman at Docharnea pushed me out of a runaway horse's path. However, the horse hit him and he sustained injuries."

"Did the incident take place in Ardrishaig?"

"In the main street."

"James told me it happened in Ardrishaig."

Elizabeth stared at Adam.

"What is it, Elizabeth? You've gone pale."

"He is the coachman I painted years ago! His height, build, hair and caring eyes – his first name. The beard and a two-decade gap threw me."

"Are you sure?"

"What would you put his age at?"

"Around forty."

"The same as our coachman."

"How can it be the same person? Due to the war and severe hardship, people have aged considerably over the last two decades."

"It's the same person, Adam, my instinct was correct. After all those years, why did he return and at this particular time?"

Adam stared at Elizabeth.

"What is it Adam?"

"Perhaps fate is why he came back."

"Fate?"

"It would appear your life is not the only one he has preserved."

"Go on."

"I tried to end my life Elizabeth. I had become depressed and cut both my wrists. James came to the gallery, found me and an ambulance rushed me to hospital. If it had not been for him, we would not be having this conversation."

"Adam, why did you not tell me?"

Adam bowed his head. "Too ashamed of what I did."

Elizabeth reached for his hand. "Both of us owe a debt of gratitude to James."

"Yes, we do."

"There's a rumour that Docharnea is haunted by the former coachman."

Adam smiled. "James is not a ghost, Elizabeth."

"Why does he not age?"

"Why has he saved both our lives?"

Elizabeth smiled. "Maybe he is our guardian angel."

"I'll wager he has gone to save someone else, that is why he has vanished."

"Perhaps we will meet him in the future."

"And have intriguing questions to ask him."

Elizabeth smiled. "No doubt he will still look the same age."

Adam laughed.

Elizabeth lifted her glass of wine and drank it. "Adam?" Elizabeth laid her empty glass on the tablecloth.

"Yes?"

"There is something of a delicate nature I must discuss with you."

"Delicate?"

"It concerns Evelyn."

"What about her?"

"Perhaps you should refill our empty glasses."